PATER ET FILIUS

Also by Mikulas Kolya

The Animal Mutiny/Electric

Men-Art-War

PATER ET FILIUS

MIKULAS KOLYA

iUniverse, Inc.
Bloomington

Pater et Filius

iUniverse books may be ordered through booksellers or by contacting:

iUniverse
1663 Liberty Drive
Bloomington, IN 47403
www.iuniverse.com
1-800-Authors (1-800-288-4677)

Because of the dynamic nature of the Internet, any web addresses or links contained in this book may have changed since publication and may no longer be valid. The views expressed in this work are solely those of the author and do not necessarily reflect the views of the publisher, and the publisher hereby disclaims any responsibility for them.

Any people depicted in stock imagery provided by Thinkstock are models, and such images are being used for illustrative purposes only.
Certain stock imagery © Thinkstock.

ISBN: 978-1-4620-5340-7 (sc)
ISBN: 978-1-4620-5341-4 (ebk)

Printed in the United States of America

iUniverse rev. date: 04/11/2012

Filius pars patris est.

A son is part of the father.

Was hat mein ganzer tag gefrommt
Wenn heut das blonde kind nicht kommt?

Of what use is my entire day
If the blonde child doesn't come this way?

There was a man.

His life was one of confused wandering . . . years of mazes and forked roads and false turns . . . bramble-covered paths leading to the edges of cliffs . . . beasts lurking at the edges of forests . . . stumbling through an enormous labyrinth alone, without directions . . . forced to find his own way through a wilderness of doubts, of regrets, of mistakes . . . It was a pathetic search for happiness, the man not realizing that happiness was reserved only for those beasts lurking at the edges of forests. It was a fruitless search for security, the man not realizing that security was unattainable to those who thought and lived as mere individuals.

This search took place in the diminishing light of a dying star, in a poisoned land amid a weary people. Like these people he followed the creed of the zeitgeist's god in desire for things, for material riches, for comfort. Like them he shambled halfheartedly through rotten fields of decayed corpses, attempting against all biology and dignity to stretch his adolescence into eternity. Like them he ignored what the gods of life and of mighty nations decreed was necessary – propagation at any cost.

Then, one day, he emerged from the labyrinth.

*   *   *   *

The man, having followed the advice of the Seven Sages, having followed the advice of the inscription on the walls of Apollo's temple, finally knew himself . . . all weaknesses, all strengths, were now obvious . . . He gained

1

this insight from the lonely decades spent in the wilderness, wandering as a starving child, stealing like a Spartan youth when he could, taking whatever nourishment opportunity presented him. Over the course of time he realized that the energy he expended on himself must be directed toward others or he would be destroyed in the flame of self-interest . . . burning brightly during a youthful holocaust before fading inexorably to coals, then embers, then ashes . . . This realization of the necessity to banish his selfishness, this awareness of the obligation to redistribute concern, was known by greater men during more promising times as *duty*. They grasped the simple truth denied to so many – that by sacrificing the ego of youth one could transfer that youth, could safely remove it from the shell attacked by Time and pass it to a new generation, thus becoming immortal. By extending this ethos of unselfishness to the larger tribe, one could become not only immortal, but invincible.

All healthy organisms possess the inherent urge to procreate. Like millions of other moderns the man was not healthy. He was sick, he eventually realized, infected by *Kulturkrankheit*, the disease of civilization. This realization of his state and situation slowly grew over the years. During that time he watched as, like dying trees, fellow victims of the disease flaked and crumbled to the woodland floor. He watched as their once solid shapes decayed into the soil, there to be consumed by other, more virile life forms. Eventually a sturdier forest, brimming with vibrancy and strength, would arise upon the rot of the other. He knew this through long observation of woodland ways. Readings in the annals of history provided the same understanding. The man did not want this fate for himself. He didn't want to flake and crumble anonymously into the soil or be shunted aside by encroaching invaders. He didn't want to be sick. He wanted to be healthy, he wanted to *live* . . . and so, armed with the gleanings of history and knowledge of the woodlands, he decided to remedy his grave situation and act . . .

Thus it was that after thirty-three years the man finally made the first steps – dutiful steps – toward immortality . . . toward healing himself . . . toward releasing those lives that were imprisoned inside of him as he was once imprisoned inside others, all of them nesting together like an infinite number of *matryoshka* dolls . . .

He was to become a father.

*   *   *   *   **

When one spends unsheltered years in the wilderness, one learns to grasp reality . . . to sees things as they are . . . The man has learned that as Time begins to have its way with men, chipping away at the mind as stealthily and insidiously as it does the body, the joys of youth diminish as surely as the eyes ultimately dim. When finally this youth is left behind one slowly realizes, among other things, that there are few genuine instances of wonder remaining in a finite life. All previous experience has been gathered, categorized, and shelved. There it remains, always at hand for instant comparison to all subsequent experiences. The sparkling thrill of newness has forever gone, washed away by waves of information and familiarity. This is knowledge, the enemy of wonder.

This recognition of the loss of wonder in his own life spurs the man to eschew what other moderns perceive as benefits. He refuses to utilize the science of Faustian men to ascertain the gender of the fetus growing inside his wife's womb, choosing instead to await his child in an anticipatory state of unknowing. Of course he knows what he wants. He is the descendant of slaves and conquerors, of farmers and sailors, of freemen and serfs, of savage women and refined barbarians, and he wants what they all wanted for their first-born. He wants a son.

For months this is what he dreams of – a boy, made in his own image. As he watches his wife's stomach wax like the growing moon, he tries to will whatever lives inside it to become exactly what he yearns for. The primitive fear that he'll somehow be tricked by fate is what finally reins him in. He begins to restrain himself, denies himself the pleasure of imagining, tells himself he'll not get what he desires most . . . a dream of a dumpling isn't a dumpling, said the Litvak Jews – it's a dream . . .

The day arrives. The baby is turned the wrong way in its mother's womb, its head trapped beneath the ribs, necessitating, so experts say, the slicing open of that very womb. It is a time of perpetual war. There is no peace, no safety. What better way for the child to learn these truths than to have its only refuge gashed and violated by surgical steel? All is intrusion, all is mechanical in the rusting, robot Occident. That is the child's first lesson.

Rudely yanked from the slit in its mother's belly, past the layers of oozing flesh, the infant comes into view. Fate plays no tricks on the man. He is given a boy. Squirming and fighting in the middle of the sterile room, purple and ugly, no clot clenched in his wrinkled hand as the newborn Temudjin had, no blood pouring through his tiny palms like the newborn Timur . . . nothing to set him apart from millions of others . . . No matter. Wonder courses through the man regardless of the lack of silly portents. The feeling he experiences is unexpected and overwhelming. Tears hover at the edges of his eyes. He is unsure if this indicates weakness, removed as he's been from the emotional displays involved with the renewal of life. Certainly it seems natural, but crying males are lauded now, hailed by the mouthpieces of that rusting Occident. This gives him pause. He reminds himself that he is in the presence of capitalists disguised as doctors, and that only the most diluted emotions are to be revealed to such types. So he hides his ecstasy behind a reserved grin and watches his boy struggle and listens to him scream and thinks to himself, "You are finally here, son. Millions of ancestors, an infinite amount of combinations, all to make you perfect. The enemy of the Last Man — the First Man."

With steady hand he cuts the cord.

*   *   *   *

The second lesson the boy must learn – one it took his father decades to grasp – is that this Last Man is everywhere. It is he who populates the earth now. It is he who hastily sutures the gash in the groggy woman's abdomen, anxious to make it to the golf course before rain comes. It is he who wheels the newborn infant away from the delivery room, talking about college football games to the silent man walking alongside the gurney. It is he who scurries along the sidewalks of the murdered land just outside the hospital walls, well fed and content. He is everywhere. He dwells in valleys and on hilltops, in bloated cities and in the obese countryside, in mansions and condominiums and tenements . . . standing with poor posture in his kitchen, his den, his garage, his media room, his board room . . . slumped in overstuffed chairs, surrounded by kitsch and plasma television sets and white walls and financial charts . . . Across the West he laughs and cries, he buys and sells, he rules and he follows. He can't be identified by profession. Annual income level yields no clue. Social status is no indication. Race or religion or class cannot be used to identify him. The quantity or quality of his possessions is no dividing line. His geographical location does not distinguish him. The Last Man is everywhere.

In the hallway outside the recovery room of the man's wife another man walks back and forth, loudly speaking into his cell phone. His own wife has given birth to a girl earlier in the day, and he proudly repeats his new daughter's name several times to the party at the other end of the call. It is a novelty name, sugary sweet, filled with vowels and exotic inflections and pops of air. This man thinks himself clever, unique in his and his wife's attempt to set themselves apart from their friends, neighbors, and coworkers, all of whom also make the effort to be different, straining in unison to deny similarity between themselves and the other members of their social circle. Great pride is taken in the degree of obscurity, the uniqueness, the *bizarreness* of the names given their own children.

In different parts of the country – less enlightened parts – others who are more cognizant of their lockstepping fondly smile down at their newborn Jordans, their Dylans, their Hunters, their Jacobs and Madisons and Ashleys and Rileys. They shamelessly pluck such names from online "Top-Ten" lists or best-selling books sold in malls. They raid the character names of favorite television programs, they pore over entertainment magazines, searching for what's coolest . . . a celebrity's name, a professional athlete's, a musician's . . . something everyone knows, something everyone's comfortable with . . .

Most uncommon or most popular – these are the primary criteria considered before doling out children's names in the Kingdom of the Last Man. It doesn't matter if the parents sup on grass-fed beef tenderloin or hamburgers slapped together from the ulcerated flesh of Midwestern feedlots. It makes no difference if their refrigerators contain sulfite-free organic wines imported from central Chile or the canned swill of corporate mega-brewers. Rabble above, rabble below – at root there's no distinction. One will have a daughter named after a Nepalese flower, the other will have a daughter named after the plucky heroine of a kids' show on cable, but neither will have a ceremony for the presentation of that name, neither will celebrate the arrival of the child beyond the profane, neither will offer depth to their creations. What is a daughter to these people, what is a son? An extension of themselves, a continuation of the family line? No. A child is a fantastic pet. That is all.

They have no rules for their lives, these people . . . and rules are necessary . . . The man knows the name must not be something to merely mark the boy, an identification tag attached to a tightened collar. It must be an echo of the eternal, it must recall kin living and dead, ancestors silently judging and awaiting. A name must give meaning, must make the past the present and the present the future. It must lend *relevance* to existence. To thumb through stacks of magazines searching for such a thing is useless. To scour the fairy books and holy tales of other peoples is useless. Tremendous value, *sole* value for the man, is to be found only among the tribal names of those whose homeland stretched from Eire to the Urals and beyond, from the icy top of the globe to the warmth of tropical seas . . . a people who bridled the horse and bridled the rocket and will one day bridle the will again . . .

The boy is a link in a silver chain extending all the way back to the dawn – but silver chains break, individual links break, so these must be clasped one to the other, must be fused, welded into armor. Poetic twaddle, true, abrasive to the ears even, but the lyrical is relevant if it gives voice to the biological, and the biological says that the boy must be protected. He is the physical wrenched from the metaphysical. He is the First Man, the higher man, the becoming man, the recurring man, and he must be protected.

Ruddy and raw, screaming and furious, he twists in his father's hands as the nurses scrub his skinny red body. Alone he would be defenseless . . . but the man stands there, holding him and protecting him . . . all the while thinking of the necessity of rules and the necessity of armor and of how to go about linking and fusing the chains . . .

*   *   *   *

Night arrives. The man is exhausted, his head leaning against the window of his wife's recovery room. In the distant hills glow the seductive colors of West Hollywood, sparkling and twinkling along famed Sunset Boulevard. They beckon, luring one to become lost and corrupt amid their charms. Below him, on the shadowy sidewalks, are tiny yellow pools cast by electric street lamps. They illuminate the world out there, making it seem like a welcoming place. It isn't. Yet all those flaring points in the immense darkness are enticing, there is no doubt.

Sleep begins to claim him. He looks over at the bundle tucked next to his wife. He stares. The searing elation he felt earlier has cooled. A minor trepidation takes hold. Who will claim this son of his? Those urban lights will beckon to him as much as they do everyone else. They must be fought. How will the man, a mere individual in the most horrible sense of the word, teach the boy the truth about them – that they obscure more than they illuminate? How will he, alone, teach his son to survive in that world beyond the hospital walls?

Outside the moon has risen, pale and white against the grayish sky. The man's tired eyes turn upward, focusing on it. It is perfectly round. The following night it will wane and begin to shrink, and follow its predictable phases until dark, hidden, and dead.

He ponders many things, then slips, at last, into slumber.

*   *   *   *

The morning brings visitors. There is the sharing of joy and of private concerns with the welcome ones and the exchange of empty courtesies and blandishments with those who aren't. Eventually the room clears and mother and child nestle, fade, and sleep. The man turns his head about the place, staring at the pointless baskets and vases of flowers that were left. Sliced from their roots, they've already begun to die internally, their natural beauty sold cheap like blonde slaves in Byzantium or Babylon. Wherever dwells a hollowed-out people, wherever there is no longer any purpose – and Los Angeles is clearly such a place – earnest sentiment is replaced by the easy outlay of gold.

What happened the day before was sacred – so why is all acknowledgement of it so profane? It was a birth, one of the most important experiences in the lives of peoples of all cultures, and he has no way to mark it beyond some mixed bouquets and a dozen frozen images on a camera's memory card. Without truly meaningful occasions, without significant markers in life, the man and his small family are nothing. Though his son may have been given a traditional tribal name, there is no ceremony planned for his arrival – none exists for his family. The man had daubed no honey on the boy's tongue, drawing the sacred syllable "Om", as did the Hindus. When the hospital staff asked if the child were to be circumcised, as were the Muslims, the Jews, the Masai, and himself, he said no. He told himself that this was because the child's pedigree ensured his purity, and purity was not to be altered to suit the whims of a tainted world. However, this was only a belief, with no physical act to reify that belief . . . and even if he had allowed a circumcision to take place it still would have been a mere *procedure*, clinical and expedient, not the celebratory and ritual *event* it is for those others in their own lives . . .

So what, then, *is* there to denote this triumph, apart from the banality of overpriced roses and long distance phone calls? He looks at the boy, all wrinkled crimson flesh and balled fists. The child is the first in more than a thousand years of ancestors to be born free of the Christian yoke. The man has broken the bonds of the sword-imposed and self-imposed slavery, and the occasion is monumental in the history of his family and tribe. True, the negation of something cannot be something in itself. True, nothing has yet replaced the Galilean's creeping creed. True, it is the time of the great nihilism foretold by mighty Nietzsche . . . but surely the occasion deserves recognition of some kind . . . The moment has passed for promptness, yet he can still do something. He can still acknowledge the glory of the boy's arrival, even locked up here in this expensive airless room, with the delis and decadence and detritus splattered on the street below.

Gingerly he lifts the sleeping creature from its mother's arms. The child feels so small, so fragile in his hands. Ever so softly he walks out of the lightless confines of the north-facing recovery room and makes his way to the other side of the building. Here the sunbeams pour in from the southern sky, warm and bright. Nervous that his son will awaken at any second, he holds him up to the windows and allows the yellow light to bathe him, to envelop and bless him. Their people once hailed the sun as father of all things. The belief has done nothing for them, but still, an atavistic sense of pride and love courses through the man as he looks down at the golden infant cradled in his arms, sun-blessed and beautiful.

Aware of the presence of others making their way through the corridors, he hastily mumbles something about the *túath*, the tribe, and about the inescapable *geis*, the taboo of obligation, laid upon the boy by the former and future members of that tribe: the duty to persevere and propagate . . . As with the earlier imagery of armor and silver chains, the man cloaks the necessity of community and genetic survival in what have become romantic terms, trying to imbue the prosaic reality of hospital hallways and streaked windows with poetry. Ideally the rites should be taking place on a mountaintop with hundreds of reverent and ecstatic kinfolk in attendance . . . but the electronic security chip embedded within the plastic device clasped around the boy's ankle precludes rushing out to a mountaintop . . . and numerous genocides over the past centuries have seen to it that there are no hundreds of kinfolk . . . that there no longer is a *túath* . . .

Still, one does what one can. Gently kissing the child on the head, he removes him from the rays of the sun and returns to the recovery room.

* * * *

Two days later the boy is unyoked from his security anklet, a quasi-ceremony in itself, marking the release from confinement. The family leaves the hospital. Beyond its doors the city whirls unceasingly with its throngs, its traffic, its noise. Everywhere one looks there is flash, there is spectacle. Ambulances and luxury sedans and panhandlers and specialists and nurses and addicts and quacks and traffic lights and liars and thugs and shills and police cars and litter and the elite all jostle and flash and scream in the shadow of enormous buildings that blot out the sky. In the near distance, set atop a lonely hill above the turmoil, stands a statue of the healer Hippocrates, brilliant son of Hellas. His image there, amid the fumes and corruption and perpetual illness, is a mockery.

From the backseat of a taxi the man watches the statue recede into the distance, then returns his attentions to wife and child. The woman protectively holds the sleeping baby close to her breast. Outside the cab the crowded and polluted city passes by. Eventually they reach their tiny house, standing on a hill in the middle of Los Angeles. Sixty languages are spoken at the bottom of this hill . . . secrets passed in fifty-eight tongues the man doesn't understand . . . curses hurled in fifty-eight tongues the man doesn't understand . . . The chaos of the world surrounds him, the clamor of Babel reaches the very walls of his house. This is what he is bequeathing his son . . . madness . . . confusion . . .

Long ago, in a faraway place, in a very different time, the clever and powerful Choson family, rulers of what the Long Noses now know as Korea, sealed the borders of the nation-state they ruled. For centuries no foreigner could enter. The Hermit Kingdom it was called by some, a place where the man and the boy would have been instantly noticed and violently forced out. There was sanity, not madness. There was comprehension, not confusion. To this day the exemplary nation retains these qualities.

Other nations, too, seek sanity, wishing either to retain or attain it. Across vast Cathay, ancient and looming neighbor of Korea, the Han folk smile in an unpleasant way and refer to foreign travelers as *laowai*. In Tokyo, the fair-faced capitalists trying to do business in the Roppongi district sip their rice wine at outdoor tables, pretending not to notice the vans cruising the streets with mounted loudspeakers demanding the expulsion of the decadent and corrupting *gaijin*.

Around the world cohesion and comprehension attempt to reassert themselves, to the benefit of some, to the detriment of others. The bellicose Muslims transplanted to London and Rotterdam to scourge a cowardly people will, given the chance, roughly knock the man to the pavement and sneer "*dhimmi*" at him. The Armenians in Echmiadzin and Glendale have a term for him as well. It is *odar*. The Orthodox Jews of Montreal and along Pico Boulevard call him *goy* behind closed doors and in free newspapers. The epithet *gringo* no longer begins south of the Rio Grande, or over the border in sentimental old Tijuana. It is shouted from just down the hill, or three blocks east of his house.

From the Lapps in the far North to the defeated and near extinct Alacaluf in the utmost South, all peoples who are truly peoples have or had a term for the boy and the man, a blanket to throw over them and those they resemble in order to distinguish them as outsiders. It is what those who value cohesion and sanity and comprehension do . . . *dimam, odar, goyim* . . . It is what those who have retirement homes exclusively for themselves listed in the Los Angeles Yellow Pages do . . . *farang, barang, ferenji* . . . The din clatters upward from the bottom of the hill, the middle of the hill . . . *gringo, gora, laowai* . . . It clangs from the house next door, from the apartment across the street . . . All have come to the land the boy's ancestors escaped to . . . no retirement home exclusively for the man and the boy and their type . . . only struggle for them . . . only scribbles and whispers and dreams of dumplings for them . . .

Them. Us. The man will simplify the boy's life. It's a very complicated world now. There are sixty languages down there at the bottom of the hill . . . sixty different peoples . . . silly to try to understand them all – the secrets, the curses . . . no need . . . The boy will have a word now too. Heraclitus gave it to the man, Homer gave it to him . . . *herpeta* . . . most miserable of all the things that breathe and crawl upon the earth . . . a single term to maintain sanity . . . a blanket the man and the boy, too, can hurl over the world . . . It's all-inclusive, per the law of the land. It's non-discriminating. It's not just for those with different tongues, or those of different stature and countenance. It's not just for those who worship gods or God or neither or themselves. The capitalists are included, naturally . . . the communists, the humanitarians, the egalitarians, the Galileans, the bourgeoisie . . . all who aren't the man's type, welded into a single mass, joined under the same rubric . . . *herpeta* . . . "All *herpeta* are driven by blows," said inspired Heraclitus.

The boy's father left the labyrinth with knowledge. He learned the ways of the sane. He learned from the mistakes of the ancients and the tactics of successful moderns. He learned from the Los Angeles Yellow Pages.

Them. Us. That's all there is.

Except the boy is not quite "us" yet. To be so he must be consecrated, making him different from "them". Confusing? Only to certain types . . . expendable types . . . those who choose the vanishing Alacaluf as their role models . . . those who find fulfillment in being powerless, chased across continents, thrown into the dank holds of merchant ships, and scorned by every people they encounter . . . No, the boy must be consecrated, he must be made special . . . he and all who come after him . . .

*   *   *   *

Nine days after the child's arrival is when his baptism is to take place. Nine is auspicious in their varied myths and legends . . . three, nine, twelve . . . always those numbers appear, but of them all it is nine that most often promises salvation . . . For nine days Deucalion was hurled about on his ark, floating above the inundated ruins of his former world, before solid ground appeared again. For nine days Ulysses clung to the wreckage of his ship on the wine-dark sea, his countrymen all killed and a vengeful god seeking his destruction, before finally being rescued. For nine long days Odin hung screaming on the ash tree before finally learning the secrets of the runes.

In light of their current historical situation, seeking relevance in specific aspects of tales involving imaginary gods and superhuman heroes seems to be a pointless exercise for a very real father with a very real son in a very real world. The man is well aware that he and his family do not possess, as do more successful peoples, a "living" god – dynamic, pliant, and worthy. This makes him even more conscious of the questionable benefit of utilizing, or even in only recounting, the tales of outdated deities and demigods and heroes, outside of entertainment. Stories of larger-than-life entities battling sea monsters or riding eight-legged horses across the sky are meaningless and can only have religious resonance with those who set up shrines to cartoon versions of Thor or Mithras or Zeus in their basements . . . yet he employs the tales regardless . . . for along with the sound advice to be found therein, there is another thing that impels him to continue mining them . . . It is, quite simply, the fact that the stories are *theirs* – the man's, the boy's, the family's, the scattered remnants'. They belong to no one else. It is pride of possession in a world where universalism has claimed all things for all people. The man utilizes these myths and legends – *their* myths and legends – because even though there never were supernatural beings, magic weapons, or fantastic powers, there *were* ancestors, men and women linked to the present by genes and culture, striding through the fog of prehistory, struggling to survive and overcome through the use of technology and will.

As with the personalities populating the mytho-cultural tales of all peoples, the various heroes and divinities present in the tales of the man's tribe were formed from different sources and circumstances. Some of them appeared when the worldly exploits of the mightiest and cleverest among his forebears became exaggerated over the centuries, which Euhemerus long ago pointed out. Others were anthropomorphized from the combination of environmentally specific natural phenomena and the merged and amalgamated qualities and attributes admired by the tribe. These formative details behind their origins aren't important to the man, though. The possibility of a pre-euhemerized Odin, for instance, bringing his kinsmen from the hinterlands of Asia to a new northern homeland, has as much relevance to him as the shamanistic version of a psychopompic Odin conducting the souls of the dead into the afterlife. What is relevant in a case like this is the knowledge that his ancestors, in their desperate bid to continue living, attached prestige to those who brought their followers to new realms, either leading them from one territory to another or from one world to the next. It is the implied meaning of the myth itself and its pertinence to the present that carries the most importance.

However, in order that the wisdom contained in these myths and legends might be made applicable to the various situations encountered in the present, they must be known in the first place. They cannot be lost. They cannot be forgotten. Therefore the man continually combs and catalogs the ancient tales, finding much of substance and worth along the way. At the same time he hermeneutically purges them of their fantasies, diligently killing off imaginary monsters and sky gods in order that the sunshine of reality might dispel the fog of prehistory. By paring away the fantastic, he learns, the boundaries between the past and present crumble, and when this happens the landscape of one's consciousness is completely altered, unable to ever return to its previously partitioned state.

This revelatory technique, like most things, is in no way new. More than two millennia before the man undertook his exegesis, brilliant Virgil had already depicted his Sibyl showing wandering Aeneas the vanquished mythical beasts of the past, finally consigned to the realm of the dead where they belonged. The Roman knew that, in order for a people to persevere on this earth, myth must be brought down to this earth. He knew that silly creatures must ultimately be slain, buried, and left in the germinal years. The irrelevant and the false must be discarded. Talk of gnomes and Cyclopes and miracles and fairies and frost giants and magic must fade away, not even to be touched by children any longer. The man's family has antagonists and enemies more deadly than witches or demons or Satan – more dangerous because they are men, and men are real.

*   *   *   *

Nine days . . . the baptismal moment has arrived . . . Someday the child will know that he is an end *and* a beginning. He is different from the herd, from the *herpeta*. "You solitaries must become a people." So said their thundering prophet, one of three, one of twelve, let the future decide. The boy will have a tribe. It is forming even as the pressure of evolution increases. To gather that tribe, each to the other, is one of the *geasa* that has been laid on the man. His other *geis* is not one of obligation, but of proscription: to never let despondency hamper him during this difficult search. The duty of those he seeks is, whether they know it or not, to discover the man and the boy . . . to enfold them in strong shield arms . . . to embrace, to melt, to meld, to harden . . .

Discomfiture lurks within the man, however. His self-assurance is attacked by his self-awareness; his confidence is undercut by the internal nagging, by the fear of foolishness. He does not want to appear ridiculous in the eyes of imaginary witnesses. To invent – rather, *to adapt* – rituals and traditions is awkward, particularly when only a single family is involved. Even the brief moment in the hospital hallway, with the sun and the hastily muttered romantic words, did not feel fully right . . . yet the necessity outweighs anything . . . They are the hunted, and they themselves must shape the tools that will enable them to survive or they will perish. It is too painful for the man to think that perhaps they already have, and that all his thoughts are those of a ghost . . . too painful to think that those three standing there in a cramped Los Angeles yard as he prepares his ceremony are only specters . . . To selectively rummage through records of the past, to seek meaning where perhaps there is none, to attempt to rescue from ruins and debris that which only *might be construed* as having relevance – all this is disheartening in its artificiality.

The sun disappears. At the man's feet a fire has been kindled. It is the released energy of that vanished sun, giving light and heat in the night that always, inevitably, comes. In the flames rests a steel bowl, holding ice that rapidly melts to water. Constant change, yet constant existence . . . never disappearing, only altering . . . from ice to water to mist, reappearing as water again somewhere else . . . as dewdrops covering the steppes of Ukraine . . . as rain clouds over the Caucasus . . . floating to the North, to the West . . . descending as sleet over Saxony, turning to frost in the Vendée . . . on and on . . . on and on . . .

> *We are the children of Earth and Water,*
> *And the nurslings of the Sky;*
> *We pass through the pores of the ocean and shores;*
> *We change, but we cannot die.*

Their new situation calls for the creation of new narratives. All words of past poets and musicians and philosophers will be taken, turned to use, not whimsy . . . not solipsistic "insight" . . . Their deeper meanings will be codified . . . made relevant, not specious . . . exclusive, not public . . . specific, not vague . . . All of everything will be gathered, sifted, assembled, applied, tested, and lived.

Beneath the lustrous colors of the gloaming the naked lad is handed over. The words are spoken solemnly, earnestly.

"Let us look each other in the face. We know well enough how remote our place is. Beyond the North, beyond the ice, beyond death – our life, our happiness. We have discovered that happiness; we know the way, we got our knowledge of it from thousands of years in the labyrinth. We, ourselves, alone."

The freezing water is poured over the boy's head. He doesn't cry, and is returned to his mother. She wraps him in a red towel grown gray in the fading light of the sun. The man slaps a stray mosquito and continues.

"*Intelligenti pauca.*"

Few words are necessary for those who understand.

And like that, it is done.

It is synthetic. It is incomplete and amateurish. It is awkward and forced, bordering on the modern, on the craving for Druids and antler hats and the ridiculous desire for mystery. Yet it is still worth infinitely more than nothing . . . more than a congratulatory phone call and a bouquet of dying flowers . . . There must be ceremony in their lives, *there must be acknowledgement of what is important.*

It will change over the coming centuries. It will evolve, grow, be persecuted, go underground, flourish, and finally become stable . . . formalized, not ossified . . . Every aspect will be infused with meaning, every word will take on deeper value. As the descendants of the man and the boy and their comrades and kin grow, and thrive, the baptismal rite will eventually be performed in their own language, the current tongue of the Anglos left to others who choose slave trading, warmongering, or defamation as their *raison d'être*. There will be thousands of baptized children, millions of them . . . and there will be a name for them . . . These people will have a name again, as they had once, in their truncated state of becoming.

He slaps another mosquito . . . smiles at his wife, who smiles back . . . She understands the importance. She is kind enough to say nothing about how strained it seems, how glaring and weird and pointless it all seems without tribe or tradition to infuse a sense of normalcy.

Somehow, though, somewhere, no matter how small, no matter how seemingly insignificant, it had to begin again.

*   *   *   *

The man has lived most of his adult life in Los Angeles. Drawn there in his youth by the lure of the sparkling lights, the city – with its ghastly fusion of the worst the First and Third World have to offer – has grown increasingly toxic to him over time. As with the men and women who trod the earth before him and from whose pattern he's cut, the urban environment works upon him like a slow poison. His ancestors had their lives cut short in the newly mechanized world of the factory and the bomb. They died early, and they died out. He, their descendant, doesn't suffer the assembly line and the shrapnel, but rather the postmodern equivalents of choking air, incessant noise, and constant threats of urban violence.

Previously the man was able to at least seek respite from it all in the mock peace offered inside his house. However, with the addition of the newborn that luxury no longer exists. The infant, howling and screeching at all hours as it does, brings the chaos and shrieks of the outside world directly into the home. The man finds himself under constant mental assault. When the two are occasionally left alone together, the child's pale face turns red with consuming frustration over the fact that his father is not a female of the species. The urban, atomized man, long ago cut off from the reality of new life, doesn't understand. He fears the infant will scream until it dies, if such a thing is possible. He knows it desires only soft caresses and nourishment and instant succor, yet its screeching elicits no sympathy from him. Only rage. Only the masculine desire to smash until the howling ceases.

Adult males of the species should not be so involved with infancy. They should never be so close to a baby, particularly without the biological buffer of the female. The man feels this intrinsically, knows that the contrary notion is only a modern ethos, antithetical to animal law, a syrupy extension of televised melodramas that's bound to fail and fade like all such things. During the glorious becoming of the Persians, a father did not see his son until seven years had passed from the child's birth. This system, it's been claimed, was devised to alleviate a man's heartache should his boy die. Perhaps. Perhaps a greater truth is that squalling children's lives were, in this manner, saved from the rage of fierce men only recently emerged from barbarism. Perhaps, as the custom faded away, so did the once-mighty Achaemenids and their empire.

However, there are, admittedly, occasional moments of contentment. The boy's toothless smiles and bubbly gurgles and widened blue eyes do something to the man, bring forth emotions like he's never known. His chest stirs, his heart opens as wide as the California sky, and any hostile thoughts in his head are repressed, banished to dark corners. He kisses the little fingers and toes and lips, laughs long and boisterously over his good fortune at being a father . . . feels like a buoyant young Titan stomping across the earth when it was new . . .

Fantastic as the feeling is, the man never allows the heightened state to last very long. He cannot let himself be joyously lifted, then lulled to contentment, because contentment leads to complacency, and complacency eventually leads to ignoring the reality of the harsh world beyond the walls. The buoyant young Titans, it must be remembered, or whatever race they represented, ended up murdered, tortured, and enslaved.

* * * *

The boy grows quickly. Each evening upon the man's early arrival home from the office his firstborn is eagerly snatched up into his arms. Together the two head out into the streets, out where life is . . . out where beautiful things and interesting things sometimes shimmer amid the botched and the scarred . . . Their route follows, in microcosm, a course seen over and over again in their history during times of strength – an *iter ad Orientem*, a march to the East. The man exits the gate and strides uphill toward the nearby bluff that overlooks downtown Los Angeles. It is a city abuzz with the frenetic vibrancy of flies consuming an eagle's carcass . . . a city of ghouls and vanishing peoples, of gnawing termites, of mosquitoes long grown immune to poisons and pesticides . . . Its high-rises, perched high in the smoggy sky, gleam in the light of the setting sun. The orange and yellow rays reflect off mirrored windows, bleaching the concrete and brick and steel as easily as they do scattered camel bones in the sands of the Tarim Basin, that Asian graveyard where the Tocharians lay down to die . . .

Staring out over the impressive skyline, the man cradles the child in one arm and points with the other, speaking in a low baritone. "All this must be torn down, son. This civilization and everything it stands for – the slavery, the usury, the cruelty – must go away. Inside those glass buildings over there are busy men who murder people who dwell in mud huts. They do it with bombs, they do it with newspapers, they do it with numbers. Before that they murdered people who lived in brick buildings, or straw shacks, or farmhouses, or huts, or tents made out of animal skins. It didn't matter how these people lived, or when, or where, they murdered them, and when they weren't murdering them they were shackling them. We're no different in their eyes. Thralls, fit only for servitude. We must destroy it – you and I and our descendants. If we do not, we will remain slaves forever." The oblivious child raises a fat hand and rudely bats at his father's mouth. The man smiles and tickles the fleshy chin. Someday, perhaps, his words will have meaning to the boy.

That finished, the two turn north and march around the corner, where stands a tiny house that looks as if it's been plucked from a clearing in the Black Forest. Here all the city's pigeons congregate. The man tosses them healthy seeds, not the garbage bread marketed to the proles. With imitation coos he lures them closer. Then, when the moment's right, he abruptly lifts his arms to the sky . . . *whoosh* . . . As one the birds rise into the air. In that split second he quickly readjusts the boy in his arms, balances him in his hands and, as he does every evening, begins to fly him among the startled flock . . . rushing back and forth, dipping him up and down within the gentle maelstrom of the whirling pigeons . . . carefully steering him clear of the possibly diseased feathers gently descending around them . . . appropriate manna for the times . . .

The boy, as always, bursts into a laughing frenzy . . . kicking his legs, flapping his milk-plump arms and inflated feet, exuberantly attempting to mimic the creatures . . . Jaded Angelenos cruise by the scene in their foreign cars, watching, and the spirit of the moment is infectious, forcing them to grin broadly, to smile with a rare glee at the pure sight of the laughing baby boy flying with the pigeons.

One day an ancient woman emerges from the storybook house. She tosses dried grain to the sidewalk . . . nourishment for the birds, turning them into her companions in this loneliest of cities and loneliest of eras . . . The pigeons know their benefactress. Braving the annoyance of the human hatchling flapping and kicking in their midst, they return for their meal.

The old woman has a horrible hunchback. She moves slowly. The boy wants to meet her and the man acquiesces. He brings the child closer to her. She smiles as much as her shriveled mouth allows. Her eyes shine forth from the dishrag wrinkles of her face. They are lucid and intelligent eyes, so different from the foggy mirrors of the man's contemporaries, dulled by media, dulled by everything. She thrills when the boy beams at her, his little lips twisted upward in friendly greeting. She and the man exchange the pleasantries that strangers still share at times. Her name is proffered – it is the same as the boy's mother.

"What a pretty baby he is," she rasps, over and over, staring, seeming to remember something from long ago. Ever so subtly the man offers the boy for her to hold. Sadly, she indicates that something is wrong with her hands – a disease? – which prevents her from touching him.

A tinge of sorrow brushes the man, a bead of unhappiness that the world drips into him on occasion. Eventually he and his son go away, leaving the old woman rasping effusive goodbyes and struggling with neighbor-friendly hand waves. Between genuine promises to return, a sudden shame arises within him. The drips of unhappiness have become a torrent, threatening to wash away the carefully constructed seawalls he's erected about himself over the years. He is ashamed of the heartless youth he once was, ashamed of the teasing and nasty mockery he once doled out to those less fortunate than him, the same quality he now finds so loathsome in his enemies, those men who fill the skyscrapers on the eastern horizon.

The man doesn't want memories like this to appear. He particularly doesn't want them interpreted in the enervating tongue of weak moderns, but rather in the *Ursprach* of indifferent Nature. Still, he recalls his former cruelty, wonders whence it sprung, and why. He no longer falls prey to television logic, to simplistic bourgeois falsehoods versus gestalt reality. *Why* doesn't matter. The deeds of the past lie there to be interpreted any way one wishes. He will utilize these mistakes of his. He will gain strength from them. He will allow the shame he experiences to be reconfigured into lessons for the boy. The child will not be cruel in life to those who do not deserve it. There is, after all, no shortage of those who do.

They about-face, heading south now, surrounded by stucco and palm trees, by cacti and bohemians. The heavy scent of jasmine stuffs up their noses and mouths like fluffy cotton. There are quick glimpses of heavy-lidded men getting drunk in dilapidated garages. Overhead fly the omnipresent police helicopters, pointed out to the boy clearly and coldly as "enemy", which is what he calls them for years, knowing no other term. They walk on. The man explains where the ubiquitous graffiti comes from . . . explains who scrawls it everywhere, explains who allows it . . . explains the simple methods and mindset that could eliminate it . . . He speaks of the weaknesses of the world, but not yet its full horrors.

Eventually they reach a boxy house owned by a popular artist couple, its yard filled with sun-drenched, brightly colored flowers. Here the bees busily work, silently positioning and repositioning, moving from jasmine to ice plant to mock orange. The longer the man and the boy stare, the more bees seem to appear, silently revealing themselves from amid the camouflaging vegetation.

"It's a circle," the man says to his son's curious little face. "The sun feeds the flowers, who feed the bees, who help feed us – an enormous circle, and if one part is broken we all suffer the consequences." The boy gurgles and grins and shakes his pudgy fists and watches the insects intently, not knowing that across the doomed continent the bees are mysteriously dying out and disappearing . . . as if they too, like the childless couple whose ice plant and mock orange they pollinate, have lost the will to live . . .

Onward marches the pair, continuing up the hill, the man pointing out trucks and clouds and birds and trees. Finally, they reach their corner, a spot where the sidewalk's concrete is cracked by roots and weather, and the street sign pole is bent from a runaway vehicle. They sit on the curb here every evening for months, the one held gently in the arms of the other, until one night it happens that the boy is finally able to sit upright alongside the man . . . fat legs dangle over the high curb, their attached feet still not able to reach the ground . . . one chubby elbow, punctuated by cartoonish indentations and dimples, rests casually on the man's knee . . . Lightly stroking the flaxen hair so different from his own, the man tells the boy that the wind whispers secrets meant only for them. He tells him their legends, their poems, their history. He speaks of intrepid adventurers and savvy generals, of clever thieves and hardened armies and grueling slavery . . . of the accomplishments of a magnificent people for the most part forgotten, their memories only occasionally animated by the gloating of victorious enemies in skyscrapers . . . As always, the tiny creature intently watches the moving mouth on his father's face.

"You are I are different from each other, but the same as each other," the man says to the child. "I am you and you are me. They are they and we are we." Only certain types understand such realities. Only *túatha*.

The patchwork population of a city, of a civilization in its final throes, tumbles by. Burly white truckers, having taken a wrong turn, slow their vehicles and smile at the boy. Walnut-stained Indian women, up from Mexico and Guatemala, do the same. Mustachioed gay men clad in leather, returning from their bars . . . Korean students . . . skinny hipsters . . . lesbian couples . . . many stop during those many months for no other reason than to tell the man what a beautiful baby the boy is . . .

And he is . . . he is . . . a vision of heaven, painted from a palette dripping with rose and blue and gold . . . "From fairest creatures we desire increase," said De Vere, culturally incapable of imagining that one day whole nation-states would spit on such notions.

Finished with their curb-sitting they take the short stroll to the Salvadoran's house. A crucifix hangs on her garage to ward off gangs. Her eternally yapping Chihuahuas leap spasmodically behind her chain link fence. The noise draws her outside, where she smiles and comes over to greet the man and the boy. Every other week the spry old Catholic queries the man on his ancestry – was he Russian – and then eagerly relates her own lineage. She tells of Spanish, Jewish, and Indian blood, tells of the trials of life in El Salvador and Colombia, tells of her long-ago marriage to a Welsh Mormon and the daughter it produced. She worries that the boy is cold in the evening air now that the sun is setting, or comments on his startling eyes, then she goes inside to have her tea. The two leave her house and continue on their way, stopping only once more to give regards to their next-door neighbors, an old couple whose accents still recall the isolated Japanese village they left sixty years before. The wizened husband shows them his pet tortoise, nearly half a century old, and his wife proudly offers cucumbers from her garden. The boy crawls in the dirt, sniffing flowers, while together the adults talk beneath the vanishing light of the sky.

Eventually the man and boy say their goodbyes, return to the street, and turn through their gate for supper. The final sight most evenings is the aging and childless artist-owner of the flower and bee house, walking her dog and emptily blabbing into her cell phone. The appearance of the dog sends the boy into excited palpitations, while the barren biped slouching alongside it is a reminder to the man that behind all the niceties – the flowers and compliments and *gratis* cucumbers and illusory, multicult splendor – the city always lurks. It's always there, ready to bring one back to reality in a second. It stinks of sterility and selfishness and decay and looming violence all at once, but mostly it stinks of death.

$$* \qquad * \qquad * \qquad *$$

There are no children on the city block where the man lives with his wife and son. In every Neutra-designed house atop that Los Angeles hill, in every postmodern concrete and glass cube, in every flat-roofed swimming pool apartment better suited to Amman or Tangiers, in every hipster-restored Spanish-style duplex from the 1920s – in all of them dwell immature men and infertile women. There are complete boulevards of these people, whole neighborhoods of them, blithely whistling as the guillotine descends on their delicately scented necks. Whole nations of them exist now, purchasing, sipping, driving, tasting, listening, watching, eating, testing, playing, discussing, lounging, performing, observing, critiquing, protesting, dog-walking, blogging, obeying, flying, downloading, judging, screaming, auditioning, red-lining, green-lighting, voting, consuming, and laughing. Their abodes are filled with all the treasures the world can provide. They live lives of sheer self-amusement . . . lives of collecting, not of growing . . . all reaping, no sowing . . .

They're too busy entertaining and being entertained to look ahead. They don't see the approaching confrontation between themselves and the yawning beast that is Age. They're unarmed and unprepared. Time is already waging its war on them. Its vanguard attacks are nearly imperceptible at first . . . the single strands of gray on the head, the creaking knee, the mysterious pain in the shoulder . . . the wrinkles clustering in corners of the face, tiny cracks perceptible only under harsh light . . . the faint tiredness always lurking, ready to engulf one in warm slumber at any opportunity . . .

How will they cope, these who believe that youth lasts forever in a single body? They can pretend for a time that they're beyond the laws of the universe, but soon the reality won't be able to be ignored in the same way in which they ignore so many other realities in their lives. The man knows these people. He mingles with them, he hears their complaints. The songs on the radio aren't as appealing to them as they once were, the names of the new bands aren't as easily recalled, the music itself makes them feel cut off from the vitality of youth, which is all they really pine for. The patrons at the bars they still frequent seem younger than ever, and speak a different slang. Their cherished ideas, world outlooks drilled into them by university professors and supposedly subversive arthouse films, are no longer as accepted, are increasingly irrelevant and antiquated. They've sought profundity in everything except the essential, and now the dust begins to gather on their dreams as heavily as it does their accumulated possessions. They have become like objects themselves . . . stiff, no longer human . . . manufactured, bought, sold, bought again, sold again, discarded, and soon to be forgotten . . .

It will gnaw at them, the worthlessness of it all . . . the meaninglessness of yet another piece of configured plastic, of yet another bottle of imported absinthe, yet another three-chord song download . . . What will they be at fifty years, sixty, seventy, as increasingly they grow weaker, more alone, their onetime friends – never comrades – evaporating along with the rest of their faddish surroundings? Where will they gain respite from their worsening woes? How will they shake off the burdens strapped to their swaybacks by a snickering world, one that's ravenously anticipating, even hastening, their demise?

High above all of them, just off a trail winding through sprawling Griffith Park, the boy sits cradled between the man's legs, the two of them smelling the summer air and silently looking out over the megalopolis they live in. Unconsciously the man undulates his oddly crooked toes beneath the straps of his sandals, a habit of his. Happening to glance at the boy's feet he notices ten smaller toes, similarly crooked, moving in the exact manner as his own.

The man smiles. He squeezes his son, breathes in the warm smell of his soft hair. Twenty near-identical toes wiggling in unison . . . Can the closets full of ironic tee-shirts and stacks of manga and lovingly collected Scandinavian furniture of these others offer anything like the fulfillment this living boy gives him? Can their spoiled dogs act as a physical mirror reflecting the past and the future, as does a child of one's own? Do those people in that city below have *any idea* that the silence of the crypt speeds their way?

One by one the morning hikers walk by in staggered single-file on the path behind the man and the boy. Their ears are covered by headphones. Their faces are placid, the emotionless visages of a suicidal cult – which is what they are . . . a childless sect that dominates the man's neighborhood and similar neighborhoods across the land . . . They have their own carefully considered rituals and taboos, their own saints and heretics . . . their own demons and angels, hallowed ground and pilgrimages, sacred images and writings . . . For the moment, the West is theirs.

"To perpetuate was the task of life," said London, who made truth simple. "Its law was death."

The man and the boy drive home. To their right and left are yoga studios, health food co-ops, antique shops, coffee houses, vinyl record swaps, cafés, theaters, clothing stores, renovated houses, bars, live music venues, Thai restaurants, used book stores, and gelaterias. The sidewalks are bustling. The outdoor tables are full of chattering people. Everything looks tidy and pretty . . . but he is not fooled . . . He knows the shiny wonderland is but a façade for evolutionary failure, a stage erected for the walking dead. Communities such as these, lacking children, should be burned, says the Talmud. Though the law does not seem to apply to the man's people, he receives and accepts instruction, insight, and advice where he can. "Take counsel from those who are most successful," instructed Leonardo. The man does. He knows where to seek strategies in the world marketplace. He's learned how to apply knowledge to specific situations without the melting to nothingness of universalism. Though a subjective person, he's learned to utilize objectivity to garner the benefits of others' subjectivity.

Such places should be burned, he agrees, but as fate would have it, no one need even actively strike a match at this stage. The inhabitants are burning *themselves*, ecstatically immolating themselves with every wasted egg, with every damaged sperm. To a human's scaled down vision it's painfully slow, but it's happening across the decades and centuries nevertheless. An inferno, *suttee* on the grandest of scales . . . Wife, mother, aunt, grandmother – these have become useless words for many, relevant only in describing previous generations. Husband, father, uncle, grandfather – titles of the receding past . . . anthropological terms etched on tombstones and in crumbling books no one reads anymore . . .

On the other side of the ocean and the years, in a land whence the boy's ancestors came, the Communist murderers efficiently eliminated the indigenous artisans, aristocrats, and middle class. The sentence for select non-laboring possessors of clean fingernails and smooth palms was a bullet in the back of the head, and the genetic heritage of centuries was forever altered. Capitalism, Communism's bankrupt twin, didn't even need to waste the bullets. It simply waited a generation or two for the artisans and aristocrats and middle class to gladly, willingly, off themselves. Where those across the ocean were executed and tortured and worked to death in gulag camps, these Angelenos happily move into downward dog position, sip lattes, hook up, nosh on pad thai, and critique films, with the same result. Disappearance.

It is as it must be. This generation of gelato eaters and comic book collectors and media worshippers must burn and fade away. A new forest will arise from its ashes. The man is thankful for the destruction, thankful, in a way, for the mass suicide. These people have proven themselves unfit for existence. The great question is, what will replace them?

The teeming bottom of the hill, that's what. Sixty languages, marshaled against the man and the boy . . .

✳   ✳   ✳   ✳

At that teeming bottom of the hill is a park. At a park, it was once assumed, one could find clean grounds and exuberant youth, neatly trimmed athletic fields and doting parents unanimously agreeing that theirs was a nation with a glorious future because everyone shared a love of baseball. No longer. The grounds of the park at the bottom of the hill are littered with trash, soiled diapers, and the waste of dogs bred for fighting. A whole different type of exuberant youth mill about, with vibrant names like *Mara Salvatrucha* and *Calle Diez y Ocho*. Crack cocaine is smoked in dark corners by down and out black men who are being pushed across the city by newcomers – Aztecs, Mayans, and nameless other tribes who've immigrated from fecund southern realms. Among the ranks of these newcomers are those who've already given up, who've been beaten down by the Land of Opportunity as thoroughly as the despondent black men have. They hang sloppily on the periphery of the park, swallowing booze without the romantic quaintness of paper bags, numbingly unconscious by eleven o'clock in the morning.

The buildings and the swings and the climbing structures and the water fountains and the trashcans are covered with graffiti. Further west in the city more prestigious parks employ something called a "graffiti removal person", whose task is to daily scrub the spraypaint from picnic tables, boulders, and trees. This person never comes to the park at the bottom of the hill. Nor do many people who live at the top of the hill come, unless it's to hastily walk their dogs – they prefer to drive to those other parks further west. For the most part, shaved heads and obesity are the order of things at the park at the bottom of the hill . . . and children . . . The newcomers from the overflowing southern lands do not wear the reproductive straitjackets of their inventive, dog-walking neighbors. There is no novel to concentrate on completing, no studio deal in the making, no lazy pursuit of exhausted art. There is just life, and lots of it.

The park is walking distance from the man's house. No matter its run-down state, it still has trees and swings and occasional swathes of unspoiled grass. The asphalt and concrete city block the man and boy live on has little of these, so they make use of the nearby park when they can. Tuesdays are said to be the best day to visit. The city workers clean it on Mondays, so the inevitable weekly accumulation of litter is still small the day after. Unfortunately the man works on Tuesdays, so weekends have to suffice. For months he carries his son down the hill to the park on Saturday mornings, making his way through a truly incredible amount of trash before spreading a blanket on a piece of untouched ground. Here he sits with the boy, watching him play with broken sticks and rocks and the like. Then he carries him to the swing, pushing him back and forth and grabbing at his unshod feet, listening to his squeals and laughter. He tells him stories or hangs him from the monkey bars, testing the grip strength in the little hands. He kisses the child's eyelids and tickles his thighs and never forgets the reality of their surroundings.

Over the course of those Saturday mornings there is little interaction with other park visitors. Occasionally Guatemalan or Honduran nannies make their way over to the man and the boy, eager for a playmate for their own blonde charges, feeling intrinsically that like should be matched with like. The man politely smiles at the naïve young women. They've not yet gained the cultural refinement necessary to know that in their new wealthy homeland, congregation is discouraged among certain categories of people. They're unaware that "like matched with like" is an outmoded idea to the parents who live atop hills.

Such instances of tentative contact are the exception though. Generally it's just the man and the boy, alone. This lack of connection can be attributed to other reasons beside the innate shyness of the man's breed. In addition to the yawning bio-cultural divide between him and the others, there is the guard he puts up . . . the constantly emitted low-level threat signal that perhaps others can sense . . . a hyperawareness of everything taking place around him at all moments, a heightened alertness . . . He's seen the outlines of bodies spraypainted on the asphalt streets as he walks down to the park. He's seen the blatant hand signals occasionally flashed in his direction when visiting the place. Brutality is always lurking, visible or not. There can be no displays of middle-class obliviousness. There can be no earnest attempts at neighborliness. A disarming smile can't be offered for fear of it being misconstrued as weakness or submissiveness. It is a dangerous time, a time of struggle, and the shield can never be lowered too much.

*　　　*　　　*　　　*

But as the days and weeks roll on, the man begins to realize how heavy that shield really is. It weighs him down. It saps his strength. It tires him

29

out. Finally it occurs to him that there actually is a way he can safely lower it on occasion. It strikes him that he can be freer with his son out in the suburbs . . . out along the beach, among the wealthy . . . among those with different concerns and fears than his . . . less involving the threat of bodily harm, more involving a loss of privilege or economic status . . .

So he shifts venues. He drives the boy two hours south to a shining kingdom of crouching and hiding and whispering and pretending . . . a land where hand signals and shaved heads exist only in the films rabidly consumed by its pampered youth . . . a land where the people have never even heard of the outlines of bodies spraypainted on the streets by gangs . . . a gated land, a bubbled land . . . a land where he grew up . . .

He exits the freeway, making his way past the familiar landmarks, past chain restaurants and overly large tract houses and cinema marquees touting PG movies. Finally he arrives at his destination – a park close to his old house. The park didn't exist when he himself was young. There were woods then. Clearly though, to the neighborhood's residents, a park is superior to dirty, unsafe woodlands . . . and it really does seem to be an amazing place . . . There are no crack pipes dropped in the Audi-filled parking lot. There are no drunks slumped in the bathrooms. There is no graffiti anywhere, thus no need for a "graffiti removal person". The playground area is gleaming. The athletic fields are neatly trimmed. The grounds are clean and the sky is blue. All is, seemingly, as it should be.

The man doesn't fall for it though. He sees through the place as easily as he does the neighborhood of gelaterias and coffee shops back in L.A. This suburban park is as threatening and depressing as its littered urban counterpart a hundred miles north. So what if it's clean – so are cancer wards. So what if it's safe – so are sarcophagi. The whole place is nothing more than a comforting deception, and the most dangerous part of the illusion is the existence of the babies and children scattered about everywhere who resemble his son . . . for though they are the same phenotype as the boy, they are nothing *like* the boy . . . They cannot be. The infants and children crawling and toddling on the clean, safe playground surfaces have not been held up to the sun; they have not undergone baptism of fire and ice. The boy is different from them because his parents are different from their parents, and his parents are different from their parents because his have undergone some type of mutation, be it cultural or biological . . . and when mutation takes place, memetic or genetic, it indicates the budding branch of an evolutionary divergence . . . This is the reason, perhaps, that the suburban playground appears so different to the man than it doubtless appears to those others around him.

He casually surveys them. He remembers these people from his youth . . . the scented and the coiffed, sporting their designer bags and designer faces . . . They haven't changed. They are still motivated by different desires than he is. It's money alone that drives them . . . the *auri sacra fames*, the holy hunger for gold . . . They strive for it, would rend the flesh from their skulls for it. They have sold their dignity, their history, their honor and birthright for it, and would do it all again. It is their one true god, it always has been, and they desperately desire to become one with it. Their sweaty lust taints everything about their already cramped personalities. There must be another term for them, something to replace *nouveau riche*. It flows too easily, it sounds too pretty . . . something in Tocharian is more apt, something in the tongue of the Alacaluf . . .

The man stares at them, America's bourgeoisie. They are profane, as always . . . thickly clustering, monochromatic in hue and soul, covetous and base, living only to consume, consume, and devour like their childless ideological brethren up the freeway in Los Angeles . . . This must be where they come to breed. Perhaps he just hasn't understood the lifecycles, the migration patterns of those atop his hill. Here on the playground are people who seem strangely akin to those sterile urban hipsters, yet with offspring. Here they are, laying their eggs in the Pacific sand like so many endangered turtles.

Your life is lax, without dream or purpose,
Older and more decrepit than the barren earth,
Castrated since the cradle by this age which kills
All vigorous or profound passion.

31

It's been well more than a century since the Frenchman De Lisle wrote those lines. Now, after a global eradication of the sacred, the times are even worse. City, suburb – only superficial differences, really. The man is as far removed from the inhabitants of the one as he is from the other. A punch in the mouth isn't, in the end, much different from a punch in the stomach.

*   *   *   *

There is a shiny toy at the manicured playground, brightly colored and plastic. It was manufactured in an ecologically devastated town along the Huai River, hundreds of *li* northwest of Shanghai where no *laowai* ever travel. The environmental damage it did to the world when it was created, however, is not finished. Now, thousands of miles from its birthplace, the shiny toy wreaks havoc on the *social* environment of another nation, one already past the point of saving.

The man watches as the boy crawls up to the toy, drawn by its colors. Its four-year-old owner is engaged in another part of the playground. He is the son of a mortgage broker whose paternal ancestors stretch back to that once-glorious France that De Lisle saw finally die. He spends three hours a day watching television. He knows the names of twenty-two animated characters but has never heard of Merovius or Vercingetorix or Charlemagne or Tancred or Louis IX or Bayard or Napoleon.

Seated near the bauble is the child's nanny, shipped over from Ireland, maybe England. It doesn't matter. There are no differences anymore between the peoples of the self-conquered West. From over the rim of his book the man watches as she smiles at his son. It is the grimace of a corpse, which is all she knows, having been birthed and raised in a massive graveyard. The boy recognizes the expression, imperfect as it is, and returns the smile with his own, all cream and apples and sunshine, before moving forward on all fours to finally touch the thing, whatever it might be.

"Ah-ah-ah," he's admonished, at nine months old, "That's not yours. That's somebody else's." The boy, while he may have thought he understood the meaning of the forced smile, definitely doesn't understand this voice. It's rigid, it's glacial, it carries an unfamiliar energy. It's not part of his world – yet. It will be soon. It's the voice of vapid materialism . . . the voice of the crypt . . .

Unsure of himself, he halts, beams again, moves forward, reaches out . . .

The cold voice returns instantly. "No. No!" The second "no" is sharp. It startles him, freezes him in his place. "It's. Not. Yours." The pallid nanny bends forward, plucks the plastic toy from the ground, tucks it into a bag, and that is that.

This is how it is. There is to be no community at the playground. Ever. It is America, white America, and nothing is shared between people, between families. Each individual is to fill his role as atom, never becoming a compound, forever floating in a muddied solution until finally, blessedly, dissolved . . . the nanny only plays her part, performs her ordained, lower-caste duty in keeping the crypt spotless . . .

The man knows he's just breached playground etiquette. He knows that immediately upon sighting one's child merely *approaching* something that isn't personally owned by one's family, that child is to be stopped . . . and if it's too late, if the child *does* manage to get its hands on someone else's possessions, it must be reprimanded . . . The reprimand generally follows the same pattern. First, an emphatic, head-shaking, "No," is shouted. Then, in a perfect balance of control and instruction, an exclamatory explanation is made, directed at the child but meant for all to hear, about how the object in question belongs to someone else and is not to be touched by anyone except its owner without asking. Finally, wrapping the whole bit up, the child is forced to apologize for the quasi-sin. Meanwhile the mother or father or nanny of the child who's been wronged will cajole him to offer high-minded forgiveness to the rude transgressor of playground values. Mumbling, the slighted child does so. Everyone hopes that a lesson has been learned and that such a thing will never take place again. In this manner modern values are instilled early.

The boy has moved on, crawling away across the neatly edged grass. His father has lowered his book and smiles after him. "How old," asks the pasty nanny, the empty question posed on playgrounds across the continent by cardboard women and half-men, not really caring about an answer, just trying to fill uncomfortable silence.

"Nine months," he answers, his voice equally hollow, letting her know to no longer speak to him. He watches his son on the other side of the playground, sitting up and playing with a stick he's discovered, the primary entertainment he knows. All around the small boy, as far as the eye can see, are various proprietary toys brought by the other children and their parents. There are balls and bicycles . . . buckets and shovels . . . cardboard books and plastic dolls, sand sifters and dump trucks . . . There are light sabers and action figures, blocks and stuffed animals, jump ropes and bean bags and skateboards and Frisbees. The number of toys, the sheer number of *things*, on that one playground alone is remarkable. Everywhere the man looks, everywhere he goes, from the playgrounds to the suburbs to the city, is *stuff*. It's unavoidable, it's overwhelming . . . an avalanche of material goods filling houses, filling stores, factories, warehouses, landfills, dumps, forests, oceans . . . choking the world, assaulting the final vestiges of sanity . . . How is it, he marvels, that with all of this – with *everything they've ever wanted* – the people of the United States have become *even more* selfish?

On the opposite side of the globe, in an unnamed village in Pakistan's North West Frontier Province, there is a single scuffed soccer ball. It is no one's. It is everyone's. Some days all the children play with it, screaming with vivacious, reckless life of the sort the man witnesses at the park back in Los Angeles. Other days only the older kids play with it, monopolizing it, forcing the younger ones to conspire and think of ways to procure the ball for themselves. Some days they all cheer each other for a good goal, the ball bouncing between the rock and the plastic Coca-Cola bottle that serve as the posts, while other days arguments ensue and someone is roughly pushed down, learning humility, respect for strength, or a dozen other lessons . . . and no matter which child notices a goat getting at the ball, he'll always attempt to stop it, *always*, because the ball is everyone's . . . and no one's . . .

Sallow nannies don't exist there.

When did it leave, the man wonders. When did the naturalness of community disappear, blown away like desert sand? Someday he will tell the boy a story about his great-aunt. Before the bombs dropped on Hesse, before the days of flying steel and bloodied women and the burned stumps of perfect children and the rubble of the houses stacked by the survivors in color-coded piles, she stood with her sisters, cousins, and friends. They were peasants, healthy and simple. A group of nine, they stood in a rough circle, passing around a treasure recently brought back from the Leipzig Fair . . . a wooden paddle, gaily painted, with carved chickens atop . . . underneath, connected by string to the chickens' heads, dangled a weight . . . With the proper hand motion, the proper method of swaying the paddle, all the chickens' heads would bob up and down, pecking at the grain and insects painted on the paddle's surface. Tiny, expectant grins spread across every face as first one child tried it, then another. The delight each experienced was magnified by the presence of the others, all watching spellbound, passing the toy to the next open hand, sharing smiles, sharing joy.

They had community. Then came the fire and corpses and boots on the back of necks and new products to buy, and now that community is gone, now all is gone. There is no need for the man to mold himself, or the boy, to the norms of a society built atop those peasants' graves, a society where never-ending gain is the loftiest of goals, where possession of as many things as possible is the highest and only attainment imaginable. That is why he says nothing at the playground. He simply does not care about these people or their nasty customs.

Later he picks up his son and carries him back to the car, the plump body wedged into the crook of his arm. They touch forehead to forehead and the man speaks. "You will learn to take from these people all they have, without apology. You will join the rest of the world in wresting from them *every single thing* they hold dear."

*　　　*　　　*　　　*

35

They stay the weekend in the suburban neighborhood, the boy's Oma thrilled to be with her only grandson. For the man the visit is a welcome respite from the rigors of the city, and it ends far too soon . . . but time away from the house on the hill can only last so long . . . The boy needs his mother's milk and the man must return to his job. Tax slaves must labor for their masters, must sacrifice segments of their allotted earthly span to those who've assumed the mantles of gods . . . work, work, work . . . The multitudes need to eat and the man has been ordered to feed them. Public parks need to have litter picked up and the man has been ordered to pay for it. The graffiti removal person needs cable television and it's up to the man to provide it . . . work, work, work . . .

Time spent with the boy grows less. The spirit of the workplace, the spirit of the many too many, begins to dominate the man's world again. Even in solitude it attacks him. The essence of the masses permeates the very air he breathes. It's everywhere, *they're* everywhere, as rife as those toys on the suburban playground. Every day, all day, in every situation, from the office, to the grocery store, to the street, he encounters them . . . the drugged and droning hordes . . . the warmongers, the pacifists . . . the Babbits, the *Untermenschen*, the worshippers of the trend, the two-minute haters, the tolerant, the intolerant, the genuflectors to the base, the Last Man . . . He silently observes, tries his hardest not to let it all affect him, strains to block it all out, to not let it penetrate his defenses. Day in, day out, he reabsorbs the revulsion, he internalizes his wished-for responses, he bites not just his tongue, but his whole being.

When the man and the boy do have time together, early in the mornings and on a single day each weekend, the man masks everything. His disgust with the dominant culture is cloaked, and he conveys only solidity to his child. The boy has begun to change, he notices, ever so subtly coming alive to the environment around him. When the wind blows the boy growls at it now, treating it, in true primitive sense, as a force to be recognized. When the Chihuahuas yip at him from behind the Salvadoran woman's rusty fence he growls at them too, no longer content to remain passive in the face of threats.

One morning, attempting to elicit a word or two from the boy's limited vocabulary, the man asks him if he's able to say "Mommy", which he can and does. This is followed by a perfectly pronounced, "Oma". But when it comes time to give the word "Daddy" a try, all the man gets in response is the little growl, the "grrrrrr" used for wind and aggressive dogs, and he realizes that in the eyes of his son he's merely a bundle of anger, a reactionary raging against the torturous stimuli of this Tartarus, this Los Angeles. His emotional "masks" have failed, which is depressing, yet another muddy trickle into the lake of filth that's threatening to drown him. He needs to cleanse himself, to scrub away the accumulated muck of a hostile environment . . . the office, the city, the whole world . . .

So the family escapes to the mountains for a brief time, the only place where the man has ever felt true solace, a sense of peace and promise. He passes the laughing boy off to his wife, leaving the two behind as he hikes up into the forest away from it all. The trail is steep, which he welcomes . . . the more difficult the path, the less chance of encountering those who would sully it . . . Onward he hikes . . . upward . . . There is no one else in sight. He sprints. He leaps into the air. His lungs sting and his heart beats faster as he sails across the earth. He swallows the crackling oxygen, revels under blue sky unmarred by billowy streams of pollutants, inhales the prehistoric scent of pine needles, rubs his palms over rough sappy bark, and hurls jagged stones into canyons. An ecstasy comes over him, ancient, virile, untamed. He sprints faster now, to the point of exhaustion. He punches trees to feel pain in his fists, pain he can *understand*. He lies face-first in icy streams to shock himself, then sits to dry on warm boulders, grinning at the sunbathing lizards. He stares out upon distant lakes and the still more distant snow-capped peaks, and dreams of his utopia.

With elbows on knees and chin balanced on fists the man thinks of the settlements he saw fanning out across Israel, two continents and a decade away. A friend took him to one, told him it was a *kfar noar* – a children's village. In such places eighteen-year-olds were married and already having children, children without end, armed with an ideology, a beacon, a blueprint, a map. It was r-selection and K-selection all at once, not an insipid either/or . . . a lesson for those who can learn, for those who can create reality, for those who believe all words and thoughts can be reified . . . There need not always be the separation of presumed opposites – they can be equally absorbed. What's the matter with quality *and* quantity? Everywhere, everywhere, he encounters these dialectics, this Hegelian confusion, with no spot of ground for the tiny minority to stand, no dry place in the ocean for the farseeing. There's only a single area in life where contrasting duality must initially be applied – the aware few, divided from all the rest. Everything else follows from there.

∗   ∗   ∗   ∗

Back in the city, riding exuberantly on the refreshing sensation of release that took place in the mountains, the man decides that he finally feels comfortable enough to attempt a meal out of his house with the boy. He and his wife are urban dwellers, they have been for too long, and as such are addicted to many of the treats available in the modern metropolis. One of the luxuries offered to them, and to everyone who's swarmed into the First World's cities, is the restaurant, a curious establishment that arose fully formed from the ashes of France's *Ancien Régime*. In the many years since the revolutionary guillotiners romantically announced the arrival of "the brotherhood of man" this institution has grown like a parasitic vine, thriving in lands where families are dying. Many of the man's acquaintances place such priority on having easy access to restaurants that, if forced to make a choice, they would willingly forsake their sovereignty, freedom, and future for the opportunity to have pho, kebabs, and sushi prepared for them in a comfortable environment at a reasonable price.

Having picked an hour when there will be a minimum of fellow patrons, the trio sits outside on the patio of a local eatery. Their waiter is silently appreciated by the man for his efforts to keep the infant boy occupied. The boy, for his part, even with his surly attitude and intermittent shouting fits, manages to win over the food server. One or two out of the dozens of pedestrians walking past on the sidewalk also smile at the child in seemingly genuine fashion, though one can never be sure what really lies behind strangers' expressions in the land of the professional actor. The man ambivalently smiles back at them, scrutinizing them and the rest of the crowd as always, mulling over the processes that formed them. His pencil scratches along notebook paper, scribbling questions, recording insights . . .

Suddenly, in the middle of this routine act, something happens to rid his mind of all thoughts of these passersby. Observations and analyses are forgotten, for across the strangely empty boulevard, here in the middle of the city, dozens of crows have begun circling . . . murders of crows, arriving in jagged black streams from all directions overhead . . . He's never seen so many of them. Together the gallows birds caw and scream, alighting on trees whose name he never learned, filling the empty branches with shadow bodies. It's a meeting of some sort, a gathering of the tribe.

The man watches the phenomenon, enrapt, separated from everyone, from even his family, mesmerized by these animals once considered holy, then deemed hellish by the Christian conquerors. The boy, too, grows silent, his whines dissipating as the intensity of his father's observation increases. Why do they gather? The moment is odd, interesting. It stands apart from the delicate world of the restaurant, with its white linen napkins and wine decanters and imported organic olive oil. It is as if some portal has opened, revealing another land, rougher than his own, yet more soothing . . . unvisited, yet somehow known . . .

These glimpses, these rips in the seam – how, the man wonders, can they be turned into reality? How to pull aside the curtains, pull aside the poetry? He wants this other world, not just as a sound bite offered up by political whores, not just as escapist essays penned by religious gurus, but as something for *himself* . . . something for them, the woman and the hunted boy . . .

Then, suddenly, like a punch to the heart, it hits him. He must leave this place and begin anew. He must take his family and depart forever this spreading, perfumed cesspool, this land of dirty pigeons, this Ur, this Los Angeles. That other world must be sought, the world of the mountains, of the crows . . . In a flashing instant he knows that he must lead the family out . . . knows that their livelihood must be left behind, their friends left behind, everything they know left behind . . . Flee or die. These are the choices. East Los Angeles as East Prussia . . .

Once that decision is made there amid the shiny trappings of the evening meal – a decision made internally, with no proclamation, no discussion – the iron bands around his chest snap, the buzzing between his temples subsides, and his fists slowly unclench . . . for the time being . . .

*   *   *   *

When freedom seems possible even the ordinary begins to shine. Though in reality only a slackening of the chains has been envisioned, this prospect alone polishes the dullness of the events and circumstances composing the man's everyday existence. What would seem of little significance at other times becomes, now, somehow meaningful to him. His son's daily acts, in particular, gain a currency and beauty they've not held previously. Everything he does at this stage in his young life brings light back into the man's world, brings smiles to his eyes. He bounces maniacally in his saucer contraption while his mother prepares supper, his round head lolling and whipping at the end of the thick neck with the abandon of those who've never known civilization. He strikes up friendships with tattered dolls and animals, favoring simians over all others. He lashes out in anger and annoyance when forced to dress as a panda on rainy Halloween, one of many holidays that the man later learns must be taken away from the herd, snatched back and sacralized. He points wonderingly with sausage fingers at the moon, mouthing the word from between rounded lips, while the man carries him, blanket-wrapped, on chilly autumn nights.

Shouts, chuckles, perplexed glances, enraged glares, ridiculous tantrums, and ecstatic squeals fill the house. Various facial expressions, all labeled, are made on demand, a dozen masks plucked right out of Fagin's bag. He lurks in his walker behind the refrigerator then bursts into the kitchen, cracking himself up at the man's mock-surprise before scuttling off to repeat his performance. Slowly, incessantly, he reaches for the protected living room electrical outlets, gauging the reaction of his parents, pulling his hand away like a cobra when "No!" is shouted at him, only to impishly look his gatekeepers in the eye and grinningly reach back again, wondering what their limits are.

And on and on such things go, day in and day out, bringing great joy to the man. It is the very simplicity of these daily occurrences, their *lack* of a deeper something, perhaps, that gives them their true worth.

He and his wife are not the only ones charmed by the presence of the child. The amount of compliments the tiny boy receives in public is amazing, never ceasing. At times the flattery accumulates so rapidly that it doesn't even seem real, that in actuality it's all about hidden cameras and tricky television hosts and an enormous joke played on a man who's written off the masses as unseeing boors. A charm, that's what the child is, one whose magic works mysteriously and wonderfully in forcing normally restrained urban dwellers to open up. Somehow he pulls a voice from those who've been made mute or silent by multicult and fear and loathing and too much media, and those voices, in turn, act as a needed salve on the man's festering misanthropy. The people gush at the hipster grocery store, they gush at the working-class grocery store, they gush at the Mexican store, they gush at the Filipino store. The Guatemalan and Honduran nannies "ooh" and "ah" at the playground, the Armenian branch manager does the same at the bank, the Israeli cashier does the same at the carwash. Gush, tribute, everywhere they go, all for a milk-fed, golden boy.

This relentless praise, lulling as lotus flowers, eventually works as all group thought or consensus does on the individual mind – it clouds accurate memory. With the passage of time the man, basking in the overflow of the compliments, begins to gloss over all the absolutely frustrating travails he actually experiences with the child during these months. The boy's disobedience, maniacal screaming, and frequent bouts of hysteria are forgotten, while his tender approach toward animals, his love of being flown among the birds, his appreciation of the cold air, and a thousand other memories just like them remain. They sit, tucked somewhere safely inside, waiting to be fully unpacked someday to either warm or break an old heart that has reached the point where life is lived in the past, no longer the future.

*   *   *   *

Yuletide comes and goes. The man is too busy to formulate the proper structure necessary for future generations and tradition. He doesn't have the time to devise the specific parts that will ultimately form the aggregate, doesn't have the energy to fully define the holiday that will someday celebrate themselves while, simultaneously, separating them from others. What will be the liturgy, the duration, the meals, the symbols, the rituals and prayers and songs? Does it make sense to even celebrate a Yuletide, or is that reactionary romanticism? Such thoughts will have to wait. All excess energy and savings are being exhausted to complete the rehabilitation of the house on top of the hill in order that the dreamed for escape can happen that much more quickly. The man has revealed his plan to his wife, who, thankfully, seems as fervent as he is in her desire to leave the city behind forever. To hasten the family's eventual flight she and the boy ship off to the emasculated southern suburbs, land of the sterile playground and sterile will, there to stay at the man's mother's house in order that the various phases of destruction and reconstruction of their Los Angeles property might proceed.

Loneliness quickly sets in, however. The boy has become such an enormous part of the man that his absence is stinging, and the man finds himself on most weekends seated aboard a southbound train heading out of the city . . . staring blankly out of the window, anticipating the reunion with his missing son . . . annoyed that he only ever arrives at night when the child is sleeping, but excited as a soldier returning from the front to spend the following day with him . . .

They no longer go to the suburban park. The beach is nearby, and if they visit at the right time of day, and the man cocks his head at just the right angle, the sight of offshore oil tankers and military helicopters maneuvering on the horizon can be avoided. Together the two amble along the shoreline, the tiny boy atop his father's shoulders. Their faces are slapped by the sea breezes, which taste of salt and freedom and promise. The eternal waves lap at the man's ankles. His feet press the wet sand into small craters. He basks in the feeling of it all. Though the environment is, admittedly, adulterated here, it is still superior to the dreadful playground and its arid non-community of humans.

It is one indefinite Sunday, there on the beach, when the boy effortlessly rises on two legs and suddenly walks as if crawling never existed for him. He walks, he doesn't stop, he doesn't topple, he *walks*, and the man cheers and grabs him and lifts him and spins him in his arms . . . but the boy has other things to do, so upon once again touching the earth, he waddles, grabs a stick, squats, and commences digging into the shore of Balboa's magnificent ocean . . . The waves crash as they always have and the sun begins to sink as it always will and on the shore a proud father watches his only son casually poking a stick in the sand, oblivious to the change that's just happened in his life.

Curious to see what all the commotion was about a stray gull lands nearby, attracting the digging boy's attention. He glances at the seabird for only an instant before his gaze abruptly slides past it, focusing instead on the massive body of water beyond. He stares as if seeing it for the first time, or seeing some quality in it he's never noticed previously. After the metamorphosis from four-legged creature to two, one's perception changes forever, and when perception changes, so does one's world.

With a shout he rises from his haunches to attack this beast, this ocean, this thing that has just revealed itself. The startled gull flies off. Beneath its vanishing shadow marches the determined boy, clad only in rolled up pants . . . advancing toward the waves, treading through the icy water, chasing the threatening undulations with stick in hand . . . Onward he marches, straight into the dragon-roars of the surf, cowardice an unknown concept, bravery an unknown concept, as it was for all his people once, when they were all Sigurd, all unable to know fear, and thus courage, which comes only when the fear has to be accepted and swallowed and overcome. Without this courage, this will to conquer, aged tribes – those burdened with history – shrivel and die.

In the long ago, when the youthful Goths encountered Southern traders who plied them with wine and then attempted months later to collect extra payment under a concept called "interest", they laughed deeply at the preposterousness of it all and swung their bright swords, separating cheating head from delicate body. The descendants of these Goths, grown feeble and thin, grown more knowledgeable but no wiser, are unable to free themselves a millennium and a half later from the very same usurious tactic – which is, when all is said and done, something *not even real*. Frozen with fear, though pretending it's *not* fear, they wallow in slavery and wither away to nothingness. They lack audaciousness, they lack will, they lack true maturity. Smugly believing themselves shrewd and intelligent, and thus incapable of being enslaved, they refuse to see their true condition. Better the rash deeds of ignorant youth than this enlightened impotence . . . better the pure, unconscious state of *being* . . .

Fearlessly the boy marches forward, ignorant of the deceptive power of those foamy crests . . . onward, onward, his body wetter and wetter . . . He shouts defiantly, screaming at the infinite ocean. He brandishes his digging stick like a cutlass, threatening the sea as if it's alive, a pulsating creature, sentient and hostile . . . every whitecap an entity, every glob of seaweed a potential foe . . . Ontogeny recapitulates phylogeny, not biologically but bio-culturally, and in him is displayed not just those once-shining Goths but also those ancient Achaean heroes, and those who came before *them*, those forefathers, those ancestors for whom the world lived and breathed through a thousand gods and beings, now killed off by science, by unchecked knowledge, by the inexorable drive to understand. They were young on the world's stage, these amazing people. Wherever they roamed with their horse and their wheel, their cattle and their wheat, they saw with the deep-set gaze of children that nothing was false and everything was alive . . . the mountains, the forests, the sea, literally *alive* . . . but then somewhere along the way they divided their body into soul and mind, and then their tales changed, and their Odin gave his eye to know more, and their Faust gave his soul to know still more, and after that what was really left but a horrible sense of loss and nausea and a yearning for complete vision and totality once again . . .

The water rises higher against the boy's tiny body as he goes even further, deeper, still shouting, still challenging, uncowed by its power, wholly unafraid, punching the choppy surface with insignificant fists, hurling invective and war cries into the wind. He's been challenged by the gods of the sea, the gods of life and death, and he'll meet them head on. He cannot win, but he does not know this, he does not doubt his ultimate victory. He revels in the struggle, *his* struggle, ragingly displays his *Funktionlust*, gaining satisfaction from what he does best. It is both raw and beautiful, this belief in the power of the individual manifesting itself here before the man. There is no denying that it stirs one at some primal level, that it is aesthetically appealing like all fantastic works of art . . . but it is also a deadly conceit the boy will ultimately be taught to purge himself of . . . He must grow as certainly as his tribe must grow, learning as he does so that the myth of the solitary hero battling great odds is adequate for children, but not for the truly mature. For those who have gained wisdom along with knowledge over the years, this belief is to be abandoned, left to the embryonic centuries, replaced by others that emphasize the bravery of the people, the perseverance and intelligence of the group, the clan, the *túath*. The boy will grow. The boy will learn. They all will learn.

That can wait, though. The lessons, the instruction – it can all wait. For the moment, here in the gloaming under the lavender and tangerine sky, with the roar of the Pacific drowning out the screams of history, the man will merely love the boy. He bounds into the surf and scoops his son up, the two of them laughing together in the brine and the roaring. The small child is the most amazing thing he has ever experienced. He loves him. He loves him.

✳   ✳   ✳   ✳

That night, after supper, after wrestling, the man places the boy into the crib that's been set up in the room he himself slept in as a child. Just before the foreheads are touched, pressed one to another, he speaks their nightly prayer. "*Respice. Adspice. Prospice.*" It is the tongue of the Romans. "Look to the past. Look to the present. Look to the future." Look back, look around, look forward – these are their instructions. The past, the present, and the future are but a single landscape. No longer will there be false demarcations between them, no longer ignorance of the potency of each facet of the whole . . . not in the man's family, not in the coming families . . . For them a failure to acknowledge any of these temporal aspects is to be recognized as one of the hallmarks of a shameful life.

The foreheads gently make contact, the bedroom door is closed, and the man leaves. An hour later he's alone once again, sitting on the near-empty train returning to Los Angeles. As happens so often, thoughts of the son he recently left behind fill his consciousness, force the financial paper to be closed and laid aside. All the regrets he once carried have been destroyed by the boy, he's come to realize. There can *be* no regrets, there never *were* mistakes or wrong turns, because everything has led him to this child, the one to the other, and it is a perfect state. Each supposed poor decision in his life, each misguided action, each bramble-covered path followed to the edge of a cliff – all these were essential in bringing him together with his wife, and every minute of existence from the time of his own birth, his father's birth, his grandmother's birth, drew him ineluctably to that moment of conception when the boy was created. A different egg a month later, a different seed an hour later, *a second later*, and he never would have been given the fantastic treasure that now enriches his life so much.

The vagaries of fate – for fate is what it is he's describing, he knows – are not to be relied on, of course. Fate plays but a small part in the lives of those who've become aware and who've applied this awareness to life. The man has been fortunate, that is all . . . but all time is fluid . . . If the present is impressive and beautiful, then the complete past – no matter how dismal – can be seen as necessary in having brought it about. In this manner the past can be redeemed, viewed only as an essential *becoming.* Thus a glorious present, gained by circumstance or seizure, is the corrective to an inglorious yesterday. Grow this realization beyond individuals, apply it to the reality of the group, and *history itself changes.*

*   *   *   *

Back in Los Angeles the man turns down the offer of a job in order to complete the necessary interior work on the house. It is his prerogative as a freelancer – the rehabilitation must take priority over employment. Day after day he works at it until, finally, it is complete. The inside is now finished. The small family reunites, and the man reveals to his wife that before returning to work they will go on a scout . . . a mission to find a new homestead for the family, somewhere to settle after the house is sold . . . northward seems to be the trend, demographic pressure forcing many to head in that direction . . . wagon trains of hypocrites, leaving the Golden State they'd ideologically fouled . . . moving vans stuffed with double-talkers escaping the chaos currently being scribbled on the opening pages of hell . . . The man will join them . . . an Aeneas without a people and without the assurances of the gods . . .

He chooses Portland . . . a true sanctuary city for a true minority, a global minority . . . They'll give it a try, he and his wife agree . . . test it out for a bit before returning to Los Angeles . . . It would be an easy segue – still a city, yet a smaller one, more manageable, and near the mountains and forests he desires. They can't make the wished-for permanent departure yet, but they can get a taste of other possibilities . . . four weeks . . . not long, but long enough . . . Their ancestors didn't have the luxury of sampling the New World. It was leave Europe or starve or get a bullet in the back of the head. The choice is simple. Four weeks will be fine . . . a single page ripped off the calendar . . . thirty days blowing away like chaff over the Don . . .

A heady thrill of escape colors all in the beginning. Every little thing the boy does folds itself into the moist ravines of the man's gray matter . . . pointless things, stupid things . . . data so doubtlessly worthless that it's bound to be written over someday . . . He sloppily pets slobbering dogs, he screams ferociously at trolleys. He destroys wooden block towers with the insouciance of a Temudjin or a Stalin. He insolently sucks his bottle, newly weaned and proud. He admires his feet, those clawed replicas of his father's, and bursts into laughter when socks are put on them. He waves to his shadow, is fascinated with heavy machinery, and licks peanut butter from spoons. He sniffs his socks, hurls balls across the condominium, and hugs his favorite blanket. He earnestly embraces his mother, shakes his father's hand, and kisses them both before bedtime each night. He has no idea how much life he's added to their lives.

The zeitgeist can't be withstood forever, though. The outside world, with its fevers and sickness, exerts itself soon enough.

*   *   *   *

Does the man have a moron for a son? Does he want this boy to babble like a baby, to speak like a toddler, for perpetuity? Does he want him to resist intellectual growth and to cling desperately and pathetically to his infancy? No? Well, that's what others want for him. "Yes, yes, that's what we want for him, that's what we want for all of them," affirm the pallid women and stale men who control and conduct the education of American youth. They're everywhere . . . a particular type . . . a maggoty clique, a devouring swarm . . .

The man sits beside the boy on the carpeted floor of the Portland Children's Museum, thrust among the contented proletariat. Before them a malnourished woman reads an insipid tale. She is thin-armed and mousy. She is watery-eyed and dull. She drawwwwwwwwwwssss out her words, wiiiiidens her eyes, ups her voice an octave. This person wants to keep children stuck in time, thinks it best that they be mummified with language. In her personal life she bitterly complains to commiserating friends about the protracted adolescence of American men. In her public life she reads the story of Ferdinand, a Spanish bull, to two, three, and four-year-olds. She mispronounces *banderilleros*. She sticks out a sulky bottom lip, collapsing her eyebrows to show that the *picadores* in the story are bad, preparing the tiny listeners to be able to make such facile judgments on their own one day. Everything's exaggerated, everything's cutesy, everything's gootchey-goo . . . her delivery, her *life*, is Hallmarked, Hummeled, Kincaided, lollypopped . . . and she's been replicated tens of millions of times . . . not just limited to Oregon, not limited to a particular state . . . not limited to children's museums or the halls of grammar schools . . . No, her kind infest the country, every nook, every cranny, from California to the Carolinas, popping up in public libraries, acting with puppets on public television, narrating children's stories in parks and classrooms and chain bookstores and everywhere in between . . .

The man is still new at being a father. Everything is a testing ground. Listening to a story being read had seemed semi-interesting, if only for measuring the awareness and response of his son – and he is able to do that, at least. After mere minutes the boy's eyes narrow and meet his own, indicating that he wants to leave. What is this, the child seems to wonder. An adult who speaks like a baby? Why? Look at those pursed lips. Listen to that simpering condescension. Why?

The boy must learn early. This thing before him, this creepy Maenad, with her offstage talk of "potties" and "sippy-cups", with her squeaky lexicon rife with "owies" and "boo-boos" and "binkies", is a deadly tool in the hands of those who would destroy him, who have nearly succeeded in destroying him. It's her fault, hers and her horrible spiritual kin. She is one of the primary reasons that the boy is culturally hunted like a beast.

Together the two rise from the floor, anxious to escape the droning. Yet as the man carries his son away and places him before some wooden trains to manipulate and maneuver, learning more than he could from a year's worth of readings of *The Story of Ferdinand*, he feels the urge to turn back and study the scene. It is just one incident among billions played out daily in the lives of a fading people, a limp people, a *remnant* people. Yet no matter the frequency and ubiquity of such episodes, they must be examined and scrutinized . . . the nature, methods, and reactions of all participants must be dissected and disseminated as a warning to whomever's left . . .

So he watches, turning his attention from the story reader to her listeners, noting various details about the members of the pack hunched on the floor next to their wriggling offspring. They are primarily women, with a smattering of slouching men sprinkled in. Some are overweight, others rickety and thin. Some are younger, others are older – too old, perhaps. Some are trashy, some are hipsters, some are caricatured creatures of the suburbs. A few are definitely wealthier than the others . . . but none of these superficial divisions is particularly relevant . . . It is in their frozen faces where the real clues are to be found. The truth of what these people are, the hint as to why they'll accept anything, is revealed through each placid countenance . . . through drooping cheeks and empty-headed smiles . . . through the inert expression plastered on every one of them . . . Something is missing from their eyes, their miens – something is horribly *absent*. There is no alertness, no awareness, no understanding. There is neither a sign of struggle to throw off a yoke nor an indication of stoic resignation in the face of a bio-cultural assault. There is a look of casual contentment, that is all. The story listeners are satisfied with this new world they've helped conjure up. They have, in thoroughly religious manner, accepted it and their diminished roles in it. One can almost hear the chanted "oms" echoing through their skulls . . . no jewel in the lotus, but a dead insect squashed in a dried flower . . .

They deserve their new status – there is no question. Every slur the sneering whipcrackers make about them is apt. These people are nothing more than easily controlled props for ruthless slavers . . . lepers soaking in, *fouling*, the water of life . . . When will they go? Why are they still here? How are they even able to procreate? The man asks himself these questions as he looks at the squirming children, then back to their parents. Can greatness spring from such as these? Can anything healthy *at all* come from them?

Yes. It's not a case of *ex nihilo nihil fit*. Something can be made of those little buds out there, tender offshoots of blighted flowers, attempting to germinate, their roots only just now being set down in the culturally depleted soil of the Twilight Lands. A skillful gardener can cull, can cut, graft, tend, fertilize, and grow. But how? Would words alone suffice? If they could, which is doubtful, then these children, not yet dulled, the indoctrination only in its nascent stages – this is what they must be told, whispered in passing from beneath pillows and through partially opened windows and on pages of *samizdat*:

"You have no allegiance to these so-called parents, to these who see themselves and the peoples of the world as vibrant blobs of paint on a sloppy palette rather than as groups of ideologically-linked tribes engaged in perpetual struggle. You have no allegiance if they're not preparing you for a life of war and conflict and strife through aeons. You are *allowed* to rebel, ordered to do so by broken skeletons that once knew the truth and by the shades of the still unborn, the trapped, the screaming. The scripted voice of the figurehead who traipsed through Galilee of the Gentiles, with his magic shows and admonitions, was even more adamant. 'If anyone comes to me and does not hate his father and mother . . . he cannot be my disciple.' His followers destroyed one creaking world, now you must do it to this one. No longer can you remain a possibility, no longer can you prefer the shadow of *potential*. You must once again become the kinetic blows of reality, of thousands and millions of brains and fists. Join in the destruction, hasten the collapse of this civilization, for from these ruins will arise new possibilities and new realities.

"Gauge them, test them, these guardians of yours. If they've not taught you to recognize the reality of your current servitude, if they've chosen to leave you forever outside the realm of consciousness, well then, throw the groovy words of the one 'prophet' so many of them claim to admire back into their faces:

We children are not your children.
We are the sons and daughters of Life's longing for itself.
We come through you but not from you.

"Utilize this rebuke only in the aftermath of cankerous generations. When power has been wrested back, when honor has returned, the admonition will become irrelevant and can be hurled on the bonfire along with every other bit of cumbersome baggage, replaced by 'honor thy father and thy mother'. To gain the strength you need, to find the examples of perseverance necessary to overcome your current lot, you will now draw on the millions of the past, not the two whose house you currently share. Remember, *remember – you are not preordained to be diseased yourselves.*"

The man turns away. Ultimately, no matter the slim potential of the next generation, he has no hope for the unpromising people before him. Like that day at the suburban playground back in California, he is again struck by how different he and the boy are from these creatures . . . not only different, but completely opposite . . . Though the gape-mouthed story listeners may look roughly similar in form to the man and boy, even that will change over the years, as their outer bodies take on the characteristics of their sickly inner ones. It will change as the external forces of social evolution continue their pressure. Rural folk were handsome specimens once . . . then a centralized and hostile government, taxation, property theft, endless imperial war, and a hijacked food supply caught up with their Baptist brains, and today the hillsides and country roads crawl with obese monsters as if the land were but a backdrop for primitive myths . . . so it is with these on the floor . . .

The boy must beware them.

*   *   *   *

Sadly not all threats are so easily identified as the slumping story readers and story listeners. At the grocery stores where the family shops, shoulders are rubbed with those urban types who are fit, healthy, and attractive. They seem crisp and with it, bright-eyed and cognizant of the world around them. They verbally toss back and forth the gamut of new buzzwords and phrases that, in a truly healthy society, never would have had to come into being – *sustainable, organic, fair trade, green, think locally-act locally, free-range, pastured, community-sponsored agriculture*. Unlike their cruder, dopier cousins outside the city limits there are certain beliefs that they hold in common with the man – and this makes them more dangerous than the others. The child must not confuse them with true allies. They simply happen to share a sliver of the same ethos with his father, and the resemblance ends there.

The night after the museum experience the boy proudly trots through the aisles of the local organic market. He proudly carries a tiny bag of chamomile, and is met by giant smiles at every turn. The man smiles back at his fellow shoppers, all the while listening to their conversations, as he has for years. Though these people are self-anointed champions of social equality, he's learned that there are massive groups they would leave out of their socially equitable society. As one they join in condemnatory chorus and, like him, mock the outlooks and tendencies of their suburban and rural counterparts, those sports bar clods who are too socially coarse to ever *truly* be their equals. The fact that these righteous consumers, with their carts full of soy milk and brown rice, fail to notice the psychological similarity between themselves blindly rooting for one of two neutered and acceptable political parties and those warehouse shoppers they so disdain rooting for a particular football squad is just one glaring example among many of their actual obliviousness . . . *another* quality they share with their supposed inferiors . . .

There are so many subsets for the man and his family to contend with . . . so many types, so many different attributes . . . There is hypocrisy among some, unquestioning belief among others . . . lack of dignity among some, lack of humility among others . . . specialized knowledge to the point of irrelevance among some, ignorance to the point of ridicule among others . . . They aren't really at odds though. The apparent dichotomy is false. At heart, it is only the degrees of profanity that vary between these varied enemies of theirs – who are, the man knows, but a single enemy.

∗　　　∗　　　∗　　　∗

On an overcast day, at a local playground ringed by patches of deteriorating forest, the barefoot boy tests his burgeoning balance, strength, and speed. The man watches him, gauging progress, occasionally offering a wave or a smile to the child as he tramps across mock bridges or scuttles over woodchips. Just beyond the boy are two older women in business garb, their demeanors wintry and nasty. In another world citizens would shout "unclean" whenever such as these ventured into a public place, but in the inverted society of today they are lauded and fêted for their silly protest against evaporating sociopolitical signifiers like "gender stereotypes" or "the kitchen" . . . too hostile, too mulish, to realize that they're merely another type of order-follower . . . soldiers in a cult of death that has nearly triumphed . . . useful lackeys to interests beyond their limited imagination . . .

The two ladies make eye contact. They know each other, but it's obviously been some time. Each is in the company of a single, small child – a boy and a girl, respectively.

"Your granddaughter?" asks the first, her voice flat and passionless.

"No. Grandniece. It's the closest I'm going to get."

The man listens, picturing the imminent loneliness awaiting this essentially family-less woman and her Western clones, picturing the looming cobwebs poised to appear in condominium corners and mercury-warped brains. He thinks of the bestial state apparatus that, at the proper time, will consume this creature that once so willingly fed it. Television, film, radio – all media, in fact, with one voice, have led the spinster to believe that she'd stay young forever. It is only now, already late in her life, that she begins to doubt, begins to question. Such is the way for the myopic, for the most fanatic of followers. Now, between the fantasies of Jamaican sex vacations and volunteer archaeological digs in Bolivia, unwelcome images of retirement homes occasionally intrude. Un-hip terms like "assisted living communities" vie for a place in her vocabulary alongside "glass ceiling" and "oppression".

"Yeah, I was worried," says the other. She indicates the shy boy by her side, a towhead looking timidly about the playground structures molded in the shapes of castles and battlements. "My son was forty before he had him. Isn't it great though?" This final sentence does not vary in tone from any of the others. A smile doesn't cross her face, a hand doesn't fondly pat the shy boy's head when stating how "great" it is, doesn't tousle his hair or stroke his jaw. The sight of a woman robotically displaying no emotion is even more disturbing than that of a man displaying none. It cloaks the playground in the fog of science fiction, makes the scene seem that much more unreal.

"It's the greatest," replies the old acquaintance, secretly jealous of the woman across from her. Grandson trumps grandniece, she knows inside. The relationship is more direct, more possessive. As a grandmother, her rival *owns*, while she – with no direct lineage – merely leases.

Later the boy trips in front of this same woman. He cries from the shock of the impact. Standing three feet from the crying child, she continues her conversation on her cell phone, glancing blankly at him as if he's an annoying gnat or mosquito. The man comes and picks him up. Sometime after that the little girl manages to escape her liberated great-aunt's gaze for a second. She ends up playing near the man, on a portion of the raised play structure that is without protective railing. Realizing the moderately iffy situation she's put herself in, he leans over, reaching to retrieve her and place her in an area where there isn't the possibility that she'll topple over the edge. It is at this moment that the great-aunt realizes that her only link with immortality is missing. She shouts the child's name and nervously twists her head about, instantly noticing the little girl's precarious position.

"Don't worry, I have her," the man states as he lifts the child up under the arms and repositions her a few feet away. The frenzied woman, displaying more emotion than she has since the presidential election, rushes up to the bridge, plucks the child from her new location, and carries her back down to the ground. She is desperately thankful that her sole shot at genetic continuity hasn't toppled from a slightly elevated playground bridge onto the protective matting below . . . though not thankful enough to say anything to the man . . . To harpies such as these all males are as Phineus, existing only to have their person and sustenance fouled daily.

Ignoring decorum – that stultifying concept that was killing the West more thoroughly than all its fratricidal wars had – the man speaks loudly to the barefoot boy.

"Look, son. Boorish self-interest – that's all you can ever expect from the bourgeoisie."

The pinched face of the woman turns upward toward the man and his robust son. It is a confused look she gives, cramped and reactionary. She's bewildered that someone could mistake her for a bourgeoise. Clearly, she must have heard him wrong. After all, she lives in a city, a *progressive* city. The bourgeoisie is other people.

*   *   *   *

The family is eating dim-sum lunch in Chinatown. During the man's travels through the vast land of Cathay, he never came across any thriving neighborhoods that indicated a corresponding bio-cultural incursion from West to East – no Irishtown, no Ukrainian Quarter. In those urban sections of the awakened Oriental nation that once upon a time did house *laowai*, there to ply the mercantile or missionary trade, only attractive buildings stood as a reminder, their one-time inhabitants long since shoved out. Chinatowns, on the other hand, are bustling everywhere across the Orient and Occident alike. Yet who is he to draw secret comparisons of vitality and health between countries and peoples? Just a nondescript man, eating a dim-sum lunch in a popular Chinese restaurant with his wife and whining, fussing, annoying son . . .

The sour disposition isn't the boy's fault. The noise, the clatter, the compressed crowd – all of this is unnatural to him. He's still of an age where he's unable to communicate his emotions and unable to deal with situations as he sees fit, thus he indicates his displeasure through bratty behavior. The woman has taught the man to understand such things. Expressing hostility toward surroundings that somehow seem threatening is normal in a healthy creature, she pointed out. She's right, but regardless of the truth behind it all, the boy's occasional ill behavior still takes its toll on the man. Thankfully the restaurant is noisy enough inside that he is able to ignore his son's mood in this instance, simply allowing the angry outbursts to be masked by the buzz of dozens of conversations while he buries himself in an old newspaper grabbed on the way in. It is called the *Asian Herald*, and it is edifying, like everything.

While his wife chooses items from the food carts wheeled around the room by rough Han women, the engrossed man reads coverage on supposedly leaked military reports documenting the chaos hovering on the world's horizon. Climate change will usher in Siberian winters to New York and England. Southern California's water will dry up. Millions of immigrants will attempt to break into the "stronghold" nations of the West, an insane way of describing them. Massive typhoons are on their way, enormous tidal waves imminent. It's simply another version of the literary plot first outlined by that embittered son of Judah so many years ago, furiously scribbling his screed outlining the heavenly punishment in store for Rome. "Revelation" the Galileans call it today. Of course, if the man could put faith in bureaucratic or journalistic fantasies and be assured of such pending catastrophes, he'd be much better off. In the throes of unleashed, natural violence at least there'd be something physical to struggle against, visible forces to wrestle with instead of the banal softness he currently battles.

He puts the paper down and retrieves a fork that his angry son has hurled to the floor . . . looks around the restaurant . . . stares at the customers casually wielding their chopsticks, casually wearing their blinders . . . Stronghold nation? In what sense? Where? These people welcome typhoons. They've been hit by wave after wave for centuries – Carthaginians, Christians, Huns, Muslims, Mongols, Turks, Nipponese, Bolsheviks – and each time a progressively smaller remnant still crawled back to *terra firma* to sip tea and mindlessly natter as if typhoons didn't exist . . . blithely babbling as if their dwindling numbers weren't, every year, being inexorably driven to higher ground . . . not a single one of them building seawalls or shelters, not a single one making plans, but rather *sipping tea* . . .

A bland pair sits next to the man – a sexless female and a typically effeminate male of the type he calls *hemianthropoi*, half-men. The two are well into their thirties, stylishly shabby and unattractive. They yawningly talk about the songs on their iPods. They chatter about non-profit organizations and teaching English overseas. They blither hackneyed tales that are so predictable strangers can guess their dénouements by the time the second sentence is muttered.

Their conversation climbs into the atmosphere, joining scores of others. They merge, not into a cacophony so much as a whine . . . the sound of rats' feet over broken glass . . . It claws at him. He hates that he's among them. They are empty. At the front of the room, at the back of the room, empty . . . These people, these *whites*, always white, are so maddeningly *void*. They're bland, they have no fire, no spirit, just a vacuum at their core. At least the black or brown folk they ethnofugally worship from a safe distance have a spark in them. At least their favorite social target "white trash" is breathing and kicking and tying cans to cats' tails and fist-fighting and smashing bottles and the like. Not so these two slumped at the table next to the man, struggling with their chopsticks, poking at their potstickers, discussing politics as if they're something real instead of an elaborate stage show set up for types just like themselves. Not these two, shooting lizard-like glances toward the boy when he throws his fork on the floor, the actions of a child completely foreign to their chalked-in world. Where have they come from, evolutionarily? How did they end up, after hundreds of thousands of years, sitting at a table directly next to his own?

The boy's screaming notches it up enough to be noticeable over the din. Promptly taking advantage of the situation, the man scoops him in his arms and leaves. Outside they breathe deeply and wait for the woman, both glad to be away from the buzzing voices of the hive. Unprompted, the child fills his cheeks with air and bulges his eyes, making a preposterous face directed toward the patrons within. The man bursts into laughter, which makes the boy laugh, which precipitates more laughter in response, and in just seconds the man's rotten mood has changed completely.

When viewed from emotional distance, either through the eyes of a perceptive stranger in the present or through the hazy gaze of the man himself looking backward from the future, a pattern clearly emerges. The man encounters the masses and is filled with contempt. The man spends time with his son and it's all washed away. The man encounters the masses and is filled with contempt . . . and so on and so on and so on and so on . . .

*　　　*　　　*　　　*

On the days he is not visiting real estate agents or language immersion grammar schools or libraries containing economic data pertinent to the city's future, the man is with his beloved boy. He cherishes his allotted time with his child, knows it will lessen upon their return to Los Angeles, knows he won't witness as many of the boy's mental and physical strides. It is during this period in Portland that the child begins to recognize letters and to gain an increasing fondness for books. He demands that the man read to him about beasts, and the man does, careful to keep all contemporary tales away, utilizing ancient myth and fable to introduce relevant social lessons, or only telling stories that accurately portray animals' actual habits and traits. The cutesy animal books so adored during the current era are avoided. Such narratives are useless for instruction, are ridiculous in the way the gray-breathed West makes everything ridiculous, equal, and false. Bears are not best friends with children, tigers do not play with deer, and owls do not chum around with field mice. Encyclopedias are utilized to illustrate that threatened bears will attack children, that tigers tear the flesh of deer, that owls feast on mice, and that nearly everything must kill something else in order to live.

Together they pronounce the animals' names in Latin and English. Together they imitate their roars, their caws, their howls. Together they sit on the floor and point at pictures of squirrels and pigeons, horses and swans, wolves and ravens and crows . . . but the man recognizes the pointlessness of it all, particularly when elsewhere in the world children of other tribes, *herpeta* tribes, are repeating the ancient dicta of instructional and inspirational holy books rather than the hoots of owls . . . There is a feeling of speciousness to this gawking at photographs, a removal from reality. Therefore he brings the boy to a large park, a place where they can see crows as they actually are, a place where they can hear their throaty voices as they actually are . . . If others are studying and memorizing the instructions of sacred texts to advance themselves, the boy and his type can, for the time being, observe the workings of nature and reach the same simple truths by proxy – there are predators and prey, in-groups and out-groups, and constant maneuvering by all species engaged in the eternal and lethal battle for resources and survival.

Walking barefoot at the edge of the woods ringing the park, they spy the crows floating on currents over the pines, a troop of blue-black bodies with spread wings, not illustrations on a page but actual flesh and blood. Ecstatically the boy shouts, "Caw, caw," while the man thinks back to the Los Angeles restaurant, the odd gathering across the street that so stirred him. *Corvus* was what the Romans called the animal. It was also the name they gave their revolutionary invention, shaped like the bird's beak, which slammed down from their amateurish boats onto the decks of rival Carthaginian warships. This enabled the ever-determined tribe to rapidly board the vessels of the seasoned Levantine merchants and sailors, stealing their enemies' renowned ship-ramming skills away from them while giving the advantage to the sword and dagger they themselves used so perfectly.

The man has learned much from his Romans, from their rise and their fall. Always the fight must be with your strengths and on your terms, the strengths of your enemies mitigated, their employment denied. All conquerors came from underneath at some point, all have redefined the rules of engagement. No owner can expect to hold on to the world forever, for as soon as it's taken he finds himself in the position of having to *defend*, of having to fight off those who also clamber for a piece of it. Once booty is acquired, once riches and power have been gained, the attempt is always made to have the current status remain static for eternity. It is vainly demanded that evolution itself come to a halt.

But it never does.

*   *   *   *

Within the boundaries of the Portland park lies the zoo. The man has been asked by friends, Los Angeles expatriates with children of their own, to join them there sometime. "Please come," they insist. "Your son loves animals. It will be great for him."

Zoos are championed by all types. They're cheered by grandparents, worshipped by illustrators, and touted by teachers. Zoos are benign and whimsical, instructive and fun. Glossy brochures rave about them, chambers of commerce blow bugles, and housewives pass the word. There is no better outing for children than a day at the zoo. There they can witness a penguin – only a five-minute walk from the tiger enclosure! There they can see an animal from the other side of the world – right in their own backyard!

The man turns down the invitation. The friends, though nice enough, are not comrades. They do not know what the zoo means to him. They do not know that to him such a place is but a mass prison filled with kidnapped life . . . display after display of slaves, ripped from their homelands . . . taken from the tundra, the veldt, and the desert, and brought to subsist in the damp clime of the Pacific Northwestern rainforest, forever . . . magnificent examples of evolution now existing only for the amusement of human crowds, offered up cheaply to the glutinous mob . . .

One day, returning to the parking lot after walking through the park's woods, the man and the boy hear the giant blasts of Portland's captive elephants, trumpeting their uniquely elephant call. It's a melancholy sound that shouldn't exist in that part of the world. The boy turns his eyes to his father's, awaiting an explanation, but the man can only shake his head for the time being.

Slavery is *sad* to witness, he wants to tell the child . . . a sordid, dismal spectacle . . . Penguins, apes, lions, elephants – these do not choose to be caged, unlike the debased spectators gawking at them. The amazing *Gattungswesen*, that perfection of a creature's essence, is tainted, is inverted, when lives such as these exist only for japery, for goofy episodes of cheap amusement. It is horrible to see the wondrous beasts of the earth turned into fools for the profit of jailers, their lives worth nothing when judged on their own merit, apparently, but only having value in relation to the drooling bipeds gaping outside their enclosures. Zoos, like cities or civilizations, redefine the reality of the natural world. What significance has the roar of the lion any longer when it takes place behind plastic? The might of the rhinoceros means what, exactly, when the animal is stuck in a pit encased by concrete and steel? Regardless of efforts to replicate particular habitats, from patches of grass laid down to warmer air emitted by heat lamps, the environmental phenotype extended at the zoo is not that of any of the captured or clinically bred species, but is solely man's. This is his world. The cement and iron, the glass-fronted cages, the troughs with their listless water – all his. They are all examples of the power he has attained on earth, and of how he's chosen to use that power.

The boy will never go. In his life spent with the man he will never go to such a revolting place. The boy is the lion, that glorious *Raubtier*, that beast of prey. He must empathize with the plight of these animals and understand that he too exists now merely to amuse others. He too is caged. He too has captors, jailers, feeders, trainers, and handlers. Escape won't give him his freedom. True escape is impossible, there is nowhere to go. The environment outside the zoo is as hostile and alien as the one within. For him to be free, for all like him to be free, the very world itself must be changed.

✳   ✳   ✳   ✳

The man begins his final day in the sanctuary city with a brief, brisk hike in the wooded part of the park where the crows sail. This park, unlike those he's used to, has not yet been marred, tagged, littered, overrun, or destroyed. Since humanitarianism and environmentalism are at odds, and since humanitarianism is the prevailing doctrine of the sanctuary city, someday – and someday not far off – the Northern park will resemble the places awaiting him back in Los Angeles . . . wounded landscapes, scarred by beer bottles, filthy diapers, plastic bags, piñata paper, cigarette butts, fast food wrappers, soda cans, and a dozen other forms of trash left to molder and make the world ugly for the twelve people remaining alive able to recognize what ugly is . . .

But the ugliness hasn't arrived yet, the man acknowledges gratefully, looking around. He breathes the sweet-smelling morning air, stretches his arms and legs. This park, with its forests and fields, is as pristine a place as one can hope to find in a modern city. It refreshes and heals, and he's glad to be able to experience it. He sets out, still not conditioned to being struck by the disappointment that always seems to come. Only minutes into what is meant to be an invigorating morning wakeup the first contact with humanity takes place. A yuppie, reeking of perfume, reeking of *privilege* like the universities teach, saunters by with her unleashed terrier, which unloads its bowels there on the path . . . the same path the man walks on, the same path the pampered pet-owner walks on, the same path hundreds walk on . . . She doesn't pick up the dog's waste. Blissfully she continues, *innocently* she continues, insouciantly checking her fingernails or her wedding ring, making it seem as if the man does not exist . . . trying to pretend as if what just happened did, in fact, not just happen . . .

Her performance is amateur and unconvincing. Slight shame colors her face . . . not shame over her failure to clean up after her pet . . . just the shame of being caught . . . He hurls a sarcastic, "Thank you," as the woman hurries by, feeling the tension zipper through her overly tanned body. There is little satisfaction on his part – he knows that in some small way his life is diminished by the pettiness of it all, made smaller by the fact that he feels he even has to respond to such a thing.

Next up come the scrawny joggers, gaggles of them plodding along beneath the overcast sky . . . measuring their heart rates, listening to their music, plastic buds wedged into their ears . . . closing themselves off from the world around them even as that world rises against them . . . content to die with moderately healthy lungs . . . and though they can't hear the crows cawing in the hemlock trees, can't hear the movement of a squirrel or rabbit pattering through the underbrush, these people are still happy they have their woods . . . they're happy to have their sweet-smelling flowers and bronze statues and tinkling fountains and beautifully landscaped park, a place magically brought forth from the earth by men they fervently condemn . . .

They are blind, these jogging Last Men, willfully so. They are uncurious about the domestic reality of the country beyond their sanctuary city, or perhaps just frightened. They've never seen graffiti scrawled on a park bench, let alone seen it sprayed across the bark of venerable oak trees, a common Los Angeles sight that even the graffiti removal person can't fully remedy. They've never seen such a thing, but it's still coming for them . . . once again . . . the tsunami . . . They can't jog away from it. They'll sip tea and try to explain it when it does arrive, these descendants of the bastardized men who carved and hewed and created the park and made it lovely. They'll shout about abstractions even more loudly than they currently do – rights, equality, respect, tolerance, understanding – but that won't stop the realities of physical encroachment and transformation. They'll march emphatically down the same beetle-ridden trail as their forebears, right into their unmarked graves, cheered by all, missed by no one.

The morning fog begins to burn off. The man climbs into his car to head back to the condominium his family's been in for the past month. Portland's streets are empty, which puts him in a good mood once again, and the thought that his wife has made blueberry pancakes puts him in an even better one. Every minute of every waking hour can't be spent obsessing over the decline, the destruction, the loss, the lies, the future, the past, the bleak present, the propaganda, the possibilities, the injustice, the helplessness, the hypocrisy, the dilemmas, and the solutions. Sometimes, if only for preservation of sanity, the thoughts have to be of blueberry pancakes.

He drives, following the normal route back to the condo. His stomach rumbles and his mouth moistens from images of the breakfast painted in his mind, when suddenly orange plastic cones appear in front of him . . . an unexpected barrier . . . Shaken from his reverie he turns, goes down a block, and is again met with the sight of orange cones impeding his progress. This time an official-seeming young lady stands nearby. She walks to his open window and the man explains that he has to get to the other side of the cones where his condominium complex is. The route is closed to traffic, she politely informs him. A performance of that beloved urban ritual, the 10-kilometer run, is being staged in the area. However, residents of the man's neighborhood are permitted to drive their vehicles in the forbidden zone, he's assured. He gives a wave and cautiously proceeds . . . onward, onward, nearly home, closer to the pancakes . . .

A bit further on, at an intersection where participants in the race pad soundlessly along emptied streets, stands a police officer . . . thick neck, fat gut . . . uniform . . . He holds up his right hand, palm out, indicating that the man should stop, and with his left vaguely gestures toward the ground at his feet. It is somewhat confusing. The man slows, unsure, but the police officer emphasizes "stop, stop" with his right hand, so he does stop, ten feet away from the public employee in the uniform. But then the public employee in the uniform gestures furiously to move forward, to the spot he's now distinctly pointing to on the ground. So the man does, expecting to be given some further direction on how to proceed. This seems as if it will be the rational sequence of events . . . yet rationality holds no place in the day-to-day dealings within the American carcass . . .

"You hit me, there's gonna be a problem," shouts the cop, the protector of something, the server of something. The man is baffled.

"What?"

The voice, as it drools from between thin lips stretched across a porcine face, is accusatory . . . arrogantly condescending . . . "You go a few more feet and I'm on top of your hood! *Then* you got a problem on your hands! Understand? You wanna spend your weekend in a cell?" His words make no sense with regard to the situation. There *is* no situation. The man is unsure as to the full implications of what the belligerent cop is saying, but instantly he seethes. Rage courses through him. He wants to harm this pig-eyed aberration, this *symbol* standing here before him, with its drooping moustache and snake brain.

"Not if I'm going three miles an hour," he replies, hoping to puncture the fantasy of the municipal hero, the adult bully currently attempting to make someone's life worse simply because he *can*.

The thick-necked police officer ignores him. "You see those runners there," he asks in an obnoxious tone, pointing at the dozen people moving directly in front of them, as if maybe the man can't see them. "When I say go, you go, and not before. Understand? And don't hit any of 'em!" He steps away. An enormous gap presents itself, and the cop lapses into the histrionics of an L.A. actor playing an enemy of democracy, commandingly shrieking, "Go! Go!"

Acid churns inside the man's gut. He drives forward, livid. This prop of the state, this enforcer of the arbitrary law, who gobbles his T.V. dinners two at a time while fantasizing about handcuffing runaways, is having some kind of bad day, and so he ruins someone else's. Day in, day out, he lords his authority over anyone he's allowed to. The man, not being part of a protected class, is a permissible target . . . and that reality, in turn, crushes him . . . because he knows, the scene makes clear, how utterly helpless he really is . . . at the complete social mercy of "legal" cops and "illegal" criminals . . . of ethnically cohesive multinational corporations and ethnically cohesive street gangs . . . of entrenched politicians and enabled immigrants . . . Rabble above, rabble below, the attack continues unceasingly, from the boardroom to the alley, without end. It's not new. He's seen the old posters from a dying Europe. What is new is having no one on his side, having no comrades, no brothers. The only option remaining him is to run away, because there's nothing he can do against this behemoth, this technological Leviathan, this golem state erected by default geniuses and run by sycophantic functionaries. All he has left open to him is flight. He knows this, he accepts this . . . but down deep, down at the base of it all, it's the other evolutionary option he prefers – not the fleeing, not the scampering off into the brush, but the *fight*, the *fight* . . . Nature endowed him with chemicals and muscles and fury and rage for a reason – to kill all that stands in his way, to destroy anything that threatens his survival . . . but these ancient gifts have become curses in this society . . . the excretions of glands and the pulsing of the limbic system, unable to find physical outlet – and thus purpose – bring him only pain . . .

When he returns minutes later to the condominium the boy shouts in excitement. He toddles up wearing a little flannel shirt and jeans, beaming at his father. The man is incapable of pretending, barely managing a weak grin. Inside he is frozen, feeling his powerlessness like one of those mighty zoo animals locked away behind steel bars. When the boy's giant smile shines on him that awful sense of powerlessness quickly turns to shame. He's ashamed that his son has been given such a father, one who's unable to make a different world for him . . . ashamed that his own child will have to start at zero, just like he himself did, just like their people always have . . . thousands of years, one weak generation after another, after another, after another . . . no mending, no repairing . . . just bitter acceptance and acknowledgement of impotence . . .

The small family heads back to L.A. Portland will not be the place to begin anew. It will not be their Alba Longa – the Willamette is not the Tiber, the boy is not Iulus, the man not Aeneas . . . and though comparisons might be drawn between the burning, sacked, depopulated, and repopulated cities of Los Angeles and once-magnificent Troy, the greatest element of the ancient poem is missing in the man's cheap equivalent . . . In his modern knock-off, there are no sign of refugees who have it in them to someday become Romans.

*   *   *   *

For the first time since the boy's arrival the man and his wife will be working simultaneously. The woman is pregnant again, glory be, and the need to gather funds for the move overrides their compact to always have one or the other be with their son. With no family other than the three of them, with no community, with nothing at all as support, the only option is to place their beloved child in what is euphemistically called "daycare". Had the man thought of Los Angeles as an existential Troy? He was wrong. It is Aulis, where desperate Agamemnon offered up his own beloved child as sacrifice for strong winds to drive him onward.

Depression infects the household at the thought of handing over the boy to strangers. How has it come to this, this splintering, this separation of families? Have the people of the West irreparably broken down, exhausted themselves? Or have they been deliberately broken? The diagnosis is moot. None of it matters at this stage anyway. The man cannot resuscitate the dead – that lesson has been taught from the dawn of civilization. Gilgamesh wasn't able to raise Enkidu from the tomb – he had to learn to accept the passing with courage and resolve. The man cannot heal wounds that run thousands of years deep. He can only focus on what is at hand, can only attempt to fix what is immediately in front of him. All that matters currently is that a place be found for the boy.

Pickings are slim though. The same folks who have their own retirement homes in the Los Angeles Yellow Pages, the ones whom the man and the boy must learn from, have their own daycare centers. Such types are never without a clan, never without quality nearby. Nothing of this kind exists for the man and his family. Nothing of this kind exists for helots who should have learned their place by now, down in the blended underclass. The overlords are always on the lookout for them attempting to establish such places. They know that muttering together in the field eventually leads to insurrection, so they keep their eyes open for any hint of congregation, any display of protective unity. They dub such things "hate".

The man is only too aware that he and his tiny family are clinging to a piece of flotsam in the middle of the ocean. There's no land in sight, and their desperately-kicking feet can only attract the ever-present sharks to their helplessness. How to survive the travails of the oceans without drawing attention to yourself? This is a question never pondered by the Seven Sages. As with everything, seemingly, he has to learn as he goes.

Reports from the boy's mother on facilities she visits near her offices are discouraging. "He'll be a 'Little Duck' here," proudly states one daycare woman on the phone, "And there are a lot of people in your industry who utilize our services." It sounds promising. "Little Duck" and all that . . . but when she visits she feels physically repulsed, she later informs the man . . . multicult dumping grounds . . . televisions blaring in rooms for infants, one room dedicated solely to retarded children . . . overweight employees waddling around with that blank gaze so familiar to Angelenos, a zombie look void of all discernment or erudition or wonder . . . These are the lackluster eyes, the *horrible* eyes, meant to daily watch over their son?

Of the small handful of friends of the man and his wife who've had children, only one couple remains in Los Angeles, a wealthy lesbian pair who've entrusted their adopted son to a Central American nanny, that ubiquitous sight at playgrounds citywide. Perhaps this is a better choice than daycare. The man walks to their house to ask them about specifics – they, too, live atop the hill, their back deck overlooking the littered city park far below. Together the two women speak to him in code, as do most peers and acquaintances of his. It's a code everyone is expected to understand, its terminology woven into everyday speech, and if one doesn't know it one will never grasp the true motivations for the actions undertaken by those who fluently speak it. It is doubtful the women's nanny understands it. It is doubtful the speakers themselves grasp all its nuances, as with any speaker and his native tongue. Over the course of the conversation the code is used quite liberally, though. The two tell him that for the benefit of their child they'll eventually have to leave the City of Angels for someplace with "better schools". They bring up "cleaner air". Not once do they mention the park at the bottom of the hill. Not once do they mention the outlines of bodies spraypainted on the streets near the bottom of the hill. Those realities, and many more, are encoded in the phrases "cleaner air" and "better schools".

The man isn't sure what the constant lying does to such people. Directing falsehoods outward to confuse rival groups in the struggle for resources is a useful strategy, but when internalized as truth must surely warp and shrivel you. As usual, though, conjecture and analysis are useless. He needs to know about childcare, that's all . . . about the costs of nannies, the quality . . .

It's too expensive though, as he feared. After hearing the numbers he realizes that he and his wife can't afford a personal nanny. He returns home and tells her. Their search becomes more desperate, the replies from the facilities more disheartening.

"Do the children watch any television at your place?"

"No, none. We do show them educational videos though."

Ugh. No television? What do they think that thing they watch their "educational videos" on is called? And what is an "educational video"? On three different instances he hears either that term or "good children's programming" posed as some sort of superior alternative to the regular videos or "bad children's programming" that other, presumably less discerning, childcare providers allow their charges to watch . . . as if the developing brain of a one-year-old can distinguish between the programming aspects of two-dimensional on-screen images, quick cut and flickering in the ether . . . A child's brain is still forming until two years old, until *twenty-five* years old, shaped in part by its external environment. Neural pathways in the gray matter form, fuse, and harden. The pliable wires for the reception and relaying of information ultimately become stiffened cables, perfectly constructed for the transference of data absorbed from the outside. When the eyes are focused from an early age on the flatness and machine gun-editing of the televised world, rather than the three dimensions and angular consistency of the real one, the flowering neurons within the skull are forced to creep along unknown paths. If they're laid wrong in the beginning, not strung out properly, the future is mayhem . . . the buzzing of incomprehension, the inability to concentrate . . . This is what he wants for his child? This is what *anyone* wants?

A hollow hopelessness begins to settle in his stomach. With each conversation, with each daycare talked to, the reality of their situation clubs him over the head. Then, as if scripted, during the depths of his despair he gets a callback. A message is left on his voicemail, along with a phone number. He rings back, chats with a woman. She offers childcare and lives nearby. He and his family meet at her house a few blocks over. No television for the kids, she says . . . no sugar and no garbage food . . . cloth diapers are okay . . . She offers her pedigree . . . four generations in the country . . . Russian *shtetl* to Lower East Side tenement to uptown Manhattan to Los Angeles . . . More random chat follows, and then it's agreed – the boy will spend his days at this woman's house, along with other sons and daughters of hilltops. It is not a community . . . not a *túath* . . . but it's the best they can do . . . For their kind, in this era, no situation will ever be the best – only "the best they can do".

The man hates having to leave his son. He hates having to drop him into the arms of a stranger. He hates the pitiful cries when he abandons him in the mornings. He hates that pieces of the boy's life will go missing. But this is the price one pays in the robot Occident. This is the way of things for those who've not managed to gain control of their own destinies, those who meekly wait for the world to change instead of changing it themselves.

*　　　*　　　*　　　*

The sting of the daily separation begins to lessen over the following weeks. The amazing adaptability of children comes into play and the boy begins to actually enjoy his time at the daycare. Slowly, though not completely, the man's guilt fades. Each evening upon arrival he hoists his son in his arms and listens as the daycare woman recaps the boy's day: his clamoring for books to be read him, his contented playing with toy trucks, his various interactions with other children. The man listens approvingly, thanks her, and turns to go, the boy invariably waving and shouting, "Bye-bye," at both the woman and his new playmates.

"Bye-bye" is one among many words that have joined his expanding vocabulary, the most utilized and favorite being "no". His time spent among other children emphasizes the importance of the word, letting him fully realize its use as a power syllable. "No!" he shouts at the little girl who tries to touch or kiss him. "No," he says, adult-like, when he knows something is amiss, like a kid ripping her own diaper off or a dog nosing into the garbage. At the park he passes a Filipino woman, nanny to a red-haired boy, and believing something wrong with the matching of the two, scowls and commands, "No!" The man makes a light-hearted crack, anxious for his son not to be stigmatized for noticing variation and difference in peoples. "No!" uniformly shout media and universities and the zeitgeist when the urge to acknowledge such realities is acted on.

One morning the man is asked by the daycare woman to secretly watch his son's reaction to a particular toy, a plastic jack-in-the-box consisting of four media characters that pop their colored heads out of covered holes and shout an obnoxious phrase. The man recognizes some of the characters from his own youth. Such things have been deliberately kept out of his home in order to shield the boy from characters and objects mass-produced by capitalists. Merchandise comes from merchants and merchants are the boy's masters and masters must be overcome, and to be overcome they must be weakened, which is what happens when their livelihoods are ripped away.

However, outside the sanctity of the home lies a different world. At the daycare toys of all types are scattered about. Most, like the one the daycare woman places in front of the boy, are designed solely to appeal to the broadest target audience – the colors are exceedingly bright or the eyes in the goofy faces are overly large. They are the products of a makeshift culture, one consisting of equal parts marketing, consumption, and downbreeding, and though the man wants his son to have nothing to do with either the products or the culture that births them, this is currently impossible.

The daycare woman steps aside, allowing the man a better view from the window he's looking through, and the first of the annoying characters reveals its head from the jack-in-the-box. It shouts its catchphrase. The boy is aghast. Though nearly every child and adult in America knows the quartet of puppet characters, not only is the boy unfamiliar with them, he is oddly hostile toward them. His little fists strike out immediately, fast and hard. A second squeaking head pops up. Furious, he looks around in a weirdly funny rage and finds a tiny wooden hammer, then attacks again. The grinning daycare woman makes eye contact with the equally grinning man through the window. She tells him later that the bizarre attack is great amusement for her employees throughout the course of the day.

That night the man brings the contraption home to show his wife their son's odd reaction to it. He begins to add his own platitudes to the words of the plastic heads. "We're all brothers," or "Accept everyone!" The boy, horrified at seeing the four creatures there in his own house, performs on cue, making a rapid crawl forward to smash the toy before hurling it across the kitchen floor. Eventually all the man has to say is "one world" or something like it and the child anxiously begins to look around whatever room they're in, anticipating the presence of his foes and the punishment he'll dole out.

The man's time with the boy is now limited to a couple of hours each evening. After their meal they take their nighttime walk together. With his pudgy, character-pounding fist wrapped around his father's long index finger, the child waddles along under the purpling sky, pointing upward and shouting, "I want moon!" over and over. The man suggests they lasso it, and mimes the act. Intrigued, the boy follows suit, awkwardly moving his little arm, and there they stand, the father and the son in the middle of the city, vainly attempting to reel in the symbol of all that's cold and pure and accessible to few. It takes a minute for the man to realize that the boy *actually believes* his father is going to bring the moon down to their feet.

The power he holds over his son during this sliver of his life is incredible, is limitless. A thumpety-thump indicates the child lumbering down the hallway to his father's bedroom-office. The door swings in and he enters, concern on his plump face. He shyly hands a toy bear to the man, a gift from his Oma. It has a small opening in its back, an empty space meant for the insertion of batteries. "Hurt, hurt," he explains, pointing to the slit. The man nods his head in understanding. He assiduously examines the bear, turning it this way and that, gently probing the wound while the boy gazes on. Finally, his voice full of assurance, the man pronounces the creature okay. The smiling boy takes the stuffed animal back into his arms, his eyes shining like the sun. "Bear okay," he repeats to himself over and over as he walks off. "Bear okay."

The man watches him disappear. This, he imagines, is what it must feel like to be a benevolent god. There is a cleanness to it all, a deep satisfaction. The child trusts him implicitly – his words, *mere sounds coming from his mouth*, are assurance enough to the boy that everything is as it should be in the world. Yet as his little thumps recede down the hallway, the man can't help but note that in their simple exchange was reflected the tragedy of millions of eternal children, his own people, those who've never tribally grown into the role of adults. They vaguely sense that something is wrong, but are unsure exactly what it is or how to remedy it. These sad paedomorphs bring their concerns to those who are more mature, those who smile at them, guarantee them and promise them. They hope, as they have for a long time, that someone else can solve their problems; they hope that someone else can simply make their worries vanish.

> *Hot moons fled swiftly through the gates of time.*
> *Is your hope your sole possession?*
> *Will you continue trusting in their words,*
> *Pilgrim with your staff in hand?*

How many more millennia before they grew up, Stefan George wondered, as does the man. When will they begin valuing wisdom as much as they do knowledge? Will the day ever dawn when they finally become men? Will the day ever dawn when they finally take it upon themselves to fix their own problems?

It has to.

*   *   *   *

The cleaning ladies at the daycare on top of the hill, along with the two girls who help with the children, are Mexican. All four are warm-hearted, laugh much, and are fond of the boy, which raises anyone in the man's estimation. Yet living where he does, as he does, when he does, he often dwells on the psychological aspects of an implicit racial servant class and the hostility eventually engendered by this type of economic relationship. He thinks of the Chinese in the Philippines, the Boers in South Africa, the Jews in Germany, the Hindus in Uganda. What were his grandmothers' feelings when they cleaned houses on the East Coast decades earlier? Was there any resentment felt by the young Italian and the young Teuton toward the Anglo-Saxons they labored for? His whole life he never asked, never heard anything, never thought about it. Now he wonders. Is there secret resentment among the girls at the daycare for their charges, for their employer? There doesn't seem to be, quite the opposite in fact, but who can ever truly know another's heart? Who can ever know what will happen the following generation, who can ever fully grasp the subtle social and economic and environmental changes that take place incrementally in the interacting lives of different peoples? How many Poles slit unsuspecting German throats on Prussian estates, how many quietly seething Turks stabbed their Armenian employers throughout the cities of the Ottoman Empire? History shows that a tipping point is always reached. Los Angeles isn't immune. Nowhere is.

This blanket hatred of the other, secret or overt, is clearly the way of the world, and clearly always has been. The man can suffer no delusions; he's not isolated enough nor protected enough to allow himself this luxury. He knows his debility – that his hatred isn't as vicious as the members of the rest of the world's tribes, that it isn't ingrained. It hasn't been passed down to him. He was raised with different rules. It still feels unnatural to judge a whole people, as apparently nearly every other person crowding the globe does with practiced ease. He's had to train himself, has had to approach it from the standpoint of duty – the duty toward himself, the duty toward his family. When he scrutinized the world's thrivers, laid them under the same microscope they'd strapped him under, he noticed that they knew how to hate and mock and scorn and mistrust "the other" with an ease that was wholly unfamiliar to him.

Who is "the other", though, for the man? Who are the *herpeta*? It always goes back to this. The first necessity in making a comparison is having articles, objects, to compare. Before there is an out-group there must be an in-group and if there must be an in-group, there must be a name for it, for things without names cannot exist. In order to safely guide his family through the tempest of time, this problem must be solved, this question must be answered – who is his group? Regardless of what once was and of what might be again, he's part of no extant tribe in the true sense of the word – he's found no one who shares his views, goals, lineage, and beliefs. There is nothing in the yuppie society he's lumped with that he finds redeeming. Where these people experience giddiness he feels contempt, what they consider valuable he finds pedestrian, and what to them is meaningless he knows to be of great worth. This is not the silly contrariness so beloved of self-professed iconoclasts, safely ensconced in hipster enclaves from Williamsburg to Wicker Park to Silver Lake. It is simply the healthy reaction to a sickly culture and a corrupt breed. Therefore it's clear, and has been for some time, that along with those babbling, varied inhabitants at the bottom of the hill, all the neighbors atop the hill who look and speak like he does are also included in the out-group. The bitter truth that follows is that, if his family wants to ultimately thrive like others, they must realize that not only are they, alone, the in-group, but that *the world itself stands against them.*

Such a position is daunting. A single family cannot hope to challenge such a powerful force. It is insane. The man understands this. Nor can the burden of standing alone fall solely on the next generation of the family. It is unfair and unrealistic to expect the boy and his future siblings to fight this fight on their own as they grow older, this wrestling with a wretched world-spirit that seeks to enslave and cripple and stunt all life in its bid to equalize. No, for a struggle of this magnitude allies are necessary. It is impossible without them. Yet just because something is necessary does not mean it's easily attained. The man has a fierce conviction that there's little, if any, human material left to work with. What can remain after centuries of internecine wars, each successive conflict amplified by technological applications into greater carnage and greater eradication? Industrialization, class schisms, sterile diets, state-sanctioned discrimination, gender battles, dysgenics, and celibacy have also taken their toll alongside the staggering genocide. He looks around at the members of his generation and sees nothing of caliber, sees only the broken and the botched . . . and even if that weren't the case, the thought of proselytizing, of trying to enlist others, is an appalling one . . . To actively seek out possible adherents to one's particular creed is an exercise in long-term futility. If a prospective convert is malleable, amenable to all suggestion, then what sense is there in trying to form something solid out of him, only to have it melt away at the charming words of the next person with a more attractive message?

It all seems so pointless. It all seems so hopeless. Nothing about the reality of the everyday world he inhabits indicates in any way that he'll be able to fulfill his *geis*. Nothing.

And yet he cannot succumb to the nihilism . . . perhaps if he were alone amid the rubble and the bleakness, but not now . . . The boy has honed the man's purpose and his ideals, impelling and inspiring. He knows that even if his disgust and dismay are natural reactions to the current situation, he must not allow them to thwart him in his bid to survive. He and his descendants *must* survive, must survive and spread in order to one day bring about *their* world, a cleaner one, a healthier one, one where they won't simply endure, as they do in this one, but flourish.

These are just words, though, words and thoughts. It is a fight against extinction he's waging, the fight of every species, and fighting is done not with words and thoughts but with action. The idea of the Christ-figure wasn't anything without fanatics burning down libraries and stabbing in alleyways. The genius of Marx would be but the sound of one hand clapping if not for the millions of trigger fingers that drove his theories home. Always it is deeds that make the difference – *facta non verba*, said the accomplished Romans – and the greatest deeds to be undertaken today are to silently build clans and to link these clans through bonds of kinship. It must always be borne in mind, however, that although fecundity and procreation are the highest form of action at present, they are only a part of the solution, and a miniscule one at that. Anyone can make offspring. The trick is in making the right type, locked arm-in-arm, driven by purpose and ideology. He will do what he can, seek where he can, in order to gather and lock arms and grow.

"It is proper to every gathering that the gatherers assemble to coordinate their efforts to sheltering; only when they have gathered together with that end in view do they begin to gather." So said Heidegger, who understood everything about the new world that has come about.

*   *   *   *

The man's sister and brother-in-law live in Los Angeles as well. They've made a pact to never have children. All the reasons of the day back them up, pouring from their mouths as easily as they do the mouths of his neighbors atop the hill . . . yet the boy's uncle occasionally shows glimmering signs that he can buck the trend . . . He expresses genuine joy when chasing the squealing child, or reading to him, or simply watching him go about the odd routine children follow, with their quirks and curious logic. The man takes the opportunity during such moments to explain that there is nothing more stupendous than having a laughing, intelligent, beautiful son in your life. It's a happiness that can be experienced by almost anyone, this thrill of being in the presence of a child whom you love more than anything and who loves you more than anything . . . a child who lessens your own struggle by not knowing anything *about* that struggle . . .

The man speaks earnestly at these times, desperate to reveal, to impart. Seeing the world through his boy's crystal eyes fills him with so much contentment that descriptive words are entirely inadequate . . . culturally-specific sounds whose authentic, deeper meanings are available only to true comrades and kinfolk . . . He attempts, with bourgeois politeness, to point out to his brother-in-law that both he and the man's sister are forsaking the cycle of life for material ease, that this self-imposed sterility of theirs is selfish and self-defeating. When the boy laughs or runs or throws a ball, something in the man responds so profoundly, he says, that he almost feels immortal. What he wants to make clear, but holds back for fear of some social misstep, is that though the world oppresses them in every way, and though, in truth, they're little more than serfs, there is still the Logos, and this he's able to touch more than ever through the life of his son.

His exhortations have no effect. His brother-in-law smiles, replies that it all sounds great, and climbs back into his Lexus to return to the west side of town. He and the man's sister, while enamored of their nephew, are adamant in their choice to forego a family. This world, which they too seem to despise, has no place for children such as they'd produce, they later tell him. The reasons they give, over Burgundy and steak *au poivre*, are logical, are thought out. He senses that they, like he, are trying to impart something . . . that with the same bourgeois politeness he himself obliquely used, they're telling him that he and his wife have made a mistake in bringing a child into this hostile realm . . . that yes, they've made something precious, only to one day see it crushed by the tidal wave poised just beyond the horizon . . . that only hell is going to pour forth from the man's oh-so-precious Logos . . .

It is a stinging defeat. The reformer Zoroaster – shunning the peasants and shunning the princes – found his first followers among his own family. The man is not so blessed. He will have to look elsewhere.

*   *   *   *

Spring arrives. The jacaranda trees bloom, decorating the city. The time with the boy follows its predictable rhythm and pattern of morning drop-off, evening reunification, and rare weekend days spent together. "Knock-knock," he says in his little voice as he and his father approach the daycare's front door each morning, instantly motoring across the floor to play with his temporary friends the second it opens. There are effusive thanks offered to the British boy for handing him a green car, laughter over the German boy's crazy sounding "*neins*", and punches doled out left and right by tiny, possessive fists clenching wooden trains.

Much emotion bubbles up during the daycare woman's nightly recaps. The man is angry when he hears that his son, in a cowardly move, has pinched another child for some transgression. There is disappointment when he hears the boy wouldn't leap from a table like some of the more rambunctious children. There is pride when he hears that the Mexican girls asked him if he knew his alphabet and he quickly replied, "A-B-C." There is sadness knowing that the friends being made at the place will be lost to the child when the family leaves Los Angeles. No tribe, no community, no longevity, no solidity, no organism, no future. The theme repeats itself like the yearly flowering of the jacaranda in the toxic and polluted city. One day, if the status quo persists, neither the complaint nor the tree will exist.

*   *   *   *

The man's in-laws are flying in from Massachusetts, his father-in-law coming to L.A. for business. It is the man's task to pick them up at the airport and bring them to his house. As a surprise it's decided that he'll bring along the boy – their only grandchild – to greet them earlier than expected. He tucks the child into the crook of his arm and walks to the street where his car is parked. It's eleven years old, with nearly 120,000 miles on the odometer . . . one accident away from the junkyard . . . dirty from the filthy Los Angeles air . . . Something akin to embarrassment briefly flutters through him at the thought of pulling up to the airport curb in that car, an embarrassment he never suffers other times. In a flash the feeling turns into something else – a comparison between his father-in-law's accomplishments and his own. Quickly he pushes the thought out of his mind, putting the boy down on the sidewalk in order to open the trunk and make sure it's empty.

"Daddy's big, black car."

The man turns his head to the voice. His tiny son stands there before him, patting the dirty vehicle admiringly while staring at his father with enormous pride. His eyes are shining. His face is beaming. It is daddy's car. Daddy is great. Therefore, daddy's car is great too.

The man's face breaks into a smile nearly as big as the boy's. It is this that cannot be explained to his brother-in-law. There is nothing like it anywhere, this purity. He basks in the beauty of the boy's naïveté, revels in his awesome *innocence*. He savors it while he can because he knows how fleeting it is. The child will lose it someday. He'll have to. It's necessary and inevitable. An age will arrive, a time will come, when he begins the transformation to adult, and the hardness and reality will push out this innocence until it disappears forever. Strife, as the poet said, comes with manhood, just as waking comes with day.

Continuing to smile, the kid wipes his runny nose and fondly pats the vehicle a second time. His father picks him up to strap him into the car seat. He holds him a second longer than is necessary, then quickly and gently brushes his lips along the top of the tawny head.

The man loves the boy.

*   *   *   *

By the next morning the child's sniffles have turned into a full-blown fever, the first he's ever had. The man is concerned. It is wrenching to witness a creature that is usually so powerfully alive lying supine on the bed, staring listlessly at the ceiling, looking like the personification of Europe. It is disconcerting – the total lack of energy, the slight flickering of the eyes as he falls into a restless sleep while listening to his grandmother read. The boy is easier to deal with when falling onto floors and tumbling from chairs and cracking his head on tables. Incidents such as these take place in a flurry and a flash, instantaneous release of the chaos bubbling within. There are tears, then sobs, then the episode lies in the past and life proceeds. The fever lingers though, requiring broader vision to see it through. Its longer duration allows worry to invade. The man frets in silence, concealing his concern. It is his first child. He has nothing to compare the situation to, no point of reference. His people have been hacked apart by progress, separated from the rhythms of life. Everything is brand new to them each shrinking generation. Fevers are something they read about in instruction manuals now, the basics of existence being sold back to them for a price.

The man is thankful for his in-laws' presence. His wife's mother tends to her little grandson easily, makes all the right moves, exhibits none of the man's apprehension. It's old hat, there's nothing to it – Grandma doesn't need an instruction manual from the mall, she's done it all before. She soothes the boy, takes care of him, casually displays skills her own daughter doesn't possess, skills that weren't passed on. It is comforting, but it is maddening. This schism, this failure to hand down, this loss of information, this vertical fragmentation of families and knowledge must end, must become the past, must be remembered in the near future strictly as an interregnum, an evolutionary challenge. In kinship alone lies true wealth, not in the fiat dollars dribbled by others into lonely, outstretched hands. The man doesn't want the sacrificial self-destruction, he doesn't want the extinction, it's the adaptation he craves, the *adaptation across the whole of the group*, the transformation *into* a group, but he doesn't see it happening anywhere, he only sees tar-pits filled with mammoth bones and steak bones and Burgundy bottles and instruction manuals and no one cares, no one seems to care or understand, not even those closest to him, that if they don't adapt to this social destruction that's been unleashed they will die out. That is all. There is no middle way. There is no middle way for anything, ever.

During the days of sickness and blessed recovery his mother-in-law says over and over that she sees her own eyes in this boy . . . and those eyes are her father's eyes, she adds . . . Thus she acknowledges, in the most trivial way, that the boy is not the isolated individual that she and the zeitgeist proclaim him. He is not merely composed of one-half mother and one-half father, nor is he simply a quarter of each grandparent, nor an eighth of every great grandparent. He is not an *individual* in this horrid, patchwork sense. Such thinking is epidemic among the bourgeoisie, among the man's family and friends, a virulent strain worming its way through centuries and civilizations, through rotting Greece, rotting Rome, rotting Enlightenment Europe . . . To view the totality of a human life as a series of fractions is insane. To see halves and quarters and eighths rather than whole numbers is aberrant. They get closer to reality when they assign particular qualities to the imaginary portions. "He's three-eighths German, so three-eighths serious. That humor must come from his Irish side." But even this is simplistic and odd and rooted, somewhere, in that petty nationalism that stands in the way of true apotheosis. Survival dictates that national characteristics make way for supranational characteristics just as much as it demands that the bizarreness of individualism fade.

He wants to explain all of this to his in-laws. A tree is not a tree without trees. There's no such thing as an ant, only ants. Nature doesn't know a single bee, just bees. He wants to draw them closer, to enlist them, to make it all clear to them – but he can't. He tries, it's impossible. The barriers have been erected, years of media, years of America. It is a horrible position he's in. He does all he can to strive for the health of his son, but that's the health of only a *single cell*. For the cell to function properly it needs an environment, a strong body brimming with other healthy cells, forming systems, storing information, destroying invaders. Where are those other healthy cells amid the malignant cancer of today? What stirs under the millennia-long accumulation of filth bequeathed by ancestors who chose truckling instead of standing . . . who accepted and enforced a creed at odds with vitality, longevity and, ultimately, life itself . . .

When the boy goes for strolls with his grandparents around the neighborhood – walking backward, laughing, squealing – everything seems so sweet, so bouncy, so beautiful. To a degree it is. But when he points out a cat eating mouthfuls of grass, does his grandfather reflect on his own great-great grandfather doing the same back in Ireland, crawling along the earth like a miserable cow because he and his tribe allowed themselves to be enslaved for so long, allowed their affairs to be handled by more ruthless men for so long, that starvation was the logical outcome? When the boy stamps the earth, feeling the thud shivering up his little leg and into his body like a miniature Anteas, does his grandmother recall any tales of her grandfather awakening on frosty mornings and stomping the black Ukrainian soil in exactly the same way? Does she ever wonder why he had to flee Ukraine with his family, abandoning hundreds of years of homeland and horse riding and sabers and fruit trees to slave on a railroad across an ocean he'd never even heard of? Does she ever wonder what happened to those relations who stayed behind, those who couldn't escape? Ever?

By neglecting their pasts, they're denying the boy his future. They can't see this. They have no songs, no fables, no legends, no symbols, no rituals. Their food is American food, their customs are American customs, disposable and cheap. There's no washing the face in the dew on May Day, just baseball on television. No poems of Oisin battling the Christian interloper Patrick, just Bugs Bunny versus Elmer Fudd.

They'll never test his verbal ability, never quiz him, never push him, but they will – they do – rave about how smart he is, another favorite American custom. "He knows so many words," they gasp, as if this came about magically . . . calculator, enemy, cow milk, daddy glasses, mommy book, sword . . . "Listen to his sentences," they marvel, meaning "Bye-bye, leaf," or "Oh oh, dat bwoken, daddy fix it," or a hundred other simple phrases that somehow indicate brilliance.

The man questions his own positive assessments of the boy in the aftermath of the visit. If everyone's so smart – and certainly, viewed through smudged parental prisms, there are tens of millions of little geniuses across the land, themselves the offspring of millions of more geniuses – then why in this position? Why on the verge of starvation like the grass-eating peasants back in Ireland? Why caught in this diluted version of the gulag? Why does the man have to put his son to sleep in a sweltering bedroom, unable, in their vibrant neighborhood, to leave the window open at night for fear of the child being kidnapped? This is what smart brings?

No. This is what stupidity and weakness bring, it is what false views of reality bring. These people are bondsmen, and they're in bondage because they've let themselves be put there, cooing to their children how smart they all were while others were busily and stealthily fastening shackles about their ankles and wrists. They are victims of extortion and imprisonment and theft and slander because they have *allowed* themselves to become victims. They are paying not just for the sins of oblivious parents and grandparents, but for the sins of their great-great grandparents, and *theirs*, and *theirs*, for those who washed their face in the springtime dew and told sprightly tales of Oisin.

The man is teaching the boy otherwise. Their family, too, is enslaved, but unlike those others they're in that state unwillingly. Instead of merely telling the boy he's smart, he'll also tell him he's nothing more than a thrall, and that to remedy that he and his descendants must see the world as it is and begin to somehow break the chains that bind them. The groundwork must be laid, the framework erected. It can be done. It can be done. It must be done.

*   *   *   *

The grandparents return to Cape Cod, leaving still more questions in the man's already overstuffed head. His wife ends her freelance job and flies to meet old friends in a wealthy mountain town, giving the man three consecutive days with his son, three days of bliss and memories and treasure. The boy makes "gully-gully" noises, odd chuckles rolling upward along his skinflapped throat. He shrieks when tossed into the air, he dances with his stuffed otter, he awkwardly throws balls and kicks his legs, he clumsily hugs the cat. He demands, "M'up," to be carried, he wrestles like a demon, he points out letters on street signs and magazines. He tries to sing, to draw, to read. He grinds his forehead into his dad's, he points at photos of his grandparents in albums, he bounces as he runs. He shoves grapes into his mouth, yogurt into his mouth, chicken and waffles into his rosebud mouth. He does a thousand little things every minute every hour every day, a fat, giggling, effervescent ball of beauty, and the man wonders if there's anything, anything on this earth, that compares with the experience of simply spending time with the fruit of one's loins.

Those ignorant ancestors whom he recently finds himself so often silently condemning, clinging like rats to their sick religion, wandering about without foresight or vision, he now thanks, without rancor for the moment. It's true that the window stays closed in that stifling room on summer nights because of them, but it's also true that they made it possible for this most awesome of beings to exist side by side with him, for this amazing lad to be a part of his life. For this he humbly thanks his folk. The boy is not just his alone. He's all of theirs. In the same way that honor and prestige could flow both ways in the *hutong* and the *shtetl*, the man knows that he and the boy can purify these forebears, can redeem them, by finally attempting to put things right . . . by finally striding purposefully toward the goal . . .

✳ ✳ ✳ ✳

Across the world those varied types who are already on the proper path – those who set out on it long ago, and thus currently lay claim to the title *Übermenschen* – possess many social mechanisms to allow them to retain the position they've attained. One of these is their collection of holy days, annual markers steeped in relevance, the feasting balanced by fasting, the joy mitigated by sorrow. *Untermenschen* on the other hand, the directionless, have holidays. They are shiny, sparkling, fun, and meaningless. Those who possess holy days, regardless of their differing creeds or ethnicities or cultures, are tenacious, determined, and strong. The rest simply float through their allotted span on earth, frivolous and flip, blown this way and that, leaving everything up to fate like a frog or a bug.

On a calendar in his office, in neat squares marked by the ink that's spilled over this world like Caesar's blood, the man notes that it is the 22nd day of September. It is a day called Rosh Hashanah by some, a celebration of a new year, the beginning of ten holy days that culminate in a time of self-examination, of reflection on deeds performed, of repentance, of solidarity, of standing in judgment before the ethos of the tribe, also known as "God". That same day, for those who call themselves Americans, is "Elephant Appreciation Day". It is a special day set aside to appreciate elephants. One way to appreciate elephants, it is suggested, is to look at pictures of them. Another way is to visit a nearby zoo to see a captive elephant, thus enlivening and deepening the meaning of the holiday.

An ocean. A puddle. In which does one swim, draw inspiration from, *sustain* oneself from, and in which does a person merely splash about for a moment until dirty? Which surges and thunders, swells and churns, and which evaporates in an instant under the strong light of the noontide sun?

That evening, when picking up the boy, the man finds out that Rosh Hashanah has been celebrated by all the children at the daycare, no matter the lineage or beliefs of their parents. The woman who owns

85

the business tosses the information his way humorously and casually. He smiles, goes along. She doesn't seem to understand that, by giving her own holy day away, she's made it equivalent to one that surreally celebrates elephants.

*   *   *   *

There is much talk of the moon on the part of the boy that autumn. It is a curiosity to him, a wonder, a thing he cannot touch, real yet not quite real, varying in its appearance yet carrying a name that remains constant. During their evening walks he demands the slivered crescent, demands the bulging half, demands the rounded full. The wispy voice pleads with the light-polluted Los Angeles skies. "I want crescent moon." When he speaks to the man on the telephone during a visit to his Oma's, he whispers, "I see gibbous moon, daddy," and the man looks out the back window, seeing the same sight a hundred miles away from his son, triangulating the three. It hung low and full in the sky on the boy's first night out of the womb. It will remain there throughout his lifetime, waxing, waning, waxing, waning . . .

Intelligent peoples, determined peoples, have linked themselves via their calendars to this planetary body that grows and shrinks like fortunes but that always reappears. There is genius in this. All members of the clan, no matter where they might reside on the globe, can observe holy days simultaneously, be they living within sight of the twinkling Bears at the top of the world or beneath the Scutum Sobieskii at the bottom. Seasonal changes are neither the underlying reasons nor the indicators for religious observations, and so the antipodean embarrassment of chopping down evergreens in summer or of celebrating a festival of rebirth at the beginning of autumn is avoided for the most part. Internationalism becomes the norm; the world itself becomes your tribe's home.

With the exception of the spring holiday called "Easter", no special day indicated on the pages of the calendar the man uses is contingent upon particular phases of the moon. His calendar, like that of most people in the Western world, is a solar calendar. A representation of this calendar sits on his desk. It is made in a foreign factory by the hundreds of thousands and consists of a dozen oversized pieces of paper imprinted with numbered squares. Its primary function seems to be to highlight which days of the year banks are closed for business.

Once upon a time the ancestors of the man and the boy measured the eternal, finding order in the seasons brought about by the earth's fluctuating position vis-à-vis the sun. Over their millennia of existence they discovered great poetry and truth in the summer, the autumn, the winter, and the spring. They discerned the image of man reflected in the seasonal mirror; they saw the parallels between living, dying, death, and rebirth. The most perceptive among them realized that the laws of nature are followed by all . . . that there is no difference between the great and the small, the external and the internal – *nichts ist drinnen, nichts ist draußen* . . .

Over time, like autumn leaves being blown from the same ancient oak tree, these people were spread across the earth. No matter their dreamy insights, no matter their unparalleled accomplishments, they steadily fragmented. They split, and split again . . . but as they split and spread they failed to triangulate themselves . . . they failed to constantly remind themselves who they were . . . They lacked *cohesion* past seas, past deserts, past mountain ranges. They were only able to apply their minds to the broadest religion or the narrowest nationalism, linking themselves either to imaginary afterworlds or to specific valleys or hillsides, forever incapable of fusing their genetic and cultural similarity across languages and invisible lines in the ocean. Sliced apart and hollowed out, things like Elephant Appreciation Day began to appear on their calendars. No one cared.

*   *   *   *

The days leading up to the arrival of the new child fall away, crossed off the office calendar never to return as the moment draws closer and closer. The boy hugs his mother's rounded stomach in anticipation . . . laughs in surprised delight when the creature, alive under the balloon of flesh, kicks at his caresses . . . He doesn't understand the meaning of it all. He's unable to anticipate the changes that will be wrought when the woman finally gives birth.

The man smiles at his son's laugh, notices that the voice is already less babyish. Life is constant change, there is no stasis. Every worthy culture noted that from the beginning. The search for solidity is what plagues him, the constant seeking of ways to build a ship sturdy enough to cross the eternally churning ocean, not just muddied puddles . . . one that can be sailed by all generations, from the dawn to the dusk . . . "Build such a ship and survive," the gods warned Deucalion, Utnapishtim, and Noah, "For those without a vessel are slated to be destroyed."

He and the boy take their evening walk, unaware that tomorrow is the day they've been awaiting, the one where more glorious life arrives to bless their family. The son he loves so much is wrapped tightly in a blanket and carried in his arms as together they meander through the cool September air. There is no time to breathe in the beauty, the perfection of the union, however. A car whips by full throttle. Bass-heavy music booms from its windows as it screams past. It is a terrible sound – ugly, vicious, sadistic, and hateful . . . a sound unprecedented in the whole history of humankind . . . a sound that is, without a doubt, the utterly apt expression of the era . . .

They walk a little more when suddenly screeching sirens fill the dark. There is no respite. Discord is the normal state of things. "Fire engine," the boy says, followed by, "Woowoowoo," his high-pitched imitation. He doesn't know that life isn't meant to be like this. He doesn't know that there's supposed to be silence at night. He doesn't know that his father is supposed to be able to love him without being molested by the strident anger of the modern world. The man's every waking minute is tainted, stung by the tentacles of random violence and jarring mechanical and electrical noises. All around him lurks the presence of psychological torture and forced submission and brutality . . . and still, even with all this – ignoring every single warning – he mulishly continues to bring more children into the chaos . . .

*   *   *   *

The woman's water breaks the next morning and everything follows from there. Midwives of the postmodern, less effective sort, arrive at the house on the hill. Hours later the new child emerges. It is a girl. All the nascent traditions are followed, all sacredness observed, as she is welcomed into the fold. But this is not her story.

Change comes over the boy. It was inevitable, perhaps. There is intense vacillation between moods, the man alternately his ally and his enemy . . . piercing shrieks . . . slicing shouts that razor into the atmosphere when he's reprimanded or disciplined . . . It is the fervor of existence, not yet faded and worn, not crushed or tattered. That fervor is overwhelming, though . . . exhausting . . . The same child who exuberantly welcomes the man home with a boisterous, "Hi, dad! How are you?" also writhes around in such furious fits that he bites his tongue or mouth and covers his chin in blood, or leaps from his crib and gashes his stomach, or bashes the back of his head on the floor in public places, or rolls around on the sidewalk with an indescribable rage generally reserved for the insane.

It is hard on the parents, both to witness and to accept. It hurts the man to see the pain the boy is in, yet it also infuriates him, stings his ears, makes his stomach churn. The depth of his son's anger at this tender age is unfathomable to him. Clearly it is a reaction to the presence of the baby girl, but it all seems so psychotic. There are times the man feels like hitting him, which is internally disturbing to someone who's not completely purged himself of prevailing mores regarding the physical punishment of children. He takes to walking around the neighborhood alone at night in order to avoid the shrieks. Often, though, the urge to return to the house and roughly shake or strike the rabid boy walks along with him. The day finally arrives when, much to his sadness, disappointment, and relief, he finally acts on his primal urges. He slaps his beautiful son, his jewel, his love, across the howling face.

*   *   *   *

Always on the lookout for things to do together in that city that caters to all except them, the man decides to take the boy to something called a Fire Department Museum. Such flavorless diversions exist not merely because of the shallowness of the culture, but because they aren't a threat to those who profit from that culture. The thralls can be entertained without the possibility of forming dangerous thoughts. Dinosaur books, princesses, toy trucks, stuffed animals, cartoon characters created whole cloth by Writer's Guild members, fire department museums . . . all hollow . . . all for sale . . . all permissible . . .

It's an exciting place for the boy, however. The world's brand new to him. He's thrilled to see the antique engines, to press the button which makes the red lights spin, to wear the plastic fireman's hat handed over to him by retired members of the Greatest Generation, those who birthed the Orwell Generation. He's happy, and that makes the man happy, or rather some inexpressible variant of what's termed "happy", rooted in the privilege of witnessing a piece of oneself able to once again draw pleasure from sources long abandoned.

Upstairs they find a room filled with wooden fire trucks and puzzles and other toys . . . all, like the shiny hat atop the boy's head, manufactured in China . . . The boy plays contentedly for a goodly amount of time . . . becomes slightly possessive, slightly upset, when another lad attempts to join in . . . Of course, since the setting is a museum, and only particular types visit such places – fading types – it's merely a matter of seconds before the newcomer is admonished by his bourgeois parents for daring to grab what another child already has. The man grimaces, bored by the typical reaction he's grown to expect. When his son, too, finally becomes equally bored, they leave the playroom and enter another, lined with glass cases filled with a collection of miniature emergency vehicles. Thus begins the horrible end, the deterioration of their entire day.

The boy demands that his father remove the toys from behind the locked glass. It can't be done, the man explains. There's no key. Back and forth they go, the demand followed by the explanation. Each time the boy becomes more upset, more rude. The man leaves the room with him. The hysteria increases. He counts to ten. He orders the now bratty boy to get himself under control. Finally, after the writhing, the shrieking, the screaming, and the lashing out, he can't take anymore. It is time to leave the museum. He yanks him off the floor and carries him rapidly down the stairs while the child screams directly into his ears. On they go, through the main room, past the looks of the public, who never seem to fully understand or approve of what's going on. Finally, finally, they're out in the parking lot, out in the calming air, which is where the man has anticipated an ending. It hasn't crossed his mind that the scene can get worse.

As he unlocks the car door the boy throws himself on the ground, just as he did outside the daycare when being picked up the day before. There he lies, frothing, rolling on the asphalt like a snake-handling Baptist speaking in tongues. The man opens the door, lifts the child up to strap him into the car seat, and the shrieks become even louder, which seems impossible . . . two minutes of torturous screaming, nonstop, up close . . . two minutes of arching his back, twisting his neck, kicking his legs . . . all enveloped in that maddening screaming, that screaming, that screaming, that screaming . . .

The man slaps him.

Instantly the boy shuts up.

Instantly the man feels a tinge of sickness in his gut.

He wants to pretend he's done it altruistically . . . old helpful dad, aiding in the cessation of hysteria . . . but he hasn't, he knows . . . It's been done in anger. However, any further reflection is impossible, because as soon as he begins to drive away the screaming returns full force . . . The boy kicks his little legs out, makes desperate attempts to unbuckle himself from his car seat. The man's concentration is shattered. He thinks he might crash the vehicle and yells at his son like he's never yelled before. It has no effect.

The time in the car drags. Traffic forces him to exit the freeway early. The surface streets are jammed too. The screaming continues, though less forcefully. He tries calming the lunatic, right arm stretched to the backseat, rubbing the tiny foot. It's to no avail. The shrieking doesn't cease until daddy's big, black car drives up out of the land of sixty languages to the house on top of the hill.

As they pull to the curb there is, finally, silence. His psyche shredded, the man walks around to the passenger door to remove the boy, who sits staring at him, eye-to-eye, adult-like, strong. He hates the man. The man in turn grins an embarrassed grin, overly aware of the reddened cheek on his son's face. Suddenly the tiny boy smiles back, his previous glower instantly washing away. "Daddy wear hat?" he asks. The man fulfills the request, puts on the fireman's hat. All seems forgiven. He carries the boy inside, where he immediately runs to his mother and begins crying. She takes him to his crib and lays him down to sleep. At the kitchen table the depleted man cradles his forehead in his hand. He exhales until empty.

When the woman returns he tells the story, admitting that he not only slapped the boy, but slapped him hard. She knows. The child told her from his crib, sobbing, "Daddy hurt my cheek." The recounting hurts the man. There is irony in the situation. This person at the table, this secret monstrosity among his surrounding bourgeois-hipster class, this aberration who's fought with fists for a good chunk of his life, having bled and made bleed while they shirked and shunned and mocked and socially looked down on "violence", this man who in his darkest moments would gladly purge the world of all of humankind with no feeling other than a profound sense of duty to every other form of life, sits quietly holding his aching head because of a single, isolated smack.

His wife pulls out a chair and sits across from him. She says that, as she laid the boy down to sleep, she explained to him that mommy and daddy didn't know what to do about his behavior lately, that his incessant shrieking had worn them both down. The man, still frazzled, snorts at her words . . . middle-class "explanations" to babies barely on the threshold of consciousness . . . a waste of time, he tells her, blind to his own manner with the boy . . . She takes offense, angrily asks him if, when his son awakens, he plans on apologizing for what he's done.

No. He will not do it, he says. Such a response would be simply more *Bürgersprache*. He will not tell the child he adores that his actions were wrong, that he let an emotion control him, that he let anger impel him. The boy can't distinguish between motivations, between being slapped for just cause or slapped due to the weakness of his father – and weakness it was. Perhaps it's human, perhaps a fallibility of many men, but that's not an excuse, because as he well knows, *man is something to be overcome*, and to overcome anything one needs self-discipline, which he did not show. That is an issue for him, personally, to deal with, not to be shared with a mere child. If the boy is to be told anything, it's that he was slapped for a reason, for unacceptable behavior, which he must at some level have grasped to begin with.

This is the beginning of something in the child's life . . . a shift . . . The time of punishment and of discipline has crept up on all of them. Though these repasts are not to the tastes of the bourgeoisie, they're necessary if the boy is to become a man in any sense of the word. He has to be poured into the mold of the indomitable Roman, has to be forged into something that can withstand the assaults of the whole world yet be noble enough not to fall prey to its sickly charms. However, to even approach that insane possibility the man will have to be harsh at times; unyielding, terrifying, threatening. There's the probability that the child will not understand, that he'll believe his father desires merely to harm him rather than prepare him. Such a misreading has severed many a tie between a father and son. The predictable outcome of the individualism that's made his former *túath* both amazing and obsolete is nowhere more glaring than in the rocky historical relationship between these two familial roles. It is there, in the legends of the past, in the reality of the present, pointed out by both allies and enemies alike – a regrettable tendency toward intergenerational male conflict.

The man grasps the danger of his situation. With no community, and by extension no communal laws, his fervor to instill order and discipline into the boy's life will merely be viewed as tyrannical, the natural expression of an authoritarian personality. The intellectuals who've targeted the man and the boy – men who actually had the *privilege* of coming from a community – have built the framework, have created the vocabulary and the sympathy and the phony commiseration designed solely to splinter, sever, and deconstruct their vulnerable family.

He has no holy books to consult, no wellspring to drink from, no tribal elders to give him advice, no comrades to assist in enforcing his decisions. He needs to breed a man from the boy, but all his admonitions, all his lessons and warnings, will be for naught if the respect and admiration dissipate – which they will, eventually, amid the bubbling hormones of sulky adolescence. The man, in his role as sole punisher, will eventually make a logical target for the boy when he reaches the cusp of young adulthood. Without a community, without each family following the same laws and policing the same social transgressions, a father ultimately becomes, in the eyes of his son, simply one opinionated man standing among millions of other opinionated men. When those laws are created and enforced by an individual, rather than a group, they don't resemble laws at all, but personal expression . . . and since this personal expression is linked in the youth's mind with hurt and anger, the tenets contained therein are most likely to be ignored when carried over into early adulthood . . . Only with age can the youth finally recognize the law in his father's voice, but by then, it's often too late.

His wife listens to him speak. "Nature's made it so that he won't understand my lessons until long after I've lost my vitality, driving us right back into the cycle of having to relearn every generation. This is wrong, wrong, we're living wrong, do you understand, do you see the flaws? These single bonds, father connected to son, these aren't the right way to traverse time. They're *weak*. Thousands of bonds, that's the right way, this family to that one, that one to this one, vertically and horizontally – and not just connected to each other, but to the *law*. Do you know how alone we are, our little family? Do you know how vulnerable we are, how there's no safety net any more, no guide? Do you know how long the descent's been? We can't even see the cliff we marched off, it's been so long. Thousands of years of never-ending murder, the total annihilation of our *very best*! Every tool necessary for our survival has been broken, every weapon we need to defend ourselves has been *thrown away*!"

He sinks his head into his hands. The woman softly replies that she does understand, though it's clear that like most of her kind she is unable to move into the nebulousness of the *idea*, unable to converse at the level of the sky, unable to internalize the framing of eternal truths. No matter. It is the chthonic nature of her sex, and it is necessary for survival. Stolidly and admirably she turns the discussion back to the concrete matter at hand – their son was slapped in the face because his father couldn't control himself. Such a thing must never happen again.

She is correct.

*   *   *   *

Over time, as the girl grows and meshes with her family – becoming a sister to the boy rather than a resented rival – the boy's anger begins to subside. His personality gradually returns to the one his parents have grown used to, and weekend mornings follow a regular pattern once again. The door to the man's bedroom-office is shoved open, while simultaneously a loud voice shouts, "Knock-knock, daddy." Off they go to the park, early, before the trash-hurling hordes descend. They practice running in the grass. The man trips him, throws him to the ground, steamrolls him. They discover dirty tennis balls and throw them back and forth. They do kicks in the air and stare up at the clouds. There are piggyback rides and knightly accolades with sticks substituting for swords. They breathlessly listen for the screes of the dwindling hawks. Tiny seeds are gathered to present to the boy's precious mother and pinecones are clutched in fat hands to offer his tiny sister. An apple is eaten. A story is told, "The Three Billy Goats Gruff". In the shadow of the trees the man explains the meaning of the tale to his wide-eyed son – you always work together to attain a goal, and if an enemy wants to stop you then you bide your time until you're strong enough to challenge him. Such a tactic is called *Taqiyya* by the Muslims, a technique they learn from some of their most sacred teachings. The man must convey the same message through a ridiculous peasant story about talking goats and imaginary trolls.

Once again the boy's grandparents come from the other side of the country to visit, this time in order to see their new granddaughter. As always the event is dreadfully secular, two individuals staring at a third individual. To the man the happiness displayed seems only an approximation of happiness, a shadow of what it could be if vision were broadened. The joy is circumstantial, incomplete. He tries to forgive his in-laws their various weaknesses. He forces himself to remember that they have suffered also, that they are products of their time, that though they cannot identify symptoms of the prevailing sickness, let alone causes, they are the reason for the appearance and existence of his children.

Still, the interactions are maddening at times. The manner in which they speak to their grandson is bizarre, the words aspirated and elongated, a virulent meme replicating itself across the Twilight Lands . . . the spirit of the reader of *Ferdinand* making its unwelcome presence felt in the man's home . . .

"Where's the cat? Wherrrrrre's the cat," asks his grandmother. The boy turns to look at the cat, three feet away, then returns his face to hers. He's perplexed. The cat is obviously in front of them both.

"Don't you know what a cat is? Caaaat. It's right there." She points. The boy, believing his grandmother to be initiating some type of game, points to the animal, then to the old woman, then smiles broadly.

"No, grandma's not a cat. You were right the first time. Thaaaaat's the cat." She points again. Confusion stretches across the boy's face. It stays there the whole week, as his grandparents applaud and cheer him for the completion of the simplest tasks. He's unused to such displays. His mother and father take his awareness and verbal aptitude as a given, and speak to him in a regular tone. These grandparents however, as they did on their previous visit, marvel at his burgeoning intellect but don't seem to fully understand or accept it. They believe him to be smart, but from a modern perspective, where no stupid children exist in reality but only as straw men to be used as comparisons. A previous desire of the man's – that his wife's parents lived closer in order that they might enrich and vitalize their grandchildren's lives – is, by the end of the week, thoroughly quashed.

On his last night in Los Angeles the boy's grandfather reminds the man and his wife, in his East Coast way, of the importance of drawing up a will. It is a necessary precaution to take, he intones, in the event that something unfortunate should happen. The man meets his wife's gaze. The subject of a will has – naïvely, he realizes – never even crossed their minds. Now a *possible* nightmare scenario plants itself alongside the very *real* nightmare scenario of his daily existence – the infinitesimal chance that he and his wife should die suddenly and simultaneously.

He lies in bed the following night, unable to sleep, his father-in-law's words ringing in his ears. Certainly when it comes to the macabre possibility of his and his wife's premature deaths, legal and financial issues involving the children are important. However, concerns like asset distribution and unbreakable trusts are easily dealt with, and hardly worth losing sleep over. What keeps the man awake is the terrible, terrible fear of his children being raised in this world without him . . . their morals pruned by someone else, their intellects unchallenged, underfed, unshaped . . .

To imagine the boy, in particular, brought up by either pair of grandparents is a harrowing thought. To be handed over to those who haven't made the necessary changes, who've not adapted their thinking, their *lives*, to the realities of the current historical situation, is unthinkable. To be raised by those who've internalized others' struggles as their own is unthinkable. To be raised by fiddlers amid the flames, whistlers walking past graveyards, those who never question anything, who've incorporated the nature of the slave into their very fabric so that kowtowing and self-debasement have become virtues and living honorably something unknown and alien – *this is unthinkable*.

Their children would be shoved back into the muck, there to suffocate until drowned . . . perfect acorns, hurled willy-nilly into the windblown sands of the desert, never able to take root, never able to send out the necessary tendrils to become oaks . . . This is the fable of their *túath* in microcosm – the impossibility of becoming what it had the potential to be due to an incompatible environment . . . the inability to grow to perfection because of a poisonous shift in the cultural soil . . . Entire forests exist in a single acorn, thus each one must be nurtured and protected in order that that potential be realized. The boy and girl must likewise be nurtured and protected, which simply will never happen if reared by their grandparents. When people don't notice that whole forests are burning down around them, they're not capable of nurture and protection. Simply put, nothing can be *allowed* to happen to him or his wife.

The man turns in the dark of the room, caught in the throes of insomnia. His family, its existence, is so fragile. Granted, it is an incipient cluster, something that has the potential to grow, yet mathematically it's as close to zero as a solitary individual, and an individual without a people might as well not exist. The all-important sense of *being* unfolds among others sharing the same beliefs and responding to stimuli in like fashion. That tiny family of his is not enough. He needs others to join him, cemented together by culture and struggle. He must gather those who will help him, as he will help them. Together they will protect each other's offspring, together they'll reseed devastated forests.

But where are they? He's always going back to this. Clearly they're not among his relations, but where? He's not sure where to search, or how. He cannot think of a recent encounter with anyone who even approached the qualities needed, someone with the fortitude and foresight to submit to rules, to delay gratification even unto the twenty-seventh generation. The remaining people of quality seem to be all spoken for, and are already in arms against the man and his offspring.

It has become the dominant theme of his life, a paradox he must somehow solve. To survive he must find an imaginary Grail, yet accepting that the Grail is imaginary means he cannot survive, yet he must survive, so he must find an imaginary Grail, and on and on and on until exhausted and dead. Therefore, if he is to function in the present, in order to serve the future and honor the past, he must accept that the Grail he seeks does exist and that there are others out there like him, also floundering, also treading water. The manifestation of himself in the person of the boy, that different aspect of his own essence, will not allow a middle-class, solipsistic wallowing as response to the challenges issued by life. There *are* others who have nothing, who *want* something, and are seeking a way to get it. Five hundred families fled west from the wrath of the Mongols, coalescing to form the beginnings of the Ottomans. Fifty families, according to the sociobiologists, were all that were needed to keep a community functioning amid the hardships of rural antebellum America. Give the man thirteen families, nine . . . anything . . .

*   *   *   *

Days later he sits on the corner curb, unconsciously rubbing the boy's tiny hand between his palms. His eyes sweep over the glass walls and Spanish tiles of the refurbished houses on the block. The occasional screenwriter saunters by with a mixed-breed dog yanking on its leash. The electric cars flash their "Free Tibet" bumper stickers. It's all so tedious. He knows that wherever those first families will come from, it isn't here. They won't come from his mother's processed, suburban neighborhood and they won't come from this one, this urban habitat of barren mares and geldings. He is depressed by his prospects. Resolutions and fantasies concocted in dark rooms are difficult to maintain in the smoggy light of day.

The talk with his sister and brother-in-law, the silent rebuke, had disappointed him. He'd thought of Zoroaster and his frustrations and tribulations then. He thinks of him now. The lauded reformers of the past, the calumniated ones of the present – before they spread their creeds they all searched first among their own *túatha*, their regions, their shared cultures. For the atomized man, this is impossible. The only thing he shares with those around him is a zip code.

He sits, deep in thought, dreaming in the sunlight. The Santa Anas blow, the palm trees sway. A discarded newspaper comes rasping down the boulevard like a leper without its warning bell . . . garbage, always garbage in this garbage city . . . there it rolls, semi-crumpled and festering with agitprop and advertising . . . there it rolls, a loathsome rag owned by criminal billionaires . . . there it rolls, a piece of inked trash whose final act will be to tumble drunkenly into a filthy river and choke the remaining fish . . .

He watches it, disgusted, preparing to return to his interrupted thoughts . . . and then—

"Look, daddy! The newspaper is dancing down the street! It's doing somersaults! Look! It's dancing! Bye-bye, newspaper. Bye-bye!"

The man turns, and smiles, and watches the newspaper dance away down the street.

Oh, what this child does, what he does . . . Beside him sits an adult, one who's grown to manhood during a time of incredible struggle. He's seen so much, too much, in this marathon through hell . . . cancerous lies, screamed and whispered, broadcast and loudspeakered and scrawled in those newspapers . . . ugly slavery, bloody-backed slavery . . . the befuddled glances of proles as they stared dumbly at the welts on their torn and swollen bodies . . . or, worse, failed to even notice the welts . . . The destruction of his whole world, that's what he's witnessed . . . a demolition of all that was dear . . . the beautiful replaced by the malformed . . . aberrations everywhere, changelings everywhere, slurping on grime, swimming in pus . . .

The small boy, though, his only boy, magically makes it all clean for him. Somehow he hoses off the sludge and baptizes it. The man's disgust for the newspaper, for the city, for the *era*, is washed in the boy's innocence, scrubbed, expelled. For a moment all is forgotten, all is pure for him again, and in that moment the man is the boy, *forever* he is the boy, and the boy is him, and the man is his own grandfather, and the boy is his own great grandson, and they both know what immortality is, what biology is, what truth is. The fevered followers of the Christ-figure tried to eradicate their past. The ruthless soldiers of Marx tried to obliterate it. The worshippers of modern democracy are trying even as those warm winds blow from the honeyed South. They've all succeeded, to a degree. Many people have been cut off. Many have withered and died. Yet for a few, for those who must be gathered and united, *it has failed completely*. Their roots go deeper, thirstily seeking water from subterranean streams and rivers and unknown sources untapped by those who withered and died. The man, the boy, they will prepare the soil and nurture the seedlings, they will sink their own roots deep into the earth, and thus their branches will bloom and their seeds will drop on fertile ground, loamy ground, and grow into beautiful things themselves, limbs raised against the sky, forever reaching for the sun.

The man looks into his son's glowing face, staring at the long-lashed eyes as they watch the newspaper dance into the horizon. No matter what the boy's grandmother says, the eyes are the man's eyes . . . but where his are drained and tired, the boy's are twinkling and vibrant, still incapable of perceiving ugliness . . . Likewise, beneath the child's sturdy nose the man sees his own mouth come back to earth again, a mouth designed for extremes, for feasts and famines, for hollering and whispering, for screaming in triumph and screaming in pain. Though this mouth of his has long-since grown grimly taut, he is able to recognize it as it once was, etched there on the boy's face, bending upward and beaming in awe at the wonder presented him by the world.

To see the murky waters of his own visage reflected so clearly on the little face across from him is an inspiration beyond explanation. What do the man's neighbors atop the hill have to compare to this? What do his sister and brother-in-law have to compare to this? What device do any of them have that transforms lead to gold and the possible to the real, *a posse ad esse*? Without the child the man would be made impotent by the objective sense that nothing can be done to end the slavery, that it's useless to attempt to repair the destruction. Now he is forced to find a way – it is himself impelling himself. To will is to *have to* will.

This boy has meant everything to him.

*   *   *   *

Over the next weeks the man's life is dominated by work. There is so much sacrificed to those who are not his own . . . so much labor offered up to his conquerors, so much tribute given . . . How much of his life, of *everyone's* life, is hacked away, never to return? There are nights when he doesn't even see the boy now. He comes home late to the silent house. The kitchen light reveals the child's miniature blue and white shoes standing empty beside the door. The man places his own giant black ones alongside them, staring for a second at the two contrasting pairs, then walks down the hallway toward the bedrooms. Outside the boy's open door he stops to listen. Eventually the soft sound of deep breathing makes itself heard in the darkness. Reassured, he continues on to his own room . . . to the uneasy sleep that always awaits him . . .

The Puritans' New World Seder passes. His search for comrades is futile. The ninth month of the republican Romans passes. His search remains futile. He diligently combs both his personal and professional environment but continues to come up short, constantly running up against the wall of voluntary childlessness. Groovy hipsters though his friends and workmates might be, with their pretensions toward creativity and artistic expression, they are people unable to master the infinite. Children are a burden to them, not an extension. Avatars are something they remember from comparative religion classes, not something they themselves might create for perpetuity. So it goes.

Autumn and its warm winds come to an end and so, finally, does his job for the time being. Christmas is coming to Southern California. That's what the older relatives call it. The younger ones simply mumble a bland, "Happy holidays," meaningless in its inclusion. Its only merit is that it negates the Christian name for the expropriated pagan festival.

The new breed though, the propagating mutants, refer to the season thereabouts neither as "the holidays" nor as Christmas, but as Yuletide. No more lies that don't benefit them. "They stole one of our holy days," the man tells the boy. They stole all of them. They must be taken back. But who will sit, who will gather in groups of three and nine to define these new holy days, which are the old holidays purged of their tackiness and universalism and infused with the essence of the tribe-to-be? Holidays, *holy days*, the way they should have been from the beginning. The man simply has not the strength to carry the burden, has not the energy to do it all. The world of the future is calling for guidance . . . for men and women of direction and resolve . . . not for reactionaries, not for dreamy pretenders, but for steely visionaries who understand what's happened, what's happening, and what must be done . . .

A new calendar is needed for this new breed . . . something meant to complement the tenets of the group, something *exclusive*, not something designed for multicultural empires . . . not something like Sosigenes gave Caesar's Rome . . . not something like the replacement calendar instituted by Gregory, the one that currently links the planet's serfs, followed assiduously by both hippies and CEOs equally clamoring for "one world" . . . no Elephant Appreciation Days, no homage to zombies, no fireworks, no goat slaughtering, no corporate candies . . . simply a religious unifier for those who've regained consciousness . . . It is necessary.

*　　　*　　　*　　　*

The girl and her mother have already made the holiday trek south to gather with the family. The man and boy ride the train the day after to join them. The boy can't believe it. A train. He points, he grins, he shouts from the windows, thrilled by the experience. His ecstasy colors everything. Even the massive stretches of industrial waste and the ubiquitous graffiti make little impact on the man, their harshness softened by the child's enthusiasm. Such is the way with him.

At the next morning's breakfast, that most splendid of meals to the ancient Greeks, the boy's Oma attempts to feed him a particular brand of bacon, sliced from the corpses of cruelly abused animals and soaked with chemical preservatives. The man puts a stop to it. The boy begins to cry, eager for the deliciousness of the meat. His Oma mutters under her breath several times that the bacon won't hurt him. Calmly the man tells her that, as an adult, she may put whatever she wants into her own body, but that he decides what his son eats, and what the boy eats isn't scraps of poisoned flesh tossed his way by techno-capitalists. She looks at him as if he's insane – bacon is bacon, after all – then sullenly goes about her day.

German peasant types never change. They'll never understand the forces out to harm them, even as they're being sent to the gulag or reeducated or methodically surrendering everything their ancestors worked for their whole lives. They still retain all their old stubbornness, gullibility, and fairytale belief systems, but their better qualities, the ones that gave them a chance, have been eradicated by modernity. Once upon a time their stubbornness, gullibility, and fairytale beliefs were offset by the fact that they could grow rye or build a mill or graft fruit trees or shod a horse or make sausage. Suburbs and refrigerants and discount stores have changed all that.

He watches as his mother leaves the kitchen, saddened by the reality of their relationship. Long ago she was rescued from the steppes of Ukraine by forces she didn't understand. Long ago she and her family were driven from the banks of the Dnieper by forces she didn't understand. Even now she doesn't understand, doesn't *care* to understand. She calls herself American, sometimes, German others. Both are words from the past, linking people to the name of a land. That era has gone. She does not realize that a new world has arrived, that the old badges no longer mean anything . . . Factory-farmed chemical bacon, vacuum-sealed in plastic and sold out of massive warehouses, no longer means what "bacon" once meant. English, Irish, French, Dutch, Italian, Russian, Spanish, no longer mean what they once meant. They are shadow terms, fading terms. The interregnum between destruction and rebirth is here. From one they became many – *too* many – and now, from many, again one.

There are shadowy Yuletide celebrations performed there under the roof of his mother's house. The man and his family keep mum about it for the old Catholic's sake, faded as she is, worn out as she is. She senses something has changed and, as is entirely natural, does not want it to. Her house has all the empty consumerist trappings and she's anxious to continue the parallel consumerist "traditions". She wants to purchase something for the boy, one of the many splendid gewgaws offered in the land of merchandise and debt. She's been bringing it up for months, and once again approaches the man about it. "No," he says, trying not to hurt her feelings. No gifts of the type she has in mind. On Christmas day, the day that will one day have no more meaning to the man's descendants than Elephant Appreciation Day, the boy is to receive only tangerines, grapes, raisins, almonds, peanuts, or the like . . . nothing else, there is no need . . . He will already be receiving a tricycle from his parents, and accumulation of material goods will assuredly begin to make him as American in spirit as he is by geographical circumstance. The fruits and nuts are enough, particularly at this age. He tries to make her understand, tries to make her an ally. He speaks respectfully, brings up her own austere childhood, warns of the spoiling of character brought on by possession of too many things.

Yet she presses, this woman who brought the man into the world. There is a *need to buy* somewhere deep inside her, an overwhelming urge to consume. It's about more than just her grandchild, he realizes. Purchasing something fulfills her in some manner. So he considers her feelings, balances them against his own, and finally accedes to her wishes. He will allow her to give the child some coloring books, though there are rules for that small concession as well. No zeitgeist images crafted by corporations, nothing to drag the boy to the moron level. She agrees. She doesn't fully understand, but she agrees, even if in her mind she's being wronged like the poor old grandmothers she sees on televised talk shows or reads about in the advice columns, all of whom are forced to suffer the rudeness of the unappreciative ogres they've raised. Imagine, being denied the right to give her own grandchild a toy! What's the world come to?

So on Christmas morning, that day of greed and lust and ridiculousness, what lies there beneath her artificial tree? What lies there, despite her promise? What does the boy, wide-eyed and excited, reveal when, with surprising reserve, he rips open the colored paper of an enormous box? A crummy plastic train set that he enjoys for a total of two days before moving on to other things, like yogurt containers and kitchen spoons.

She has handed over money, money that could have benefited her grandson, to a capitalist enterprise that siphons wealth from the local populace, denies that populace any type of employment, enriches a foreign land filled with people who sneer at the boy, rapes the environment in the production of its empty product, and uses a portion of the profits to disenfranchise the boy in the very country in which he was born. And for what? To prove how much she loves him? The supposed highest of emotions proclaimed through a piece of molded plastic? Has she always been like this?

Yes . . . or at least the potential was there . . . The German peasant who manages to make money is always bourgeois, always the silliest type of materialist . . . so eager to accumulate stuff, so ready to amass objects . . . Brilliant Spengler knew this about them, knew that under the right circumstances – material success in a permissible clime – they were as crass as any Levantine or Oriental "other" their scholars used to so desperately contrast them with . . .

Of all the problems in the man's life, of all the barriers to surmount, this is one of the greatest. To make a mighty people, a strong people, a woven people, a forged people, there must be mutual respect, a shared sense of destiny, duty, and danger. There must be family worthy of emulation, worthy of love. What is there in reality? Sterility, consumption, pedestrian values . . . contemporary outlooks, not eternal ones . . . The man's parents, his wife's parents – he can't find a single point of cultural reconciliation with them, a single point of essential commonality. It's imperative that family be cherished, that it mean more than the fading nuclear clusters so beloved by marketers and plutocrats, yet the further one stretches from the core, the weaker the outlying entities seem to be . . . the more detrimental to evolutionary success . . . It's why the Christian revolutionaries became their own family – their *Weltanschauung* was utterly incompatible with the worldview of so many of their biological relations.

The man has reached an age where he can grasp the intricacies of ideas. The boy has not. He will unquestioningly do whatever his father tells him to do – love his Oma or view her as yet another hindrance to achieving goals. The latter is the wrong lesson to teach a susceptible young mind, particularly one that must follow rules for the future, the greatest being to grow your kin and put all faith in your kin so that you might empower your kin. Therefore the man will not say anything at all and instead focus on actually reaching that future. It will be an agonizing process within the ranks of his tiny family unit. He suspects that his wife and children, in order to reach the next world, will have to be dragged along unwillingly at times. There is pain in leaving behind the known, and great sadness no doubt awaits them. When all sentiment is stripped away, however, the man knows that before family becomes sacred again, it must be torn asunder.

$$*\qquad*\qquad*\qquad*$$

There is a shopping mall in the suburb where the boy's Oma resides. Perpetually packed with humanity, it is one of several such places that the man generally avoids, like a pit of vipers or a tenement filled with cockroaches. "*Odi profanum vulgus et arceo,*" said the freed slave's son, Horace. "I loathe the unholy rabble and I keep away." The man generally follows suit. However, the nearby mall happens to have a play area, an oasis in the middle of the herding grounds. It is a place where the boy can happily play during these rainy days of Yuletide, away from the battery of "nos" constantly blasted at him as he explores his Oma's house. "No", the daycare favorite, the negative refrain that reverberates throughout the lives of the children of the wealthy West . . . they internalize it . . . meekly obey its command when their betters bark it at them as adults . . .

Together the man and the boy enter the mall. There is a disconcerting sheen to it, a luster, as if a corpse has been painted and sparklers jabbed into its rotting flesh. Faint nausea bubbles up through the man, letting him know that the environment isn't good for his type. For others it seems fine – judging by their grinning faces and armfuls of packages, the *herpeta* wandering about find the place to be nothing short of heaven. Even the boy – unable to see the ugliness surrounding him – wears an excited smile.

At the play area there are climbing structures, miniature vehicles, giant building blocks, and the like. In the center of all this stands an enormous contraption, its transparent walls revealing whirring gears and churning motors within. Colored balls are transported along various axes – X, Y, Z – and lifted via Archimedes screws or by automated buckets connected to pulley systems. The boy is fascinated, drawn to the intricacies of movement and function that are inherent to the device. Any child would be fascinated, one would think.

One, however, would be wrong . . . for even as the boy stares and concentrates, the other children thronging around him pay no heed to the machine . . . Ranging in age from ten months to ten years, they focus on nearby objects for seconds at a time, one minute at most, before rapidly moving on to the next bauble like frenetic dragonflies. They are the flitting children raised on sugar and bred on television . . . on the flat screen of two dimensions, on quick cuts . . . They're the expendable products of the new Ice Age . . . "Little Ducks" . . . creatures entirely removed from the way the world operates . . . not just the Occidental technological overlay, but the *real world,* the one lurking just around the corner, waiting for them – waiting for many – when there's no one left to run the crumbling system . . .

The man turns his eyes from his spellbound son to the nearby escalator, packed with the adults that have produced these flitting children. Carried up the automatically ascending stairs, they clutch their sleek bags in hand, ready and eager to purchase still more stuff . . . a bigger pair of pants, some extra dinnerware . . . a plastic train set . . . always on the verge of finding that one thing that will finally complete their lives and make them whole . . . He spies on them, watches how they move, notes their every motion, every act. Each time it is the same routine; a single step onto the bottom escalator stair, and then – nothing. Instantly they go inert. Voluntary motion stops. For the busy *herpeta* of the suburbs the mechanized tool isn't used to facilitate movement – it's used to supplant it.

"Ease is inimical to civilization," said overrated Toynbee. The insight needn't stop there. Ease is also inimical to life itself. The end of struggle means only complacency, softness, and death. Thankfully the man and his family have been presented with the greatest struggle he can ever imagine.

He allows the boy to play for a bit before scooping him into his arms. Together they walk up the staircase, past the stationary shoppers riding up the adjacent escalator, and leave.

$*$ $*$ $*$ $*$

That evening, on a stroll through the homogenous Southern California wonderland, the man is spotted by the neighbors from across the street. They've long insisted that he pay a call, and now do so again. "Come visit, bring the family." He has nothing in common with them . . . no interests, no likes, no dislikes . . . nothing . . . Why should they want him to come over? What is the point? He doesn't understand.

Still, constrained by the suffocating morality of the area, he nods, says okay, and on the last day before returning to his Los Angeles home takes the plunge. Family in tow he walks across an overly landscaped lawn, past a mass-produced birdbath, past two SUVs atop an asphalt driveway, and approaches the neighbors' giant house, meant to be a "piece of Tuscany" transplanted to the Pacific. "It's been in *SoCal Magazine*," his mother excitedly let him know the night before.

They're greeted at the door with hyper-effusive welcomes. The boy tightly holds his father's hand as they cross the threshold. Inside is as typical as outside – thoroughly modern, oozing dullness and oozing chemicals, from the toxic white paint on the walls to the hormone-fluctuating beige carpet stretched across the floor. The man's wife comments on what a nice home it is. Their hostess artfully brushes off the compliment, then casually offers to put the boy and his baby sister in front of the television with her own children. She talks as she walks, maintaining a nonstop chatter, a deadening white noise, *Bürgersprache* about how she's bought all these "really educational" videos at some store in the mall and they're *great* for kids and they just *love* them and her own children don't even know they're *learning* and isn't it sneaky, isn't she such a *bad* mom, teaching them by letting them have fun, pulling the wool over their eyes, teehee, teehee . . .

Everyone follows as she strides into the next room. There they are, these children of hers, sitting silently hunched on the floor and staring at the antics of animated characters on a gigantic flat screen. There they are, two drones, a pair of living, breathing creatures that are meant to be inhaling great gulps of oxygen and standing in the beating rain and lolling on hillsides under summer suns and hurling rocks into waves and swallowing big mouthfuls of milk and building dams across creeks and catching frogs and caterpillars and toads and racing across fields and spinning until they fall down and shimmying up trees and wrestling each other and reciting poems and eating cherries and tying knots and singing songs that their ancestors sang nine generations before and stalking squirrels and picking through junk and learning to whistle and snapping their fingers and sprinting down sand dunes and poking in rabbit holes and peeking in bird nests and floating armadas of berries atop puddles and living, living, living, living, not this dying, this cloistering in caves with that luminous square casting its pale light on their terrible, glazed faces . . .

"No thanks, we don't let them watch television."

She feels the sting. The man tries to mask his disdain, tries to not let such people know his views, his family's views, because he doesn't care about such people, doesn't care about those who don't care for themselves. Anything against their way of thinking, or non-thinking, is a slight to them, and the man is in firm agreement with them here, is solidly on their side. To this lady, to her husband, to her family, such statements – "No thanks, we don't let them watch television," – are a rebuke, to be met immediately with the suburban equivalent of the old American, "You think you're better'n me?"

"Not even educational programs?" she parries. There it is again . . . the daycare mantra . . . the middle-class mantra . . . education . . . edjukashun . . . ugh . . . The two families meeting together there in that house live in what policymakers and professionals decry as the stupidest industrialized nation in the world, a corpus of idiots the likes of which has never before been seen on earth. *Stultorum infinitus est numerus.* Yet this word, "education", is on everyone's lips. A ball bouncing across a screen is education. A puppet singing about the letter "F" is education . . . a dinosaur dancing . . . a comic book from a fast food joint . . . Anything is education, which is only natural in a land, a culture, where anything can be art and anything can be called bacon and anyone can be a citizen and any boy or girl can grow up to be President with enough billionaires behind them.

"No. We don't like them staring at a screen just yet. Maybe someday . . ."

"Oh sure, sure, I understand."

But she doesn't understand. If she did, the conversation wouldn't be happening. If she did, she'd already know that children's brains don't stop growing when they leave the womb . . . that different stimuli have different effects on mental development . . . She'd know that she and her husband have lessened the possibility of their sons ever being able to merely watch a bird soar across the sky . . . to wait silently for the sun to set, the moon to rise . . . to be able to debate, to join the great conversation . . . to grasp essential elements of literature, foundations of mathematics, the rudiments of philosophy . . . If she did understand she'd know the man was lying when he said, "maybe someday". There will never be a "someday" for his children when it comes to the world's slave screen, its moron producer. There will never be a "someday" for them to cozy up with this subduer of peoples and rotter of nations. He's seen the mall. He's seen the Little Ducks, seen a world rampant with them, *teeming* with them.

Back in Ukraine, that land of mass graves and mass chains and concrete tenements and brothel fuel, the boy's ancestors long ago called the radio "the metal liar". Who could know then that an even more awesome destroyer would soon replace it? A few foresaw the potential power of the flickering televised image, seeing the possibility of molding and pacifying both serfs and heroes alike. Kindly Uncle Joe, that smiling ally to those balding champions of liberty passing out hats at the Fire Department Museum, was one. His Georgian intuition proved on the money – television worked like gangbusters for a time. It sold soap flakes, it lulled, it stupefied, it made Little Ducks . . . but mutation and adaptation never end . . . For those overlords of the future, those whose success will be edged with an abhorrence of luxury, to own such a thing will no longer be looked at as a boon or a display of prominent status. The people who utilize televisions primarily for entertainment and time-filling will be smirked at, their choice linked with low breeding, the giant screen at the center of the room a symbol of irresponsibility and self-abuse. This social schism, with its correlating evolutionary consequences, has already begun. It is taking place in that very room, at that very moment.

The afternoon drags on – one long, undeclared struggle on both sides to force their ideas to mesh. As in most bourgeois encounters, where no dissent or argument can ever take place, the discourse invariably levels out to a bland stream of agreement . . . so while the others discuss immigration and school districts in obfuscatory language out by the massive barbecue and the tiled swimming pool, the man takes the opportunity to walk through the house . . . Ostensibly he's searching for the boy, who's disappeared for the moment, but actually he's gathering data. He's curious about the lives of these types who swarm the graffiti-free playgrounds and malls.

Silently he walks up the stairs, looking to glean a little information about his hosts from the subjects of the books they own . . . but it's difficult . . . With eyes wide open, and occasionally shouting the boy's name, he encounters shelves constructed with books seemingly in *mind*, but occupied instead by DVDs, framed photographs, and meaningless department store knick-knacks. There simply aren't any books in the numbers he imagined. By the end of his brief walkabout and room-peeking, his tally is six – five about becoming wealthy through real estate transactions, and one oversized illustrated edition of *Mother Goose* used as décor in one of the kids' bathrooms. This last is being pored over by the boy, who's never been introduced to the collection of rhyming drivel so beloved by the Anglo-Saxon nations.

Six books total. Oh well. Aggregate numbers of such things can't offer a particularly accurate intellectual assessment, no matter what good liberal psychologists and good conservative I.Q. defenders preach. After all, every hipster abode he's ever visited back in Los Angeles is stuffed with dust-gathering volumes encompassing all manner of cerebral and important subjects – Tibet, cubism, Japanese cinema, Palm Springs architecture, the history of beatboxing, astrology, Indian cooking, traveling in Thailand, colonialism, Monet paintings, screenwriting techniques – and their owners still got mugged in neighborhoods they thought were safe. Granted, the guy who lives here is an absolute boor, but in late-stage America there's no qualitative difference between the boor owning five books on real estate and the trust fund "political activist" owning five hundred books on ephemera. The two are simply different manifestations of the same lousy type the man encounters everywhere. For one illiterate warrior-farmer he'd trade them all.

He returns *Mother Goose* to its display area next to the sink, lifts his son, and returns to the patio. The remainder of the visit is suffered in tense acceptance . . . an up-close peek into an organism's abscess . . . a true sociology class . . . an excursion up the Congo to find Mista Kurtz . . . Relaxation doesn't come until his family's finally safely back in Los Angeles. He grasps the irony.

*　　*　　*　　*

Both parents are off from work for the time being. The man's wife stays with the new baby while he himself works on the exterior of the house, trying to complete the renovation. The boy remains at the nearby daycare, happy to be there. An air of contentment once again surrounds the man. His naked son shouts at birds, attempts headstands, demands songs, laughs at the deliberate mix-ups his father makes when reciting the alphabet, slips into naps on the newly constructed deck, listens enrapt to his mother's stories, demands that books be read to him, hugs his sister, stares at pictures of wolves, chugs his milk, repeats matter-of-factly that animals in zoos are sad because no creature wants to live in a cage without its family, cracks up over the way the British daycare boy pronounces his name, pushes away the man's overcooked pork, insanely erases the letters "p-a-t-e-r" from his chalkboard, and screams with ecstatic glee when he's hurled into the air.

The two march around the neighborhood as they have from the beginning, the child blessedly barefoot and alive. No shoes for him, for as long as possible. His father wants him to spring across the ground on the balls of his feet, to drag those feet through the dew-sprinkled grass, to squish-squash the mud at the edge of ponds, to stomp the earth and feel it in himself like his people did on the steppes before the Purge. He wants him to harden his soles like Spartan lads and harden his soul like Chinese . . . balance while walking, balance in all things . . .

Both the old Salvadoran woman and the old Japanese woman admonish the man over his little son's lack of shoes. Even the odd blue and white ones with soft soles that they've seen him wear on occasion are better than nothing, they cluck. He smiles, nods, moves on. It is the silent examples of the natural world he allows to instruct him on what's proper for the boy's well-being, nothing else. There is no need to study the works of the evolutionists or the primitivists to understand that growing feet shouldn't be shod, or that sunlight should be welcomed, or that water should be bubbling and pure and untouched by chemicals. The rewards he receives for following the examples presented during millennia of formation are immeasurable. To watch his naked boy throw a rock or balance on a ledge or jump for a fly is like seeing first man returned to earth from some golden age, lithe and tan and strong and agile. *Der Leib sei der Gott* agreed those bookend peoples the Greeks and the Germans – the body is the god. Although they were off in their multiples – it is *combined* bodies that constitute divinity – the man still takes the maxim to heart.

However, as the world endlessly turns even gods can ultimately be made to suffer. The boy rapidly hurtles along the neighborhood sidewalks while his father walks behind him, cringing, awaiting the inevitable falls, the *painful* falls, that will eventually teach him to lessen his speed on concrete. Evolution, nature, God, call it whatever, meant for the boy's kind to bound across savannahs unhindered . . . to sprint with toughened feet across springy earth, to feel wind through hair . . . to have no fear of falling to the ground . . . It's not like that in the city. This creeping world of concrete progress devours everything – and there's the rub. The boy is slowly adapting to the urban environment, following the same path as those millions of other hominids that have already adapted to it . . . those who've become something less alive, something aberrant and weird . . . Don't run on the sidewalk. Wear stiff shoes while you're still crawling. Drink soy formula from this plastic container. Get these shots. Be careful.

The hobbled, the foot-bound, the timid, the inert – these are the physical types being fashioned here in the city. The man offers up his concerns at the boy's daycare, listens to the parents' responses, analyzes them, always waiting for that one hint of agreement that will allow him a chance at finding an ally. Instead he gets the same old social head-nodding, courteous and uncomprehending. Other topics are more important to them. Nothing he says sinks in. Over and over he hears the same chanted chorus: No hitting. No climbing. No running. No living.

It becomes increasingly clear that he's made the right choice to flee Los Angeles. Now he just has to make the right choice for their destination. Much as he'd thought Portland would be an option, with its easy transition between differing degrees of urban environments, it just hadn't been the right place – in the end, it too was a concrete city. It too was filled with the stunted and the effete. It's the countryside the boy has to go to, the mountains like the man originally envisioned. For better or worse, a godlike creature cannot mesh with a hell-like world.

> *But for my children,*
> *I would have them keep their distance*
> *from the thickening center;*
> *Corruption never has been compulsory,*
> *When the cities lie at the monster's feet*
> *there are left the mountains.*

Jeffers knew.

*   *   *   *

He drives in his car, alone, to the north and to the east . . . through deserts and mountains, for days . . . utilizing his time off, searching for a hidden Shangri-La, an Ultima Thule for his family . . . Where will they go? How will they survive once they get there?

The long, straight miles are filled with the sound of the radio. The airwaves are unfamiliar territory to him, filled with the babbling of Baptists, the screeds of warhawks, the insipidity of the masses. He switches channels, considers their content, floats through them . . . snatches of music, catchy songs . . . A woman's voice croons, "They don't love you like I love you," over and over. Who's she talking about? He likes her message. It's the same as his for the boy. They don't love him. The man has the deepest urge, the need, to explain that to him. How can those automatons out there – those shells, those pods – love him when they can't even love themselves? They can't. Only if he plays the fool, only if he crawls like they do, only if he hurls his dignity away like he hurls his tiny pebbles into the road. How can the others – the manipulators, the liars, the whipcrackers – love him when he's not one of them? They can't either. None of them can.

His family loves him. The man loves him. He has brought focus to his father's future. Always the man is looking there now. That is why he's driving across this place, this United States, this malignant subset of an abstraction called "Western Civilization". Does it even hold a future for the boy? The man looks at the snowcapped mountains of Nevada passing by outside the window. Small towns, ugly towns, the residents drained . . . no greater ideal, no nothing . . . What are they called? Indo-Europeans? How bland, how academic and empty. Their outposts scar the land. These people mar the wilderness just by *existing*. The foulness the man drives through in Nevada or Utah or Montana or wherever is the perfect environment for them, the army of the botched. Sullenly the soldiers of this volunteer army march along with rheumy eyes and wheezing lungs and splotchy skin . . . hating for no reason . . . murdering for no goal . . . He can't avoid them. They're everywhere. All he can do is attempt to lessen their impact and to make the boy understand who they are and what they represent.

What do they represent? A world that despises him. A world that wants to make him and his family and his future tribe crawl, wants to keep them as the most abject of slaves. The boy's enemies, his owners, will do everything they can to divide him from his family, to cleave them one from the other with the practiced precision of butchers and diamond cutters. They want to enlist him in that horrid legion of undermen out there. They'll lie to him. They'll try to convince him to throw away everything his father's given him, every weapon, every tool.

They'll tell him to hurl it all over a cliff like an errant knight does his sword before becoming a childless monk. They'll entice, they'll cajole, they'll lie, they'll lie.

He must believe the man who loves him. The boy must believe his father when he tells him that he's only cannon fodder to them, a body to stop bullets or a body to murder other slaves less easily controlled. His baby sister and his mother are whores, *marocchinata*, prizes in a global brothel, parceled out during war and peace . . . and in between the murders and the rapes and the devastation they're all expected only to work and to buy things . . . to purchase hard plastic and colorful rags, meat and diamonds and beer . . . the little bonuses that make life so wonderful for the content thralls . . . the things they've built their prison out of . . .

The temporary goal of the man is to find a location where the happy members of the proletariat aren't so many . . . thus a place where the prison bars aren't as close together . . . The mountains, he knows, have always brought him peace. So he concentrates on exploring towns in this type of terrain . . . driving, inspecting, crossing possibilities off his list . . . Infinite rows of unappealing houses zoom by in the near distance, hurriedly erected by unskilled laborers using the shoddiest materials. They seem inches apart from each other, as aesthetically jarring as the garbage scattered across Los Angeles parks. Day after day he encounters them, dropped haphazardly across the countryside, biting savage mouthfuls out of the forest or desert . . . more evidence of America's "libido for the ugly", the phenomenon noted by Mencken that still haunts the country . . . There the houses sit, waiting to be filled with that army of the botched, waiting to have pizza delivery magnets stuck to refrigerators and plasma screens hung on walls and packaged meals heated in microwaves and cheap toys strewn across inappropriate lawns and knobby-tired quads crammed into overflowing garages.

Within a few miles of every one of these tumor-like settlements are the gas stations and the mega-merchandise stores and the corporate food places, all doing a fevered business. These last, the kitschy fast-food restaurants and family-style eateries, loom largest when seeking out examples of a degraded, defeated population. It is shocking what the people put into their bodies during these days of evolutionary bottlenecking . . . not just the swill they consume in their franchised strip mall establishments, but the meals prepared in their very homes . . . The man has seen their kitchens. He's seen the cabinets stuffed with the imitation food they feed themselves and their kids . . . odd creations brimming with sugar, destroyer of bones and teeth . . . surreally-shaped concoctions infused with chemicals to please both capitalist manufacturers and capitalist doctors . . . strength-sapping products created solely with the idea of maximum shelf-life and maximum profit, nutrition an afterthought usable only as an advertising gimmick . . .

He's seen what they drink, the enormous plastic containers and the aluminum cylinders crammed into their refrigerators and cupboards in units of six or twelve . . . cans of poison, bottles of poison, their exteriors emblazoned with clever corporate logos, symbols to the world of the commercial empire that produced them . . . a land of smooth-talking salesmen and velvet-gloved oppressors, marching first with media, then with bombs if needed, then with media again, then with products . . .

He's seen the meat they serve their families, the same meat they tried to serve his own family at the *SoCal Magazine* house get-together, the same his mother tried to pawn off on her grandson . . . hacked from the bodies of wretched animals that were treated like all prisoners were treated in the industrialized empire's never-ending war . . . hacked from diseased carcasses, microcosms of the only type of state these new imperialists could ever erect . . .

The devastated national landscape begins to make sense once one knows what grotesqueries the land's inhabitants put into their bodies. Their fluoridated, chlorinated water is the oil slick on the ocean. The forced air circulating through their particleboard houses is the polluted sky over the valleys. The outer reflects the inner, *is* the inner. *Nichts ist drinnen, nichts ist draußen.*

It's been argued that this nightmare simply happened to these people, that forces beyond their grasp and control foisted this dystopia upon them. Perhaps. Overlooked is the fact that many of them *want* these tidy slums crowding the road on either side, they *enjoy* the putrid food offered them, they willingly *choose* it over better fare. It becomes clear to the man during his drive that in a thoroughly adulterated society, anything that is accepted *en masse* – not just lauded or touted, but merely *accepted* – is deadly. That is the way to view it all, from art to history to what to have for breakfast.

Those few who want nothing to do with any of it, those who shun this current world as a temporary aberration, are forced to make their own dietary laws, allowing only purity into purity. No Sigurd can ever come, no nation of Sigurds can ever come, if allowed to subsist on impurities . . . and with the advent of dietary laws, specific commandments for an aware few, comes the germination of a new people growing amid the old and broken . . .

*   *   *   *

Finally, after a week of disappointed driving, he makes a discovery . . . high in those protective mountains he loves, near rivers and lakes and forests . . . a place where perhaps – perhaps – he and his family can duck and wait it out . . . a place where deer walk through the middle of town and wolves howl at its edges and ravens perch in the ponderosas and only a single traffic light hangs over the narrow streets . . . a place where he can pretend that they are free . . .

He stays there a few days to observe. Others are converging on the town as well. Elite policy directives are forcing hundreds of thousands to flee the cities for the countryside, destroying what little wilderness remains. The flood is arriving, the exodus of conquered California. The refugees come with money and disease. Their influx has inflated the cost of everything . . . food, utilities, real estate . . . It's obvious that the area will rapidly be eaten by "development" and all its offshoots: overpopulation, cheap labor, crime, congestion, pollution, laws, higher taxes, economic stratification, wildlife destruction, environmental devastation, yuppies, politicians . . . all of which conspire to eventually bring about flight once more . . .

The family of the boy's great-aunt – his ancestors – inhabited the same Hessian village for at least seven hundred years. Already in his life the man has lived in eight different locations. This will be his ninth, if indeed they move here. It is tiring. Still, what can be done? There is nothing great in store for the near future. There will be nothing beautiful tomorrow, no movement, no surge, no uprising, no reversal. This tiny town chiseled out of the boreal forest is merely a bit off the path of attrition. The war was won generations ago, centuries ago . . . mopping-up time is here . . . one can only hope to delay at this stage of the aftermath . . .

So with mixed feelings he buys a piece of land, joining everybody else in the pecuniary parceling out of the world. There's a view of the Rockies . . . a river for the kids to swim in . . . trees to climb, woods to explore . . . They'll build a house on the property when they leave Los Angeles. But that's all it will be – a house, a *shelter*, not a home in the old sense of the word, the seven hundred years in one location sense of the word. Homes are in a homeland and a homeland doesn't presently exist for the man's family. Only inside of them does it survive . . . only as a dream of dumplings . . .

He cannot expect more than this. Always he must keep in mind the reality of the zoo – that just because a beast breaks out of its cage doesn't mean it's any closer to its home.

*   *   *   *

It's a long drive back to Los Angeles. Hours after returning to the squeals of the boy and kisses of his wife, a neighbor comes over to warn the man to "keep his eyes open". There are burglars about. "They wedged my doggy door shut with a chair," mews the potbellied bachelor. It's a clever technique that prevents the animals from exiting while the house is being cased. There are hundreds of little tricks like this in use for robbery, rape, assault, and murder in the City of Angels.

The man thanks him for the warning, then gravely asks, "They didn't take anything, did they?" The concern is feigned, of course. He feels no sympathy for the former 60's radical before him. His is the type that comprises the bulk of the exodus the man just witnessed . . . the enfeebled, the gelded . . . passels of existential eunuchs primed to be wiped from the map . . . members of a dwindling majority populace that is genetically programmed to become ill and die, unprepared for what's been unleashed . . .

"No, I got lucky," the paunchy fellow replies. His jazz albums are safe.

A new job begins. It is downtown, near Little Tokyo, which is adjacent to Chinatown, which is somewhat near Historic Filipino Town, which sits somewhat between Little Armenia and the Byzantine Latino Quarter, but is not next to Thai Town or Little Ethiopia. Headspinning Los Angeles. In the 60s, the heyday of the man's nervous neighbor, the city had more Protestants than any city in the United States. That's a sure sign, the demographic a definite guarantee, of approaching decay, dissolution, and extinction. The only Protestant churches the man passes on his morning commute have long since been re-ethnicized, the ghosts of the Anglo-Saxons barely remembered by the new all-Korean congregations that have replaced them.

He spends the next months driving through squalor on his way to work and back . . . driving through the reminders of a dead past . . . In Libya he stared at the still-standing architectural remnants of the Romans, their amphitheaters as solid and beautiful as when they were first raised two thousand years earlier. In the shadow of these magnificent structures weathered Arab women wearily lugged buckets of water back to their makeshift hovels, looking mean and slapdash next to the monumental remains. Likewise, during his morning drive to the office – a place encircled by razor wire-topped fences and guarded by men with guns – he sees the Victorian mansions and the once-neat yards that are telltale stamps of those vanished, upper-class Protestants. They are slums now, filthy with garbage, teeming with life. It's the way of the world, of Libya and California and Europe . . . an ugly way, a way that wounds him internally, but the way nevertheless . . .

Time trundles on, the months go by. A day eventually arrives when he no longer notices the graffiti, the trash, the broken windows, the throng. With a gloomy awareness he realizes he's become inured to it all, that he's finally, after years, grown desensitized to what previously assaulted his psyche day in and day out. He arrives home, finds his wife and children already asleep, and walks out to the deck in his backyard. He lies down, stares up at the sky and searches for solace in the stars . . . but no stars are visible . . . He squeezes his eyes shut, trying to retrieve some banked memory of what they look like, when out of the darkness shrieks the high-pitched whine of the pot-bellied neighbor yelling at his dog, shattering the silence.

There is never true peace in the city. The man hates the neighbor, wishes that his type had never been formed on the globe; the believers in political parties and political slogans, the dog screamers and incense burners. They *have* been formed though. They're here, the descendants of shirkers, of toadies and weaklings. They cluster atop his hill, they fill the flats and hollows of his land, presenting themselves as iconoclasts, relishing their phony role of system buckers . . . alone in houses, dogs as soul mates . . . framed posters on their walls, jazz on their authentic turntables . . . doing everything they can economically, socially, ideologically, environmentally, and politically to destroy his family's future . . . Why does he have to suffer for their sins? Why should the creepy little neighbor be the man's problem, the boy's problem? Why are men such as these, *hemianthropoi*, half-men who lack honor and testosterone, of relevance to his personal struggle?

Because there's no such thing as a personal struggle. Individuality is an illusion. Somehow, the man knows, this crawling, spongy, cowardly thing yelling at its dog is his cross to bear.

*   *   *   *

The job goes on. The boy grows. May Day comes. *Sumer is icumen in* . . . May Day goes.

A carnival arrives at the bottom of the hill, part of a larger street festival. The man carries the boy down. Swarms of *herpeta* mill about, faces angry, or sullen, or slack-jawed. It's the mall crowd, any crowd, massing with blank eyes . . . narrowed, shifty, suspicious eyes . . . The boy, thrilled by the smell of cotton candy and the sight of the carnival rides, laughs and wriggles excitedly in his father's arms. He does not see what the man sees. The horde bubbles all around them. Spoiled brats masquerade as bums. Shaved-head Salvadoran gangsters posture and roll. Women with neck tattoos secretly drop heroin needles into the gutter. Vicious cops intimidate everyone by their presence, dreadlocked poseurs shuffle along like broken toys, and the world of the obverse celebrates another victory here in the toxic froth of Los Angeles. Even the carnies blend in, where in ages past they stood out.

A flier is handed to him. Later that night a gathering of bands will be taking place down the street, self-styled "urban guerillas", meaning the private-school children of those Protestants who've fled to the suburbs. There's a drawing of a black teenager with an automatic weapon and bandolier, looking menacing. Bold Helvetica font reads: *"But I didn't know I was a racist," you'll all say as you die. But that ain't no excuse.* Hinting at genocide is edgy if you're talking about the right group. The man folds the flier. He supports these trust fund kids. He appreciates the honesty . . . the pointing out of hypocrites . . . the war against their parents . . .

As he tucks the flier into his pocket a fat Mayan boy, a diabetic, points his new toy at him. It's a cell phone that takes pictures. The man feels like a Comanche or a Tatar of long ago, having his soul stolen by another despicable invention of the disappearing magicians of the First World. Domination through technology is an age-old theme, and that technology being turned around and used against the former conquerors is a theme just as ancient. The man wants to harm the kid for robbing him of something indefinable. He can't. He'll just have to let the modern diet take his revenge for him. A daily insulin needle puncturing the pudgy arm is compensation enough.

He continues to carry his precious little boy through the chaotic crowd, the lunatic extras in a Brueghel painting. Beauty doesn't exist here, not even as a memory. They pass the affordable housing booth, then another for the local chamber of commerce. The traditions of the man's neighborhood are touted . . . innovation, harmony, and diversity . . . On the cover of the organization's pamphlet are twenty-one innovative people, harmoniously posing for the group photo. The diversity is a single Asian woman. The other twenty are palefaces, potential targets of the bold urban guerillas, no doubt.

Next up is the Green Party booth. Their political platform, a placard reads, is based on social justice, gender equality, a woman's right to choose an abortion, and a living wage. There is nothing about the environment in their literature . . . and there is nothing even remotely odd about that . . .

He walks with tightened grip, musing. He came from this scene. It's all familiar to him. Many of his former friends are here, eager to mingle, to watch bands or drink margaritas in the afternoon. There's even one at work behind the Green Party booth – they exchange brief smiles and waves. The man, too, was once a part of this hipster community. He once found the pointlessness so thrilling, so wild. What's changed? Has age caught up with him? Has it been the incessant reading, focused, finally, for the last five years? Has it been the thinking? The traveling? Maybe. But clearly the most obvious answer is the boy. In the heavens themselves he'd shine, but here, juxtaposed against the lonely and the damned, the hopeless and the vicious, he gleams even more brightly, a brilliant lodestar drawing the man ever onward.

He puts the boy on a ride where turtles mechanically spin in a circle. The child grips the bar in his serious way, looking straight forward and straight-faced, and the ride begins to whirl around and around and around. Finally a smile appears on the little face, and when it does it's like the breaking of the dawn over the sea. It's huge and toothy and wonderful and pure, the kind that adults are no longer capable of flashing due to decades of beatdown and civilized life. The man's heart kabooms, and all the sounds of the cacophonous herd fade for an instant as he watches his son. He's so happy staring at him, so happy that a life actually exists somewhere that still remains unburdened . . . no mindset, no worries, no thoughts of the future . . .

The ride ends and the boy scrambles off, pulls his father's hand, tries to rush ahead to the next one, an inflated slide. He steadily climbs the ladder to the top, flashes the man another knockout grin, and ecstatically descends, laughing the whole time in a state of unchecked bliss. By his third attempt he switches things up and goes down on his stomach, amazed by the sensation, laughing, shouting. He tumbles to the ground, gets to his feet, and again snatches the man's hand, yanking him along to the adjacent bouncy castle. He clambers inside and immediately begins to leap and jump, sprinting, tumbling, bouncing to the four corners, meeting his father's eyes in rapturous glee, boisterous and unbridled and alive, alive, alive, so alive and so ineffably beautiful.

What's this, though? They notice. The living dead take notice of the boy who's oblivious to all but his own joy. He beams like a miniature Apollo, glowing golden and warm, and people are smiling at his exuberance, their eyes as tender and fond as the man's. Why, why, what is it, what makes them do this? The man wants biological answers, evolutionary answers, not poetry, not sociology. Why that big drag queen, why that Michoacán mom, why that pasty junkie? Why do they see what the man sees? Or *do* they see what he sees?

How can they possibly?

$$*\qquad*\qquad*\qquad*$$

By the middle of summer the man's reserves have run dry. Even on days when he doesn't have to make the draining drive to the office the city has its way with him. The carnival has never departed. Every day is a celebration of the mediocre, a victory for the enemy, a protracted rape. He has to escape, as is his way . . . has to somehow hose down, wash himself, scrub his senses . . . He gathers up the family and heads northwest out of Los Angeles, along the fabled coast. For two hours there is only sprawl. There is traffic, choking and eternal . . . asphalt, petroleum, subdivisions, and cell phone towers . . . It all grinds away at the brain, it churns the stomach. It is sublime torture, a whole new type, embedded in the everyday . . . selective in its workings, choosing only psychologically-specific victims, but otherwise unnoticed and unfelt by nearly all . . .

He tries to ignore the stimuli, tries to return to the semi-inured state he'd reached back in the city, but it's impossible. The nasty taste of bile fills his mouth and refuses to go away. It's a natural reaction to the trappings of civilization, he knows, one he's grown used to, but today the bitterness remains on his tongue even after he reaches the campground and the previously comforting forest. Above him airplanes leave odd streaks across the sky that don't dissipate. Around him other campers blare radios or watch television in their enormous metal and plastic campers. They slouch at picnic tables, pouring blue concoctions down their throats, blind to the scarring of the sky, blind to how alien they are in the woods. Everything is marred by their presence. The purpose of the Last Man is clearly to drive the man insane.

Then, a gift from the gods – they depart. They actually leave for some crazy reason, and the man and his family are alone. It seems impossible. Loveliness returns to his life for a time. Leaves lazily drop from trees. Woodpeckers sound, stars appear, a breeze gently soughs through the branches and the leaves. Insects hum, crickets chirp, a skunk or chipmunk rustles in the underbrush. The Milky Way, denied him for so long, gleams overhead. The boy is enrapt. His father has always promised him that there were more stars in the sky than the two or three visible above the house on top of the hill. Here they are. They find the Bears, find Draco and Aquila and the Swan. The man points out their people's star, Polaris, hovering over the North they came from so long ago. The black dome above them is spackled with relief, the relief that comes from the awareness of the total indifference of outside forces. They will win their desired place on this earth or they will not. They will survive or they will die. It is all so calming. This is the comfort he'd sought lying on his deck that night. This is what civilization has denied him.

One weekend, that's all. For the childless, the dead, it's no time at all really . . . a pleasant excursion, nothing more . . . glasses of wine and walks in the woods . . . For the man, though, the two days are stretched beyond their finite horizons, stretched into eternity, to the North Star and back and back again, forever. It's that son of his who does it, that gem who twists time just by sailing sticks down streams, by catching lizards and inspecting spider webs, by tossing rocks and swinging baseball bats, by sloshing through the surf, by chasing squirrels and sprinting across fields.

The man's friends have forsaken the possibility of experiencing this. His sister, his neighbors, all of them have . . . They've chosen lives that will become increasingly empty. They will ossify and putrefy from too much entertainment, too much leisure. To witness the boy shout, "No!" at a perplexed squirrel, followed by, "Don't eat my watermelon!" means more than a thousand arthouse screenings of Palme d'Or winners. To hear him ask, "Daddy, what those people have in there – a monkey? They have a monkey in that cabin, daddy?" is worth more than a lifetime of indie concerts in smoky scenester clubs. What's their life now, all of them? What are the good things in it? Eating at restaurants? Ironic jokes? Exotic vacations? Momentary diversions? Don't they see it? Can't they see it? Can't they see how their lives can deepen? Broaden? The little boy points out the Milky Way stars as they appear one-by-one above, and in his raspy, beautiful voice begins singing, "Twinkle, twinkle . . ." to the speckled sky. Do those others not recognize the value of this? Solitude? Is that what they crave? The comatose existence of the monk? The loneliness of the crypt?

The indomitable Romans, during the centuries of their awesome becoming, loathed celibacy and childlessness. Who are these moderns compared to those men, who are these urban lotus-eaters who've forgotten their past and can't gauge their bleak future? Why do they not have it in themselves to strive as the sons of Romulus did, to pattern themselves after those for whom Jupiter fixed no boundary in time and no limit to accomplishment? Why do they not have it in themselves to learn about the hell that descended when these men and women finally broke their own laws and succumbed to the scourge of childlessness?

*　　　*　　　*　　　*

And yet there are still some, it must be admitted, who've not been touched by the affliction. There are a few who aren't sterile, a few who aren't barren. Some of them are procreating, even outside the boundaries of cushy suburbia and the shoddy countryside. Back in the city the man gets a call from a former co-worker. They've grown apart over the years since she left their mutual line of work, yet now that both have children there is a presumed bond. It's not so ridiculous an assumption . . . a birthday party, he's told, for a one-year-old . . . Come to our house. It'd be great to see you. My husband would love it. He misses you. We'd love to meet your kids.

This might be it – the time when he'll finally find fellow travelers . . . comrades instead of the fleeting automatons encountered daily at the daycare and the office and life . . . He's always liked the girl who's called him. There's been little contact between them since she first gave birth a few years earlier, but it doesn't have to stay that way. He feels a bit ashamed he didn't think of reaching out to her first.

So the man accepts the invitation. He has not yet questioned the concept of birthday celebrations at this point in his development. Ultimately he realizes the sickness it is. In old Japan all children of the nation were credited with being birthed on the same day of the year, a single day for boys to share, another for the girls. In this way was emphasized the greater importance of the organism versus that of the cell. Back in Mother Russia, that linchpin land of history, a saint's name was attached to each day of the calendar. This saint's name was included in the name given every child born on that particular day, uniting the Orthodox across *versts* and generations, distance and time. Not that it worked in preserving the nation, but still, the concept was superior to that of a special day set aside to commemorate the anniversary of a solitary birth. This is simply more cult of the lone figure . . . more acclamation of the individual . . . more dissolvent social forces pushing the Western precipitate into the grasp of empty consumerism . . .

The man is met at the door by his old friend and her spouse. He knows, without her even opening her mouth, that she's changed . . . or rather, that he himself has changed . . . They hug. Immediately she begins to burble over the boy's blue eyes.

"They're beautiful. Look at them. You're beautiful, kid! We were hoping for blue, but we got brown – gotta settle for contact lenses." She indicates her own child, then sighs, then laughs. But she is not joking.

He smiles. He nods. What else can he do? Leave? Harangue? No, just smile and nod and stifle his feelings. Contact lenses? If that tiny child holding his hand there beside him had been born with the coal black eyes of the Bedouin he'd have loved them. His father's cruel mouth . . . his mother's peasant nose . . . these are attributes handed down by ancestors through generations . . . This woman disdains features her children inherited from their forefathers? Hazel eyes and she wants to mask them? Why? Universal ideas about beauty? Are universal ideas about anything worth their salt? Is she quite sure everyone even *likes* blue eyes? They sure don't in the Atlas Mountains, or in Iowa schoolrooms, or in Cambridge lecture halls.

This is the very beginning of the party, and the rest follows suit. It is hard to reconcile the bright woman he once knew with this event. The day is like nothing he prepared for. He's quickly overwhelmed. It's arduous to stare into the vacuous faces of pale blonde women nattering about the rising price of gasoline, or to listen as they drone on about poignant episodes of the televised reality shows they've recently seen. It's draining to be in the presence of emaciated candlewicks blabbering about how hot the weather's been lately, or to politely smile as they compare the benefits of shopping online to doing so at Santa Monica boutiques. It is not genuine conversation that takes place among them, the man realizes, but a jungle-like mimicry, a mindless repetition.

Skulking nearby are the doughy husbands, cuckolds and cowards, their sweaty hands clenching sweating bottles of watery beer . . . calmly discussing their jobs, their director or V.P. positions at candy companies or film companies or pharmaceutical companies . . . subtly boasting of their functionary roles as cogs in massive machines . . . machines erected merely to manufacture products and convince others that they sorely needed those products . . . These men, reeking of malnourishment of one sort or another, gladly assume such roles in order that they might earn enough income to purchase the essential products made by other companies different than their own. They contribute portions of their salary to their retirement funds and cheer the great dental plans provided, proud of where they've ended up in life . . . proud of the many perks they've accumulated, proud of the little treats they're tossed like the fish thrown to captured dolphins to entice them into performing humiliating tricks . . . In between their bourgeois braggadocio they plead with their three-year-old sons to stop running inside the house or to please stop throwing toy trains across the room, careful to show the children the deference and respect that all three-year-olds command.

The offspring of these female mannequins and emasculated males bounce all around the place, hyped up on sugary snacks produced by corporations presided over by men and women who would never feed such things to their own offspring. They're rude kids, inattentive kids . . . already materialistic, already lackluster in a thousand ways . . . They don't respect their adult fathers because the men use no authority with them. Their mothers' curious method of preparing them for the harshness and ruthlessness of the world is to give them everything they want the instant they demand it. The boys are a decade away from being pummeled, academically or physically or both. The girls are being groomed to be fashionable whores, to hate family, prudence, heritage, and self-respect.

Escaping the air-conditioned house, unhealthy in so many ways, the man makes his way to the backyard . . . goes out with the boy into the 105-degree heat . . . It's like a furnace. The whole city's been turned into one enormous parking lot . . . no soil anymore, no fruit trees anymore . . . only asphalt and concrete and internal combustion engines and plodding bipeds . . . "Underneath all this is the beach," blustered those permissible revolutionaries in Paris, those puffed up '68ers. So what if it is – they haven't even been able to take care of the beaches that are left.

There is buzzing behind the man's forehead. His skin is beaded with sticky sweat that captures the omnipresent toxicity in the atmosphere. When he wipes the perspiration away the napkin is stained a dull gray. The air is polluted, physically and metaphysically. Already exhausted he stares at the outdoor crowd, smiling occasionally to throw them off . . . to assure them he's one of them, in no way different . . . He smiles to make them believe that he thinks their thoughts . . . to make them believe that he reads what they read and sees the world as they see it . . . It is the smile of the tuk-tuk driver in Chang Mai, the smile of the fruit vendor in Wutan or the functionary in Singapore. It is a lie. Behind it he is judging. Everyone in that yard, everyone standing atop that plot of earth that once produced oranges and lemons and walnuts, is an enemy.

Finally the heat becomes too oppressive, and the boy has had it. They move indoors again, the child running off to explore, the man taking a seat on the floor. He props his back against the wall like a gangster in a steakhouse, trying to be as inconspicuous as possible. Across from him, adjacent to an enormous display case that houses ceramic figurines of angels, giant letters neatly hang on a wall. They're brightly painted, made of treated wood, and spell out the birthday girl's name. D-A-K-O-T-A. Has anyone in the family's ancestral line been named Dakota? Is Dakota an historical figure they admire or have some cultural bond with? Does the name hold a cherished spot in their religion? No. But Dakota sounds nice. There's a popular series of films starring a loveable moppet character called Dakota. A popular web site recently trumpeted that Dakota is one of the "coolest names on the scene". Two popular celebrity couples have named their daughters Dakota in the last year. It is, undoubtedly, the perfect name.

Dakota, who is turning a year old, has clothes by the boatload and toys by the truckload. She has more personal belongings at *one* than most people around the world will amass their whole lives. To such people it would be difficult to comprehend not only where all of this loot came from, but also how it managed to end up in the possession of someone who cannot yet even speak.

However, the number of possessions of the one-year-old girl seems meager when compared to the amount of things her older brother has. At Owen's last birthday party, when he turned four, he received seventeen gifts, most of which are broken or forgotten by now. Among those gifts were toy trains, his favorite, modeled after the talking train on a popular television show. Scattered through the house there are, literally, hundreds of these wooden trains and accoutrements. Some are in boxes, some in bureaus, some atop tables. Many are strewn across the floor. There are locomotives and cabooses, passenger cars and coal cars. There are trains that whistle and trains that transport circus animals. There are sections of track, straight and curved. There are bridges and tunnels, station houses and mock trees. The pieces are everywhere, oozing like poison from pores. In such enormous quantity they have ceased being mere toys – they are symbols of the profligacy and unquenchable desire of the age.

Across town, in the sparse room the boy shares with his baby sister, hangs an enlarged photograph. It is of an orphaned child in the orphaned land of Austria, a land where the boy's own kin once lived in stables after being driven westward from their Ukrainian farms. The child in the photograph sits on the edge of a curb, awaiting the coming winter. The shoes on his feet are full of holes. In his hands he holds a second pair of shoes, brand new, a gift from something called a relief agency. The expression on his face is one of sheer delight, reflecting the unmitigated elation and gratitude experienced when a true need is somehow fulfilled. This black and white photograph is a constant reminder before the boy goes to sleep each night of what is actually important in life. It is, among other things, a silent rebuke to the debilitating materialism that accosts him whenever he ventures out into the shallow world.

The man watches his son happily playing with some of Owen's trains. He turns, clutching an engine in each hand, and excitedly totters across the floor to show his father. The man puts the boy on his lap and together they inspect the locomotives while the party goes on around them. He is glad for his son's company. It lessens the possibility of being dragged into further conversation with any of the other adult attendees. He turns the toys this way and that, pointing things out to the boy, when "cake time" is suddenly announced. They rise to their feet and walk to the kitchen to fulfill their social obligation.

This particular child's birthday party, like so many others, has a theme. The people holding such events can't apply themes to their lives, but for an infant's birthday celebration there's no stopping them. Elephants or toy trains, ballerinas or conspicuous consumption, the ideas are virtually limitless. Dakota's party is all about fairies . . . winged, fluttering around toadstools, carrying little wands . . . There is no reason to assume that parents who wholeheartedly believe in unrealities in their own lives will not foster similar beliefs in their children.

Poor Dakota sits in the kitchen. She is propped in a highchair with dozens of adults gawking at her, digital cameras at the ready. A conical hat is awkwardly strapped to her head and a song protected by copyright laws is sung to her. Slowly, proudly, an enormous cake made of refined white flour and sugar and food dyes is carried toward her highchair. At its center is a lit candle in the shape of the number "1".

"Make a wish, then blow," she's exhorted. She is being taught early the peculiar customs of her people, "wishing" being of particular importance to them. It is something they do on special occasions and something they do in their day-to-day existence. They wait for magic to strike, for fairies to wave wands. They wait, they hope, they pray – unaware, it seems, that there are other peoples who walk the earth, more powerful peoples, more *dynamic* peoples, who don't wait for fairies to wave wands . . . who long ago traded empty wishing for the will to power . . . people who make wishes come true themselves . . .

The man looks around. All the adults wait in anticipation for Dakota to blow out the candle, eager for a slice of birthday cake . . . maybe two, even . . . He squeezes the boy's shoulders and silently sighs. This is what's left of his world – eating cake. Eating cake, arranging playdates, making wishes . . . electronics sales at big box stores, conference championships on television . . . stupid wives and consumptive sons . . . He has nowhere to go to escape the stench. It permeates the age, the soil. When the increasingly effeminate Englishmen became too much for Richard Burton to stomach he was able to run off into the maelstroms of Asia to be among his rough and honest Arabs. Millions of the sons of these wishing fairy people have made the same metaphysical choice, turning away from their parents and toward the virility of American black subculture . . . printing flyers calling themselves urban guerillas and the like . . . The next wave, a far smaller demographic wave, will choose *narcocorridos* and graffiti, will enthusiastically surge toward where life exists, will choose *anything* over this numbing existence on display before the man . . . yet another generation lost to itself, yet another generation desperately seeking fulfillment in all the wrong places . . . only able to catch glimpses of its reflection in broken, dirty shards . . .

"Come on, honey. Blow out the candle. Make a wish." And as the little girl, the *one-year-old* girl, finally bursts into tears from the pressure, neither blowing out a candle nor making a wish, the man decides to play along and make one in her place. He closes his eyes and, echoing the desire of those more powerful and more dynamic peoples, calmly wishes that these sickly creatures surrounding him would be wiped off the globe forever.

It is a wish he has no doubt will come true.

The cake is doled out on Styrofoam plates, speared with plastic forks, and crammed into dozens of mouths. Politely refusing any either for himself or the boy, the man stands in the air-conditioned kitchen silently suffering the accumulated disgust of the day. These people don't need holy books. They don't need a new calendar. They need a cataclysm.

*   *   *   *

The afternoon sun glints off the boy's hair, gets caught in his eyelashes as he naps on the deck the day after the party. His father sits beside him, eating a late lunch, while across the fence the pudgy ex-hippie screams at his dog to the accompaniment of the sloppy jazz that eternally plays on his stereo. The man's thoughts turn from the events of the previous day and travel back to his student days in Paris, also a city where jazz spills from windows. He remembers a cemetery, tiny and brooding, unvisited by tourists. A tilted headstone stood there, sunken and gray like the remaining French themselves. Across its face were chiseled the words, "The Sons of the Crusaders will never surrender to the Sons of Voltaire". Alas for the future. If the twain had recognized they were brothers things might have gone differently – the might of the Crusaders' sons coupled with Arouet's genius would have been unstoppable. As it is, the man and the boy are left alive during the fulfillment of one of the Frenchman's many prophetic insights: The history of the world is but the sound of hobnailed boots marching up the stairs and the sound of silken slippers descending them.

Are the man and the boy and their family doomed to be replaced? Is it historical law? Only the insane rail against the coming of winter. Only the deluded struggle against the inevitable. Must all, then, be lost? On the surface it seems so, for how can such a fate be avoided with men like the jazz neighbor filling the ranks, with men like the birthday party attendees dragging them all down? When the man's wish for these people's future finally comes true, when the cataclysm he so desires for them does descend, must his progeny go as well? Why? What if he were wrong about having to bear the genetic cross of the cowardly neighbor? What if a deliberate effort were made instead to hurl that cross onto a trash heap? What if all the superfluous fat that's congealed over centuries were simply scraped away and incinerated? Perhaps after decades of the unconscious separation that's currently taking place – that biological exodus of the disgusted from the ranks of the complacent and complicit – it will be revealed that enough scattered stock remained to solder. Perhaps, with the unfit pared away and the right elements in place, *the unconscious separation can finally become a conscious one.*

He cannot leave this to chance. He cannot leave it to "perhaps". He is not allowed to. The consequences are too dire. No, he will continue to seek those others he needs, searching for the quality necessary to rebuild Rome not as city, not as empire, but as family, then clan. Others will come. From the hunted males will arise Romulus after Romulus, while every bourgeois woman who accidentally possesses character and quality will lustily be considered a Hersilia, there for the bold to seize.

It may not work. He may very well be another Turnus, fighting against what's already been decided. No matter his success or failure, however, he must never forget that it is the boy who pushed him to this state, that it is this bright Balder asleep beside him who motivates him and that he, at least, might be trained. The man must not despair before the leaven of the age – whatever may threaten and impede him, *he must instruct!* For even though he lacks a circle, he must still entrust his seeds to the ever-blowing zephyr, the eternal wind that will carry them further and further, until one day, in the future, tender shoots of the greatest quality will be awakened. Thus was the counsel of farseeing Herder, one of thousands of whom the masses know nothing, one of the many men of the past who, even though offering no specific advice, still gives solace and encouragement to the man and his son in the present.

$$* \qquad * \qquad * \qquad *$$

Weeks later the man stands with the boy outside the Pasadena children's museum, awaiting the arrival of a former workmate of his whom he'd run into at the birthday party. It was this ex-colleague's suggestion that, since he too had a child now, they get together here with their kids. Naturally the man agreed to the meeting, though under no illusions that this guy would finally be the one, the first to join him in the crusade against Them.

His old chum, never really a close friend, shows up soon enough with wife and son in tow. The child's name is Dylan. He's three years old. Still wearing diapers. Has a corporate cartoon character on his shirt. Is whiny. Ill-behaved. Eating candy. It's immediately depressing. Instead of being formed into an interesting human being, something alive and purposefully striding across the universe, the poor creature is being turned into something pathetic from the get-go. The man glances at the kid's soda-sipping, gum-chewing mom and dad. Until mutation and environment decide otherwise, like will always produce like.

Due to Dylan's poor conduct and attention problems – a mystery to the sugar-swallowing parents, who are themselves incapable of understanding links between diet and behavior – the man's old workmate and his family leave early. The man then turns his attention to his own son. The boy is riding what he reverently calls a "big humongous tricycle" into an area where he's been warned by his father not to go, and the man shouts for him to return immediately. He hurries back, quickly and obediently. Oh, the many eyebrows that are raised along with the man's voice. On every pale face is a flicker of disapproval. Commanding a child to follow instructions is frowned upon by the desexed soy males and soccer moms. Time-outs are better . . . gently explaining . . . begging . . . please, *please* listen to mommy or daddy . . . The parents know these ways are superior to anything else ever devised in history. Television and magazines have confirmed this for them.

The man and the boy sit down to eat the lunch they brought from home. An open pamphlet sits on their table. It asks that money be sent to assist the downtrodden children of other countries. Donors can check a box to indicate which nation they'd like to grace with their contribution. This particular pamphlet is partially filled out. The man doesn't know what happened to the concerned citizen who began it, doesn't know why this person checked "Indonesia" and "Somalia". But here's the proof in front of him. For some reason these places weighed heavily on someone's mind. Indonesia. Somalia.

There is no manner or form in which these arrogant First Worlders are not laughable. The folk of Indonesia or Somalia or Whereveria, with all their supposed disadvantages – the woeful poverty, the taboo of lower intelligence quotients – are managing to shape stronger kids than all the Dylans in California. Their youth train in the *madrassah*, gaining a discipline utterly lacking in the West's media-nannied, antidepressant-fed brood. They don't shirk duty. They're not on any useless quest to grasp "what life's about". They don't waste their time seeking constant entertainment . . . and yet some visitor to the Pasadena children's museum still took pity on them, much like a blind man pitying those with sight . . .

It is bizarre, this condescension . . . some form of insanity . . . "He whom the gods would destroy they first make mad", said flowery Euripides long ago, himself a harbinger of the madness that was descending even then. Why has it taken so long for the destruction then? More than two millennia and plenty of them are still mucking along. Sure they're on their way out, but they have tens of thousands of years behind them to unravel, so their evolutionary annihilation won't be happening tomorrow. Those whose thoughts occasionally flit over such possibilities in the cold light of day need not worry overmuch about witnessing the demise in their lifetimes. Slots will still exist in tomorrow's society for the boys and girls of the Pasadena children's museum. For the time being the world needs public school teachers and porn actresses, pastors and real estate agents, politicians and dental assistants, race car drivers and news anchors and voter registration activists and soldiers and timeshare salesmen and professional golfers and cops and liberal arts majors and missionaries and prison guards and Methodists and protestors and drummers and metal sculptors and beauticians and performance artists and lecturers on good and evil. Sure, the remaining positions, the meaningful ones at the levers, aren't open to them anymore, but they don't care, they don't care. It's the choice they've made, a preference for the second rate, and it suits them perfectly.

The man and boy depart. On the way out they pass a family of Central American *herpeta* walking through the museum's entrance hall. The Mayans are wowed by the hall, with its tinkling music spilling from unknown sources and its alternating convex and concave mirrors and Tesla coils and mosaics. While well-heeled parents of private school children hurry by without stopping, having seen such curiosities a thousand times, these others shuffle through the entrance hall amazed, as if they've suddenly entered another universe. The man has seen this look on their faces before. He has long watched them at the park at the bottom of his hill, newly arrived from overcrowded Guate or the Honduran countryside, driven by poverty, lured by opportunity, their eyes glimmering at the playground structures . . . marveling over a little piece of nothing – slides, monkey bars – built by the disappearing fungus people of Los Angeles and the world . . .

There are men among the fungus people who arrogantly believe such examples not only set them apart from these newcomers, but also *elevate* them culturally. They take pride in these technological wonders, see their own *superiority* reflected in a playground or a multi-sensory museum entry hall. Unable to reflect on themselves or their place in the world, they never consider that it is they and their creations that are out of place. So what if these others cannot erect such clever rubber and plastic structures, so what if they can only ogle or destroy them – they aren't the ones who *need* to build something for their children to play on. The youth in Bahrain or Benin or Bangladesh play with whatever is around them . . . sticks, rocks, garbage . . . If the shared soccer ball in the Pakistani village is ruined somehow, a goat's bladder will be used instead. There's simply no need to take unnatural materials, things that shouldn't even exist in a healthy world, and erect this artifice, this world of playground slides, colored ball contraptions, and escalators. The constant, busy creation is just one more step on the long march toward oblivion.

It wasn't the bombs that spelled the devastation of the one-time community of the boy's kin . . . not the airplanes, not the bullets, not the decades of reeducation . . . No, the answer lay in that mass-produced, pecking chicken toy from the Leipzig Fair. The imminent destruction came about when their people first began to construct a totally different world from the one they were born into without thinking about where this new world would take them. It arrived as soon as they realized that, somehow, they had the capability of creating another environment, one that more fully reflected the fantastically false one that was carried inside their heads. The seeds of their ruin were planted when shoes were first made from the skins of animals, when the first grains were sown and cultivated, when the first lyre was strung. It was the creation of a wholly material civilization, coupled with the inability to harness such a civilization, which doomed them. The slope toward oblivion dramatically increased when the pecking chicken toy stopped being made by a local wood carver and began instead being mass-produced in factories . . . when every kid could eventually afford his own pecking chicken toy instead of passing a single, shared one around in a circle . . .

What has to be done then, in order to ultimately survive on modernity's terms, is to somehow live within this material civilization while not succumbing to it. Instead of a craven quest for *things*, which seems to lead to inevitable downfall, a desire instead to consistently deny oneself those things. "I do not want gold. I want to rule over those with gold," said the Roman emperor. Let those others take the luxuries, the ideologies, the plagues, until they too become infected and sick. The man and the boy and those who will follow will take their mighty power of creation – the power that enables realities to spring forth from ideas – and temper it with discipline, utilizing it to abolish this world that has now grown inimical to their existence. That amazing quality that has led to both their rise and their subjugation will now, if used correctly, be their savior. From this point on, whatever remains of their creativity must be used in the service of destruction.

Long ago, Virgil put into Aeneas' mouth the proclamation that if he could not bring heaven down, he would bring hell up. It is the duty of the man, the boy, the coming families, to follow the same course of action – since it is impossible to build their world at the moment, they will turn their attentions to tearing this one down. They neither have nor will have swords to swing . . . only their minds . . . but they will do it . . . Their motivation? The driving force behind the generations of creative destroyers? The thing that will impel them toward their goal across the centuries? Simple. It lies directly before the man. Here, on the playground outside the grounds of the Pasadena children's museum, his son goes down the slide and is kicked in the back by a bigger child coming down behind him. Without a word the boy waits, then quickly follows the other boy up the ladder, slides down again, and kicks *him* in the back. Revenge . . . an impetus older than history . . . older than civilization . . .

Only one question needs to be answered – revenge against whom?

*   *   *   *

Pusillanimous modern Christians easily lend themselves to a certain trifling revulsion, like discovering something decaying at the back of the refrigerator that should have long ago been discarded. They come in a thousand varieties these days, most not even going by the name Christian. Many, lacking the smallest bit of insight, even profess a supposed *distaste* for their Jesus-worshipping brethren. Unfortunately, in this era of sloughing, in these decades of evolution where population transfers and media are the winnowers rather than sleet and ice sheets, those who will breed the strength of the future still have connections, familial ties to that most horrible of all creeds, that which has gone by many names but which always shares the same basic article of faith – equality in everything, equality in tigers and lice, equality in treasure and trash.

The boy has a grandfather – one would not call him a blood grandfather, but who, in reality, isn't bonded by blood in these days of dwindling? He abides in the suburbs of Southern California, having years earlier married the man's widowed mother. He is a peculiarly modern type of grandfather, one who feels that he should be venerated for his advanced age alone rather than for any particular displays of accrued wisdom.

This ersatz grandfather often struggles between which figurehead he should submit to more fully – the Pope in Rome or the President of the United States. On the rare instances when these two mouthpieces make contrasting proclamations, the victory for the grandfather's slavering allegiance goes to the President, who has more media outlets at his disposal. When one believes in God as a bearded, talking man in the sky, one easily makes the transition to believing the scripted words of coiffed news anchors blasting from a glowing box in the corner of the living room.

His morality is a particularly American amalgamation of prudishness, acceptable conservatism, and Vatican II Catholicism, wrapped in the flag of the Republican wing of the wink-nudge, liberal-democratic, two-party system of the United States. If an enemy is hyped as a threat – from foreign nation-states to homegrown individuals – the grandfather believes it . . . every time, no exception . . . and as long as he doesn't have to take any type of personal action, he knows that all threats must be dealt with, and harshly . . .

The grandfather's global bloodlust, which is always sated by the empire's actions, is matched only by his hatred of the human body. Such is the way of Christians, and has been since their unwelcome intrusion into the dying body of the classical world. While a dinner guest in the house of the man and the boy he expresses shock over the sight of the bronzed, healthy child heading outside naked. It is unfathomable to him that this should not only be permitted, but desired. The flesh is evil he knows – the body given mankind by his ripped-off god is to be covered as much as possible. There was the whole expulsion from the Garden of Eden and all that. Thus a flabbergasted look crosses his face when, after he worriedly informs the man that the boy is walking into the backyard without clothes, the man replies, "So what?"

The grandfather is confused. "Well . . ."

But that's all that comes out. Before he can get a thought together the man states, crisply and matter-of-factly, "I thought you knew, Daniel, we're not Christians."

This sets the stage. It lets this ridiculous has-been know flat-out that there are now people who look just like he does but who don't identify with his religion, and yet somehow aren't hippies or Jews. What can they be then? And say, what the heck do Christianity and nakedness have to do with each other anyway?

"What the heck does that have to do with it?" he asks, offended.

The man answers casually, nothing in his voice indicating any emotional wavering . . . nothing implying that he's trying to convince, to win a convert, to challenge, to point out moral lacunae . . . It is not stated as an opinion, as something he's formulated himself. It is simply stated as fact.

"Christians hate life. Their world isn't here on earth, their life won't be fulfilled here on earth, so they despise it. They'd sooner drape the body than celebrate it. That constant self-loathing, that mock-morality – it's just absurd, don't you think? I know how this probably sounds to you, Daniel. You grew up in a different time. Did you know, though, that you and my mother and her brother and sister are actually the only Christians I know? You're going the way of the dinosaurs, old-timer." He play-punches his stepfather's arm, seemingly trying to lighten his message, but actually trying to confuse.

"But let's not talk about this now. I think the food's almost ready. Smells like the girls have made gravy." He walks into the kitchen.

The words are relatively benign. They're simply softer versions of the man's thoughts, filtered by decorum. Silently, though, he seethes. He peeks under a pot lid, feeling the steam rise up into his face, and the rage whirls inside his head. The very presence of his stepfather in his home offends him. Whenever he calls the children his "grandkids" the man's stomach knots, and whenever he opens his mouth it's like a television that can't be turned off. His vaunted Christian pedigree repulses the man, linking himself as he does to the feral slaves formed from the scum of antiquity, bubbling up from the insanity that transpires with the dissolution of greatness, birthed from miracle-believing hicks and hysterical, hair-tearing women. It's all too much – the phony humility, the everyday hypocrisy, the "next world", the proudly taken position of choosing faith over reason. These inverters of the values of Rome, these wish-makers, these babblers of bastardized Greek beatitudes, these and those like them, *no matter what they call themselves*, are what will motivate the man and the boy and the rest. These are the kick in the back on the slide that will keep them going, these who've harmed the man's type and will continue to do so, eternally, until one or the other is finally eliminated forever.

*　　　*　　　*　　　*

The summer nears its end. Along with some other parents and children from the boy's daycare, the man and the boy take a trip to the library downtown. It's big and beautiful, built by the same specters that made the lovely gardens in Portland. There is a program scheduled about lions this afternoon, with stories and a puppet show. The boy is excited. He rides on his father's shoulders as the group makes its way through the cavernous building . . . so many books . . . So much scholarship and effort and struggle went into their creation, and for what? The land is dotted with public libraries containing more bound pages than the world's ever seen and yet somehow, according to the headlines, the national population still borders on idiocy.

A man and a woman are the library's story presenters. They are cramped and ghostly, typical specimens for their profession. When the program's finale takes place – the puppet show – it is disappointing, not even able to be called anticlimactic. How can the tale of Androcles and the lion be made pathetic and boring? It's easy. First, make sure the narrator is the proper gender – that is, neuter. Then, double-check that the sexless narrator has blended its ethnicity with the air, letting it disperse harmlessly into the atmosphere. Finally, verify that this odd professional will always condescend to the audience, treating every single child as if he's the most moronic creature to ever walk the earth. There you have it. Death extracted from life.

Afterward the disappointed man and boy walk through the designated children's area. Displays are set up throughout . . . suggestions on the proper books to read, all flashy and colorful and fun . . . Mother Goose, naturally . . . nursery rhymes . . . important tales from Vietnam or Chad . . . Dr. Seuss . . . Children snuggle uncomfortably in enormous chairs, their mothers sitting beside them reading large-print text in flat tones, exact word for exact word. A world of nonsense is what they offer their children, a world of gigantic illustrations and gibberish. Only this abnormal people could create such ridiculousness, only this abnormal people could *perpetuate* such ridiculousness. Little Bo Peep means what? Does what for a child? Teaches what? Tom Tom Piper's Son? What is that? Does a healthy culture retain that which is superfluous, keeping it around like a dirty box of old report cards in a musty basement? *The Cat in the Hat? Goodnight Moon?* Sugary pap, cooed over by mothers whose eyes are set too close under their low brows, whose voices are too high for discussion of reality. Little Golden Books? Void of relevance; fluffy commercial patriotism cloaked in the most sterile civility . . . chuckled over by grandparents who had no culture to pass on to their progeny even if they wanted to, which they didn't . . . All of them, a complete society, are choking in the accumulated dust of centuries. The house must be cleaned. If something – a story, song, picture, anything – doesn't assist in the eternal struggle, doesn't help strengthen, then it's worth nothing. It's filler. It must be tossed, left behind. They must learn when to let go, learn what to let go, learn what to refurbish . . . an organism that cannot rid itself of waste cannot survive . . .

In the library the parents of the boy's daycare pals have chosen cozy chairs of their own. They've hunkered down, they have the right books opened. The Romans believed that one was supposed to learn from teaching, that the act itself was more than a one-way street. What have these parents before him learned? What are they learning as they read these stories? He doesn't know. What is it they're even trying to teach?

*   *   *   *

Autumn returns. The wheel continues to spin . . . more swallowed frustration, more working toward their escape . . . more eternal seesawing, from the top of the hill to the bottom of the hill, from the city to the suburbs, from the hatred of the external ugliness to the love of boy and family . . . a cycle, rhythmic in nature, maddening at times, soothing at others . . .

The boy continues to blossom and grow, beautiful in his becoming. His fit little body sheds its plumpness, his features become even more exaggerated. Walking through a public space is like strolling the boulevard with a planet at one's arm . . . tousled blonde hair, milk-fat face . . . the brushed red lips and the buttery skin and the beaming eyes . . . There is a sublime healthiness to him, reflecting on the outside what he is on the inside, an Aristotelian insight ignored by the purveyors of egalitarianism, who screech and broadcast that every slob hides an inner Parzival just waiting to burst into the world.

The heat makes its final appearance of the year, and the family escapes the city and heads to some seaside town. Casually the boy says, "I want to get naked and go in the ocean." Even as he mouths the words he's stripping off his garb, and in an instant he's down at the surf. The girl squeals with delight over seeing her brother prance naked in the waves, the sea foam the color of Venus's skin, the distant water the color of Minerva's eyes. The man lifts the boy up and swings him, whirls him as if the two are the navel of the universe. He puts him down, and there the child stands, thigh-deep in the ocean, golden and glowing, a sight that doesn't belong to this age, an image of ancient Hellas. The man turns away and the strangers stare, as always, with fresh-faced smiles . . . but in a split-second a wave rises and the man, spinning about, sees it too late, instantly knowing it will knock the boy to the ground . . . It does, and the child is violently slammed down and rolled in the surf.

145

Immediately the man is there, quickly snatching him from the water and praising him for his "swimming", singing "For He's a Jolly Good Fellow" as if the boy's just done something spectacular. The tears and shrieks and fears are gradually vanquished, and the man explains to the boy that weak people get knocked down and stay down but strong people get knocked down and get up, they rise again and again and again, no matter what. The child listens and begins to smile, then laugh, while his father dries the shivering little body with the shirt he's peeled off his own back. Everything is put right again, and away they go to the waiting arms of mother and daughter, the boy walking on the sand, the man, in love with his son, in love with life, walking on the air.

*   *   *   *

Two years after making the decision to leave Los Angeles, the man and his wife finally put their house on the market. The renovation is complete, the bank accounts are padded. The man takes his evening walk with the boy he adores, silently comparing other residences that are also for sale and in competition with theirs. Every month there seem to be more. Why are these people leaving? He doesn't know their particular reasons. He can guess, but doesn't care. His mind is only on his own family's escape.

The boy peddles his tricycle alongside his father, focused on the sidewalk in front of him. A car slows, low-riding, bass thumping . . . windows tinted . . . hairs rise on the man's neck, but he remains calm . . . looks around, spots a chunk of asphalt, good for breaking cheek bones and chins . . . smoothly picks it up, tosses it in the air, all so natural . . . tells the boy to stop peddling, then squats next to him, talking about nothing, waiting . . . The car drives away. He exhales. The guard must never go down. It's a hunt to extinction. Survival calls for violent instincts to return . . . not for selling your house and running . . .

Later in the week the city's unlikely coyotes throw the body of a half-eaten cat over the fence. The man takes the opportunity to talk to his son about death. The boy didn't fully understand the concept when the old hunchbacked woman died earlier in the year, but now he's brought outside to see what it can look like. He stares down at the shredded animal, its ribs exposed, its back half missing. Oddly unfazed, he refers to it as "the bad cat", intrinsically realizing, perhaps, that for the healthy there's nothing good about losing life. "I'd rather be a farmer's slave up there in the sunshine than be down here in the gray with these dead people," said the shade of rash Achilles, grasping it all too late.

*   *   *   *

Yuletide approaches. The man is given two gifts from the gods. The first is presented him at the boy's daycare. There, after seeing a curly-haired, older kid hit his son in the stomach, he gets to witness the boy retaliate with such a sudden and hard punch to the chin that the other child tumbles from the couch the two share and falls to the floor, bawling.

A day later, the house sells.

Everything is tying up. His long job is coming to an end. His life in Los Angeles, his life atop the hill, is coming to an end.

The process of departure gets underway. The man and the boy and the family go down the hill to the local J.C.C. to say goodbye to friends and neighbors at the seasonal Festival of Lights celebration, touted as an all-inclusive gathering for the local community. There are empty promises to keep in touch, to visit often, and the like. While his wife takes the kids off to play games, the man chats with an old friend, a college roommate once. The guy is really talking. He's a bachelor, so perhaps something's eating at him, here among the couples and one-child families. He speaks of his childhood, speaks of Hebrew School with scorn, speaks of his instructor with derision. "He told us that all the Jews there ever were and ever would be were with Moses in the desert." He looks to the man as if the words were insane.

It seems impossible that the ex-roommate doesn't understand. It seems impossible that he doesn't grasp the continuum implied in the phrase, "We were all at Sinai." Doesn't he see the underlying biological reality, or at least the *implied* reality? The man does, *wholly*, *implicitly*, and the boy will too one day. Their Goethe said it – they, too, came from somewhere. As soon as that's acknowledged, as soon as one's *own* timelessness and accomplishment and relevance and suffering are understood, as soon as self-worth reveals itself, then the only thing left to do is to gather the tools to build the future.

*   *   *   *

It is the morning of the boy's third birthday. He is euphoric – there are other children coming to his home and there is an inflatable castle on the lawn, something he loves. It is his first and last party in the house on top of the hill. It will take place despite the misgivings of the man about having celebrations that glorify individuality. He's justified it this time by combining the event with a *bon voyage* party for his kids, because a week later the new owners will move in and the small family will leave Los Angeles forever.

Alone, before anyone arrives, the boy bounces in the castle on the grass . . . higher, higher, higher, abandoned to the glory of temporarily defeating gravity . . . "I'm three, I'm three," he shouts, over and over . . . but the fricative floats from his ruby mouth as "free" . . .

"I'm free! I'm free!"

From behind the trees the boy's father watches the scene. His breast aches. His eyes are tired, their corners wrinkled from stress and age, their edges brimming with tears. There is the boy, his only son, tasting the sugary happiness he once knew in his own life when he believed himself free . . . when he was still ignorant of the forces at work to destroy him . . . The boy knows none of that. He lives in the moment, not in the devastating nether-realm of the Fates, passing their single eye back and forth, seeing the past, then the future, and so on. He is three, and thus is afforded the luxury of dealing only with the present.

The man treasures this gift before him. As he recognized in the spring, there on the sidewalk next to the family's beat-up black car, the day will come when the boy, too, will become a man. His innocence will be discarded, his brilliant glee dulled, the simple love for a stuffed fox or a piece of cheese washed away by the slaps of a wretched world. All will be twisted out of him by the unremitting injustice of the times. The day speeds closer when he'll learn that he's not free . . . that he's been birthed into slavery like his father and others . . . he'll learn it, hate it, and help prepare the ground for the day when their descendants will, after hundreds of years, live as they wish once more . . .

*   *   *   *

And suddenly, just like that, their life in the house atop the hill is consigned to the past. The waves of time are washing over the man and his family. Los Angeles is submerged, sucked into the ocean of memory. New crests arise, some caressing, some threatening. Mexico is the present, a tiny farming village along the shining Sea of Cortez . . . a place for release . . . for the binding of wounds and the carving of arrows and the sharpening of swords . . . reluctantly preparing for the inevitable return to it all . . .

Back in Alta California, when the boy was knocked to the sandy bottom of the Pacific, something happened to him, unnoticed at the time – fear finally entered his life. The sea he once loved now makes him nervous. The salt spray splattering his face makes him cry, and when the rolling waves crash onto the shore he rushes away. So day after day the man sits next to him in the wet sand and tells him tales of blood-linked men, and arms, and ships . . . of Jason and Ulysses and Aeneas, of Leif Ericson and Christopher Columbus, of Vasco DaGama and Barend Fokke and Davey Jones and the mighty Spaniard Hernan Cortez who, because of his bravery, stamped his name on the very sea tickling their toes . . . After the stories the man strips and enters the chilly water. He swims and shouts to the boy that fear will always exist for him now but that it will make him a slave forever if he lets it, and eternal slavery is only for those with no culture, no history, no dignity, and no will. He emerges, dripping, and dries himself. They walk together along the coast, hand in hand, the cushioned foam swirling around their feet, just a bit, just enough to get him used to it all again . . . slowly, slowly, steadily . . .

It works. After three weeks the unbridled joy returns. The boy throws smooth stones that plop and sink in the water. He hurls chunks of driftwood that the friendly waves always graciously return. Every cormorant sailing by becomes a messenger, every whale on the offshore horizon is a portent, and every object found on shore a mystery. Hands clasped, he and his father march in unison into the surf, leaping, daring the waves to become higher and higher.

At night, under the stars, as those waves shush shush, the man speaks of English pirate-thieves robbing the galleons of the industrious Spanish. He tells the boy of Deucalion surviving the flood. He whispers of Neptune and his brother Jupiter and the white foam bull that bore the lovely Europa to the shores of the continent now named after her.

"Who is Europa, son?" His voice grows solemn, the sounds of the surf filling the spaces between his words and thoughts as he answers his own question. "The mother of us all."

Other times, under the glare of the afternoon sun or in the orange glow of the evening campfire, he grabs a handful of sand, carefully extracting a single grain, which goes into his left hand. "This is not sand," he says to the watching boy, indicating the virtually empty palm. He spills the handful from his right. "*This* is sand."

The weeks amble on, the salt air cleaning their heads and eyes, the sun warming their skin, but still, the departure is fast approaching. All the ills of the world begin to knock at the man's mind again. His own fears return on creeping feet. Vacantly he watches the children playing on the shore. The boy teasingly pinches his sister. She laughs and asks him to do it a second time, which forces the boy into guffaws, an amazed stare, and a quick sprint to his father. Here he breathlessly recounts what just took place.

"Dad, she *wants* me to pinch her *again* – like a Christian! Ha!"

He walks back to the fray, chuckling, shaking his head at the insanity of it all, as the man does in his daily life.

The horses running through the surf . . . the sloppy farm where the boy learns about strength and weakness and struggle and death, all through a runt pig . . . the ramshackle kayaks floating across the glassy surface of the water . . . the fish and tortillas for supper . . . the rhythms of the day, of the sun, the winds, the clouds . . . they fade, they fade . . .

*   *   *   *

Thus the brief respite from it all ends, and the man takes his family to the North, to the town he's chosen for them to live in. Now when the moon appears in the sky it rises from behind mountains instead of skyscrapers, and shines down on vast coniferous forests and ranches instead of slums. Somehow the orb seems larger, more familiar, than it had in the city. The boy, mesmerized by it, says that he'll "be like a Titan" and climb onto the mountaintops to yank it down. Already he thinks differently than a year earlier, no longer leaping or jumping for it, no longer asking for it, but making a plan, utilizing his environment to attain a goal.

The man, too, has made a simple plan for the time being. They've earned enough money on the sale of their Los Angeles house to not worry much about employment for a while. Therefore, while his wife works part-time from their rented house with the tiny girl at her side, he will deal day-to-day with the construction of their permanent house. The question of what to do with the boy, however, is not easily answered. It has plagued both parents since before they left Los Angeles. The new town, like the enormous city they left behind, doesn't offer much in child-rearing options. They've not been here long but the man doubts if there's a single ally, a single family to forge a pact with, to help lessen burdens, to help lighten loads . . . people who live religiously, people who *understand* . . .

The boy needs stimulus, needs friends. His mother and father want this for him. Unfortunately there are no others who share the same values as his family. He has no cousins. He has no village where everyone looks after each other – there's just a random place in the mountains where some random people have decided to live. The breakdown of the extended family in the West is, when faced full on, overwhelming. The decomposition of the basic elements of the tribe means constant weariness for those who've been cut loose. It means frustration. It means eternal *Sturm und Drang*. Individual units comprise the population now. They're no longer building blocks of clans – just entities . . . roommates . . . The pitter-patter of the silken slippers is going down the stairs and the thud of hobnailed boots is coming up. Leathery Arabs, sinewy and tough, are coming to replace them. Mayans and Jamaicans are coming to replace them . . . thud, thud . . . Armenians, Chinese, Indians . . . thud, thud . . . One can open an atlas, close his eyes, and point. Those people there, on the page under the finger, they're coming too . . . everyone . . . Hardworking Brazilians. Industrious Koreans. Indonesians and Somalis. The people formerly of Vietnam, people from Chad . . . healthy forests replacing diseased ones, beetle-infested ones . . . Move over Portland park builders. Move over Los Angeles library builders. Move over erectors of playgrounds and eaters of birthday cake and admonishers of dogs. Move over Mother Goose and *hemianthropoi* and weakness.

Once again "daycare", the normative term wafted about the land as casually as the brutal self-hatred, is considered – the boy needs companionship and his parents need free time. As is usual though, their options in this regard are few. There's no possibility of judging such institutions based on what they offer. Rather one must choose which place is least harmful, least noxious, least offensive. It is the cruel joke of the American ballot box replicated in the lives of American children.

There's no difference, essentially, between any modern daycares available to the proles. All foster the same core values. The teachings of a snitch culture, of an effeminate culture, of a helpless culture, of an incriminating culture – all begin here. The indoctrination of the children of the depleted and broken starts early, as it must. They're taught from the beginning not to handle problems themselves, not to reach decisions on how to act or react, but are instead instructed to scamper to an adult, or what passes for an adult in a nation of infants. "Let the grownup take care of it," they're told repeatedly, from day one. That's always the answer. Don't do anything on your own, young man. A four-year-old child who can't figure out the most effective way of dealing with another child who's snatched away a puzzle piece runs immediately to the adult. A thirty-three-year-old neighbor who thinks the music is too loud next door quickly calls the police. A sixty-five-year-old pedestrian who notices a man walking in an odd fashion automatically alerts the authorities . . . the same, the same, the same . . . from cradle to grave in the land of the free, where irony is worshipped except when it's forbidden . . . The soft police state is erected, block by colorful block, right there in those brightly painted daycare rooms.

None of the glories of the ancient world exist in such places . . . exist anywhere . . . the freedom of the body, the breathless revelry displayed and felt in wrestling and boxing and racing . . . "I was made to run," rapturously shouted the boy one day in Mexico, sprinting along the shore toward the distant horizon, whipping stones and leaping atop boulders. So true – he was made for the disappeared gymnasium, made for the *palaistra* and *agoge*. He was made for the discus and the javelin, the bow and the horse . . . not for Western daycare . . . Here it is all modern woman, her smallness, her constraint, her incomprehension, her complete lack of desire to understand *what the boy is*, what the male of the species is, to understand what is inside him, what motivates him. He is to be denied the physical, the glory of testing the body, the delicious struggle of competition. It is the leaden force of the earth pulling at the sky. "Don't wrestle." "Don't hit." "Don't run." "Don't shout." Command after command . . . all movement is stifled, ground to a halt . . . bodies stiffen . . . life folds in upon itself . . .

Sending his child to such a place depresses the man. It was bad enough when the boy's consciousness was just dawning, opening like the most wondrous of flowers, but the child is older now, he understands more now. The man loathes his limited options, despises the historical processes, the craven cowardice, the sociobiological devastation, the bad luck, and the miasmic myopia that have brought him and his family to such a dismal, desperate state.

They've arrived at the mountain town late in the school year. Nearly all of the daycares are full. One has an opening, however, and they take the boy to visit. It's a tiny place near the lake, its windows decorated with differently colored hands made from construction paper. The woman who runs it is a ubiquitous type in the childcare industry – the soup kitchen blonde . . . an easily identifiable type, found in many fields, and well known throughout the world at this stage . . . Her compassion is more destructive than bullets. Her mores are more murderous than hordes from the steppes, the twain alike rolling over civilizations and peoples.

The family is given a brief tour. The place is typical. There are a dozen or so children – future draft card recipients and debtors and cake-eaters, all suspiciously eyed by the boy. The bookshelves are lined with paperbacks splattered with beaming illustrations and insipid characters and poor verse. The chests are filled with obnoxious toys, poisonous plastic shapes stuffed with batteries to make lights flash and unnatural noises sound. The walls are covered with laminated posters depicting model multinational children extolling progressive virtues. Everywhere there are corporate playthings and media-propped products, helpful to company bottom lines, nothing else.

They thank the woman for her time and leave. Outside, sitting on the front porch waiting to be recycled, are stacks of magazines specially produced for kids, stuffed full of dumbed-down writing and flashy advertisements. The neatly tied bundles are the postmodern equivalent of skulls piled outside the razed walls of Merv, the man tells his wife, who laughs and understands.

In the car they talk, acknowledging the reality of their situation. What good is it to possess no world-sickening plastics in one's house, what good to possess no mindless books or superhero figures, when preschools are rife with such things? It is axiomatic that ideologies weaken when youths are removed from the warmth of family, when separated from the security of blood. The carefully constructed home environment, when compared to the place where a child daily spends large chunks of time with the sons and daughters of the profane, can quickly go from sanctuary to perceived oddity in that child's eyes. The man and his wife know this. Yet they also know that an ideology means nothing if shared alone, and since they *are* alone, the age-appropriate companions the boy needs for healthy development must come from somewhere. The misgivings they previously had about sending him to the daycare on top of the hill were, for various reasons, never realized. With that in mind, they decide to give it a try in the mountain town as well. Agreeing to reassess their choice further down the line if the cultural contamination becomes too much to handle, they phone the soup kitchen blonde and enroll the boy for morning sessions.

Still, it isn't a wholehearted decision. Over the course of the following week the man attempts to explain to his son how and why their home is different from the daycare by the lake. He knows how ludicrous he must sound, how Los Angeles he must sound – explanations, only ever explanations – but he is driven by the urge to impart responsibility and truth and immunity. He wishes, in the absence of a tribe, to forge a family bond that will be able to withstand the shock of the outside world, the one that hates them and would like nothing better than to see their tiny vessel one day shattered on the looming rocks of adolescent angst and rebellion. The man wants to sail clear of the rocks. He wants to pass on the vital lessons he's learned, knowing that the sail is torn on their ship, but also believing Seneca's maxim that a great sailor can successfully maneuver the vessel even with a ripped canvas. He is trying, against all historical odds, to fill the role of *túath* for his son.

And then – out of the blue – circumstances call for the boy's mother to depart. She must leave their new mountain town for a time, bringing the girl with her. They'll be away for months. Now the man must not merely stand in for tribe, but for family as well . . . alone in the North, no contacts, no social network . . . nothing . . . It is just the two of them. Now there's no longer a mother or a sister to pay attention to the boy when he's home during afternoons and weekends, times the man is usually working. He fears that the sickness of the solitary will affect the child – playing in a room by himself, exploring the yard alone – so he often puts off his work until nighttime, when the child is sleeping, and joins and engages him throughout the day . . . constantly trying to ignore the visceral warning that such actions are not healthy either for himself, in the short-term, or for the relationship between the two of them, in the long-term . . . Something tells him, as it has from the beginning, that there is a failure of some sort in this frequent act of playing together, the adult male and the three-year-old. He feels the jabs to his self-esteem. Where can future respect come from when a boy knows his father crawled on the floor alongside him instead of working like men should? Is there any wonder regarding the scorn once felt for the *melamud*? For him whose duty it was to instruct little children? True, there are many who claim that "such are the times" . . . but the man cannot live in the same sense as these others . . . there are no "times" for him, only *time* . . .

It all boils down to options, of which he has few. Therefore he ignores his atavistic warnings, tiredly plays with the boy during their time together, and attempts to teach while doing so. He must make the most of the situation.

*   *   *   *

There are toy knights, ten of them, blue and red. Some are mounted on horseback, others stand on foot. All carry weapons. Though they are identical in facial features they are given the labels Franks and Saracens . . . no goofball names, no imaginary names . . . Charles Martel, Charlemagne, Roland, Dagobert, and Robert Guiscard the Norman are in blue. The Saracens are Mohammed, Hasan, Akbar, Saladin, and Seljuk . . . Arabs, Kurds, Turks – many tribes can be united under one name, it is taught. Thus "*herpeta*" . . .

The battles between the two sides, spanning time and space, fought among wooden blocks and on living room rugs, are not biblical. There is no undue defamation of the enemy, whomever it might be. The man realizes the potential weakness in this tactic but feels compelled to adhere to certain principles promoted by those he is most comfortable with, especially in the boy's early stages of development . . . the *Iliad* when young, not the *Book of Joshua* . . . Give credit to your enemies, learn from them, destroy them out of duty, not odium. Understand their position, but do not allow it precedence over your own. Take their winning concepts and techniques. Is it ignoble to suddenly begin utilizing stirrups if the enemy is using them and your men are not?

No, of course not. Ridiculous. And how to deal with traitors? The man makes them pop up frequently among the boy's chosen army. What is the best course of action? Is there any good that can come from them? "What if a traitor from the opposing side brings you information?" he asks his son, "How should he be treated?"

The boy struggles with his father's challenges and learns.

"Dad, why do some of them have the Christian cross on their shields?" Thus opens another conversation, scaled down to his three-year-old mind. He is taught about the constantly morphing nature of this odd sect . . . birthed by fanatics, destroying the remnants of a civilization gone corrupt . . . shaped into a crude nobility by an infusion of fresh blood . . . stabilizing and unifying a continent . . . the growing life force within it, burning the original sickliness away . . . the ignorance of those who failed to understand this was happening . . . the civil war of Europe, of a people who never recovered . . . the weird cultists of the present era, more akin to those original founders than those who came later . . . The man continues with the questions. "Was Hernan Cortez the same type of Christian as these found in your mountain town, son?" "Did Charles Martel's Christianity have anything to do with the version of the man who's married to your Oma?"

In every pretend battle the boy learns. When he chooses to be the Franks he is never allowed to have more soldiers on the field than the opposing Saracens. When he chooses to be Saladin astride his mount he is always outnumbered by the infidels. Life is struggle, he's taught, and his coming tribe will always be a minority. Victory must be gained regardless of the paucity of numbers. The focus must be on how to attain it.

Then there are decisions to make. He's captured some of the enemy. Should he ransom them (does every man indeed have a corresponding monetary worth), execute them (what will be instilled in the remaining enemy combatants, hatred or fear), or enslave them (mighty nations have always operated on slavery of sorts, but does that slavery ultimately destroy them)?

There are the philosophical questions rooted in the historical. The Crusaders drove to the East – when nations and *túatha* are expanding, are they rising or falling, healthy or sick? Karl of the Franks was known as "the Great". Does "great" to some mean "great" to all? Was he right to murder the Saxons and turn the brooks red? Does such a thing – killing recalcitrant kinsmen in order to bring about unification – make a people stronger or weaker?

"Talk out loud, boy," the man tells him. "Think. Challenges are coming. Learn to meet them."

The events of the past are played out there on the floor. Roland is ambushed in the mountains of Iberia. Can he escape? Mohammed makes the decision to charge the Kuraish at Badr rather than safely launch arrows at them from a distance. Was this the right choice? Robert Guiscard, feigning death, lies in a casket full of swords and is borne by his unarmed comrades into a monastery. There he'll leap out, pass out weapons, and slay for loot. History is vibrant, exciting, and alive. Yet if it doesn't offer examples on how to get out of this current mess it's useless. If it has nothing to say about the present it's useless. If, as it's popularly portrayed, it shows the man and the boy no greatness in their people, then they have lost, and hostiles sit atop the throne. This is clearly the case today. So whatever is broadcast as somehow antagonistic or unworthy is to be examined and studied, for these things opposed the forces that have brought the man and the boy to their present state. The study of history in their family is to be the study of the currents, the trends, and the deeds that have deconstructed all that was necessary for their type to thrive, and of the crucial processes needed to restore the proper environment needed for them to flourish.

In time the man will make the instructional shift with the child; from talk of loose tribes barbarically hacking with blades in order to gain land and easy riches, to discussion of Machiavellian means of controlling a state, to talk of Clausewitzian ideas on policy expansion and realpolitik, to – finally – the encapsulation of it all, the Nietzschean exhortations on truly becoming a people and the worthlessness of all prior actions without the fulfillment of this necessity. The pretend warmongering is just playing to the boy's primal lust for physical conflict. After all, battle is of no use when others control the technology of genocide. There will be no silly talk of sacrifice – there are none to sacrifice for yet. No bombastic talk of glory – there is no glory in being carpet-bombed. The nature of struggle and conquest must be brought to a different plane. His son will not flail about like raging Ajax, slaughtering defenseless sheep in the dark, believing them actual foes, until the clear light of dawn brings realization, shame, and suicide. No, they must *learn*. They must learn – as if time is just beginning for them – who to fight, how to fight, why to fight, and when to fight.

*   *   *   *

In a late-stage capitalist society, where no dignity or honor is imputed to physical labor but only to those who manipulate and monopolize this labor to enrich themselves at the expense of the state, new workers must always be imported . . . expendable chunks of nothing, plucked from the myriad nations of the globe . . . Chaos is inherent in the very economic theory itself, with its terrible cycles of boom-bust and peace-war. Stability is sacrificed and the price of bread, or whatever has replaced bread, increases as surely and stealthily as the new labor force supplanting the previous exhausted one.

On certain days the man brings the boy with him to the building site, where men who are a part of this new, imported labor force are erecting the family's house from the ground up. He wants his son to witness examples of how things come to be, of how the conception becomes creation. He wants him to see a wall arise where previously there was nothing, wants him to see lines on a piece of paper be transformed into stairs he can actually stand on.

Most days, however, the man arrives at the house alone, working silently alongside the construction crew hired by the contractor. It is satisfying, the lifting and carrying, the handling of tools, particularly after years of enervating deskwork. Yet he often thinks of the once powerful Persians, they of the warlike sons and stunning wives, and how, when they finally decayed, their bellicose Greek and Macedonian cousins were there to sweep them away. They despised the Eastern dandies, luxuriating in shaded gardens, biting peaches with gleaming teeth under lips that had never known chapping from winds cold or hot. Their hands had grown soft, their muscles flabby, unable to wield lance or sword. The stench of their perfume smelled of sickness and weakness to the toughened phalanxes of Hellas or Magna Graecia or Asia Minor.

Thus it is that in the spiraling, semi-repeat of history, the equally soft-handed man acknowledges his own role as an updated Achaemenid Persian, diligently toiling alongside Greeks, though these Greeks now hail from Mexico. They, too, mock effete weaklings, as the Greeks did the Persians, the Romans did the Greeks, the Teutons did the Romans, and the world does the Teutons. The man never lets on that he understands the tongue of these Mexicans, but he does, and he listens knowingly, unable to find fault with their derisive views of the flaccid people of the wealthy North.

Like the man, one of these laborers also has a son, born in Alta California and brought further north with his father and mother as they followed the economic opportunities offered by those selling their houses and fleeing the state. This migrant boy, a child of the Azteca, attends the same daycare as the man's son. The soup kitchen blonde and her assistant, docile as young cats, smile at him, fawn over him, attempt to speak his tongue in halting sputters. To these mewling *Nachbewohner*, these has-beens, the brown boy of the South, and his father, and his family, and his tribe, are harmless curiosities, exotic animals from far away meant to be nursed, coddled, pitied, and admired. This is not how the man and the boy see them. To them they are Aztecs, a conquering tribe once, a conquering tribe to come. They are dangerous, and to be respected. The grinning maternalism that pervades bourgeois America cannot exist in the man or the boy. To refuse to treat other men as men is a death sentence.

The Aztec boy, with his flat nose and coarse black hair, is not being bred to be a eunuch. He is not gelded by too many material goods, he is not castrated by a mother whose only desires in life are to be entertained often and to never offend. Though he, too, will eventually fall prey to the lassitude brought on by consumerism, for the time being he is raw and physical, the romantic notions of those who bastardized Rousseau irrelevant. The child from Alta California is an enemy like all the others, but an enemy who doesn't disgust. He is, in a word, healthy. Therefore the man is pleased when he hears that his son is attracted to the Aztec boy's energy and personality. Finally he has a companion who will engage him fully, someone whom he can poke and kick and wrestle and expect a normal response from. It is a welcome turn of events.

But manifestations of health, it must be remembered, seem like aberrations to the terminally sick. Having been infirm so long, any display of vigor is an affront to them, a bitter reminder that they themselves are crippled, unable to ever be cured. This has been seen time and time again through the millennia, from whole nations on down to individuals.

While checking out books at the local library, the man is engaged in conversation by the librarian. She sends her son to the same daycare as the boy and the Aztec child. The mountain town is small. She chitchats idly – what do you think of this, what about that. She knows that since the man comes from Los Angeles he must be urbane and learned. With sagacious nods and appropriately spaced smiles, he gamely plays along with the empty chatter. Talk soon turns to the establishment where their children play. He somehow informs the woman of his son's friendship with the Mexican boy. Her face clouds. There is concern. Hypocrisy colors the bland skin.

"Be careful with him. He's rough . . . boisterous . . . I try to keep my son away. He's younger, you know – I don't want him to get hurt."

The man gives yet another sagacious nod.

Every other Saturday this woman before him reads simple stories in Spanish to children of immigrant workers. She feels good about offering this service to the community . . . to the world . . . She feels *superior*. When equally struggling local laborers, themselves descendants of impoverished migrants from Germany and Sweden, complain of their dropping wages due to the influx of the Aztecs, the Mayans, the globe, she sneers inside. She makes cracks to right-thinking friends about rednecks. She has a Master's degree in English, these rubes barely got out of high school. They pound nails and lift things, she catalogs books and decides what subtitled film should be shown in the back room on the first Monday of every month. She knows xenophobia when she hears it. Like the shelves of her mountain town library, her compassion is compartmentalized.

She continues her now-whispered conversation with the man, urbane and learned like her and her circle . . . continues with her covert warning about, in reality, the threatening *masculinity* of the boy from *down there* . . .

"You understand," she says, wrapping it up and smiling airily, believing the man is familiar with her code, her double life.

"Sure," he says, nodding. He does understand. He *is* familiar with the code, fluent and practiced from years spent in the city. He knows that none of its speakers really believe the zeitgeist's creed – they only ever believe that they believe.

His son continues to engage the Aztec boy. Their relationship is crude. They are rough with each other. It does not bother the man. It does not bother the Aztec boy's father. Physicality only bothers the other parents . . . those pale, delicate, Northern parents . . . those *Persian* parents . . . It bothers the soup kitchen blonde who runs the daycare. And, of course, it bothers the librarian. Even after particularly violent episodes the boy is fond of the *herpeton* as he is of no others. The man knows that this son of the Azteca will never be a librarian. He will never be a judge or a mortgage broker, he will never visit a therapist or stare wordlessly at an Impressionist painting or try to vanquish malaria somewhere. And for this the man thanks whomever men like him thank.

$$* \qquad * \qquad * \qquad *$$

One of the coworkers of the enlightened librarian also gives back to the community. Since she doesn't speak another language, and is thus unable to read exclusively to immigrants, she gives a weekly storytelling at different preschools around the mountain town. Each Thursday the children of the boy's daycare gather on the floor to listen as a book for modern sensibilities is read to them. At the conclusion of the tale one of the lucky students is always selected to bring the book back to his or her home for a few days.

Mediocre books, like mediocre people, make their way into the life of the man's family far too frequently. They come from chatterbox acquaintances, myopic relatives, and hollow daycare employees and volunteers. Over time he has learned to mask his exasperation over receiving such things. Earlier in his life he would roll his eyes in private and hurl them into the garbage, ridding society of another drop of laudanum. Yet he has grown along with the boy. He now thinks, weighs, studies . . . grows Talmudic in his choice of stories for a three-year-old . . . realizes that everything can be a lesson . . .

One afternoon the boy returns home bearing a shiny book with a lion on its cover, a young male cub. Like all books produced for the children of the straw-stuffed, it is filled with pictures. A colorful scene covers every page and oversized words are printed across the bottom. The tale – specifically geared toward families, it is explained on the dust jacket – tells of the lion cub's reluctance to hunt like his father, preferring instead to play with his friends. His friends aren't lion friends, as one would assume. They are, instead, the wildebeest, the zebra, and the animal so appreciated by Americans one day each year, the elephant. Initially Lion Father disapproves of his boy's playmates. By the end, however, he not only learns to be tolerant of his son's choices, but gives his pacifistic child some credit after the cub proves that it can actually roar quite loudly – which is, obviously, the vital barometer of being a successful lion.

From the boy's first days on earth the man has fastidiously avoided exposing him to false books on the animal kingdom. Yet here he is, just such a thing in hand, it having been shoved into his consciousness by one of the billion bio-cultural saboteurs who fervently roam the Occident . . . so that evening the man breaks a household rule . . . his son is permitted to watch video images on the television screen that lurks in a cabinet in his parents' bedroom . . . footage from spectacular Africa, from the beast-carpeted veldt of the Serengeti . . . He watches lions – real lions – attacking and killing their prey. There is no friendship with other animals, no kinship – only minor acknowledgement and long bouts of truce, followed by murder. The wildebeest is but a meal to the lion, relevant only for energy and life. The lion is but a reaper to the wildebeest, a necessary predator who improves the stock of the prey's herd each generation. The egalitarian principles so beloved by second-tier elites, if applied to the vast plains of Africa, would only result in the starvation, weakening, and slow eradication of lion and wildebeest alike.

When the boy's people were peasants, connected to the land, the *Gattungswesen* of a beast – that particular *something* that defines the essence of each species – was accurately noted in fable and song. There was no need for falsehood. Qualities possessed by particular animals which, viewed through a biocentric lens, were admired within the national culture, were considered good, while ones the people frowned upon among themselves were considered bad. Such was the way of things the world over. Eventually those rustics left their fields and forests and mountains and coasts and made the move to the beckoning cities. Outside of rodents and birds, they stopped seeing wild creatures in their daily existence. The day came when qualities that were considered "good" or "bad" for millennia were scrutinized by all these newly industrialized and politicized and educated city dwellers and startlingly found to be anything *but* good or bad – indeed, what was previously held to be good was seen to be a somewhat antiquated and naïve belief, and what was formerly considered bad didn't really seem so bad anymore. As a matter of fact, they suddenly realized, their ancestors had been wrong all along. So the old fables and songs were no longer meaningful. They needed to be overlaid, marginalized, and universalized to make way for the new era . . . and they were . . . Now, shorn of the little they once had, they exist only to propagate falsehoods and spin untruths about the mechanisms of the world.

"So," asks the man, after the image of dead prey and bloody-faced lions has made its impression on the boy, "who wrote this book they sent home with you? Someone who would tell you the truth? Or someone who would lie to you – a liar?"

"A liar."

"Can we trust everything that comes from a book?"

"No."

The man nods. "That's right. Very good." He grabs the lion book from the nightstand and hands it over. "Our civilization has become infested with liars, son. They fill every niche, they guard every gate, they sit wedged behind every desk you'll come up against. They may actually believe the lies they tell us or they may be actively trying to deceive us – we'll never know which. But as long as among ourselves we know what's true, we can let them say anything they want."

*   *   *   *

That night they stay up late, the man telling the boy of his time spent traveling across Africa years before. He tells him of the fascinating panorama of life there beneath the endless skies, a thousand interactions and struggles, every species refining itself, always changing, influencing, shaping, never sedentary, never set, forever shifting like the Symplegades. He tells him of the ruins of Zimbabwe and the White Lady of Namibia. He speaks of the fierce Zulu, the stalwart Boer, the noble Masai . . . the great migrations, the *difaqane* . . . the last German farmer in the paradise at the bottom of the Ngorogoro Crater . . . cattle raids . . . interspecies watering hole battles . . . the Portuguese versus the Arabs . . . capitalists crushing independence, as they had all across the world . . . communists pretending to give it back, as they had all across the world . . . missionaries and mercenaries and animists . . . on and on, until the child finally falls asleep beside him . . .

The next morning at breakfast, as the nuthatches and crossbills sing their springtime songs, the boy takes a bite of bacon, feeds a bit to his stuffed otter, and looks across the table at the man.

"Dad, was I with you in Africa?"

The man smiles at the question, which runs deeper than it seems. How can the child even begin to understand the answer at this age? How can he ever grasp that if he's with his father now, sitting across the breakfast table from him somewhere in the Rocky Mountains, then he's *always* been with him, *ab aeterno*. Seven years ago they trekked across Africa together, and six decades before that they escaped the killing fields of Ukraine with the boy's great grandmother and her children, and five centuries before that they and their families ambushed invading Turks in the Balkans, and four millennia before that they ate pork with their kinfolk in the woods around Lake Peipus. They battled the Mongols side by side in Poland and died as paupers in Eire and counted the stars in Bactria and sang bitterly about the might of the Legions in Gaul and suffered from the intrusion of the railroad into Russia. They swept down from the steppes together, they spread across the world and the years; the boy, his father, his mother, his sister, his tribe, all of them, one after the other, one next to the other, one as the other. They slaved and were enslaved. They destroyed and were destroyed. They fought outsiders and they fought each other . . . but always, whether they acknowledged it or not, they were one . . . all the fighters, the priests, the scholars, the thieves, the peasants, the artists, the traders, the charlatans, the poets, the illiterates, the horsemen, the slaves, the laborers, the monks, the inventors, the victims, the geniuses, the craftsmen, the pirates, the refugees, and the brutes of the past . . . all one . . . and not only those of the past, but *all those to come*, those who are already struggling and avenging in the future, trying to put right the mistakes of their kin who came before them . . . They too, are part of it all, linked to these others by the man and the boy and the family and, perhaps, some few silent and aware others, hidden away in the present . . . tenuously linked, but linked nevertheless . . .

This is what the man's old roommate didn't understand back in Los Angeles. The boy is the descendant of millions and the ancestor of millions and the same as millions. In the misty past he used a bronze blade to stab a Pelasgian foe and in the misty future he'll be standing atop a mountain holding his newborn son up to the sun. He helmed that ship and hid in that cave and wrote those poems and he *will* helm that ship and hide in that cave and write those poems. He's eternal, the man is eternal, and through them their *túath* is eternal. Though they've gone by different names over the millennia, they won't forever. One people with many names, that's the only difference between their history and others' . . . but when they finally give themselves one, when they finally identify themselves, to them will come once again the North and the South, the West and the East, the past and the future . . .

The child takes another bite of bacon, awaiting the answer to his question. The man grins, thinking of the right way to put it. He exists. The boy across from him exists. So they've always existed. It's that simple.

Now he just has to make it clear.

"Yes, son, you were with me in Africa. You see—"

The boy interrupts, his eyes wide, his face lit up with excitement. "I *knew* I was! I *thought* I was there!" He nods his head up and down at his father. "That's where we first got Otter, I think!" He squeezes the stuffed animal, and smiles a smile bigger than his face. The man, his heart bursting, returns the boy's smile, and lets the conversation end there.

✶   ✶   ✶   ✶

The house continues to rise, to take shape and gain form. The man continues to work, to cook, to raise his son, but the pair of them yearn for the womenfolk of the family. Domesticity is different without them, the dynamic different. Life is more direct, more angular, less rounded. There is no softness, no coddling; it is all testing and questions and answers and explanations.

A tomato hiding in the boy's salad or eaten sprinkled with sea salt as a summertime snack fills its role. The man points it out, quizzes his son. "Tomato – Old World plant or New? Who conquered the New World? Aztecs? Mayans? Toltecs? Incas? Spanish? French? English? These latter groups, why did they come? Did they really conquer? Did the most farseeing among the Romans believe they'd conquered when they took a new region by bloodshed and added another province to the empire? What does "farseeing" mean? What did Pliny the Elder mean when he said, 'Through conquering we have been conquered.'? Your friend from daycare speaks Spanish. Why do so many people speak this language? Is it in a conqueror's best interests to teach a militarily defeated people his own tongue?"

Pop. In goes another tomato.

"Who were the Men of Cajamarca? Do superior weapons guarantee a military victory? What does 'superior' mean? Is a military victory a victory for all time? What's more devastating – to lose your land and sovereignty by force of arms or to lose your culture – thus your land and sovereignty – by force of propaganda?"

Pop. In goes another tomato.

Every single object or incident, meaningless as it might seem – every mountain, every sunrise, every traffic accident or building passed, every piece of technology, every assassination, every political gaff, scrap of garbage, living room wrestling match, falling star, crunch of boots on gravel, splash into glacial lake, shake of the salt – is explained, tied to something else and brought back to them, to their situation or their history. It is the nurturing of a *Weltanschauung*, a worldview of the particular springing from the experience of the group, not watery universalism or the blandness of free-floating individualism.

Everything they see, everything they experience, is linked to the web of their culture. A crossbill, a fir tree, Polaris – these mean something different to the man and the boy than they do to others and, compared to most, they mean *something more*. A mayfly isn't just a bug. To them it means Irish folk tales and May Day celebrations and spring lamb and political movements and on and on. The appearance of a single, greenish insect can allow them to swim in an ocean, *their* ocean, dive deeply down and never reach the bottom. Not so the bourgeoisie. They're left with only the shallowest of puddles. They chose to take the rich culture of fantastic insights and brilliant accomplishments given them by their ancestors and throw it away. Many not only threw it away – they presented it, with much fanfare, to those hobnailed boot people they so oddly pitied, while simultaneously robbing these people of their own cultures. The hobnailed, questioning the value of anything given them by spoiled brats, subsequently hurled this gift to the ground like an aluminum can reeking of yeast. There this culture lay, waiting for the man to eventually discover during his years of wandering through the labyrinth. Plucking it from the gutter like Napoleon did his crown, he polished it and reclaimed it. He is now passing it on to his children, who will pass it on to theirs, and so on and so on, never to relinquish again, never to blithely hand over. It might be stolen, it might be copied or wrenched from their grasp, but never never never simply *given away*. They need it to explain the world. They need it to make the puddle an ocean. Without this gift the mayfly is a mere bug, Notre Dame is simply a building, *Gattungswesen* is just some foreign word, and Rome only a polluted, modern city.

✳　　　✳　　　✳　　　✳

Art. The boy is steeped in it without believing, like the placid burghers, that it's somehow supposed to be separated from the life force. Civilization is here now, consciousness is here, and though the world might be better off if they weren't, the existence of art lessens the horrors and gives inspiration for the fight. From the strains of Strauss and Borodin playing in the child's room as he falls asleep, to the poetry of De Lisle recited to him in the car, to the sculptures and paintings of the European masters shown him in books to help bring alive folk tales and myths, to photographs of the unsurpassable architecture of the *Moyen Âge* he'll one day visit and weep over, he is surrounded.

The modern tendency to view art as something for its own sake doesn't exist in their household. That is for others. Art for them is a material extension of the beliefs of a people. Good art has the further benefit of having its aesthetics resonate with the observer. And great art – obviously rare – is when timeless, ideological relevance is imparted through the aesthetically inspiring piece; that is, a work of genius that is not constrained by the sociopolitical boundaries of eras. After all, what are ability and industry, what are talent and diligence, if not put into the service of an ideal, and what worth is an ideal if it is not reaching for the eternal?

On the living room wall of their rented house hangs a somewhat pretty oil painting of an anonymous landscape. It is often pointed out to the boy as an example of bourgeois emptiness. No one knows what part of the world the painting is meant to portray. No one knows if something happened there or, if so, what impact it had on today. No one knows if it was significant in the historical consciousness of a people. It simply doesn't *mean* anything. It isn't art. It is decoration.

The child is taught that his are a people that have produced the greatest artists the world has ever seen. He is also taught that juvenile boasting about this to others is worthless, particularly since those others are healthy and feel as healthy *túatha* do – that *they* are the remarkable ones. Subjectivity in peoples is to be admired and understood. It is those with an inability to judge at all that are oddest. When the child comes home from daycare with a special "art issue" of a children's magazine, along with some of his own artwork, the man takes the opportunity to explain this. He points to a prominently featured photo of San cave drawings.

"What do you think of this?"

"Well, Ms. Blanc said it's good."

"What do *you* think?"

"It's good."

The man points to a photo of a Botticelli painting, directly next to the first.

"Is this good too?"

The boy nods his head.

"Did Ms. Blanc tell you guys that?"

"Yes, she said all the pictures are good art."

The pages of the little magazine are filled with pictures of works by Monet, Klee, Picasso, DaVinci, and Warhol, along with the obligatory examples from Japan and elsewhere in the world. Smiling, the man grabs a handful of the birdseed they occasionally put out for the juncos and chickadees, places it on top of the magazine, and tells the boy to eat it. He screws up his face, grudgingly takes a bite, swallows, then sticks out his tongue and groans. The man laughs.

"Did it taste good?"

"No."

"But it tastes good to the birds, right?"

He nods his head. The man continues. "Is *all* food good?"

The boy wrinkles his face again, looks at the birdseed and shakes his head no.

"All food can't be good to all creatures. If it doesn't *taste* good to you, then you say it's not good, right? You're not a bird, you're a boy."

The boy nods. He understands. Bird food tastes good to birds, not to boys.

"Forget what Ms. Blanc told you – she'd probably say she likes the bird food, right? – but tell me, out of these two on this page, which picture do you think is better, son? If you had to choose."

He points — to the primitive San drawing.

"It looks like mine," he explains matter-of-factly.

The man laughs again. It's not what he expected, but at least the boy is learning subjectivity and opinion. Already he's moved beyond the daycare woman. He'll be beyond most of the world when he further understands that the San drawing, coming from a healthy people, is superior to the empty painting hanging on the living room wall.

"Ms. Blanc says she's an artist too. She's a sculper," the boy says.

The man laughs a third time . . . a sculptor who sees no difference between a Botticelli and a cave drawing and a Klee . . . thus unable to see the difference between anything, in essence . . .

"I'm sure she is."

The sculpting daycare woman can be a great example to the boy someday. She is one case among millions of a people with a bio-cultural urge to create, to shape and to form – and to what end? These urges have become – and perhaps always were – still more wasting of time, more wasting of resources, more wasting of life. If the myth of transcendence is ever to be overcome, then the lust of these natural-born sowers must be redirected and turned to the relevant. Art must become action. During these days of dwindling there is infinitely more poignancy in creating actual human beings than in sculpting their form. Carefully chipping marble with hammer and chisel can't be as fulfilling as chipping away at the slave state they all toil in. The passion needed for breeding strong families and purging one's life of frailties can't be wasted on merely painting sunrises on canvas or composing music. No, the mediums currently worked in must be exchanged. Splattered canvases must be thrown away and replaced with the earth itself. Beautifully sung song lyrics must be traded for iron deeds. Clay and marble must no longer have any meaning for them – only flesh and bone will do.

Goethe pulled the concept of *Erlebnisdichtung*, a poetry of subjectivity and experience, from the depth of his being, remaking the art itself. Eliot did the same in his turn, revolutionizing the field. So, too, can all of these busy modern artists. They can create a poetry no longer confined to books or memory holes or *samizdat* . . . a poetry of action and struggle and destruction and rebirth . . . In teetering Russia, Blok recognized that art was indivisible and inseparable from politics and life. The best of these remnant people, the most aware, must grasp this as well. They must make their very *being* a total work of art, a *Gesamtkunstwerk*. Body, mind, spirit – this is where they can mesh, this is where they can become whole again, the ridiculous internal divisions finally fading away . . . and they must keep going . . . the remnant people can't stop here, with the cohesion of the individual, but must continue the process, bringing their unified lives into alignment with others who've unified theirs . . . totality is what must be sought, not simple and egotistical expression . . .

Art as it was once known is dead. No longer can the remnants apply themselves to creating the traditional plastic forms. In this miasmic swamp they all dwell in, the artist – hack and genius alike – is held in thrall like everyone else. When a work by Botticelli is considered no different from a scratching on a cave wall, then what good is it to pursue art as classically defined? The one-time blustering and boasting of conservative reactionaries about being a "people of artists" must be forgotten. Certainly it's true, to a degree, but what benefit has it had? Now the world is run by those who cannot create beauty in the plastic forms – who, indeed, see no need for it. They've redefined what art is. They've made talent mean — nothing! Dedication — nothing! And if power can redefine the essence of art, the essence of a *people*, then power is what these remnants need to create, not art. Only, power can't be created. It must be taken, wrested away like the Palladium from the temple at Troy. Together the boy and man and the gathering families will learn how to take.

Nietzsche laid it out. The Last Man does not train the will. The new breed will train the will.

*   *   *   *

Sitting in their vehicle outside the local drugstore, a nationwide chain, the man speaks calmly to the boy. Briefly he retells the story of disguised Ulysses at the Trojan temple of Pallas Athene, pocketing the Luck of Troy in the midst of war, completely demoralizing the beleaguered city when its loss was realized. The building in front of them, he explains, is also a temple of sorts. Inside, displayed under noxiously weird light, are thousands of gleaming, colorfully packaged goods whose purchase will bring buyers a bit closer to salvation. It is a place erected and owned by those who would crush the man and the boy, who *have* crushed them . . . men who utilize the depleted peasant base as oxen or shields, either bearing yokes or taking shrapnel . . . Today they march this remnant peasantry into service jobs or Mesopotamian slums, yesterday into sweatshops or the front lines of Passchendaele. They are for the most part managerial types . . . bureaucrats, dispassionate and leaden . . . That is their weakness. When unforeseen crises arise they are less sure of themselves. Crises confuse, offer opportunities to the enslaved.

"When one cannot yet defeat one's enemy, one does everything one can to weaken him. Do you understand that?"

The boy is three. He is dwarfed by the sweatshirt he wears.

"Yes," he replies, serious and earnest.

"In there, in that store, are the things your enemy's power comes from."

Of course this is not true. The enemy's power comes from the dwindling life force of that debased peasantry it rules over. But such a thing is too ephemeral for his son to understand at this point. Instead the man will let the child believe, for the time being, that their oppressor maintains supremacy due to the existence of the material objects on the shelves, and that if these sacred objects are somehow forfeited then the power of the enemy will, correspondingly, begin to wane.

He continues talking, telling the boy about Spartan lads not much older than himself who needed to steal food to live, who suffered beatings and shame if caught. Therein lay a reality that must be learned – only the apprehension and the applied laws of the stronger make one a criminal. Writ larger, a tribe is criminal only if defeated. The man, the boy, their kind, have been defeated time and time again over the centuries, and thus are criminals. If they'd won, their enemies would currently be the criminals. So it goes.

What did those Spartan lads learn from stealing? That life was hard, not easy . . . that to survive, all things were permitted . . . that to be caught was not an option . . . that a crime to one was life to another . . .

that you shared with your comrades . . . that you worked as a unit . . . They learned to steady their hands, to move in shadows, and to make no sounds. All these lessons will be relevant to the boy one day.

The man drills him on what will happen inside the store, going over and over the plan like a Prussian Field Marshal. Once they enter, whatever object he points at is to be placed by the boy into his sweatshirt pocket, but only *after* the man winks at him. That will be the signal that all is okay. The man will physically block the scene so that no one can see. If, horror of horrors, he does get caught, the man will pretend to be angry with him, and then the only words on his part are to be those of apology, over and over and over, to his father and the apprehender. But he *cannot* get caught, because then the police will take his father away to jail, maybe forever. He'll be saved, but his dad will go away. Purposely the man exaggerates, gauging reaction, judging character . . .

"Is it all clear, son?"

The boy is scared, nervous, determined, excited. He nods his head yes. From this theft he will learn, in some small manner, the ways of the world. They climb from the vehicle and together enter the drugstore. They walk up the aisles, searching. The man picks up a pack of pencils to purchase, as he told the boy he would. They turn down another aisle and go directly to something the man knows the boy will have no trouble with . . . a smallish tube of candies, made of dyes and high fructose corn syrup and chemicals . . . He glances around. A week earlier, when looking for something the boy could easily pocket, he scanned for surveillance apparatus . . . hidden cameras, mirrors . . . There was nothing. Now he makes sure there are no employees about.

The people who toil at such places are weathered . . . bleary-eyed . . . They're the working poor . . . riff-raff spat at by the powerful . . . mocked in cineplexes, mocked in books, mocked in Ivy League conversations . . . unable to understand the forces that shape their lives, the forces which have stepped on the broken corpses of their kin and completely altered their previous existential norms . . . Like their urban counterparts, the rural serfs are not reproducing much. They too are withering, yawning, and exhausted. Soon there will be nothing left of them. Men grow tired of decay. When they go, the whipcrackers who live off of their lifeblood will perish also. Until then, until the blessed demise, a thousand diversions jostle for their attention . . . a thousand taxes grind them down . . . Do they really care if a three-year-old takes something from their faceless employers? It's doubtful. They don't care that their dignity's been taken, they don't care that their self-worth has been stolen away, so why would they worry about the harmless actions of a mere boy?

Yet the man must still be on guard, must be rapid of eye and, if need be, glib of tongue. Among the broken continue to exist those who've always been the greatest enemy, the confused moralists, those who apply tribal values to the universe and universal values to the tribe, those who do not see the world as it is, with its divisions, its in-group and out-group reality, but who live only in the foggy realm of concepts . . . "stealing" rather than "taking back from those who steal from us" . . . "killing" versus "saving lives by stopping those who would kill us" . . .

Luckily none of these *Gutmenschen* are anywhere in sight at the moment. The man steps to the side of the boy, blocking him. He points at the target and winks the signal. Fumblingly, yet quickly, the child crams the candy tube into the big sweatshirt pocket. He's done it! It's a success, it's in there . . . no mistakes, no creeping eyes of skeletal Puritans . . . It's in. They walk casually together to the counter, pay for the pencils, and exit. The early summer air bathes their faces. The eyes of the younger member of the duo are shining, the eyes of the elder display hinted pride. To the world the act is nothing, or silly, or odd, or most likely, utterly condemnable . . . a moral failure on the part of a despicable father . . . To the man, though, it is something else – a test, a beginning. It is completely laudable, an act that few can understand. There are no moral phenomena, one must remember, only moral interpretation of phenomena.

At their home, drinking milk in celebration, they cheer the boy's accomplishment and relive it in detail. Mercury is the god of theft and commerce and children, the man tells the boy, and there's a reason for this . . . but that lesson can wait a bit . . . For now, what to do with this horrible thing that passes for food? Neither needs it, neither wants it, so how can it truly be beneficial to them?

Everything must be a weapon. Every situation must be turned to an advantage. So it is decided that on Monday the boy will give the candy – with its vitality-stealing ingredients, its bone decaying sugar, its toxic dyes – to a bratty kid at his daycare who tattles a lot.

∗   ∗   ∗   ∗

Something called Independence Day comes. Together the man and the boy fly on an airplane back to the megalopolis they'd escaped. The boy is ecstatic, a caricature, laughing, pointing, bubbling, amazed that he's actually *sailing in the air*. They land in the city, there to visit the womenfolk. There is great happiness and excitement. Both of them lovingly kiss the little girl and both slowly, carefully, run their hands over the woman's stomach. In there yet another child forms, being put together as perfectly and methodically as the Northern house.

After a few days, however, the man soon remembers the reasons he fled Los Angeles, and begins to dream of his distant mountains.

∗   ∗   ∗   ∗

Upon their return to the Rockies he attempts to rid his mind of the tsunami they've just left behind . . . the buzzing of electrical wires, the honks, the steel, the sirens, the *herpeta*, the graffiti, the pollution, the heat, the asphalt, the eternal crowd, *die viel zu viele* . . . Tranquility soon returns. Yet even in his eyrie, even back among his aspens and firs, even here in the presumed silence, rumbling jets cross high overhead. Some leave weird trails etched on the sky, never dissipating, only stretching into something resembling clouds in the same way the country he lives in resembles a nation . . . reminding him once again of what he realized back in Portland – that there really is no escape anymore . . . that to

177

believe in the possibility of geographical flight from this overcrowded robot world is delusional . . . that an era cannot be fled from . . .

Still, this place is all he has, all they have, for now. In the forest there is at least occasional quiet. There are still numbing blue lakes and the soothing screes of hawks and the nests of ospreys and the warbles of cranes and the wind punching down pinecones and the sun-stored warmth of boulders not yet ripped from the earth and turned into countertops. The unseen voles dig their tunnels, the ducks wing along the rivers, and even if some of the streams gurgling by are polluted from various sources, he can ignore them. He was right to move his family here. It's the closest they'll get to Arcadia in America – but it won't last. The natural world's been wrested away from them, and everywhere it's being turned against them. Thoreau, Löns, Giono, Williamson, Leopold, Jeffers, Carson, Abbey, Shepard, Hardin, Wilson – all knew it, all said it, but no one ever listens, no one seems to even have the ability to hear. Why must it always be about what's wrong? When will something finally be *right*? If a single stream is dirty and polluted then the whole social system is dirty and polluted . . . and if the whole social system is dirty and polluted then the people who run it, those who have the power, are as well . . . and if they're dirty and polluted then the governed are at fault for allowing such people to be where they are and do what they do, and if the governed don't care about any of it then they're dirty and polluted too and have nothing to complain about when only dirty, polluted water remains . . . When will this be understood? How many prophets must appear on earth, tearing their beards and screaming from cliffs and saying the same thing, over and over? How many must scream raw-throated until things are finally fixed?

Near their half-built house the man and the boy hike upward, onward, feeling the joy of exertion in their lungs and thighs. The man allows the scent of pines to transport him back to youth, back to the California woods that were destined to become a playground. The boy unknowingly locks the smell away somewhere in epithelial folds for the distant day when he'll do the same. They surprise a fox trotting along the path, a headless squirrel in its moistened mouth. Contrary to library book assertions, the bloody-mouthed predator and decapitated prey were never chums.

They climb and climb and finally reach the top of the mountain they've been assailing. The afternoon light trembles on the waves of a distant lake and the cleansing hint of an early autumn wafts on the breeze, pinching the ears, the eyelids, the brow. The man inhales, fills his lungs, allows them to expand and press comfortably against the inside of his chest. Standing atop a boulder, he spreads his arms, tilts his head back, imbibes. The boy follows suit, and there they stand, the one, the other . . . living statues, carved by Praxilites, by Donato, by Clodt, by Claudel, by their unmentionable heirs . . . carved by mutation and isolation and struggle . . . In the valley far below them the evergreens and chokecherries and mountain ash stand firm, the seemingly devastating forest fire of years before having only temporarily purged them in order to form new, healthier growth.

The resurgence of life after devastation – this is the man's deepest desire.

*   *   *   *

He is so alone in the quest to fulfill the *geasa* that have been laid on him by the future, the obligation to gather and the corresponding proscription against succumbing to despair during his attempt to do so. Regardless of his fantastic natural surroundings, great weariness, frustration, and sadness are his lot most days, particularly when realizing the ubiquity of the forces opposing him. At the playground he observes how older children inspire the boy, lift him up, force him to make leaps of intellect as much as they do leaps from monkey bars. Naturally the desire to emulate and to compete motivates the child. These hardwired tendencies are meant to spur growth. Without their expression the development of the organism is stunted. Without all ages surrounding a youth, without kin at every turn, the maturation process is slower, as clearly demonstrated in atomized modern America, a place where millions of people display an unsavory puerility that would have been completely foreign to their Old World ancestors of the previous century.

The awareness of this breeds bitterness in the man. He knows he cannot give his child a tribe at this most crucial stage of development, knows that he can't link arms with anyone here, knows that his desperate attempt to stand in as *túath* has been knocked to earth by reality. He cannot be his son's primary comrade. The physical competition the boy craves cannot always be with a middle-aged man. Certainly it is instructive to race or wrestle with one's father, but doing so with other boys, both older and younger, impacts a hundred times more. The dilemma, as always, is the paucity of available material. Sure, the occasional footrace or game of tag takes place between children, but outside of the Aztec boy, who is visiting his grandparents' village in Mexico, there are no boys who are even *allowed* to come into contact with each other, let alone wrestle or box. The playground parents frown at displays of physical interaction, and whenever a hint of contact presents itself their intrusion is instantaneous.

The man watches as his boy hurtles by, rushing demon-like to the slide. Another boy, racing in the same direction, accidentally brushes against him *en route*. Down swoops the mother, stopping her son's progress, exhorting him to say, "Excuse me," for something so trifling as to be barely noticed. It's relentless. Everywhere the man turns he sees the offspring of the well-mannered being turned into cripples. The more he studies these parents and the various ways in which they squelch the *élan vital* of youth, the more it becomes apparent that the suppression of their sons' natural urges to grapple and jostle is simply social adherence to the commandment they've been issued: "Thou shall not offend." Confrontation avoidance is what lies at the heart of it all. It's the cornerstone of their ethos, much as it once was with the Alacaluf . . . and though these playground parents have almost surely adopted this principle as some form of adaptation to a global society where they're supposed to work quietly, keep out of sight, and go away, there are no long-term benefits to it . . . The very basis of survival is predicated on confrontation, be it with the elements, the terrain, beasts, or other tribes. Whatever tries to avoid confrontation for too long soon disappears.

These people, however, are an order-following breed, and their current orders are to not offend, ever. Any potential conflict, therefore, is to be avoided or minimized. This has been temporarily accomplished not only by stopping all physical contact between their children and others but also by universalizing their previously beneficial system of manners. "Please." "Thank you." "Sorry." "Excuse me." They use these words and phrases to prove they're not a threat, that they mean no harm. Their manners served a different purpose at one point . . . acknowledgement of altruistic kin behavior through verbal reciprocity, enabling a better chance at survival in harsh climes, perhaps . . . but now that there are no tribal boundaries to their use, they often just come across as ridiculous . . .

Near the bench where he sits, the man hears an overweight woman say, "Thank you," to some balding man for some minor act. The balding man replies not with the traditional "You're welcome," but merely repeats her words back to her. "Thank *you*," he says, earnestly, thanking the woman for — saying thank you? It seems so. Preposterous. Everything about these people has become preposterous.

The man's gaze continues to sweep the playground. The boy is at the slide again. It is the nexus. It is here that all children and admonitory voices eventually converge. To the well-mannered adults of the mountain town the only acceptable way up the slide is the ladder, and any attempt at a different approach is immediately thwarted.

"Ah ah ah, that's not how we do it, Tyler."

"Don't walk up the slide. Go the right way. Say 'excuse me'."

"Please use the ladder, dear!"

"We don't climb backwards, Dakota."

Conformists in all the wrong ways, conformists to the point of death . . . straining to defeat plasticity, vibrancy, and movement . . . If life is to ever reassert itself throughout the nation these children must climb up the slide a thousand ways. They must rise to the top, crest the summit any way they can; running, crawling, stretching, grasping, pulling, heaving, screaming or silent, shoving or leaping, barreling or maneuvering, they must just rise, rise, get there, and never pay attention to those reedy voices of the previous generation, those fifty tones of *moralizing*, those millions of whispered asides.

These rules of theirs have long proved suicidal. They must be forgotten.

*   *   *   *

The glorious summer stretches and glows. The man works, the boy goes to his daycare, and in between their time is spent together. One afternoon they build toy boats. The man paints his red, the color of the sun sinking in the west. The boy paints his blue, the color of the all-encompassing sky. On the sails are drawn the *sigilia*: the diamond for power, the sky-pointing arrow for justice. Shattered symbols will reenter the world through youth.

A desperate race takes place at the pond, the man's red "Power" against the boy's blue "Justice". Propelled by puffed breaths the boats wobble, they list, but move forward nevertheless, somehow wending through the ripples of the muddy water. The man's boat wins. The boy does not sulk. He smiles and cheers, thrilling to the action more than the results . . . a boat race to him, that is all . . . the inevitable questions follow . . .

"What must come first, son, power or justice?"

He thinks of what he's just seen take place before him.

"Power."

"Why?"

"Umm . . ." No reply. Confusion. "Because . . ." Desire to please, but unsure what the answer is . . . unsure, really, what the question itself means . . .

The man answers for him. "Because a people can never obtain justice without having power. Any little bit of justice they *do* receive, tossed like a scrap from the master's table, is given them by others. Others who have—"

"Power."

"Right."

"What is power, dad?"

The man thinks. And thinks. And answers.

"Possessing and wielding enough group strength to ensure you're not enslaved by other groups."

*   *   *   *

A dead dog lies on the side of the road, hit by a car. The man stops his vehicle and he and the boy climb out to observe the carcass. They look at the blood pooled on the asphalt and thickening on the animal's face. It is important that the child see it. It helps separate him from the cake-eaters and the well-mannered, those who never set eyes on blood any more . . . those whose meat is presented to them in irradiated slices sandwiched between Styrofoam and plastic wrap . . . those who've never slit a bull's artery or taken a hatchet to a chicken's neck . . . It separates him from those moderns who pretend that the violence necessary for the continuation of their lives does not exist.

Many years before, while in the labyrinth, the man made his way through India. One day, through the dirty window of a shop, he noticed a painting for sale . . . a long-ago battle between Muslims and Rajputs, between the rising strength of a new religion and the waning strength of a decadent race . . . In brilliant colors, scimitars sliced through limbs, sharp lances pierced bodies, decapitated heads littered the ground, and warriors ensconced in canopied howdahs looked down upon enemies trampled beneath the feet of their elephants. Yet despite all the carnage there was no blood to be seen in the painting. Curious, the man asked the Hindu merchant why this was so.

The answer was simple. The Westerners who made their way to the desert cities of Rajasthan, those who bought such paintings, no longer wished to see blood. It didn't matter if they were staying in bedbug-ridden hostels or expensive international hotels. It didn't matter if they carried dusty backpacks or had leather luggage toted by bellhops. *No blood* – in this the travelers from the West stood in unison. So, adapting to his customers' psychological changes, the merchant made a simple decision, and the red disappeared from hacked-off arms and headless necks.

Such indicators are relevant beyond business applications. Repugnance at the sight of the life force itself is surely a sign of exhaustion . . . of withdrawal from existence . . . and so the man stands next to his small boy on the side of a country road, staring down at a broken mongrel's bloodied muzzle, helping his child to avoid the same fate as these others . . .

Gently, the boy squeezes his father's hand. "Everything dies, right, dad?"

The man nods. "Everything that lives will die. Death comes from the sky or the forest or down the road to take whomever it chooses, whenever it will. Individuals can't counter it. That's their destiny, as mortals." He points at the tattered corpse. "But that right there is only a single dog that's been killed. A dog is dead – dogs themselves are not dead. Only in the species can we approach immortality."

The boy remains silent, staring, then turns his head up.

"Dad, why do cars kill all the animals?" Over the course of the spring and summer, they'd witnessed a funereal collection of furred and feathered corpses littering the roads . . . foxes and crows, raccoons and cats, even a smallish elk . . .

"Well..." He hesitates, unsure how to answer... unsure how to make the boy understand that mass eradication is the logical outcome of technology and industry not held in check by a prudent hand ... unsure how to make him grasp that, unfettered, these two together are destroying not just the wildlife he's witnessed dead these past months, but those ill-equipped creator people who indiscriminately foisted them on the world ...

He's saved from giving an answer, though. The boy, still looking down at the corpse, says, "You said animals could communicate. That dog's dad should have told him to pay attention crossing the road. He should have told him stories about how dangerous it is."

How does he tell him? How does he explain that such a thing would have done no good? Even their own species, those absurd apes with flappable tongues to pass down tales and opposable thumbs to record the wisdom of their ancestors – even they don't listen to warnings. Those thousands of beard-tearing prophets on the cliffs and those millions of instructive pages from the past might as well never have existed. All those cautionary words, all that insightful counsel, and still the young of the species have writhed under the wheels of chariots, had their hearts stabbed with iron blades, their throats pierced by crossbow bolts, their bodies sprayed with hollow-tipped bullets, their cities put to flames by machines sailing in the sky. Nothing ever seems to work.

"The dog knew how dangerous the road was, son. But he crossed it anyway. Maybe he had to."

*   *   *   *

The man is deep in thought as they eat their supper. He vacantly stares out the window at the blue spruce trees under the blue sky, thinking of the missing half of his family ... of the new baby within the woman ... of the dead dog and of the seemingly inevitable doom that awaits them all because of their inability to put sound advice into practice ... His gloomy reverie is interrupted by his son across the table.

"Dad, I like diamonds," he says, smiling.

The man frowns. Where's the boy even heard of diamonds? The daycare lady? Some parent? This is just one of the hundred reasons it seems they can't escape the cycle of pointless self-destruction – the lust for ridiculous baubles and trinkets, for collecting shiny gewgaws like a fox or a crow. True, this lust is merely a desire to display higher social status, but it's a pitiful society where one's position can be implied by possession of an insignificant rock. It's certainly been an odd course of historical development when a collection of gauche entertainment stars and moon-eyed brides-to-be support an unsavory network of diamond traders, diamond cutters, diamond appraisers, diamond retailers, and diamond advertisers . . . men who have, in their bid to enrich themselves, enflamed a childish desire among the masses, leaving nothing but broken laborers and an eviscerated earth in their wake . . .

The capitalists who hawk and supply such things can't share sole responsibility for the damage, though. No, from their first appearance on the globe, they have been *enabled*. The world's pasty consumers have always blithely fed that which enslaves and destroys. Even today they've learned nothing from their whipped up lust for heron feathers, ostrich plumes, alligator shoes, beaver hats, mink coats, and pearl necklaces. They've learned nothing from their poisoned landscapes, their depleted oceans and forests, their polluted water and rancid food and mortgage debt. It must be recognized as an immutable characteristic of theirs, the fact that they either *cannot* learn from their previous actions or that they do not care to, and the resolute men and women of the future must take this into account in their dealings with such types . . . and when these resolute men and women of the future do arrive – when the man somehow manages to fulfill his *geis* and gathers and sows the seeds – sparkly rocks won't designate status among their kind . . . the amount of time spent in the rain will . . . the health of one's family will . . . Diamond rings will be replaced by iron bands, and iron bands will be replaced by naked fists.

But for now he must deal with this grasping consumer world wrapping its tentacles around his child, already sleazily reaching into his young consciousness. Gently he covers the boy's hand with his own. "Diamonds look pretty, son, and I can see why you might like them. You should know, though, that every one is soaked in blood. Not just a few diamonds, like some people claim – all of them. It doesn't matter if they come from Russia or Australia or Africa or anywhere else, our family has nothing to do with them. They should be a mark to you, whenever you see them on someone, that you've encountered an enemy. Okay?"

From across the table the boy shifts and swallows. His smile has vanished. He is perplexed, sensing reproof in his father's words, but unsure why it's there. Carefully he replies. "But . . . you painted a diamond on your sail."

The man pauses. Ever so slowly it dawns on him. The boy's not talking about the *gem*—

"Are squares okay to like, dad? Are they?" the child tentatively asks.

—but the *shape*. The *shape*.

The foolish man, separated from adult companionship for too long, internally groans, then bursts into laughter . . . rises from his chair, smothers his son with kisses . . .

Every once in a while, all perspective is lost.

The boy is three. The man must remember that.

He is only three.

∗   ∗   ∗   ∗

The man lies awake in bed. Sleep is unable to come. Three years old, that's all the child is, still half a year from four. He's brand new at life. Is it too much for him, his father's incessant indoctrination? Constant talk of enemies encircling and threatening is beneficial for groups, uniting them, but the child is not a group. He is a small boy, alone, with not even a mother currently.

Brand new at life, just now tasting it, and yet already his games are ones of death. The pair play at it together, pretend battles with war cries and wooden swords . . . Zama, Teutoburger Wald, Lepanto . . . The man dies, the boy dies, and always they return to life, a dusting off, a rising to their feet, only to begin all over again. Their foes are always conquered, the numbers or caliber never matter. No fortress is impregnable, no army can withstand them. When shackled they escape, when enslaved they kill their captors, and never do they not ultimately stand in triumph.

Yet the man knows that someday the childish games have to end. Slowly, over the coming years of the boy's youth, he'll have to reveal the whole truth . . . that their triumphs have been few, their victories singular . . . that even those mean nothing anymore . . . that all their ridiculous wars have been but battles in a wider war that they never understood until too late, a genetic one, and now they've been driven over the edge of a precipice and lie broken in the dust . . .

Somehow, methodically, he must teach his son to take knowledge from these losses . . . to not fall into the same trap, to not slaughter indiscriminately, to identify his true enemy . . . He must teach him not to cross the road that the dead dog tried to cross.

And then? When all of this is taught, what then? Because this Leviathan that dominates them can crush with its breath . . . kill with its gaze . . . always on the lookout for the merest movement, the slightest whisper . . . scanning the ground for a worm to lift its head . . . What good is training and perfecting his body when whistling bombs destroy whole populations of cities and nations? What good is teaching him love of beauty when ugliness has nearly obliterated it? What good is pointing out to him injustice when injustice seems impossible to remedy? What good is honing his character and mind when there are no others to join these with? What good is telling him about his tribe when he has no tribe? *What good is pretending?*

*   *   *   *

The man awakens the next morning with heavy eyes and heavy heart.

He forces himself to climb from bed . . . lets the rising sun shine on his face as he let it shine on his baby son's years before in that Los Angeles hospital . . . He attempts to rid himself of the strangling depression. The seeming futility of actions in the present, of the role of the individual in the struggle for group redemption, must be ignored if life is to be lived. There will be no change seen for generations, true, but the future still must be served, and mental and physical health is essential. He tells himself this over and over as he stretches, exercises, and allows the chemicals released by his body to relax him and lessen his angst. The many thoughts that drive him to despair will, he knows, never leave him, will wash over him in gray waves for the remainder of his years. He must not submit.

He goes downstairs and prepares breakfast, pouring large glasses of milk for the two of them. One loss they've suffered by moving to the mountains is the inability to legally procure the untouched milk they used to consume in California. While the section of the plutocracy that deals with pollution of water, soil, and atmosphere is remarkably cavalier about the sicknesses imposed on the citizenry by corporate transgressors, another section – that which deals with "public health" – is so concerned with people's well-being that it denies farmers permission to sell animal milk that hasn't been heated. Someone might get sick, the department warns, in the sickest land in history.

For millennia the boy's ancestors consumed cows' milk. From the unknown healers and pastoralists in the *Urheimat* all the way down to his own mother, they culturally and genetically adapted to it. It's a simple process – the soil and the sun feed the grass, the grass feeds the cow, and the cow feeds the man and the boy. They want no pasteurization, which destroys the life-enhancing antibodies and the enzymes. They want no homogenization, which steals the milk's lush cream. They want, simply, milk. So, through whispers and queries when they first arrived in the mountain town, the man eventually discovered a renegade farmer in a nearby valley who kept clean stables and pastured his Guernsey cows, allowing them sun-warmed grass most of the year and root vegetables and hay in the winter. Bags of oats are swapped by the farmer's customers for gleaming jars of milk, plucked weekly from the communal refrigerator.

The boy has drunk untouched milk since his weaning. He will continue to drink it until it's finally, logically, eliminated by those who despise health in their subjects. He is strong, bright-eyed, and vigorous. His teeth are straight, his hair is soft, his skin is smooth and pink. Compared to other children he is like a Deva alongside Asuras. Everything put into his body is meant to elevate, not degrade. He eats eggs from chickens that have never been injected with hormones, that live normal lives roaming barnyards and gobbling insects from the leaves of plants that have never been doused in pesticides. Their yolks are globular and orange, bursting with vitality and nutrition. They're scrambled in a pan in thick, healthy butter. They're salted not with the sickening powdery substance proffered the proles, but with the fruit of the sea, born of the waves, dried in the sun, delicious and fortifying. Salmon and huckleberries, bison and sauerkraut, venison and beets, broth and porridge and raw honey and apple cider vinegar and coarse black bread – all these are part of his diet. Cod liver oil, one of many discarded treasures of the past, is spooned into his mouth frequently, the screwed-up expression on his face almost a cliché.

The man's generation is one of the first to fully suffer from the experiments of capitalists working hand-in-hand with government and mass media, all bearing down on an uneducated populace. The deleterious effects are apparent walking through any town, any city, any hamlet. The shores of the West are awash with human debris. Is a return to cod liver oil – with its benefits for the brain, the eyes and the nervous system – a panacea? No. The goal is to preserve what has value and to let the rest rot away around them.

✳   ✳   ✳   ✳

Summer fades. The yellow hair of the boy turns darker as the sun heads further south. His mother and sister finally return. The girl is taller, the woman's stomach rounder. There is great happiness in the family . . . for being together once again . . . for the coming child . . . In various nondescript buildings around the world policies are being formulated to push them off of the earth. They can do nothing to stop this.

∗   ∗   ∗   ∗

Halloween is on the way, yet another meaningless holiday, the only type permitted the helots of the Occident. Desiring nothing more than boorish revelry, such mindlessness is fine for the masses, but it is no longer adequate for the aware. There must be relevance, something that goes beyond buying tacky decorations at a drugstore or watching a favorite show on television. Holidays must metaphysically become holy days, the *levitas* balanced by *gravitas*, the capitalist exploitation ended, the juvenility expunged.

It is the same concern he had years before, the question of how to create such occasions. Trying to search for something other than vapid consumerism leads one only to the previously more somber Christian holidays – All Saints Day, Christmas, St. Valentine's Day, Easter. Digging deeper one is able to reach the sacred days of the pagan world the Christian conquerors built upon. Many stop there, believing that greater significance is to be found in indigenous customs than in the alien ones that usurped them. This might be true, but because everything is colored by postmodernism, any attempt made to resuscitate these native traditions and feast days simply offers the world the spectacle of the modern shaman, the Wiccan, the difference for difference's sake, the dressing up in skins and the drinking from goblets and the dancing at Stonehenge on the solstice. The elevation of non-essentials and the trappings of nothingness are to be found everywhere, seeming just as insane as the rites previously instituted by those who believed that a human could walk on water or return from the dead.

Much as he appreciates the early pagan holy days, they were clearly inadequately constructed to withstand the Christian onslaught. To celebrate them once again in some theatrical approximation of what they might have been is pointless posturing. The truth is that his ancestors failed to note the necessity of conscious adaptation of holy days to biological reality, choosing instead the object over the subject. A harvest by itself means nothing – it feeds a specific group, that's where its merit lies. Seasonal changes and equinoxes take place regardless if humans walk the earth – the celebration should be for the *particular people* experiencing them. Thumbing noses at the might of the coming winter is great fun, but the survival of the clan itself is the reality on which the festival – all festivals – should be based. Therefore it isn't merely a question of restoring these former holy days, but of refurbishing them. They need to be tribalized, specified, and justified. In order that continuity can be ensured in a constantly shifting world, new meaning must be infused into the old, meshing where possible, retaining when needed, discarding when necessary.

On paper it's easy. They are one people. They are unique. They are historical. They've shared oppression and they've shared triumph. There should be feasting and fasting, there should be symbolism and meaning in everything related to a holy day. Each sacred occasion should be a reminder of duty, where bonds are strengthened and resolve renewed, with both youth and the mature sharing the pain of the past and the promise of the future.

Looked at this way – an unreal, academic way – the task is simple. Of course, in reality, there is no "one people" any longer, only an unconnected global collection of superior individuals. For the restoration and refurbishment of these holidays a certain lack of self-awareness is called for, yet this is impossible to expect among those who, by their very nature and position, have become the *most* aware.

Resurgence can never come about without community, and a community needs shared traditions, and since there are no shared traditions remaining that have value, they must be created, but in order to be created, a community is necessary. Once more he encounters this eternal loop that offers no solution, only dismay and resignation. It is depressing. Something has to be done, though. The man knows that *something has to be done.* Ritual springs from necessity. All tradition began somewhere, began in response to something. He cannot quail.

*   *   *   *

His experiment is put into motion nine nights before Samhain – that's what they'll call the holiday, the old name. Nine is chosen for the same reasons he chose it when he first attempted such things, back during the boy's baptism. The number, like the holiday, once had meaning to them, there's no reason to believe that it can't again. Nine nights before Samhain – the time for carving the pumpkins, New World crops for an Old World people. The man sticks in the knife, slicing open from the top, always counterclockwise for some reason to be figured out when he has more time, maybe something to do with the path of the sun or the migration across the ocean. The innards of the gourds are removed – the family is stealing the brains of their enemies, he tells the children, leaving them immobilized. With enough force this can be done – the proof is in the inert citizenry around them. When the intellect of adversaries has been taken away they are always left powerless.

The children laugh as the brains squish between their fingers. The seeds are separated from the pulp, washed, baked, sprinkled with salt made from the seas their ancestors once crossed, sometimes as conquerors, more often as refugees. Next the carving begins, turning the pumpkins into representations of those who would destroy them, those who've enslaved them . . . representations, specific or general, of the enemies of the *túath* . . . a minister, a commissar, a traitor . . . the names of these criminal *herpeta* are known only to the coming families . . .

Thus carved, the pumpkins have been transformed into *morcaputen*, death heads. They sit on the porch, the windowsill, the stoop, anywhere, one for each adult and child in the family. For the present their people will blend, like their *morcaputen* do with the jack-o-lanterns of Halloween, no outward difference. Only among themselves will the truth be known of how widely separated they are from these others.

✳   ✳   ✳   ✳

Some days after the carving, the preschool woman tells the man that the young Aztec struck his son in the head with a lunchbox that afternoon, making him cry. She offers bourgeois reassurance – the boy "did the right thing" by not hitting back. The man nods his head, smiles, takes the boy to the car and straps him into his seat. Silently he drives to the post office. The sky is gray, the green of the pines fresh and dark.

"Why didn't you hit him back?" he asks.

The boy, visible in the mirror, fidgets. His cheeks are flushed.

"Because Ms. Blanc said hitting back isn't nice."

The reaction of the man is dramatic. The vehicle brakes, the arm is flung over the back of the seat, the head whips around. Fanatical eyes blaze at the thought of enemy values – *victim* values – making their way into the body of his family.

"Ms. Blanc is an egalitarian! Those are the words of an egalitarian, a Christian! Are you any of those things?"

"No."

"Is your family?"

"No."

"Do we subscribe to the most insane ideals the world's ever come up with? Do we *ever* believe what egalitarians say, what *herpeta* say?"

"No."

"What should you have done?"

"Hit him."

"Yes! And harder than he hit you! We are forced to come into contact with all the peoples of the earth, still vibrant peoples, strong, and they will hit you again and again and again until you strike back!"

There is silence. Outside the windows the October winds whistle. Leaves tumble down the street. Tension begins to thin, and the man and the boy discuss what to do.

The next day, when no one is looking, the boy punches the older Aztec boy in the face with a clenched fist. An observer would say he was unprovoked, but when humans no longer suffer from myopia or ahistoricity, such terms become meaningless. There is justification for everything. Everyone can be blamed for some past transgression. The only ultimate truth is force. The Aztec boy cries, and the man is later informed by Ms. Blanc that his son acted inappropriately that morning. He disapprovingly shakes his head and admonishes the boy in front of her – just as he earlier told him he would do. Once within the privacy of the vehicle the boy is praised, his hair tousled, his cheek caressed. The man explains, again, that enemies like Ms. Blanc can always be lied to, that to tell the total truth is a detriment to their own survival, that it threatens their very existence. Lying is a weapon, like all things are if need be. That is what the world has taught them.

At home the child is allowed a warm mug of apple cider after supper. He sits nestled in his father's lap, listening as the man tells him that the replaceable bourgeoisie – the overly mannered confrontation-avoiders – believe that their children are never, *never* to strike first, that they're rarely allowed even to retaliate. Such a precept is useless within a global society . . . a belief as dispensable as those who preach it . . .

"Their ways are not our ways, boy." The man puts the empty mug on the table beside him and turns his son around so that their eyes stare at one another. "They'll never be our ways again."

*   *   *   *

Samhain arrives the day after the first flurries of the winter. The questions are many still. They nag. They bite. How can any holy day linked to the seasons of the North, linked to the extant solar calendar of the Christians, have any meaning to a people spread around the earth – because if they exist at all, they *are* scattered over the earth. It is one unresolved question among many. It gives the man no peace, pulling on his sleeve, whispering in his ear. There is always too little time to apply the necessary thought. Where are his committees, his *minyanim*, his quorums, his *curiae*?

The visages on the *morcaputen* are wrinkling. They sag like old flesh, the candles within making the hollows of the eyes flicker and waver. They've been lit each night at the setting of the sun, now tonight the candles will be removed, their flames used to ignite the bonfire at the sign of the first star. The arrival of rain or snow won't change the ceremony. The wood has long been dried, now it is properly arranged . . . the arrow, the justice *sigil*, sits atop the diamond shape, representing power . . . The pile is small, like their *túath*, but is the foundation of something bigger. The candles are finally taken from the death heads, and the bonfire flame is kindled, blown, watched. It wisps and flares. Under the darkening sky the *morcaputen* are smashed on the ground, broken into pieces. The Latin command is given – "Leave this earth." Once, twice, again, again – four *morcaputen*, next year there will be five, a growing family, a beautiful image. The chunks of pumpkin are gathered, hurled into the flame, yellow and orange and gray with smoke. One can imagine, for only a second, that this smoke links with other tendrils somewhere . . . links with the embers of others who are hiding, waiting, biding their time . . .

Hand in hand the man and the boy leap over the fire, earth to air to earth. The womenfolk follow suit. What is the meaning? What is the relevance? All this must be thought out, explained, performed without self-consciousness. There is joy, true. It is great fun. Yet there is the feel of novelty, not Dionysian abandonment.

They return to the house. For the past nine days work has gone into the disguises, called "costumes" by the profane. Why do the boy and his sister wear them? Together they make themselves comfortable in the man's arms as he tells them a tale.

*   *   *   *

"Once upon a time, in the Twilight Lands, there were three boys who were neighbors. Each lived with his mother and father and brother and sister.

"The first boy was very selfish and nasty. He told everyone that he had nothing in common with his family, or with anyone else in the whole world for that matter. He was an *individual,* completely different from his sister, his brother, and his cousins. He had to worry only about himself, he said. This boy had a whole shelf of books that his parents had bought him, all of which agreed with him, reinforcing his belief that he was indeed unique in the world and that there was no one else like him at all. When he became a man he amassed great power and became a mighty industrialist and controlled all sorts of things.

"The second boy was very soft and mushy and cruel. He told everyone that he was no different from any other boy or girl. He was just the same as a child from the jungle, or from the desert, or from the taiga, and so were his sister, his brother, and his cousins. There was no difference between any of them, he said. This boy had a whole shelf of books that his parents had bought him, all of which agreed with him, reinforcing his belief that he was indeed no different than any other child in the world. When he became a man he amassed great power and became a mighty leader of workers and controlled all sorts of things.

"The third boy was strong and silent. He thought that he was different than other boys and girls from the jungle or the desert or the taiga. He said that he was most like his sister, his brother, and his cousins. He had no books on his shelf that agreed with him because there were no books made that agreed with him. But he did have stories in his breast given him by his father and mother and aunts and uncles.

"When the third boy became a man he amassed no power, yet he did mighty things. He could create music and run like a deer. He could carve images from stone and compose beautiful poems. He could build boats and climb mountains and pull fish from the waters and bring forth grain and fruit from the earth. He was accomplished in all arts and in all sciences and made a splendid life for himself and the people around him.

"The first boy and the second boy – adults, now – did not like this. Though outwardly very different from each other, they were of one accord when it came to their views of the third boy. Both agreed that there should be no man swimming in rivers and singing songs and picking apples for his family – that all men should be working, working, working their whole lives long, not for themselves and their own families, but for others. Men, they agreed, should be working for *them*. Therefore the two decided to hunt and kill the third boy and his sister and his brother and his cousins and his father and mother and aunts and uncles, as it would never do for the other men they controlled to think and act as he and his family did.

"When he heard of this plan, the third boy – also an adult now – warned his family. He realized that he was wrong to have been silent in his youth, and wrong not to amass power, for now the minions of those others sought to destroy him. Knowing that he could not withstand this, knowing that he and his family were too weak, he had them disguise themselves. They forced themselves to blend in with others; they projected false images of who they really were. And though they could have easily surrendered to the hunters and lived their lives in the prescribed fashion, they chose instead to retain their identity, for they did not wish to become like those others. Therefore they had to *be*, but to not *appear* to be. They became a hidden people, always conscious of who they were, and always working toward the day when they no longer had to wear their disguises to survive."

∗   ∗   ∗   ∗

The man takes the children trick-or-treating, walking among the costumed throngs out celebrating their shallow holiday. A great time is had by the boy and his sister – the evening out in the neighborhood is a success as far as they're concerned. Yet with the most hollow of feelings in his breast, their father accepts that he is failing in creating meaningful holy days. Blending in? Disguising themselves among the world's crowds? Trick-or-treating doesn't even exist in most countries. The concept of hiding, of moving through the public as one of them, even as you're not one of them, is a fine one, sure. But to gain something from it, to strengthen a family by it, to recreate a people through it, to lend historical relevance to it – these seem impossible.

He empties the collected corporate candy from the pillowcases, preparing to replace it with items that aren't poisonous to the children's health. The kids squeal in anticipation – and that seems to be the extent of the holiday's effect. Adults can garner no deeper meaning from it because there is no deeper meaning. Quasi-mystical talk of linking smoke in the skies on the night of something zombie-fearing primitives called "Samhain" will not be viewed as prophetic or essential by his growing children, but as eccentric, to be laughed off and discarded as they sink into the magma of the all-devouring world. It is all so discouraging. It all feels so cutesy, pushing him into the camp of the hippies, the hobbit people, the rune guilds, the dungeon masters, the magicians, the dreamers, the silly believers in a "collective unconscious" and a fearful Odin tucked away into the recesses of every Christianized soul. He must offer his children something, *something*, but the concrete confines of reality do not allow him the necessary freedom of spirit. His scientific materialism, his *historicism* – they don't allow him to breathe . . . and so the stomach stays knotted and all the problems remain . . .

✳   ✳   ✳   ✳

Four weeks after the emotional failure of the Samhain venture, the family has grown. A second son arrives. Two boys and a girl – the starting point for the ideal Hindu family, yet still one daughter shy of Shammai's ruling for his people. It is bio-cultural norms like these that they lack. Can such edicts, such measures, simply be appropriated? Why create whole cloth when the answers lay there before him? The survival of the man's family and their descendants will have to be predicated on a pastiche culture, a plucking from here and a pasting to there. It's obvious, and there should be no sting in it – it's how every group functioned and formed in a world of finite solutions. When the dreidel was a mere German gambling game, it had no relevance. Adventitiously drawn into the Judaic fold over time, it became something more. The profane can be made sacred – unified determination lessens the self-consciousness of actual origins. He must simply take the Greco-Romano-Celto-Germano-Slavic, jettison all the superfluous cargo, and proceed, adding a bit of this and that along the way from those others who possessed viably tested and proven survival skills. The more families eager to seek an alternative to the emptiness of the current world, the more solid burgeoning traditions will become. If historical longevity is the only criterion for meaningful holy days then the task is, indeed, impossible, but belief and victory are able to impart equal validity, as they always have.

The weeks fly by. There is the baptism of the new baby, his welcoming into the fold, which is more important than any holiday or holy day the world can offer. There is the fourth anniversary of the birth of his first-born son. Before they know it Yuletide is nearly upon them. It will begin on the darkest night of the year, the longest night . . . twelve nights of celebration, family, goose, holly, logs, ivy, wassail, mead, mistletoe, games, ham, gifts, moral instruction, candles, songs, fire, remembrance of the dead, eggnog, tales . . . these can be worked with . . . All components rearranged, no longer merely revelry in the cold of the northern winter, no longer limited to celebration by only one half of the globe, no longer just for single families, but something more, something more, something more. Something for a few, and no one else . . . something personal, yet something to be shared . . . Diwali, Eid, Hannukah . . . the man wants what they have . . . wants *something*, where currently there is nothing . . .

In a flurry of cloth diapers and midnight squalls and excitement, the holy days arrive. The candles are lit every night, the newly composed Latin prayers uttered, the feasts consumed, the sparse gifts given. It is what it is. There is nothing profound. To seek depth in it would be to mimic those moderns the man mocks, those who find relevance and spirituality in everything from desert petroglyphs to collegiate sporting events to Asian cartoons. There is, instead, comfort . . . a bliss brought on by the food, the warmth, and the presence of the family . . . He realizes that, when all is said and done, this has to be enough for the time being.

* * * *

Throughout the cold of the winter the man continues his work on the house-to-be. The boy learns to ski, to ice skate. Now that the child's mother has returned, the man's desperation to spend extra time with him has lessened – more can be devoted to finishing the task at hand. Still, early mornings and evenings are theirs, and weekends as well. There is rudimentary instruction in mathematics, penmanship, phonics, drawing, and chess. Then there is preparation for that most efficient of languages, Latin.

Why does the man teach the boy the extinct tongue of the Romans? Is it for the same reasons as the homeschooling Galileans, who seek to understand it in order to lie to themselves not in one language, but two? Is it to be used as they use it: to ridicule those pagan leaders and philosophers who were smarter, nobler and – ultimately – weaker than they were?

Does the boy study Latin for the brilliance and clarity of its structure and the benefits it provides a spatial mind, a mathematical mind, a categorizing mind, a discerning mind? Or does he do so in order to understand and fully appreciate the lives and thoughts of those Roman overmen whose voices are still able to instruct millennia later? Or does he do so in order to never forget the mistakes made by these men?

Is he made to study the language in order to more clearly grasp the reality of antiquity, to be able to "see it as it was", per Herder? Is it to forge a link between *his* past and *his* present – not simply *the* past and *the* present? Why care about those – the man and the boy are subjective people after all, as are all robust *túatha*.

Is it to fully make clear the message that Rome is eternal – not the city, but the morals? Is it to fully make clear that Rome lives within them, that Rome is but the garden and the boy and his tiny tribe the seeds?

Yes. No. These are not the driving reasons. They are merely benefits. The boy is taught Latin because he no longer possesses a language of his own. Sold as the final commodity by the Anglo – and sold cheap – English has fulfilled the universalism-inspired dreams of Esperanto creators and spread throughout the world with mercantilism and seduction and war. To have as one's sole manner of communication the language spoken by every cosmopolitan on the globe is as incapacitating as a noose around the throat.

*   *   *   *

"The capitalists want to destroy Grasshopper Field."

Winter is ending. The snowpack is still deep, still thick and heavy, but the days are lengthening . . . the chill of the afternoons is less bitter . . . The man and the boy are out walking when a neighbor is encountered and the boy mouths these angry words to her. The neighbor dyes her hair with a chemical to make it blonde. She wears a diamond ring on each hand. Her daughter has a novelty name not rooted in anything at all. Her husband is a dullard, lacking passion, lacking curiosity. Their vacation house is enormous, approaching four thousand square feet. It is filled with the soulless American *things* Rilke spoke of, though the echoes sounding through the cavernous rooms make the place seem as hollow as the occupants' consumerist ideology.

The woman's been out for a jog with her daughter, who sits safely inside a device specifically designed for jogging parents with small children. A defined purpose for every item in existence, meaning and use for cans and can openers, pencils and pencil sharpeners, yet specific lives, *life itself*, has no purpose for these people, no point . . .

"What's that, sweetie?" she asks the boy, the puff puffs of air leaving her warm mouth and lungs for the chill without. She displays something like a smile, not really interested.

"The capitalists want to destroy Grasshopper Field. They destroy everything."

Grasshopper Field is the name of a small stretch of open area remaining within the boundaries of their mountain town. In the summer there are wrestling matches between the man and the boy. Magnifying glasses inspect spittlebugs and anthills while tiny Saracens do battle with tiny Franks near miniature Antiochs and Acres. Ground squirrels seek cover from raptors, garter snakes slide through the bent fescue grass near the tiny pond. The eponymous grasshoppers leap in bunches, insectoid arcs against the blue sky. Balls are kicked or thrown, broken branches do for sword or lance. At night, when lying on their backs lazily chewing on sharp sedge grass, the stars sweep the broad sky. The welkin is spectacular and soothing. Together the man and the boy hold hands and drift like Buddhists there in that tranquil bit of meadow.

In the winters the plot transforms itself, becoming some Northern Elysian dream. Children of a vanquished people create elaborate ramps, jumps for their sleds and saucers and pieces of cardboard. Speed and vertigo, thrill and collision, all act in collusion to jar the senses and heighten mundane existence.

It is a ridiculously small piece of earth, threatened like everywhere else. The man and the boy have named it Grasshopper Field, and it is special, as special as any ground can be in this centuries-long era of forced separation from the soil. It gives peace, excitement, and joy to the community. But these are intangibles, they cannot be measured, and so they might as well not exist. The field is to be turned into a swimming pool. It doesn't matter that another pool lies two hundred yards away. It doesn't matter that an enormous alpine lake is six minutes' walk away. What matters is the decision of the board of directors of the nearby condominiums. What matters is the board's consensus that a second swimming pool will enhance the value of the property and increase the allure of the unsold condominiums that are still on the market.

Swimming pools instead of ponds and fields . . . children's museums and playgrounds in lieu of communities . . . the constant seeking of comfort and ease by those who have forfeited their right to the true spoils of the earth . . . It's a theme playing out around the world. They don't fit in any more, these marauders. The forest is nothing but paper to them, the savannah nothing but a crust over oil. They are capitalists; they measure in fiscal quarters, not in generations of folk. They terrorize through banality, they shout progress as loudly as any deracinated hippie or sermonizing politician.

The woman with the dyed hair is forty years old. She has never once in her life heard any criticism of capitalism and its adherents' destruction of the world. She believes a swimming pool is superior to a pond in a field. A pool has chlorine to keep things clean – never mind what it does to her hair, her skin, and her health. A pool is fun for children – never mind that fatalities for them are built into its very design. She is indifferent, obtuse, and pampered. Her blandness, her acceptance – these are the things that grease the world's axis.

"Grasshopper what?" she asks the boy.

"Never mind," he says, glumly. Already he learns the barriers, not of speech, but of thought.

*   *   *   *

The house remains unfinished. Money is needed. A job offer comes from the other side of the continent. It is accepted. The lingering winter of the far North will be traded for the balmy breezes of the Carolinas for a time. So a plan is made. The woman and the new baby will head back East a week early to prepare for the family's four-month stay. The boy and his sister will have a brief visit with their Oma in California, a thousand miles distant, then be retrieved after the man wraps up business in their mountain town.

It's not easy, this rootlessness. Theirs is a life of chaos and movement. They are animals pushed to the margins of ecosystems . . . a *Völkerwanderung* without a *volk* . . . but the boy knows nothing of this . . . He is excited. California to him means his grandparents, means pieces of chicken roasted on the grill, means organic restaurant pizza eaten by the slice like an adult. It means wrestling on manicured lawns, visiting fantastic parks, and relaxation of the incessant rules laid down by the man. There are excursions to arouse curiosity, sandals instead of snow boots, fruit plucked from backyard trees, and throngs of noisy people always nearby, fulfilling his biological yearnings for a true tribe. Greatest of all is Balboa's ocean, with its gulls and waves, its sand and dolphins and memories. Truly the state was a blessed land once. Now it makes the ugly descent into barbaric hell. This is what happens when there is perpetual summer . . . thus went sunny Africa Vetus, breadbasket of the Empire . . . thus went Rome, thus went Byzantium . . . thus went, finally, Europa herself . . .

Yet in the boggy hell of the Golden State exist islands of make-believe, seemingly pure, seemingly safe . . . the suburbs . . . "ocean communities" . . . For six days the boy and his sister stay in one of these havens, comforted by the presence of their kin, enveloped by the protective womb of family. Like the safety of the enclave itself, though, all of this is also an illusion. During these times of dissolution, family more often promises betrayal than security.

Against the man's specific instructions, the grandparents bring the boy and girl to a church. His beautiful, untainted, unsullied children are gently led by the hands into the dismal halls of an anachronism . . . surrounded on all sides by cloying incense and genuflecting old women . . . surrounded by the babbling of maniacs and the myriad symbols of subjugation and submission . . . It's not enough that his parents have rubbed their own faces in soot . . . torn their eyes from their sockets and trampled on them . . . It's never enough. Instead these people, every generation, under whichever name they call themselves, under whichever guise they present themselves, must also attempt to yoke the following generations to their cherished death creeds. Instead of looking for an alternative, instead of assessing the situation at large, they continue to cling to what's passed its zenith. They continue to send their youth into battle with spears against men with machine guns.

Then, on top of it all, the grandparents attempt to keep the incident a secret. They don't even possess the courage of their convictions, acting like smugglers for an outlawed cult rather than followers of the most popular faith in the world. Centuries removed from its ghetto origin and the sect is still furtive, its devotees still sneak through dank catacombs with mildewed walls, hiding from the gazes of straight-jawed Romans.

The man comes down from the North to gather the children for the next leg of their journey. His mother greets him, earnest but stiff. Though they love each other, she knows a divide exists between them, has for a long time, but attributes it to something "modern", to something that "happens these days". She doesn't understand the evolutionary significance of the widening gulf. Tiny markers in history pass her by, enormous megaliths in history pass her by.

Later, after the meals and the chatting and the catching up, the boy – far more aware of the world around him than his grandparents think – tells his tale to the man in private . . . the children taken by their grandparents to the Galilean's church on Sunday . . . the weirdness of it all . . . the kneeling, the magic water, the creepy pictures of the bleeding Christ-figure on the walls . . . his blonde head even touched by a priest, one of those black-garbed *things* the man abhors with the fury and passion of Voltaire, of Nietzsche, of Lenin, of Media . . .

He listens to his son's recounting of the odd smuggling. Eventually his anger over the deceitful act diminishes. He becomes less livid than disgusted . . . more disappointed than dismayed . . . Why would his mother do this? It's simple – because such types have always done it. When the pagan Richard Burton died, his simpering wife had him buried as a Christian, buried according to the laws of a sect he'd loathed forever. At one time the man sympathized with her dilemma and her subsequent actions. She thought she was saving her beloved husband from the damnation of eternity. Such sympathy evaporates now that a similar backstabbing is happening in his own life.

He tucks the children in, feeling more alone than ever. Now he must struggle against not only the well-armed soldiers of the zeitgeist, he realizes, but his own mother and her perverse need to force her grandchildren into the same ideological shackles she herself wore – the ones that led inevitably to the metal shackles they locked around her father's ankles before carting him off to labor and die in Siberia. It's never crossed her mind that her ancestors' way of life has, like her own, condemned their descendants to torture, slavery, and eradication down the line . . . that the flimsy walls her folk erected as Christians are no protection against the hell that's been unleashed on them . . .

> *The fault is not in our stars,*
> *but in ourselves that we are underlings.*

De Vere's words say it all.

*   *   *   *

The man and the boy and the girl leave California behind.

During the long flight east, while the girl sleeps, the man tells the boy a story. It is about a Christian bishop named Elphegus who, once upon a time as a prisoner, tried to convert a rough tribe of invaders to his watery doctrine in the hope of not paying a ransom. For months this man lay in chains while his rude captors rolled sheep knuckles, ripped greasy flesh from bone, swallowed stolen wine, and sang rousing songs of murder and pillage and swords and vengeance and glory. When at last the chance was given him to buy his freedom, he refused to burden his fellow countrymen and Christians with the cost of the demanded ransom, hoping that the mercy and might of the Galilean alone would be enough to ensure his release from the pagans. Rather than raise the money he would rely on his tongue to set him free.

Perhaps the bishop spoke to his jailers of turning the other cheek. Or perhaps he was too astute to offer up that unpalatable tenet of his faith to the Vikings, and instead waxed rhapsodic over miraculous returns from the dead and the possibility of everlasting life for those who believed wholeheartedly in his god. Regardless of the actual words spoken there is no question as to the response of the raiders from the sea. Seeing that the silver they demanded was not going to be handed over, the disgruntled Norsemen dragged the bishop from his prison, hurled him to the ground in front of their comrades, and smashed him with stones and ox skulls and axe handles to make him reconsider.

What did the Christian do in response? Exactly what his religion commanded – through bleeding lips he asked his god to love these misguided men, and to forgive them. Then one of his recent converts walked up and split his head open, and the pagans left his corpse for the ravens to feast on. Soon afterward the neighboring Christians paid the amount of money the Norsemen originally asked for. Getting what they wanted, most of the pirates subsequently sailed away.

Now, did these war-like men respond in such a way because the message of Christianity was abhorrent to them, an alien faith which they knew would surely destroy them if they allowed it to infect them? Or did they take offense at the bishop's gospel of self-slavery not so much for its message, but for the artless way in which it was described, an offense to the ears of those who valued dexterous and poetic speech? Of course not. These vaunted Norse sea wolves, these slavers of their own kind, imprisoned and beat and killed the missionary because they were greedy and drunk and they wanted their shiny, sparkly Danegeld. That's all, nothing more . . . nothing farseeing, nothing lofty . . . They weren't noble or righteous. Their character wasn't particularly better than the Christian's whom they sent from the earth, a man who knew how to meet death just as bravely as they did.

But at least when their time to die *did* come, they weren't praying for their enemies.

In his heart, the man knows that it isn't Christianity he so abhors. Strip it of its fantastic elements, make it an in-group philosophy, toss the proselytizing overboard, ditch the meekness and the Eastern incense and the afterlife, draw up a code of honorable conduct and marriage laws, keep it within logical demographic boundaries, and it'd be okay. One could argue if such a thing would still be Christianity, but nevertheless the creed is, in the end, a concept like anything else . . . words to be accepted or rejected at will . . . At root, it's not Christianity that's the problem. It's Christians. And the problem today isn't even fully that they're Christians. It's that they're the same as everybody else.

*　　　　*　　　　*　　　　*

The world is blooming in the Southeast. Gentle zephyrs waft along the lemony scent of the magnolias and strum the boy's long lashes. The harshness of winter in the Rockies is behind them, though ahead lie months of labor for the man . . . imprisoned between office walls, beneath chemical ceilings . . . slowly sickening, like all First World moderns at work . . . hunched, toiling in a cave . . . Where the sun, where the sky, where the lemony scent of magnolias?

While his father works the boy spends his days with his mother and siblings. He continues to grow in stature and intellect. Reading has become a part of his life. He can focus on the chessboard long enough for a simple game. He climbs higher in trees. He sprints faster across fields. His laugh becomes louder. An aura of loveliness shines from him. He is bright. He is confident. Like the world around him, he, too, is fresh and blooming. It is the same with all things in their state of becoming, whether rose or boy or nation.

Near a pier jutting over an inlet of the Atlantic stands a park. The air is breathy-sweet and alive. The man, off for the weekend, watches as the boy runs across the grass with his sister; barefoot and shirtless, bronze and gold, their faces all garnets and lapis and ivory. They are bursting with color . . . children of color from a people of color . . .

Surrounding them, like some gruesome fence, are citizens of the new world . . . humanoids as behemoths, bipeds as pods . . . slouching troglodytes, hateful of light . . . stuck to benches, jowls sloppily drooping, veins exploding in columnar legs . . . hair like wilted lettuce, teeth as rotten as the culture that made them . . . These festering hillbillies, these bloated farmers, have atrophied. They are the rusting cogs of democracy, the machine that eats the world. They are the detritus of this vaunted civilization, living examples of what one becomes when one follows insane creeds, when one slurps on grime and swims in pus.

He continues to observe. A few of the vaguely sentient beings stare at his children, following them with bleary eyes stuck in slow-moving heads . . . defanged crocodiles at a watering hole . . . He'd like to believe that something, maybe, flutters inside the best of them . . . that they recognize *something* in the boy and the girl, something recalled from their own mortgaged pasts, when their bodies weren't yet prisons and their minds weren't yet raped . . .

He'd like to believe it. But he knows he'd be wrong.

The girl comes and sits hand-in-hand with her father. The boy continues his exertions, a heavenly creature, an immortal, a swan among bats . . . barely touching the earth, unaware of the sullen semi-glances, unaware of the pseudo-awareness of derelict blobs dripping through wooden slats and fading inexorably from this globe like fat burned over a campfire . . . melting away, melting away, candles in the summer . . . the juxtaposition of health and disease, of light and dark, of motion and stasis is glaring . . . sparkling eyes, reptilian orbs . . . lustrous skin, pasty flesh . . . Ahura Mazda, Ahriman . . . Zoroaster was correct to sweep away the gradations of paganism and bring the contrasting dualisms to the table . . . the Christ-figure, Mani, Mohammed – all of them were right in that respect . . . To be or not to be, that is the only question. No more seeing shades of gray, no more boasting of the supposed gift for grasping nuance. From now on only black and white . . . only binary, only eternal opposition . . . the boy and the bench people . . . the boy and the priest . . . the family and the parishioners of that Southern California church . . . the coming families and the World . . . the Greeks and the barbarians . . . the Romans and everyone else . . . the *túath* and the *herpeta* . . .

Difference. That is life. That is the world. That is everything.

✱　　　✱　　　✱　　　✱

Should it inspire fear, this difference? No, not by itself. Loss of resources, hollow stomachs, threats of brutality and slavery and genocide – these are more compelling. *Does* it inspire fear? Of course.

In a world of difference, fear is a part of everyday life. Fear cripples, maims, lashes out. It builds whole nations, it destroys others. The man does not want misplaced fear for the boy . . . does not want the kowtowing, the fawning, the avoidance . . . His time is limited with the child, the lessons perhaps not lasting without the constant reinforcement of the group. He must shape him while he has the chance . . . introduce antigens while he still can . . . Mutation is evolutionarily worthless if the beneficial traits selected for aren't successfully transmitted to the following generations.

That weekend the two drive across town to the amateur boxing matches. A buzzing crowd fills the gymnasium. It is overwhelmingly black. The boy, his hair shining like a star against the backdrop of night, stands out. He is different here within the walls of the gym . . . different, too, in the world . . . He must grow used to this, must acclimatize himself to this society he's inherited as the descendant of a conquered people . . . no hiding in the Northern mountains forever . . . no artificiality for him, living in an ersatz land behind rusting gates like so many others . . . willfully pretending the world looks completely different than it actually does . . .

They climb the bleachers in what is a fairly typical high school gymnasium in the American South. They take their seats, the man thinking of the enormous suffering of this blood-soaked region that means so many things to so many people. Down below them the bell dings, and in the ring the punches begin to fly. They watch. The young men throwing blows are not as they're portrayed on television. They're not diluted versions of exhausted Europeans. Life is a struggle for them, not a comedy, all laughs, haha, we ordered the wrong kind of wine with our meal. They haven't the *luxury* of being removed from it all, they haven't the means to pretend, they haven't the urge to imitate weakness. They are, it is true, as sick in their own way as the rest of the land's residents . . . yet they have at least managed to retain some spirit of the *pankreiton*, which is more than most have . . . There is health in this, at least.

The brutality is at a minimum; headgear, pads, short bouts. The blows are muffled, the violence softened. But the fervor is pitched – the screams and the taunts are a world away from the hushed sepulchers of the bourgeoisie, a world away from the hypocrisy of the teetering liberal-conservative spectrum. The boy watches and, slowly, learns. He sees what happens when the black kid fights the white kid in the fourth bout. The crowd cheers for him. They don't boo the white youth – they scream for their own. A victory brings pride and smiles to a community. The young man with his arm being raised in triumph looks like they do. He comes from these people, he *is* these people. The crowd huzzahs, hollers. This is what must be attained . . . this naturalness, this normalcy, this essence which others have never lost, or never allowed to be wrested away . . .

"That white boy was a good fighter," an old gray head says, acknowledging the merits of the defeated, thereby enhancing the prowess of the winner. Others nod around him. The man's son is confused by it all in the beginning. At first the division is seen as solely between wearers of differently colored headgear. The "red guy" and the "blue guy" is what he calls them. Quickly this odd description, this indicator of a flaw in their kind, expires amid the shouts and the comments. The world inside the gym is honest, with its sweat and yells and sideways glances at the man and his son. There are no red guys and blue guys.

"Son, why did these people cheer for that black kid down there?"

"Because he's like they are."

Which is true. But the defeated opponent who stands in the ring below hugging the victor in an overly effusive way – a vaguely compensatory way – is *not* like the man and the boy. That is one of the many problems to wrestle with. It is still one of the toughest things for the boy to understand. The man knows it is a chink in his philosophy – all the types he most disdains, from bloated dirt farmers to cake-eating candle-wishers to neighborhood dog-admonishers to watery-eyed storybook-readers, in some way physically resemble him and the boy. Even though these people are the man's greatest enemies they can somehow claim kinship with him. Therefore, in order for this ontological problem to be remedied, all of them must disappear one way or another. Either they will change into true kin – sharing not just overrated phenotype but *Weltanschauung* as well – or simply vanish . . . which is exactly what's happening . . . Time is neatly taking care of both functions. Evolution itself is patching the chink. The steady transformation of the outside world into that of the gym's environment is forcing the needed psycho-intellectual change onto some, while *Kulturkrankheit* and its low average birth rates is ensuring the disappearance of the rest.

*   *   *   *

Always at the front of the man's mind is the necessity of gathering, of building a community, not only that his own family's problems might be alleviated, but also that he might reciprocally aid others in solving their own dilemmas. Before arriving at the new consulting job he'd thought that, compared to Los Angeles or the mountain town, he would have better success in a region that has suffered so much destruction and manipulated scorn over its history. He was wrong. The task is as daunting in this place as it is anywhere else, maybe more so. His new workmates, drawn from the elite of the area, are bookish and banal. They've never heard of the amateur boxing matches at the school gym in the bad part of their town. When he brings up the event, most of his coworkers nod their heads and grin, transparently feigning interest . . . others respond in amazed wonder, barely believing that such alien happenings could actually take place so near to where they live . . . He can't even socialize with these types, let alone hope to build communities out of them. Family seems to be of little importance to them. Few have children, and of those that do he gets the sense that they're the same spoiled, milquetoast variety found in the mountain town on the other side of the continent.

Still, the man asks around about children's activities and groups and the like – three kids in a corporate apartment is a tricky situation for his wife to handle alone. He'd like for the boy, in particular, to be around other kids occasionally. The only decent recommendation he gets comes from the president of the company. It's for a preschool that his own children attend, one that's gained a somewhat groovy status among the professors and artists in the university town . . . television isn't emphasized, diet is a concern, ecology has a prominent position . . . Again, there are certain shared beliefs between the man and a segment of these people . . . beliefs which imply a connection that just isn't there . . .

So he and his wife drive out later in the week to meet the directress of the school. Prayer wheels and Tibetan prayer flags festoon the grounds. A "Coexist" bumper sticker adorns the front door. They enter, sit, and listen to a healthy-looking, well-dressed brunette woman. Creativity, they're told, is what the curriculum revolves around. Almost immediately his mind shuts her out. This word – creativity – is on everyone's lips, bandied about at every weird play date, discussed at every community Montessori school and yuppie blog. Can such a thing really be taught? Don't ask them. Sure it can, and it must be, because nothing is inherited except looks, and these parents need creative children – children with *imagination* – so they *have* to teach it because every child, from Vietnam to Chad to California to Somalia to Indonesia to the Carolinas, is but a *tabula rasa*, brand new, formed from nothing, breaking all laws of physics, of genetics, of the universe.

"Would you say you have a creative child?" The woman's question pulls the man from his thoughts, catches him off guard. It is addressed to both parents, but unmistakably directed at him, for some reason.

He clears his throat. "Well . . ."

What does creative mean to her? Is she like the soup kitchen blonde back in the mountain town, the part-time "sculper", lumping an anonymous San person and Botticelli into a single, massive "creative" category? Does creative mean the painters in the caves at Lascaux and Walt Disney toiling in his garage and the chippers of Solutrean spearheads and the builders of the entrance to the Pasadena children's museum and the pre-Socratics and the ethologists? Or does it mean some guy whimsically serving *jalapeño* relish alongside the Thanksgiving turkey or some woman painting the exterior of her house a "non-traditional" color or someone sitting on the couch and thinking about the title of the novel they'll write someday?

Do they have a creative child? Don't all parents, among the subset of those who actually think about "creativity", believe themselves the producers of innately creative children, even if they do all claim it's something that can be taught? Seeing their kid match a striped shirt with his polka-dotted pants makes them believe it. Watching their daughter rearrange the food on her plate into a cartoon face makes them believe it. A silly play on words, an impersonation of a grandparent, a make-believe friend . . . anything fills the criteria for "creative" when that's what you're looking for . . .

Do they have a creative child?

". . . not really."

Across the desk the woman, slightly caught off-guard herself, makes a friendly comment about how all children are creative in some way, they simply need the proper environment to pull it out of them. She gently smiles as if she's presenting the parents an insight they've never considered.

On the wall behind her, ringing her framed diploma, are dozens of finger paintings of flowers. A mobile of construction paper animals hangs in a corner. Such cliché examples of youthful creativity have been made for decades at this point. Presumably the creative children of those years have, over time, become adults – and yet the land they help run is still a polluted, vapid, insolvent mess. Clearly they haven't applied their creativity to real world problems. Or has the man misread the current state of things? Is it possible that his philosophy of creative destruction has already taken hold in the United States?

The brunette continues to speak. "—so you'll find that we actively promote this type of environment here. Besides having plenty of materials always at hand, our caregivers constantly encourage the children to express themselves. There are no boundaries set on expression, except if it's harmful or threatening to others. We've found, and I'm sure many of our parents would agree, that the lack of boundaries leads to a positive maturation – I think that's something everyone wants for their children. But in order to reach that point, it's important that we not put restrictions on a child's creative freedom or inhibit the growth of self-esteem. Therefore our policies de-emphasize roughhousing and competition. All too often—"

It is at this point that the man brushes his wife's leg with his own, wordlessly letting her know that their son will never attend this place. Better a few months spent as a pioneer child – with mother, sister, and baby brother for primary company – than suffering this proudly touted, horrible repression of life's natural inclinations. Physicality is the boy's first love, and from this will blossom a vibrant intellect. *Mens sana in corpore sano.* The stiff directress obviously denies the importance of the body, placing the mind far above it in her ranking. Neither can function properly without the other. It is a tragedy that separate terms ever developed. For their family, at least, the divergent paths must monistically merge again. The sick sterility of those who've chosen the mind alone, those who've chosen modern intellectualism and academe, is not for the boy. The woman across from them, with her doctorate in education, exemplifies so much. The dust lies heavy on academia's ivory tower today, and the words of its acolytes have less and less meaning as others have finally begun to stop listening. A time will come again when intellectuals and gatekeepers will suddenly be regarded in the same way they were under the Bolsheviks . . . expendable . . .

There are smiles, thank yous, paperwork passed out, promises to be in contact, and goodbyes. That is that. Still, as they drive back to their children and the babysitter, the man is overly aware that he's yet to find what he's seeking. Family will be okay for the boy for a while. But friends, peer group, those who are needed by youth, by social animals such as humans – where will they come from for his son? Who can fill the role of worthy companion? That boy there, who shoves candy into his cavity-filled mouth and drops the wrappers on the ground? That boy there, only child, enamored of possessing as many things as he can? That boy there, who electronically murders thousands of people a day during videogame bouts because others have proclaimed them the enemy? That boy there, the foreign merchant's son, motivated only by monetary profit? That boy there, flabby and soft, who's unable to punch or climb or throw a ball? That boy there, who worships corporate sports stars and manufactured cultural heroes? That boy there, whose mother attempts through every action taken and word spoken to turn into a eunuch in all but anatomy? That boy there, hacking asthmatic, with sunken chest beneath his shirt and eyeglasses strapped across his face? That boy there, who's not imaginative enough to transform a stick into a sword? That boy there, who "wants to be a policeman", who will one day thrill to the abuse of petty power? That boy there, who prays to a peculiar god, one of debasement and psychosis? That boy there, who takes at face value everything told him by a teacher, no matter how preposterous? That boy there, whose family's cultural ethics are admirable, but who lumps the man's son in with all these others and looks at him as a filthy beast? Who will be his comrades?

Those hundreds of kids jostling each other at the boxing matches, speaking a common argot, sharing family and interests and life – the boy doesn't have what they have. It is denied him. Professionals with doctorates say those kids are poor. They say kids in Bahrain or Benin or Bangladesh are poor. They measure poverty by the absence of electricity in a community or the number of times per week that meat is eaten by the members of a particular community, but this is insane, it's First World arrogance, the condescension of dilettantes. *The existence of a community* itself is what must be taken into account first, and the dearth of it made the primary indicator of an impoverished people.

Like all healthy individuals, the man desires prosperity for his son and family, but he wants it according to the new measuring stick. He wants community, in every sense of the word . . . not the sham approximation, the falseness of the suburbs and cities . . . not mere proximity of houses, not a collection of strangers watching the same television programs and driving similar vehicles and having meetings on sustainable agriculture and recognizing each other in the grocery store parking lot . . . *He wants real community.*

✳   ✳   ✳   ✳

According to the quantitative and qualitative standards of the materialistic modern Westerner, the neighborhood the man and his family live in during the course of his consulting gig is unbeatable. The inhabitants have everything anyone could ever desire, far beyond mere electricity and meat. The houses are aesthetically appealing, the landscaping exquisite. The commercial street boasts quirky shops and eateries and bars, all brimming with goods. The sunshiny neighborhood is all it should be, per the mores of the day. Its lone blemish – a lack of diversity – is overlooked by its inhabitants because the area is packed with some of the most uniformly progressive and tolerant people in the nation. "Just look at how we vote compared to the rest of the state," they proudly remind each other, if they ever happen to see each other.

Whereas visitors from less progressive and less tolerant foreign lands – engineering students, perhaps, from the nearby university – most likely note the absence of children in this hip neighborhood's streets, the man ponders yet another missing demographic. Men. There are none. Certainly there are *males* around – he spies them climbing into their luxury cars in the morning, or retrieving the mail in the evenings – but where are the *men*? Where is the strength, the steel, the stoicism, the set jaws, the deadly stares? Where have they gone?

Like Diogenes searching through wealthy and feminized Corinth, the perplexed man walks with his kids every evening after supper, diligently on the lookout, but aghast at the caliber of male he actually witnesses. Behind the political placards and signs that grace every lawn one spies nothing but skinny necks and pastel shirts. Three teenagers of the type attending the boxing matches in that Southern gymnasium could, with no fear of reprisal, swagger down these magnolia-lined streets, mischief on their minds, chaos in their hands and chests. If they wished they could kick over garbage cans, could smash picket fences, could destroy and insult with impunity. Why? Because the owners of these historical houses – clean and beautiful and comfortable houses – would cower. Three of anything, two of anything, two of anyone who doesn't *look* like they do can terrorize the block, the street, the neighborhood, the city, the state, the nation, the West, merely by being loud, by threatening, by flashing hostile eyes. Happy slapping, assault, armed robbery, rape, murder, genocide, and displacement follow, naturally, logically . . . no mystery, no analysis needed . . .

There simply are no *men* . . . not in this neighborhood, not in thousands of neighborhoods just like it . . . Where have they gone, though? What's brought about this *oliganthropia*? Have the revolutions and wars of technology truly obliterated them all? A hundred million victims of both sexes murdered in less than a century – can any people withstand that? "Battle and death the flower of my folk have reft away," the anonymous poet had Beowulf lament, unable to even begin to fathom the insane mechanical butchery the future would bring. No, what's left is what's left – pale, effeminate creatures, crouching indoors, furtively dialing the local cops on their cellular telephones, lacking bravery, lacking sperm, lacking loyalty to their neighbor, lacking loyalty to anyone . . .

The three teenagers aren't hypothetical. They were blessedly real, and actually did come marching down the street, raucous and rowdy. An old man, not fully submerged in the new culture of truckling, came out from his garage and said something about his neighbor's gate being kicked off its hinges. Immediately he dealt with the pack, not individuals. Individualism has had its run. The old fellow, who never put political posters on his lawn, learned that no curtain-peeking neighbors of his would ever rush to his aid. He was pounded with fists and stomped with furious feet. His jaw was broken and his nose spewed blood on the very sidewalk the man currently walks along with his children.

This is the paradigm under which the Twilight Lands operate now. The aggregate cowardice of the progressive and the tolerant squelches whatever iota of bravery remains. Their spinelessness hastens the encroachment of the state, the coldest of monsters, the lidless eye. "Let the police handle this stuff," they think to themselves, justifying their curtain peeking as they dial the station's number.

The man knows the type well – they dotted the suburbs he grew up in, they crowded the faculty of the university he attended, they surrounded him on all sides when he lived in Los Angeles. They bemoan all social and governmental forms of aggression yet have been essential in creating one of the most aggressive societies and governments ever known to mankind. Never once has he heard them acknowledge their role, their *vital* role, in forging the country they incessantly threaten to emigrate from . . . never once has he heard them take any responsibility for breeding the state they claim to hate . . .

For such as these, the ennobling role of the *pater familias* means nothing. The collective potency of the *curia* means nothing. They mean nothing because the words are no longer learned, and the words are no longer learned because the realities they represent are no longer yearned for. The man despises these curtain-peekers, shielded by whimsical drapery and zeitgeist. Pushed near the edge of insanity in his personal attempts to reintroduce the sacred to existence, to formulate meaningful rituals and markers for life – daily prayers, annual holy days, milestone celebrations – these *castrati*, these epicenes, these neighborhood *hemianthropoi* muck on, content. These are the weaklings his son is to grow around? These faded examples of the males of the species, skulking in every city, every suburb, and every town? How can he allow it? Yet how can he allow the boy no semblance of community at all?

It is said of male gorillas that theirs is not a happy life, being evolutionary failures and fathers to boot. The newly tolerant, evidently, can draw no parallels, considering themselves as separate from the animal kingdom as their Christian forebears once did.

* * * *

The bourgeois circle the man and his wife move in allows an illusory feeling of belonging. It is not a community, but even if it were he would still be an interloper. He knows the members intimately. He understands them – their codes, their cravings, their pleasure sources, their blasphemies and shibboleths. He studies them, walks down their streets, mocks them in private, converses with them, seeks to destroy them, and takes what they can offer. This is the way of history.

Thus the family finds itself, toward the end of the man's employment, on a privately owned island in the ocean that was once theirs, the rough and gray Atlantic. The same man who'd recommended the progressive preschool had offered them his beach house as a friendly gesture. Desiring respite from the months spent in the college town, the man gratefully accepted, anxious to experience the solace offered by the rustling of the sea oats, the scuttling of crabs, the strength of the surf.

Yet even here, in a supposed sanctuary, his enemy's presence makes itself felt. Dreary voices and the dissonance of obnoxious entertainment assault him and his family almost immediately upon arriving. His spirits sag briefly, but he knows how difficult it is to avoid an epidemic. The grinding and thumping of atonal music floating from the adjacent beach house are but manifestations of a pervasive illness encountered everywhere. These people no longer have any culture of their own – it's been stolen, lost, and freely parceled out, leaving them malnourished and vulnerable. To counter the subsequent sensation of wasting away they've had to somehow obtain sustenance, so they've obeyed the instructions given by media and filled their starving bodies with the sludge that's been offered them. The fact that they so uncritically followed a directive from unknown sources on the proper way to save themselves is not surprising. Mass media are the only kind of authority they willingly obey these days, the electronic voices and images and text having easily filled the role of the omnipotent god they all subconsciously pined for. What is surprising, to a degree, is that the sickening gruel they constantly swallow has proved so palatable to them.

The man, his depression quickly evaporating due to the predictability of it all, points the neighbors out to his son, tries to explain the type once again. Though he understands what has led these people to their current state, he does not pity them. He derides them. They don't want anything to do with the past they share with him and his family, nor does he want them to. They are shells, the same thing the creature Grendel was forced to eat, ripped from the scrabbling bodies of muddy crayfish . . . empty, meaningless husks . . . the Kabala is right, all derogatory opinion about them is right . . . Their blue eyes look at the man and the boy, the man and the boy look back at them with the same blue eyes, and to shallow observers both sides would seem virtually identical . . . but internally the members of the two groups are vastly different . . . Those sandy-haired humanoids barbecuing on the deck across the way are as removed from the man as the Los Angeles cake-eaters are, as different from him as the dog reprimander, the Portland story listeners, the mountain town librarian . . . They are the defeated boxer lovingly clinging to his conqueror back in that high school gym, they are the suburban playground families hording toys, they are the millions upon millions upon millions who must be genetically separated from.

221

He is immune to their illness now. He and the boy walk among them as the healthy among lepers, and the man silently acknowledges that there are benefits to having contact with them, this rotting and hollow bourgeoisie. They have money, and their money, at the moment, gives him the Atlantic, gives him his desired sea oats and crabs and roaring surf. The money's all they have left though – no nation, no dignity, just a little bit of cash. They cling to it. For their offspring it will be tougher to hold on to, but they'll make do, they'll hang on another generation. They'll make it through the lifetimes of clerking that await them . . . lifetimes of managing, lifetimes of hiding . . . lifetimes of wealth without power, of luxury without purpose, of pleasure without duty . . . lifetimes of beach houses and iron gates . . . lifetimes of cultural parasitism, of downbreeding and downcast eyes . . . but then they'll be gone . . . dissolved . . . puffed away . . . They are the penultimate chapter in a book already tossed on a bonfire.

> *The time is not far away when,*
> *Lounging on a massive heap of gold,*
> *Wallowing in some corner,*
> *Having chewed away the nourishing soil,*
> *All the way to the rocks,*
> *Unsure what to do with either nights or days,*
> *Drowned in the nothingness of absolute ennui,*
> *You will stupidly die while stuffing your pockets.*

So said De Lisle during the death throes of Paris, his voice now reverberating throughout the moldy caverns of senescent America.

The man and his son and his family will not go down with these people. They might go down, but not with these revolting *Nachbewohner*. No. No. Never. They will excise these tumors from their body even if at the end of the day all that remains is a brain, a heart, and the bloody hand that wields the scalpel.

$$* \quad * \quad * \quad *$$

The next morning the man and the boy awake before sunrise. For an hour they hike along the shore, finally reaching a spot far away from the blight, a place where the civilized haven't yet arrived. Beneath the dawn they strip naked and leave the dunes behind, walking hand in hand into the ocean, the water rising, pressing and plashing on legs, groins, and chests, until finally they're in, they're treading the waves, they're shivering, but it's theirs, the Atlantic is theirs again for a time. Lashed by icy spray, determined to remain in the freezing water, they shout at Neptune, "We'll beat you! We'll beat you!" They echo their Ulysses, crafty Ulysses, determined Ulysses, and Horkheimer and Adorno and their attacks on him be damned, because now *these types* are the bourgeoisie, *they're* the dominant culture, *they're* the insiders, they've been there for a long time and all they've been able to produce is juvenile sniping, insult as insight. Their nastiness is the norm, but it's transparent now, it's clear that it lacks profundity, clear that it never was worth anything. They, their school, their type, they teeter on the edge of mockery, ready to fall into irrelevance. When the gods can be seen, no matter what kind, they can be wounded and defeated. Diomedes used his sword to do it, Ulysses used his mind . . . a thousand lessons in a pair of ancient tales, just two out of hundreds sitting there, waiting to be utilized, waiting to be applied . . . They must record them, they must categorize them and combine them and teach them to their children. They must let it begin there, with shared myth, in order that their world bloom again, in order that their Atlantic come back to them all.

The man watches the boy bashing through the waves toward shore, wind-swept salt hair, brown skin . . . a tanned blonde beast, not coddled, slathered, sheltered, weakened . . . He draws life from the sun, like an oak, like all life. Contrast those others, those clerks and managers wallowing in dank beach house corners, those who've made an enemy of the sun, armoring their bodies in the slippery chemicals of the Industrial Age. They deny the benefits of this mighty star, first god, father of all . . . they fight the power it provides, they fight anything that offers health . . . they go blind, they develop cancer, they go away . . .

On the beach, drying in the morning chill, the man and boy etch Galilean fish and crosses in the sand with their feet. Silently they let the waves wash over the images, again and again . . . each undulation chopping away at the figures, each rush of sea water grinding them down, from deep hewn symbols to illegible scratches to dim lines, until finally, foamingly, forgotten . . . Once again pristine, the shore stretches away beneath the sky, briefly accepting seashells hurled from the ocean before quickly relinquishing them when the waves roll in once more. Behind the man and boy the wind easily blows the sand from the seemingly indestructible dunes, chipping them away bit by bit by bit. Everything is allegory . . . everything a lesson for those who can see . . .

No one has arrived at their spot yet. There is peace, the peace which comes when one is abandoned to the eternal present. The graceful flight of the pelicans, the comical back and forth of the plovers – it is all too beautiful, and the man knows that he, too, has a place here, he and his son, of all *túatha* . . . the name-givers, the collectors, the organizers, the understanders, the unlockers of secrets . . . He lifts the boy into his arms and they stare to the east, over sun-painted water, and he tells the child of the motherland whence they sprung. He talks and talks, a drone, perhaps . . . talks to the boy, but only for himself, perhaps . . .

There lies our Europe,
across the sea,
broken, in chains,
but alive in Thee.

The Alps, the Pyrenees, the Urals no longer belong to the boy – the new mountain ranges are his bones. The Tiber, the Rhine, the Shannon, the Dnieper, the Loire, the Danube are no longer his – the new rivers are his blood. Anywhere their people go can be theirs, will be theirs. It all begins with *belief.*

✳   ✳   ✳   ✳

Encircling the beach house's colossal bathtub are three enormous mirrors affixed to the walls. The man and the boy have returned from another swim in their ocean and are preparing to wash the encrusted salt from their bodies. The boy leans in to stare at the foaming water filling the tub, and his reflected image multiplies into infinity.

"Dad!" he shouts. "Come see!"

The man does. He follows the boy's instructions, and leans in over him.

"We're an army!" the boy yells, ecstatic at the legions of Sons and Fathers mirrored to his left and right, diminishing in stature as they bend away into the past and future. "We're a giant army!"

An army of kin, all fighting for the same goal . . . would that there were such a thing . . . an army of passion against the bourgeoisie, of extremism against the capitalists, of fanaticism against the humanitarians, of beauty against the fetid ugliness of the egalitarians, of truth against the liars . . . an army of victory and winnowing . . . of power and justice . . . of chaos then order . . .

Would that there were. Would that there were.

The image fogs up. The army fades into mist, leaving behind just the man and the boy, who strip to bathe, on to other things.

*　　*　　*　　*

Inside one of the bedrooms, in the waning light of dusk, the man adjusts the blanket atop his daughter, then turns to look down at his son. He lies there, inert, sleeping the healthy sleep of youth, untroubled by sweating dreams of adulthood, untouched by awareness or sadness. On the pillow beside him, askew, rests a piece of honeysuckle placed there by his doting mother. On his fingers, puppets . . . tiny, furry . . . a koala and a tiger . . . All day he speaks of battling enemies, of crushing invading Huns and robbing corrupt monks, of burning castles and destroying armies – yet he whispers to the fuzzy tiger as its protector, motherly and soft and enveloping . . .

"We *are* its protector," the man teaches him. Those foes of the illusory bathroom army – humanitarians and capitalists and a score of others – have brought the beast to the edge of extinction, his old powers overshadowed, his land loudly stolen by agriculture and progress. "If we go, he goes – all like him go. If we stay, and fight, and thrive, so does he."

There is no choice. Tigers must live.

*   *   *   *

On the day before the family is slated to begin the return trek to its Northern home the man finds the boy staring at himself in the bathroom mirror. It is more than curiosity he witnesses – it is the gaze of self-love, of wonder that such a beautiful creature stands there before you, that such a beautiful thing *is* you.

The man isn't sure what to do. What is the proper response? What lesson should he impart? He doesn't know, but he ignores his uncertainty, follows his instincts, and tells his son to step away from the mirror and to stop gazing at the image reflected therein. Rather than recite the pointless, scare-technique tale of Narcissus, he instead chooses to tell the boy that he owes his features to his ancestors, that they are a gift to him, and that one should feel no sense of accomplishment when admiring a gift given by another. He fears compliments from cooing women about long eyelashes and the like have gone to the boy's head, increasing his feeling of uniqueness, which cleaves one from the larger group and weakens in the long run.

The boy turns and leaves, heading out to join the family, while the man stands there, wondering whether his words had any effect or not. He is the boy's teacher but who is his teacher? He has had to travel continents and cloister himself in libraries and expend so much energy, so much time, so much life, simply to begin to ascertain the eternal rules, truths, and falsehoods that others are taught at their mothers' breasts. Even now, after years in the labyrinth, he feels unsure of himself during particular incidents, especially when he's given no thought specific to the situation at hand. Thus, if caught off guard, reactionary mandates or moral instruction are doled out on the fly or, on the other hand, some lesson he soundly explained a year earlier is suddenly viewed as incorrect due to a different perspective. So much of his life with the boy is about learning as he goes along, which is no real system at all. There's simply been nothing delineated by others of his *túath* who trod the same path, shared similar concerns, and had a vested interest in producing a favorable outcome for their descendants.

It is one of the recurring problems he comes up against – there are none of his own who've done this effectively, none who are currently doing it . . . no re-evaluators, no calendar makers, no curriculum devisers . . . There are none to prescribe laws of action that, if followed, will allow one to wring greatness out of life. Manu and Zoroaster and Moses and Confucius and Mohammed – their words are still relevant and vital for billions. Nothing of the kind exists to mesh with the man's particular spirit. A distillation is needed, capturing the essence of thousands of years of thousands of seers he feels connected with. The past can still be remedied if men – men like himself – will but sit down and begin thinking, recording, and applying. What are the thirty ancient books that Nietzsche thundered would be the foundation of a Europe without nations? What are the fifty books, and no more, that the poet George allowed could sit on a bookshelf? They must fuse these, must make a Tanakh, a Talmud, a Zohar, a Tanya. They must make a Koran, create an Avesta, record their own Analects and Vedas and Puranas, or they'll forever be treading the same ground as those bovines that must be left behind. They'll be no different from those perpetually lost beasts, the beach-housers, the hipsters, wandering through millennia, every generation spontaneously new and confused. A compass is what is needed, not a map of contemporary nations, annually changeable due to the fluctuations of politics and time. Where went Illyricum, Lugdunensis, Africa Vetus? One should not have to know; one need only know that *North always lies that way.*

The man has never pondered, for instance, whether vanity, specifically, is a sin. Savonarola was condemned as insane when he attacked it as a moral failing. He lost, Botticelli and his talented brethren and their values ultimately won, and here, today, amid the still-resounding accolades for the victors, stands the lonely man, all the spirited output of the Renaissance having done not a single thing to halt the appearance of this squalid modern world he struggles against. It seems that one of the first steps taken by those who will devise the necessary compass will be to reevaluate all of the past's losers, study what they said, and weigh their words and ideas against the reality of the contemporary present the winners brought about.

The boy shouldn't be in love with his own image – the man feels strongly about this. But there he was, admiring himself, a simple expression of the basic human search for self-worth. If it can be hammered home that an individual's physical features, intelligence, and even personality traits are to be credited solely as temporary manifestations of the larger group's characteristics, then this need for self-worth can be filled by proxy, reflected by the greater love felt for the gifts of the *túath*. Ideally the cables of valuation would be anchored to kinfolk, enmeshing the past and present and future in a web of belonging and timelessness. Still, that won't completely satisfy. Not all personality can be subsumed by the totality of the tribe. The boy will wish to prove himself worthy one day, and as the wisest ancients have stated, the way to distinguish oneself amid the host of inherited attributes is through deeds. Individual accomplishment shines on the *túath*, a two-way street, a gift *back* to those multitudes who gave the individual the tools needed for his achievement.

Of course, as the man realized long ago, and the boy will too one day, the greatest reciprocal gift currently lies not in invention, not in the creation of "firsts", not in cultural accolades – these can all be mocked or scrubbed away by victorious enemies – but in the continuous production and forging of vibrant, fantastic youth.

✳   ✳   ✳   ✳

Prior to returning to their mountain home, the family stops in Massachusetts for a grandparent visit. The children are thrilled to see their grandma and grandpa, yearning for something that seems so natural to them, multi-generational warmth and aftershave kisses and the caresses of wrinkled hands. There is supper, there is sleep in one room and empty adult talk in another, there are morning awakenings and ticklings and laughs. After breakfast Grandpa suggests they go play at the park, and three generations excitedly head out the door. With notebook in hand the man trails them to that great socio-psychological petri dish, the American playground . . . always analyzing its dynamics, always aghast at what it reveals . . . "Study one thing and learn all things," said brilliant Virgil. Press the playground and the pus oozes out of the continent itself.

Though such places stretch from the Atlantic to the Pacific Ocean, the variation between them is minimal – the same molded structures are found scattered across three thousand miles like the ancient megaliths of some vanished race. Thousands of playgrounds exist and yet, at each, one finds the same neutered youth, the same doughy *hemianthropoi*, the same squeak-voiced women. Are there any other people that produce such doughy half-men, any other people that create women who speak so squeakily and stupidly as these?

This particular playground stands out slightly from the others – there is an old-fashioned merry-go-round on the grounds. Somehow it's escaped the fate of litigiously driven obsolescence that's befallen so many other small delights across the land. The boy and his sister revel in its speed, quickly learning the techniques for spinning, for mounting, for dismounting. This would have been impossible had they not arrived early, before the squeak-voiced women and *hemianthropoi* filled the space. As soon as these show up – with their plaster smiles and dull eyes, wearing matching tracksuits or dressed like fifteen-year-olds from television dramas – it all changes. The atmosphere rapidly fills with their cautionary shouts. It is drained by their spiritual vortices, their constant interference. With enormous expenditure of energy they suck adventure and self-sufficiency from their children's breasts, breeding the future.

Like the slide at their mountain town playground, it is the ancient merry-go-round that is the star attraction here. The children are drawn to it like a magnet, and immediately the parental instructions begin.

"Let that boy on, dear."

"Please let that little girl off, honey."

They increase in frequency.

"Thank you."

"Stop."

"Let that girl on, Dylan."

"That boy wants to get off, Ashley. Stop."

"Say 'excuse me'."

"Thank you."

"Let that boy on. Slow it down!"

"Let him off."

"Easy, easy."

Slowly they merge into a single frantic voice, alternately singsong and harsh. "Thank you. Say 'thank you', Hunter! Wait! Stop. Slow it down. Slow it down! Okay. Okay!"

Unlike earlier in the morning, the merry-go-round is no longer allowed to stay in motion. It is prevented from properly spinning. Everyone must go slowly, all momentum must be interrupted for the sake of the cautious, the crippled. Under the rules set forth by the cult of individualism and courtesy all previous joy is fragmented. The system finally breaks down under the pressure . . . and millions of shoulders shrug in unison, if they shrug at all . . .

> *O generation of the thoroughly smug*
> *And thoroughly uncomfortable . . .*

So began exasperated Pound in yet another verse hurled at the proliferating throng that, like De Lisle, he could never hope to defeat. No one can hope to. Decades later it's still here, *they're* still here, unchanged except for their clothing styles and body mass . . .

Years earlier, when still a teenager, the man thrilled to the words of an authoress from Russia. Feeling alone in the world, he found himself seduced by a creed called Objectivism . . . by a creed which seemed to offer the option of climbing out of the muck that drags so many down . . . It was a reaction, even then, to those around him, to something he sensed was wrong and base but could not identify. He merely wanted no part of these people or their sad society, and thought that by withdrawal he could lessen the impact they had on his psyche.

But as he stumbled through the wilderness and grew into a man, he left the authoress and her dead-end doctrine of individualism behind. He left behind all silly movements limited merely to the political or economic realm. He left behind all tools that were of no use in the bid for long-term survival. It was then that the man listened to the words of someone greater, a prophet who reached the pinnacle of Occidental thought . . . someone who promised resurgence if his dictates were followed, someone who commanded, "You solitaries must become a people." . . .

Certainly Nietzsche's charge was issued late in the day. After all, the wise peoples of Asia received similar instructions nearly two and a half millennia before he first laid pen to paper. The order he gave was in no way original – but this made no difference. Originality pales next to specificity, and this order was meant for the man and those like him. *You solitaries must become a people.* Following that command is the only way he can hope to attain the world he desires. Shared purpose. Shared focus. These are what make the merry-go-round function the way it was designed to function.

*　　　*　　　*　　　*

Everywhere they go on the Cape they encounter cicadas. The bizarre insects hatched two days before the family arrived and can't be avoided. For seventeen years they've hidden underground, forming into what they were meant to be, and now they've finally emerged to make a brief appearance before disappearing again.

Neighbors have come over for a barbecue, Boston attorneys staying at their summer cottage. Their child, Jacob, does not care for the cicadas. He is a product of asphalt and pavement and he finds them ugly and disgusting. He disparages them, kills them, squashes their heads. The boy is furious when he witnesses this. He shouts that the creatures are not ugly, that they're exactly as nature wants them to be, that they don't hurt anyone . . . that by the time the two of them ever see cicadas again, they'll both be grownups . . . Why kill them?

"They *are* ugly," emphatically replies the other, and he will do whatever he wants to them. The situation becomes more heated. The little voices rise. Belligerently the child Jacob kills yet another, because he can. He has a future as an enforcer for whatever regime finds itself on top. The boy can take no more. He punches the city kid in the mouth, demanding he cease harming the peculiar insects, shouting that they want to live. A fracas ensues, with screams and punches and rolling on the ground. No adults are near, no one to force the children to stop their aggression. Nature can take her course, can shape an outcome as perfectly as she shapes an insect.

The boy, at four, is noble. He defends the unjustly maligned. He battles for the helpless, for the ridiculed, for those who must dwell in the dirt to form themselves. The fight is far greater than this brief tussle with a city boy, though . . . far more intricate and involved than he can ever guess . . . It is not just the ignorant members of the herd he must battle. They can never be defeated, only controlled. Their opinions are fickle, decided by whoever has power – and that is where the real struggle takes place, beyond the reach of the rabble. It is the whipcrackers and the wirepullers he is up against. They are harsh and merciless. He'll witness this as he grows. Though his only desire may be to defend others from violence, or even if it is only to defend *himself* from violence, he'll find that such actions are not permitted . . . are ethically suspect, are sneered at even as they're made illegal . . . To rise up and preemptively attack first those who would subjugate and enslave him is even more egregious a sin – he must accept the truncheon beatings in silence. He is to adhere to a morality of inaction or be condemned. He must slave for others or commit suicide. This is the law.

The cicadas won't hurt the boy. He's correct. It is, forever, only men that will hurt him.

$*$ $*$ $*$ $*$

The big local news upon the return to their mountain town is that an asphalt plant has set up shop. The neighbors and citizens are outraged. They've escaped from wretched cities a thousand miles distant and now, blessed by the purity of icy lakes and deep forests, must suffer the same choking air they thought they forever left behind them. Vehemently they demand that this egregious polluter of the atmosphere, this fouler of the water, be closed down. They demand that the giant smokestack no longer be allowed to force their children indoors on summer days, watery-eyed and wheezing.

To understand the effect of a mobile asphalt plant on the environment and surrounding population is one thing – to understand the sociopolitical mechanisms of the system one exists within is another. These people have not yet realized that they are vassals . . . incidentals . . . They believe in the modern version of democracy and its corresponding platitudes as fervently as their ancestors believed in the Christ and one-eyed Odin. They believe themselves citizens who, with a plurality of votes, can make whatever they don't like disappear. They do not grasp that their current town government is simply an organization in the employ of plutocrats, men who don't care about their opinions or health, and so they flail wildly in their attacks, not cognizant of the utter irrelevance of their protests. They write angry letters, they make many fine speeches at community meetings, they picket city hall . . . ridiculously voicing their complaints to a system that *allows* a polluting asphalt plant in their community to begin with . . .

"We need a revolution," jokingly says one of the attendees of the asphalt plant discussions, a retired professor of some sort of social science. She makes her statement with feigned rage, and the empty quip is met with equally empty giggles and some approving head nods and affirmations – "Well they're going to *get* one," – before the matter of petitions is once more returned to.

A public meeting is held. Continuing to beat their heads against a wall, believing till the end in things like "due process" and "going through the proper channels", dozens of revolutionaries take time off from stuffing envelopes in order to complain to their elected officials yet again. Unexpectedly the owner of the asphalt plant makes an appearance. He stands at the podium, his papers scattered before him, explaining his position . . . not a devil, as many believe, but a simple scavenger . . . an exploiter of a situation . . . an example of a specific type that appears during times of dissolution and decay, filling a predetermined ecological role as much as do vultures or maggots or fungus . . . The breed arrives as naturally as all scavengers, following a mathematical model . . . collectively feasting on the carcasses of decomposing civilizations . . . Nothing stands between them and their wounded victims. Their numbers are increasing daily, indicating that something has gone unbalanced in the ecosystem. They are supported by the authorities. They *are* the authorities.

The asphalt plant owner stares out at the hostile crowd, proudly stating that he "pays his taxes", bizarrely presenting the offering of tribute as something worthy of commendation. He justifies the continued operation of the plant by the fact that "the government allows it". He's right, his logic is sound, but the citizens are befuddled – regulatory commissions and organizations exist to protect them, they're absolutely sure about this. The fact that these governmental offshoots still seem to be supporting the profits of a few men over the health of the population at large is just an oversight, a mistake, something that can be corrected with enough letters and enough outrage.

Even after witnessing how wholly ineffective their methods are, the bourgeoisie continue to slog forward, unfazed, voicing complaints and making phone calls and writing letters to the newspaper. This is direct action to them. To the man, direct action is something else. There is no buffer between the problem and the solution. The opportune time hasn't yet arrived for this direct action but it will . . . maybe . . . maybe . . . Until then though, that day in the distant future that might never come, all is pretend . . . all is imaginative release and psychological training . . . Every trip to town by the man and the boy sees the asphalt plant blown to smithereens. The begrimed vehicles parked in front of the shabby buildings are annihilated. The tar-coated innards of the offensive machinery are eradicated. The smokestack, most blatant symbol of them all, most egregious violator, with carcinogens and sickness spewing forth like the poisonous breath of six dragons, is destroyed, and the problem is solved.

"Blow up the asphalt plant!" the man shouts and two pairs of hands lift to shoulders . . . rifles, rocket launchers firmly imagined . . . BOOM, BOOM. The sounds of laughter and cartoonish explosions fill the car, a frequent occurrence, and the idea of violence as a tool is introduced at a young age, planted in a moist mind in order to incubate and grow and be passed down. Violence against those who would harm you is necessary. From somber Cato to the supposed primitives of New Guinea, from the dawn of the past to the twilight of the present, across vast epochs and diverse cultures, *all clear thinkers agreed on this*. Violence can appear as a fleet of disguised warships or a knotty club or a belching smokestack . . . as armored tanks or a domestic economic policy . . . It can be stupidly used by myopic reactionaries or it can wait and fester for millennia under the guise of pacifism until the time is ripe for its effective utilization. It is reality, not something to imagine oneself "above", not something to be painted out of pictures.

They pass the plant, and from the smokestack a river of death shoots upward toward the sooty sky, billowing down like the waste splattered from harpies. It is vile, an aberration . . . noxiously coating and poisoning the sustenance of both beasts and humans . . . How can the man pretend that what is happening is, indeed, *not*?

"Grab the owner, throw him against a wall!"

Within the passing vehicle the asphalt plant's owner is put on trial for crimes. He stands accused of attempting the murder of innocents, of poisoning the local populace, of sickening his neighbors, all for capitalist greed. He is the grown up child of individualism, one of the persecutors the boy hides from on Samhain.

"Get his family too." Pyrrhus hurled Hector's son from the top of a tower down onto the burning streets of Troy not out of hatred, but out of foresight. All kin are liable, all glued together by the sticky petroleum of the asphalt, the final crop. They're lined up against the enormous concrete blocks stacked outside the plant, still more products of the man who "pays his taxes". The boy's kin were lined up too. No one talks about it . . . only hidden folk . . . only the vanquished . . .

"This tribunal pronounces you guilty . . ." Resignation echoes in the man's voice as he announces the verdict, the asphalt plant already fading away in the rear view mirror . . . no fervor, no passion in his speech . . . a duty, merely duty, that's what the boy must learn . . . The asphalt plant owner is pronounced guilty due to the keenness of cold obligation, not fiery reaction. No matter the validity of the charges, he's not found guilty for making the proles sick . . . he's not found guilty for what he's done to the yuppies, but—

". . . for what you've done to *us* . . . to the foxes, the fish, the ospreys, and to *us* . . ."

That is the essence. That is honesty. No justice meted out in the name of "the people" until there are a people worthy of justice. The man, the boy, they cannot care about those who do not care for themselves . . . for those who believe in magic and prayers, in taboos and fairytales, in blind justice and the power of the single vote . . . people such as these are useless . . . clay pots floating down the river alongside bronze ones, doomed to shatter when they reach the rapids . . .

"For your crimes you are sentenced to execution." They cross the bridge. Two deer are startled, lifting their heads for a moment from the polluted water they're drinking. Warily they return to it, unaware of the mock drama playing out inside the passing vehicle.

Those who cannot be educated must be extirpated – this is what the ruthless men and women who changed the course of life on earth believed. No one likes to admit it in decent company, but the methods of the Communists are sound, will always be sound. The asphalt plant owner knows what the statistics say, he knows what the environmental reports say, he can clearly see and smell his factory's pollutants, and so the fact that he takes no steps to remedy the situation shows that he simply doesn't care. It is unimportant to this small-scale industrialist if cancer eats the boy's brain, unimportant if his mother's lungs blacken and char, unimportant if hacking phlegm and tear-filled eyes find a place in the home he shares with his little sister and brother, the home he shares with his miniature tribe and his dreams. This unconcerned man will perpetrate his crimes simply that he might own a larger motorboat to break the silence of lakes. He wants another snowmobile to steal the privacy of the forest creatures. He wants softer chairs and wider beds and larger televisions and to get them, to obtain these luxuries he so covets, he will steal the boy's health, his very future, with the acquiescence of a town government that the masses idiotically believe protects them.

"We do not share the morals of eternal victims, son."

The justice is doled out Soviet style . . . stiff leather jackets . . . well-oiled revolvers pointed at the base of the neck . . . The man has learned from what happened to his ancestors. Somewhere in the ever-present pain felt for the genocide of his people and his past there is an admiration for the deadly efficiency of their destroyers . . . no half-measures, that's what he's grasped . . . He is passing this knowledge along. The Akkadians took from the Sumerians and helped the latter toward their own extinction. The man, the boy, the rest, will be no different.

*   *   *   *

It is nighttime. Outside the window the sky is purpling. The man sits at the foot of the kids' bed in their now-completed house. His voice begins, low, sonorous . . .

"Once upon a time, the mighty oaks of the forest approached Jupiter. 'We live our lives for no purpose now, since wherever we grow we are in peril from men with axes,' they began. But before they could continue, mighty Jupiter replied, with some sadness and some sternness, 'You can only thank yourselves for these misfortunes, for if you didn't make such excellent posts and pillars, if you weren't so serviceable to men, the axe wouldn't bite you so frequently.'"

There is silence in the bedroom. The man touches foreheads with each of the children, says the nighttime prayer, and closes the door behind him.

Enablers or not. Miserable slaves or violently free men. Those are the options the tribes of the world are rapidly being forced to make, have *always* been forced to make. Such words are not rhetoric. Such sentiments are not meant for advertisers, for sound bites, for bland filmic utterances meant to placate paying serfs. For the man, the boy, the coming families, they are absolute truth.

Nothing will remedy this situation today. It is a process that must continue, irreversibly. The asphalt plants and dirty streams, the sullied skies and diamond mines, the broken bodies and diseased minds – all will remain until they can no longer remain. The oak trees must all be hacked down . . . the oaks, the ash, the pines – complete forests . . . different trees, not serviceable to men with axes, will replace them . . .

∗   ∗   ∗   ∗

As they adjust to their new house and lifestyles, and begin to seek new livelihoods, the man once more has spare time to deal with the boy's burgeoning education. Like Heraclitus he disdains the polymaths for their disjointed agglomeration of useless facts. When it comes to teaching he prefers the method of Archilochus' hedgehog to that of his fox; that is, a unified theme rather than a hundred unconnected subjects . . . *multum non multa* . . . much not many . . . He keeps the boy's learning deep, sharp, focused . . . every fact leads back to another, everything is rooted in that yawning history that surrounds them . . .

History is the cornerstone. The man does not make it the desiccated study of dates and dynasties. Nor does he include the exciting ethnic clashes of Chinese and Mongol, the battles of Hindu and Muslim, or the simplistic biographies of great men, with their corresponding implied message of isolated individualism. Knowing that this beast history can consume life itself, he instead attempts to subjectively *tribalize* and objectively *ahistoricize* the subject, the same as he does with their holy days, making it no longer subject to placement on a number line, marching backward to a fixed date and stopping suddenly at the point when a book is closed on the kitchen table. It is not merely the study of the past, but the study of fluid life – *respice, adspice, prospice*. In their world, Greeks are always marching east, Rome is always under threat, and the Franks are always uniting the *túatha* of Europe under a common banner.

The boy and the girl learn as they play, learn as they live. Spinning a jack on the rounded part, rather than the tapered part, is called an "Oliver Cromwell", and leads to talks of Roundheads and Levelers and regicide and the earth-shaking power of fanaticism. Popping the flowered portion of the dandelion from its stem is accompanied by the improvised ditty, "Danton went to the guillotine and they said, 'off with his head'." Questions about guillotines and Danton lead to more talk of leveling, more talk of fanatics, more talk of things they've suffered as a people and things that could have been and things that still might be.

The barrier of pillows stacked between the boy and his sister on their bed to decrease nighttime bickering is called "Hadrian's Wall", separating the barbarians from the civilized, either child wearing either label contingent upon his or her behavior that night. When the divided parties talk to each other across the barrier and the man comes into the darkened room to remind them that it's bedtime, it's pointed out that although the wall might keep them apart from each other, their voices – hence ideas and information – are still able to pass across it.

At times when the boy is occupied with a jigsaw puzzle the man sneaks pieces away from the pile, or stealthily drops in extra pieces that don't belong with the others. The child becomes increasingly frustrated in his bid to complete the puzzle, which is when the man steps in and sets things aright, explaining as he returns the missing pieces or removes the superfluous ones that nothing can be solved when all pieces aren't present or when pieces belonging to a different scene have been substituted for the correct ones. In this way the proper method for putting together the reality of the past and present, in the face of liars and obfuscators, is taught early.

During their evening games of chess the boy is occasionally forced to use only pawns against his father's full-strength army. The subsequent losses and inability to make any effective move on the board lead to talk of rules made by the stronger, and how these rules must be ignored if a victory is ever to take place. The boy listens and understands, eventually seeing the wisdom in immediately letting his king be captured in order to move on to a real game where more parity exists between sides. It is during one of these many standard chess sessions that the boy, inadvertently but essentially, challenges his father's very worldview.

"Dad, how come if I beat you last night we're playing again tonight? I thought I won." He says this casually, as they set up their pieces.

"You did win. This is a new game."

"Then your king didn't really die, he was just captured."

"Yes."

"But now he has all of his men back and he's ready to fight again. How did that happen?"

"Well, like I said, it's a new game. The old game ended when you captured my king."

"But he's back again. With all his men. I didn't set them free."

"It's a *new* game."

"But they're the same pieces we always use."

"Yes."

"I think it's just one game that goes on and on and none of us really wins or loses ever."

The man smiles. The boy's line of reasoning is tempting, and if logically accepted could bring surcease to his father's unending torment. His assertion is partially correct – everything does go on and on. Evolution never stops. Thus, if their struggle is looked at as being eternal, they haven't *lost* – they are currently *losing*, that is all, and someday they might be winning, or at least might have a better chance at winning. Great comfort can be taken if the present situation is viewed with such a broad perspective. Eschatology becomes something for others to worry about, while the pagans follow their natural course of sleeping for a while – being slaughtered, denigrated, raped, and disenfranchised for a while – and then recurring. After Ragnarok comes rebirth and the world is pure and golden until the cycle begins anew somewhere down the line. Tra-la-la.

There is a deep flaw in this naïve belief, however. In order to recur, in order to evolve, the sheer, biological truth is that *the organism must live* . . . and in order to live, one must struggle, not lazily wait it out until the magic of myth fixes everything . . . The dinosaur, the dodo, the carrier pigeon, the Neanderthal – the eschaton did arrive for them. Creatures that do not adapt go extinct, say the paleontologists, but the flipside is that creatures that go extinct do not adapt. The concept of Ragnarok, beloved by the childish, is only reified if biology agrees to it. The man's struggle, his family's struggle, is to not go extinct. They must be a beginning, not an end – or rather, a continuation, not a cessation. Therefore he searches for the health required for survival in order that they might be participants in this eternal evolution . . . in order that they might continue playing the chess game . . . in order that someday, someday, they might finally gain a victory once again . . .

Of course, the elusive victory won't happen the next match. Success isn't right around the corner. A fervent belief in immediate triumph is as ridiculous as reactionary violence – while talk of such is a decent motivator for the boy, the man has long known that to challenge the ruling forces head-on in seeking such a victory is suicidal and stupid, particularly during this juncture, the apogee of the oppressor's strength. Centuries earlier cool-headed Machiavelli pointed out the foolishness of Savonarola, who had a valid message after all, but no power to enforce it. The process of growing a powerful tribe must be amortized, taking a few losses over centuries. Every loss is minimized in eternity. Besides, in the current age, the *túath* cannot grow substantially enough to challenge its overlords anyway. In tolerant eras the growth of those who might one day defy their rulers is not impeded. Once these others ultimately gain power, as they must, they usher in an age of intolerance – as happened when the ancient world was swept away – and the subsequent difficulties in growing a tribe that might someday challenge *their* newly achieved dominant position seem insurmountable. However, even though *túatha* writhing directly under the boot do not expand enormously during such times – *intolerant* times – it is during these eras that they are *shaped* . . . assiduously taking form while above them their rulers undergo the dissolution of Time . . .

"Make haste slowly," said Octavian, as he steadily eradicated those who'd harmed his relations and his prospects. Building family. Fostering education. Teaching awareness. These are still possible during the current era, even if more direct actions are not.

$$* \qquad * \qquad * \qquad *$$

The boy's previous daycare is out of session for the summer – the blonde owner is volunteering at an orphanage in rural Colombia. Due to a downturn in the construction industry, the boy's friend, the Aztec boy, has left the mountain town with his family. The man doesn't want loneliness to engulf his son. It has been too many months with little youthful male company for the child. Human beings are, by their very nature, social. They desire to interact, they need contact with each other. Indeed, a man cannot truly be considered a man when merely acting as an individual, but only in conjunction with, conflated with, others. A naked subject without a world never *is*, as the prophet Heidegger easily demonstrated, though thousands of years too late and millions of ears and fists too few.

There is a summer camp in session near the mountain town. It is not a summer camp in the same sense as it is for other residents of the United States. Identical terms mean different things to different peoples in different places and different times. The communism extant in China is not the communism that was utilized to devastate Russia and Europe. Christianity as practiced in the slums of Ephesus was not the Christianity believed in by the Crusaders, which was not the Christianity observed by Anglo Unitarians in antebellum Boston. Summer camp for the boy is not cohesion, not solidarity, not discussion of future group goals to be attained, not rites of passage and ceremonies relevant to the inculcation of youth with the mores of the tribe. That is what it is for others, for stronger peoples. For the boy and the rest of the helots summer camp is but amusement and frivolity . . . rappelling the wall, chipping the golf ball, paddling the kayak . . . all moderately physical, all strength and tactics, but timewasters nevertheless . . . no worldview . . . no training of the will . . .

The limited options – the *lack* of options – frustrate. The man must use what he has though. So the boy is sent to the camp, his father hoping against hope that something beneficial comes from the interaction with other youth. Perhaps there are those not yet tainted by the zeitgeist, not yet infected with the death memes worming through young brains across the land. Perhaps there are some stray seeds from the dying adult plants he witnessed at the Portland Children's Museum, somehow blown off course from the culture of vanishing, and thriving in the mountain clime and soil. Perhaps evolution is at work on a different level in the countryside than it is in the cities.

He allows the boy one week of attendance before going out to meet the child's counselors. Once there the man sticks to the periphery, watching unnoticed. Any ridiculous hopes he had are quickly quashed. The caliber of the camp's attendees confirms his every observation made over the past five years. They're snotty, these wealthy children, enamored of possessions and gear. Many speak in whines. Their speech is poor, learned from television sets situated prominently in the enormous bedrooms they shared with no one. They lack solidity, vibrancy, and character.

The malaise spills from all directions. Even in an environment of, admittedly, robust outdoor activity and exertion, the cloying constraints of modern life, of economic liability, of *progress* bind the boy. They wrap around him and choke him, attempt to feminize him. There is to be no physical contact, no wrestling, ever. It is forbidden at any time during the day. Gamely he attempts to engage bigger kids when the counselors aren't watching, sneaking in tests of strength when they're preoccupied. When his actions are noticed he's lambasted . . . kneaded and softened . . . taught that physicality and competition are somehow aberrant . . . taught the values of self-made cripples and cavefish . . .

What to do, how to proceed, when so many surrounding are sick? What to do when the boy eventually shifts from the youthful inclination to please his father or himself and instead, as he matures, chooses to follow the tenets of the group, the tenets of his fellow campers and citizens? What to do when this healthiest of beasts, in order not to feel the sting of rejection, must mask its vigor and become as sickly as the others?

This is some rabid disease spreading through the American social organism, the healthy cell swamped and somehow transformed by malignant ones. Already, as the weeks progress at the camp, the man notes its advance. Meaningless episodes to others are omens to him . . . the boy's newfound interest in animated media characters he's never seen . . . his desire to sample popular garbage food fit only for political prisoners . . . his casual disobedience . . . his sudden pattern of saying, "I got—" rather than, "I have—" . . .

The shift in speech patterns is the worst of them all. It pains the man to see his son pulled downward, sucked under polluted waves, drawn into the flippant netherworld of those for whom language means nothing . . . for whom it is merely a tool to indicate the possession of objects, but not ideas . . . for those who use it to fill the air with chattering sounds rather than furthering dialogue on the most pressing issues of the day . . . These children of the empty and beaten cannot turn their thoughts into reality and thus might as well be shadows in the desert. For them there is no power in words because, as they've learned from watching and listening to their parents, words only ever remain words – they never become deeds.

It is a dilemma. The boy needs contact, yet all contact seems detrimental. These kids' weaknesses, their characteristics, will be transmitted to him – he's not strong enough to fight the power of the group. He is a lone child, unable to understand the battle for his being. He cannot be expected to shoulder the burdens of the world, he cannot play Heracles to his father's Atlas and have the enormous globe itself handed over and placed on his four-year-old back.

There must be a place. There must be some place remaining where he can grow to be a man . . . where legislative succubae haven't made his very essence, his state of being a *boy*, illegal . . . where hundreds of cousins and aunts and uncles gather to sing stirring songs and joyously dance the dances of their great-great grandparents and slap backs and eat food infused with tradition and meaning and flavor . . . where they argue, shaking their hands and swinging their arms, not for argument's sake, but to figure out the best way to plot a future for their children and their children's children . . . camaraderie without drunkenness, rivalry without rancor . . . the outsider, the *other*, as competition . . . a place where the men and the boys look like the man and the boy, share the same bright eyes and the same internal code as they do . . . a place where the adults walk with dignity and think in aeons and raise their children to do both . . . where there are people who feel the world in their breast and their bread, who are inoculated against social disease, who never forget wrongs done, who constantly shift, adapt, and become stronger from loss . . .

Without this place, without the man's desired holy people and holy books, all is fruitless, a desperate attempt at imparting a sense of the eternal to his son. Life becomes simply a series of unconnected moments, scattered dots, lone instances of ecstasy or frustration or sorrow, never mapped, never systematically charted and cross-referenced to reveal patterns, just a handful of remembered experiences thrown to the members of the next generation to decipher even as they're trying to make sense of their own lives. Fusion, a coming together, a gathering of knowledge, the harnessing of the random to bring forth the godhead – this is what the man strives for, this is what will kill him. To let his son go, releasing him someday into a world that hates him, hates *them* for everything they are, all alone with no one to assist, no one to lean on – it's a devastating thought.

Does it only exist in the past, this place? Hinted at in myth, mentioned in dusty books discarded by responsible librarians? If such is the case then it cannot be allowed to languish there. It must be dragged into the present, *it must be formed anew* . . . and to bring forth anything, to labor to produce, enormous pain is involved . . . Every great movement, when struggling to coalesce and form, has been persecuted and attacked. Some of these movements succeeded, others failed, but all made the attempt. If the struggle seems too much at this point, then only continued fading and eventual disappearance await.

✶   ✶   ✶   ✶

The summer ends, and with it the camp. The boy has made a friend there, of sorts, the son of one of the groundskeepers. He is stupider, stronger, and older. He punches and races and roughly throws the boy to the ground. That is the extent of the benefits. It is not ideal, but nothing is, nothing can be. As with the camp itself, the man takes the best he can get for now . . . for the days when the idea has not yet become the reality . . .

With the advent of autumn the slightest of separations begins between the man and the boy. It is nothing like what will take place in the years to come. It is so minor as to be nearly unnoticeable, but it is real. The man cannot identify specifics but he senses it nevertheless, notices it like the faint scent of dying wildflowers on the wind . . . knows that the time approaches when his son will no longer be as reliant on him . . . Sure, he still grasps for his father's hand, slipping his own small hand into the hollow of the scarred fist next to him. His head still lazily flops across the man's stomach on the couch, his body still nestles into the protective crook of the man's arm, his crying face still wedges into the man's shoulder. Someday, though, he won't desire any of it.

A bitter sadness wends its way through the man. He knows that on that bleak day, in the future that's closer than he thinks, as the reddened leaves fall silently from the trees and the storm clouds gather over the hills, he'll have to content himself in other ways. He will overcome his revulsion of kitsch and brush the hair from the sleeping boy's forehead, he will gently touch the child's rosy cheek as if a cliché, wistfully remembering everything, everything . . . thanking the universe for the unadulterated joy he's been given . . . nearly five years they've been together, five hundred thousand years together, and the ecstasy of being alive next to the boy is like nothing else, not the love between spouses or siblings or comrades but the love between father and son, unique, heart-crushing, tears through smiles and the gods in their heavens jealous . . .

This child is his first-born. Nothing will ever change that. But the steady separation must take place in order that bonds might be tightened elsewhere. The intense love felt by the man specifically for the boy, the painfully abundant and focused love, must broaden, must melt into the totality of the expanding family. Thus do individuals become a tribe.

*　　　*　　　*　　　*

Daycare begins once again, and the problems of the previous year, the problems of the summer camp, are amplified – a frowning on the physical, a babying of the intellect, a low quality peer group, an enervating curriculum, shoddy examples of adults, a constantly bleating message of tolerance and equality. The daycare woman not only treats all attendees the same, which is understandable, but she ideologically *views* them as all the same, every child perfectly identical in constitution and capability and potential . . . boys or girls, dull or clever, brave or cautious, Mayan or Macedonian, morose or funny, taciturn or loud . . . the same . . .

247

Beneath a calendar of differently colored youth holding hands and circling the globe, the man touches foreheads with his son and departs, depressed. Every day that the boy grows older – every day that his consciousness expands – brings new problems, new realizations, new dilemmas. The man can find no answers.

Late one night his wife finds him asleep at his desk. Even in slumber his brow is creased. The scattered pages around him are filled with observations, thoughts, charts, and tactics. She reads over his shoulder, where his pencil has scribbled a single couplet on the page, lines of De Vere's put into the mouth of Hamlet:

> *The time is out of joint: o cursed spite,*
> *That ever I was born to set it right.*

The couplet is circled. Beneath it are two underlined words, written in the man's tiny script.

> *I can't.*

She turns out the desk lamp and allows him to sleep his fitful sleep.

The following morning, before the children wake, the woman delicately brings up their increasingly stifling life in the mountain town, a place where even the books in one's personal library are discussed behind one's back. She speaks of the boy and his humdrum daycare and the even less palatable social and educational options for the following year, when he'll be too old for the place. If, as they both agree, they need a community more closely aligned with their needs, perhaps the tiny ski hamlet isn't such a good fit for them. Perhaps their options would increase with a greater amount of people to choose from. She suggests he pay a visit to his sister who, in the mad demographic purge and rush of the early twenty-first century of the Christians, has abandoned Los Angeles and moved, naturally, to hypocritical Portland.

He argues with her.

"We've already tried the place," he states. "It won't work."

"Things change," she replies.

"The countryside is superior," he states.

"Life is with people," she replies.

Back and forth it goes, until she finally leaves the room.

Silently the man stares out the window. Rain splatters against the glass. His wife's suggestion has done him no good, heaping still more thoughts onto the bonfire of an already burning mind, thoughts that deal with the future of the boy, the future of all his children. Is the mountain town the ideal place for them to grow up or is it merely a hideout for himself? Must he keep his progeny as far away as he can from the miasmic vapors of the era or must he risk all and allow them to inhale the fumes, hoping for immunity in the way he pathetically hopes for everything now?

He steps outside and lets the icy drops spill over his head. Thunder booms in the distance. Lightning shimmers on the horizon. He shivers, staring at the clouds cloaking the far off peaks, the air smelling of vegetation and bitter soil. A crane rises from its riverside nest and lifts itself into the blackening sky. Through the falling rain he follows the bird with his tired eyes, watching it fly off until it disappears into the gray.

He will go to Portland. He will visit his sister. That will be the extent of it. There is nothing there for his family, nothing hidden away and secret and magical. There is nothing anywhere anymore. He knows this now, has always known it in a way. The asphalt plant and its spineless opponents, that's who the world belongs to. There's no real difference between the two camps. They rule jointly. A world of institutions, laws, slavery, sickness, lies . . . snowmobiles and SUVs, flapping flags and summer blockbusters . . . drum circles and worldbeat, dreadlocks and performance art . . . self-loathing and pity, banks and escalators, cluster bombs and dodecaphony and usury and playgrounds and malls . . . it's theirs . . .

It's all theirs.

He attempts to push the defeatist thoughts from his mind . . . tries to imagine the two boys and their sister and his obligation to them, thinks of the *geis* he cannot violate . . . Soaking wet, he turns around and returns to the house to dry off and deal with more mundane matters . . . daily matters, business matters . . . Somewhere deep within, though, he knows the insane Grail quest is coming to an end.

* * * *

Three weeks later the car turns out of the driveway and the man and the boy begin their journey west, heading out to Oregon. The previous days have not been easy for the man. He has grown weary, exhausted by the incessant activity of his brain. He's made a desperate bid to counter the despondency that's settled upon him, but has failed. The answers he's come up with are unacceptable. They knock him down, squat on his chest, steal his breath. They make naked his violent, secret fear that no matter what he says or does there is no tomorrow . . . that no matter his actions he will end, like the Latin Turnus, defeated and broken by an unstoppable, inescapable force . . .

For the first time in his life he's begun to talk about such things with the boy, damning the consequences, slipping from his daily motivational curriculum of "certain victory" and inevitable return. He icily reveals the existence of gulags, of prisons and their deadened walls and oubliettes, where the carnal savagery of caged beasts rages beneath a fluorescent sun. He speaks of ever-present cameras mounted on poles, on cars, on mechanical insects . . . the whole world as panopticon . . . He speaks of spy satellites and infrared cameras that see through walls . . . of correspondence being read, of voices being listened to and recorded and warehoused . . . of fingerprints and retina scans and vein scans and voice identifiers and thought identifiers . . . of nanotechnology, of manufactured viruses and the splicing of genes . . . of silicon chips under skin . . . of electric shock and degradation . . . of agriculture as industry, of dead soil and dead lakes and dead skies and dead oceans . . . of forced modification at the sub-molecular level . . . of drone planes that drop genetically specific bombs . . . of robots driving cars and firing bullets . . . of invisible tanks, crushing all resistance . . . of weapons that maim, discombobulate, confuse, harm the ears, the eyes, the skin, the nose, the mind . . . of beatings with truncheons, where fighting back, where defending oneself, merely adds to future punishment . . .

When faced with such realities the path to redemption is obscured . . . the belief in the chances of their survival approaches zero . . . All the lessons he teaches his son are canceled out by the omnipotent forces arrayed against them, forces that were *created* by their kind, forces that are for the most part manned by their kind. Always this vaunted Faustian man, this kin, this cheered scientific Man of the North who goes by different historical names, has brought with him his torture, his cruelty, his subservience to power . . . crushing those he's ordered to crush, no fealty to blood, no fealty to anything, a *Fahrradler*, a bully, an eternal follower . . . a tinkerer, a fixer of what's not broken . . . a breeder of efficiency to the point of sterility . . . the best of the world's slaves, one who willingly cinches the chains around his own ankles before eagerly cracking the whip against the backs of those unwilling to bow . . .

A vicious animosity arises in the man for the very genealogical garden he and the boy sprang from, and from this animosity swarms still more confusion. He has long known that the multi-colored hands on the "Accept Everyone!" stickers he receives in the mail are unified in opposition to his family's existence. He has long known that one of the hands resembles his own and that it would willingly grasp a club and bash his brains out without a second's hesitation. But he also knows that this eternal I versus I must end, that the violent clash of like against like needs to stop. Unfortunately there's no resolution in sight. Responsive violence only begets more violence. Passivity, the turning of the other cheek, only allows one to be hit again and again and again and again and again, the boot stamping on one's face for eternity, the iron heel grinding until nothing remains but bloody pulp. It seems as if, ultimately, the cameras, the beatings, the prisons, the poverty, and the treachery simply cannot be avoided.

It is thoughts such as these he shares with the boy, unfair thoughts, even *unformed* thoughts at times – not the relationship of a father and a son, but of comrades, discussing, planning, plotting. The man is unsure of himself in this area, knows his actions smack of mushy postmodernism, but feels that the boy should know the fear his father feels for their masters, that he should know fear himself so that all his energies and thoughts can eventually be applied to survival as well. There is no longer the luxury of perpetuating an innocent childhood removed from the very real dangers threatening the family.

"We could be tricky and just walk out of the jail," the boy proclaims during one such discussion, as they drive west along the choked and tamed Columbia River. His little voice is serious, grave as a general who knows that the next morning's battle will decide the history – the very *destiny* – of his people and their world.

"Oh yeah? How would we trick them?"

"I don't know yet. But we're smart."

The man smiles at the simple response. In his child he finds inherent optimism and easy answers to difficult questions charming. Will a day ever come, though, when the grown men who desire change stop thinking like the fresh-faced youth riding in the backseat? Will they ever cease their curious, romantic assumptions of magical victory – their belief that they can simply pull down the moon from the sky – and instead deal with the difficult problems at hand like adults?

No. That day won't come.

He can finally admit it.

*   *   *   *

The time spent with his sister and brother-in-law is nice, if only to catch up and laugh occasionally. Nothing has changed with their views on propagation. They will honor their role as aunt and uncle, but that's all.

For the first time since the arrival of his remarkable children the man is envious of these two. They do not bear the burden of the future.

As he did last time he was in Portland he makes some obligatory enquiries into schools – German-speaking, French-speaking, groovy Waldorf, science-centered charters . . . even, at the very end of his rope, Catholic ones . . . but at the heart of each of them is the self-induced shame . . . the compulsory debasement, the twisting of life . . . many masks, one face . . . death . . .

Their final night is spent gathered with the urban throng, the thoroughly smug, to watch the twilight appearance of the darting swifts, fantastic little birds making their way south in the thousands. It is an event . . . something to see, something to *entertain* . . . Unattractive bipeds sit or stretch on blankets laid on the autumn ground, anxiously awaiting the coming show. As the magnificent sun lowers behind the western hills and darkness spills over dusk, the birds begin to circle an abandoned chimney, whirling, a shadowy vortex against the purpled sky. They've not many forests left to nest in on their southern migration. Loss of habitat, no more living space for a species, is an opportunity to drink wine for these moderns, avidly watching the spectacle with the same dispassionate interest they display when viewing their art.

Then, suddenly, what's this? A hawk appears from the nearby woods. It shoots across the sky, assuming a position of attack far above the diminishing whirlpool of the tiny, swallow-like birds. In the blink of an eye it descends, seeking prey, sustenance, in order to live. It is successful, as it must be if it's to survive in this world, nabbing a swift from the air and flying off with it grasped between its talons.

It is a breathtaking sight, awesome, a vision infinitely more beautiful than that of the stunted life forms stuck to the ground below. There they sit . . . fat, misshapen, skeletal, caked in tattoos, caked in makeup, gaunt, malnourished, tired, overfed, perfumed, limp, frenetic, spectacled, deprived of oxygen, deprived of sunlight. The contrast with the hawk – raw, clean, sleekly perfect, untouched by civilization – is glaring.

The man and the boy both smile, marveling at the magnificent display just presented them. And then . . . what's this? The crowd . . . it too, is reacting . . . and although nothing seems impossible anymore, the man is still taken aback by the reaction – the people are *booing* . . . They are, incredibly, *booing the hawk*. They are voicing their displeasure at *life*. They hate it, these who formerly whispered in catacombs and now arrogantly creep aboveground. Would they boo the lovely swift when, of necessity, it snatches and swallows an unsuspecting spider ballooning out on its strand of web? Aah, but a spider is not as comely as a poor swift. These despisers of action, these moldering, eternal Christians, these compartmentalizing Cartesians – they prefer that the hawk lose its feathers, that the lion die, that the wolf leave the earth, that the tiger fade into memory. It is dismaying to witness, so clearly, the dismal character of these cramped Westerners, these *emotional* predators. Their greatest desire is for the creatures referred to as "prey" to become as weak and rotten as they themselves are . . . unselected, enfeebled . . . They have an aversion to those forms of life that have carved out a different niche in an ecosystem. No matter what they claim in their free urban papers and their millions of outraged blogs, the holistic world, the natural world, is their enemy.

"They should cheer for both the swifts *and* the hawk, dad," the boy says. The man nods his head, smiles, ruffles his son's hair. They should, but they won't. They can't. They cheer for what seems weakest because they feel spiritually as one with such things. The boy will never fully grasp their insanity until it is realized that they do not look at the health of the group, but only at the fate of individuals. He will never fully grasp their hatred until it is realized that they themselves identify with prey and identify him and those like him with predators. The boy – like his father, like the caged zoo lion – is the dangerous *Raubtier*, and thus is only allowed to exist behind bars and in documentaries, as a warning.

The man stands to leave, looking out over the crowd one last time. In their numbers they are an abomination. They carpet the hillside. They carpet the sprawling cities of the West . . . of the globe . . . It is impossible to fight them. They know no boundaries. They roll over everything. They can only be avoided, for a time.

His family will never move back to such a place.

＊   ＊   ＊   ＊

Outside the vehicle the rain falls. The boy is asleep in the backseat as he and the man make the long return journey back to their home. Higher in the mountains, in their town hundreds of miles away, the rain will turn to snow tonight. Winter has arrived early.

Portland has reinforced the man's gloomy conviction. He cannot win. He's tired of the struggle, wants only to give in to the forces confronting him. He wants an end to the exhaustion, an end to the sleepless nights, when the weight of the reality is felt most forcefully . . . when mere thoughts alone seem enough to strangle and choke . . . His allies do not exist. His enemies are beyond counting. Their methods are the most brilliant, efficient, and ruthless ever devised. The dynastic courts of China, the Inquisition as manifested in *Mitteleuropa*, the Salem trials in the New World, the Bolshevik star chambers in the Old – all pale in comparison to this epoch, this time of extinction previously seen only in prehistory.

It is the time of three winters . . . three of them in a terrible row, one after the other . . . a time of huddling, of gnawing fingertips in frozen caves, of burrowing in tunnels like cicadas . . . a time of starving, a time of hacking off fingers after digging through the snow that covers everything, the snow that obscures nearly all sources of nourishment . . . attacked from above, from below, from all sides . . . the North and the South against them, the West and the East equally crushing . . . no way to win, but a refusal to lose, an inability to accept the finality of this horrendous defeat . . .

The rain continues to beat down over the valleys and farms beyond the windshield. For most of his life the man desired the country over the city. He wanted to work the land or fish the seas, not scribble and toil and calculate and think in choking offices. He wanted to be left alone, to be quiet, to bother no one as long as he himself wasn't bothered in turn. His nature, whatever it was that he was born with, screamed at him individualism. The primary sin he decries in his enemies, these leaden masses who weigh him down, also exists in him. He fights it, suppresses it, but he cannot deny that somewhere, somehow it is in him still . . . the belief, the *false belief*, in individual will . . . The quality is deadly, is only the harbinger of mass suicide. The cell cannot live without the body. Group determination is where the power lies, a tenacious desire for life, for the end of subjugation.

Yet even their long, melancholy history as a group, disjointed and rare as it's been, has been a failure. How many times have they truly arisen, only to be crushed so completely that even the truth of their actions, their very *validity*, is scorned? "I am so weary of seeing beautiful flowers bloom," said the all-seeing poet . . . and now, here at the end of all things, it seems as if none will ever bloom again . . . Does no one else anywhere share this nauseated reaction to the cowering? Does no one else experience the everyday as the most putrid of sensations? Seven hundred years of *Reconquista* for this? Hundreds of millions of lives sacrificed over centuries for this? There is not even a river to kneel by and weep for what's been lost, and even if there were, *even if there were*, there is no one to weep with. Where are they? Where are they? Where are the families to surround them, to love them, to be loved by them, to put things aright? Where are those who grasp how much has been taken from all of them? *Where are Romans?*

The miles pass. Dusk darkens to night. On the windshield the raindrops knocked away by the wiper blades freeze, turning inexorably and silently to snow. Coming from the opposite direction, in a never-ending parade of lights along the freeway, are cars and trucks and vehicles of all types . . . hundreds of them, one after the other, one after the other . . . They snake along, each with an occupant, or two, or five, not caring, not seeing, not understanding. The man can't lie to himself. There are no potential comrades among them. There are only more enemies.

This contemptible world, polluted and ugly, drained of all wonder, drained of all beauty . . . he and his family are alone in it, *utterly alone* . . . His boy, his first-born son, his *duty son* . . . his daughter, his wife and baby . . . all alone . . . All his silly proclamations, all his high-blown sentiment, his terrible understanding of the reality – it's all for naught. He does not have the ability to remedy or to heal on his own . . . does not have the ability to gather or repair, to resurrect, to create . . .

> *Between the motion*
> *And the act*
> *Falls the Shadow*

The shadow . . . it will swallow his boy, swallow his children, his genes . . . His words, his ideas, his dreams – all break on the reality of that shadow and the solid mountain that casts it. Knowing thyself? What good advice is that? How can one live life according to an epigram? What happens *after* one knows one's self? That's where the real struggle begins. The truth of Delphi, the *only truth* of the place where those words of the Sages were inscribed, is that the line of its founders died out and barbarians came and sacked it.

A solitary voice, no matter how loud it might scream from cliffs, is silent when no other ears exist to hear it. Single blows, no matter how powerful, are meaningless against a mountain. Is this the fate for his son? Is this the future he's offering him – bitter loneliness, shouting alone until he dies with raw throat? Frustratingly pounding the mountain with bloodied fists, mumbling meager platitudes, babbling about culture, seeking salvation through overly used metaphors about forests and trees and roots and plants and flowers and seasons? Poetry, that's all he's given the boy, romantic words that do nothing but inspire hope, the greatest of sins. What worth is it all, what worth poetry, what worth hope, when compared to millions of men with guns? The boy cannot grow to be the First Man, his father should never have dreamed this for him, never proclaimed this. There must be First *Men* . . . a million families, a hundred million . . . If there aren't then his son – *his son, his son, his son* – will be taken captive. They'll all be taken captive. Tortured. Bent. Destroyed. That world out there, the one that lay in wait outside the hospital walls on the day the child was pulled from his mother's womb, it's still there. It's worse than it was. It wants to take him, it wants to *devour* him. The man must save him, he must fight. He, too, swings his bleeding fists at mountains. It is a battle, a struggle, and the winner gets the boy and the family that the man loves more than anything.

He cannot win. Rationally, he knows this. But he must win. This he knows as well.

He cannot, but he must. This is the gray sky under which all else takes place. It is the fatal paradox he can never escape. He *cannot* win. But he *must* win.

"Varus! *Where are my Romans?*" screamed Octavian as the flower of his army decayed in the dirt, slaughtered in the murky northern forest of the barbarians.

Where are they? Where are the man's Romans? Are they truly just skeletons rotting in the blood-soaked soil of Europe? Does nothing remain? *Does nothing remain?* And if that's the case, if it really is a world without allies, then how will he ever remedy this pain, this deep-seated agony that gnaws him and throttles him and makes him scream tears into his pillow in the middle of the night? He cannot protect his children from what awaits. He cannot protect the boy. It used to be the inevitable flight of the child that caused parents anguish – the act of setting free the young hawk, the young swift, into the wide world. That era is gone, burned up in the global conflagration that's still raging, consumed by the inferno that the man is supposed to release his son into. The boy is at the mercy of cohesive tribes who relentlessly pound the war drums, whispering and screaming for his total destruction, his absolute eradication, as if it hasn't already happened. There is no one to save him – *there is no one to save any of them* – and appeals to mercy have no appeal to enemies famous for their justified ruthlessness, a ruthlessness the man's type have never truly possessed. They are trying to start over again, trying to survive with next to nothing. They have been defeated, nearly wiped from this earth. They have no wealth, no contacts, no folk, no power, no assets, no sympathy, no mouthpiece. They have one family, *one family*, and a father's dream of dumplings.

That is all.

There are hours to go until they reach their home. The man, lost in thought for far too long, suddenly notices that the gas tank is extremely low. Outside the snow is coming down harder and harder, the mountain wind blowing more fiercely. It's quite a storm. On both sides of the interstate the traffic has begun to slow and pull to the shoulder. An off ramp appears out of the blizzard and he immediately exits, glad to be off the freeway before the vehicle sputters to a stop. Slowly he moves along the empty road he finds himself on, searching for a gas station. In the backseat the boy begins to stir, then drowsily awakens. The child's eyes adjust to the darkness outside the windows and he realizes, suddenly, that there's a storm going on around them.

"Dad, it's snowing!" His voice is filled with wonder, with excitement. "It's snowing, dad!"

The flakes drop from the sky thick and fast. The wind plants them on the windshield more quickly than they can be wiped away. The headlights only penetrate the blackness so far, and the falling snow combines with the dark to make visibility terrible.

"Can we stop the car? Can we go out in it?"

The tank is nearly empty. The man squints his eyes and stares into the dark. It's difficult to see what lies ahead of them – are those lights way up there? Or some trick of the storm? They might be lights, but the vehicle will never make it that far with the fuel it has. He steers toward the side of the road, absently answering the boy's question from over his shoulder, concerned with other things.

"We can, son . . ."

The man stops the car. He cuts the ignition and turns off the headlights, hoping to glimpse the lights again . . . hoping to gauge what they are and how far away they are . . . On his own the boy unstraps himself and clambers up into the front seat. Wordlessly he takes the man's hand and snuggles next to him, suddenly not so eager to go out into the storm that's raging around them. The man gives the boy's hand a little squeeze. Surrounded by blackness and howling wind and freezing snow, the father and his son sit together, silently staring out into the night beyond.

If there are lights ahead in the darkness, the man can no longer see them.

*   *   *   *

Una salus victis nullam sperare salutem.

The one salvation for the defeated is to have no hope for salvation.